THE COMPLICATION

ALSO BY SUZANNE YOUNG

A PROGRAM NOVEL

Book 6

THE COMPLICATION

SUZANNE YOUNG

SIMON PULSE

New York   London   Toronto   Sydney   New Delhi

SIMON PULSE

An imprint of Simon & Schuster Children's Publishing Division

1230 Avenue of the Americas, New York, New York 10020

First Simon Pulse paperback edition February 2019

Text copyright © 2018 by Suzanne Young

Cover photographs of models copyright © 2018 by Michael Frost

Cover photographs of backgrounds copyright © 2018 by Thinkstock

Also available in a Simon Pulse hardcover edition.

For information about special discounts for bulk purchases, please contact

Simon & Schuster Special Sales at 1-866-506-1949 or business@simonandschuster.com.

The Simon & Schuster Speakers Bureau can bring authors to your live event.

For more information or to book an event contact the Simon & Schuster Speakers

Bureau at 1-866-248-3049 or visit our website at www.simonspeakers.com.

Cover designed by Russell Gordon

Interior designed by Mike Rosamilia

The text of this book was set in Adobe Garamond Pro.

Manufactured in the United States of America

2 4 6 8 10 9 7 5 3 1

The Library of Congress has cataloged the hardcover edition as follows:

Names: Young, Suzanne, author.

Title: The complication / by Suzanne Young.

Description: First Simon Pulse hardcover edition. | New York : Simon Pulse,
2018. | Series: The Program ; book 6 | Summary: Seventeen-year-old Tatum
Masterson has no memory of being in The Program, but when she starts
experiencing crashbacks she knows something terrible happened last summer,
and with the help of the boyfriend she lost, Tatum digs into the past and
future of The Program and its handlers and discovers the true cost of a cure.

Identifiers: LCCN 2017047735 (print) | LCCN 2018007741 (eBook) |
ISBN 9781481471350 (hc) | ISBN 9781481471374 (eBook)

Subjects: | CYAC: Brainwashing—Fiction. | Memory—Fiction. |
Love—Fiction. | Science fiction.

Classification: LCC PZ7.Y887 (eBook) | LCC PZ7.Y887 Co 2018 (print) |
DDC [Fic]—dc23

LC record available at https://lccn.loc.gov/2017047735

ISBN 9781481471367 (pbk)

In loving memory of my grandmother
Josephine Parzych
Always for you, Gram

ENTER THE WORLD

THE PROGRAM

The Program—a memory-wiping therapy—was created to combat the outbreak of a suicide cluster. Sloane and James will do everything they can to survive both the epidemic and its cure.

THE TREATMENT

On the run from The Program, Sloane and James must figure out a way to take down the system that ruined their lives before it can expand.

BOOK ONE

BOOK THREE

BOOK TWO

THE REMEDY

Before The Program, there was the grief department. Quinn and Deacon spent their lives as closers, offering grieving families a chance to say good-bye—until Quinn discovers her life is not at all what it seems.

OF *THE PROGRAM*

THE ADJUSTMENT

Tatum and Wes undergo the Adjustment—a new procedure to replace memories that The Program erased. But what happens when the past you thought you had was a lie?

THE COMPLICATION

After learning the truth about her past, Tatum must find a way to stop the Adjustment before it sets off a new epidemic.

BOOK FIVE

BOOK FOUR

BOOK SIX

THE EPIDEMIC

Quinn will enlist the help of other closers to save a girl she hardly knows, setting off the series of events that lead to the suicide epidemic.

PART I
HELLO, I LOVED YOU

CHAPTER ONE

I WAS IN THE PROGRAM.

The knowledge is horrifying, devastating, crushing. I gulp in a breath and lower my eyes to the paper on my desk. Moments ago, my best friend told me something that upended my world. Nathan said I'd been in The Program last summer, only . . . it never happened. It's not true.

But at the same time, the weight of it is there—a phantom pain in my chest.

The monitor, Dr. Wyatt, continues her slow pace around the classroom, arms folded over her chest, while she waits for us to fill out our weekly assessments—a relic from The Program hysteria. One the school has reinstituted on a voluntary basis. Voluntary for now, at least.

I read the first question on my paper.

Are you feeling sad or overwhelmed?

That would be an understatement.

"You think she'd take the hint," Nathan murmurs from behind me, sliding his blank assessment across his desk. "We're not going to be part of her experiment." He pauses. "Right, Tatum? We're done being experiments?"

He wants me to make a joke to show just how fine I am. I can't let on that I don't remember being in The Program; Nathan thinks I do. He might not have mentioned it otherwise.

But The Program never made its patients forget they were there. No—they wanted everyone to come out believing The Program had saved their lives. Patients were only supposed to forget the bad stuff.

I remember the bad stuff, or at least most of it. So, if I'd actually been a patient, why would the hurt still be here? Nathan claimed my grandfather got to me "early." How early?

As I try to work it all out, there's a shuffle of feet—Nathan waiting for my reply. I force myself to be normal, or some passing version—otherwise, he'll know there's a problem. He'll want answers.

I look at Nathan and flash him a half smile. "Considering I've spent the better part of a year being the caged bunny rabbit in this scenario," I tell him, "yeah—I'm done with unethical experiments."

Nathan nods his agreement and leans back in his chair. His hazel eyes glide over me, and I quickly turn around, afraid he'll see through my act. He should be able to. Then again, Nathan's

4   SUZANNE YOUNG

been lying to me since last summer. To which I'm sure he'd say, *Keeping a secret isn't the same as being a liar, Tatum.* But in this case, it is. He is.

I was in The Program, and that means everyone I love is a liar.

My entire body shakes as I soak in my shock. I look up and find Weston Ambrose still watching me from his seat in the front of the room, concern creasing his forehead. He doesn't know me anymore. He shouldn't remember—

A sharp pain strikes behind my eyes, blooming so quickly and fiercely that it's an explosion. I press my fingers against my temples, lowering my head as I grit my teeth. But I can't seem to stop the pain—it spreads across my vision until everything goes black.

And I fall into a memory.

I was standing at the bottom of the stairs in the front entryway of my house, screaming for my grandparents, who were already in bed. Men in white coats, handlers, stood on either side of me, gripping my forearms, trying to pull me out the door. Blood began to seep again from the wounds on my knuckles, and it dripped in an arc around my feet as I fought.

They'd attempted to catch me on the moonlit porch first, but when I saw them coming, saw the lights of their van, I tried to race inside. I wasn't fast enough. They nearly tackled me as I pushed open the door.

"Don't fight, Miss Masterson," the gray-haired handler said. "We just want to talk."

Yeah, right. I knew there was no such thing with them. My

head ached; my heart was broken. My hand bled. I fucking hated this life—I did. But it didn't mean I was going to give it away to The Program. I wouldn't let them erase me. I wouldn't let them destroy me. This life was mine, and I wouldn't let them decide how I'd live it.

"Stop!" I growled, kicking when I couldn't free my arms. The handler with the scar on his cheek took the brunt of my sneaker, winced, and then slammed me hard against the wall, knocking the air out of my lungs. I gasped, but with my arm now free, I swung at him.

He caught me by the wrist and twisted my arm across my chest and spun me around, locking me against him. I screamed, my voice cracking. Tears streamed down my face. "Stop!" I cried out.

The bedroom door opened upstairs, and my heart soared. "Pop!" I screamed. "Pop, help me!"

There was a flash of movement, and the handler tightened his grip on my wrists. The older handler stepped forward, blocking my view as my grandparents stomped down the stairs.

"Remain calm," the handler said soothingly to them. But it must not have gone over well, because I heard a scuffle, the sound of breaking glass, and saw shards of our entryway lamp spill across the floor.

My grandfather rushed past the handler, and I sobbed when I saw his face—alarmed, yet sleepy, his glasses left upstairs.

"Help me," I cried, getting one arm free to reach out to him, still entangled in the handler's grip. "Don't let them—"

The handler smothered my mouth with his palm, muffling my words, and began to back me toward the door. The helplessness was horrific, suffocating. I fought harder; I fought for my life.

And then my grandfather was there, grabbing my arm as he tried to physically pull me away from the handler, causing a tearing pain in my shoulder. My grandmother came running into the foyer, holding a wooden broom, and poked at the handlers like they were wild animals. She was wearing her housecoat, her hair in rollers.

"Leave her alone!" she screamed in a shaky voice, swatting them again.

But then the gray-haired handler grabbed her violently by the sleeve of her housecoat, startling her so badly that she dropped the broom with a loud clatter. My grandfather let go of my arm and raced over to his wife, untangling her clothing from the handler's fist. He put his arm protectively around her shoulders.

The handler who was holding me took his hand from over my mouth. "Be smart," he growled near my ear. "You're making this worse." But I wouldn't listen to him.

"Pop, please!" I begged, outstretching my hand to my grandfather again.

And when he looked at me, his blue eyes were so sorrowful that it made my legs weaken. The handler steadied me.

Pop knew I was lost; he couldn't help me. That was what his eyes told me. My grandmother cried quietly next to him, and she turned into the collar of his pajama top to hide her face.

The handler began moving me toward the door again, and although I still fought, my strength had left me. I would die. The Program would end me.

And no one—not even my grandparents—could save me.

Reality floods back, and I look up, my eyes wide and terrified. The classroom is a blur as I take it in. My entire body is shaking, but my headache fades quickly. I just had a crashback of memory.

Oh, God. It's all true.

Fresh tears spring to my eyes, and my nose begins to run. I swipe under it, but when I look down, I see it's a streak of blood. I quickly use the back of my hand to clear it away, relieved when the bleeding stops almost immediately. The shock of seeing my own blood pushes the memory off—letting me focus. I can't fall apart here. Not in front of the monitor. I ache for my grandparents, horrified by how scared they were. How helpless they were in their misery.

The monitor's in the back of the class, and I figure she must not have seen my bloody nose. It might be a giveaway that I'm a returner, and I'm not ready to face what happened to me. What will happen to me if she finds out. But as I look forward again, I find Weston still watching me, his expression disturbed. He witnessed my memory crashback. Did he realize what was happening to me? Does he care? Does he care the way he used to?

Weston Ambrose is the love of my life. I loved him before he was taken into The Program, and I loved him again when

SUZANNE YOUNG

he returned and was changed. But he has no idea who I am anymore.

And maybe that's why I can trust him more than anyone else in my life.

I press my mouth into a smile, letting him know I'm okay—even though I'm so clearly not. He watches me for a moment longer, doubtful, and then his lips part like he might call out to me.

Instead, Wes raises his hand and spins around in his seat. Everyone looks at him, and I have a spike of panic, worry that he's going to report me. That's the sort of thing people did to each other when they feared The Program—anything to save themselves.

The teacher stares at Wes, seeming unsure. The routine is being changed. Normally, we all sit here in active silence, refusing this assessment. The change clearly surprises Miss Soto, as well.

"Yes?" she asks tentatively. Wes waves her off and points to the monitor, who has rounded the room. Almost amused, Dr. Wyatt smiles at Wes and tilts her head.

"How can I help you, Mr. Ambrose?" she asks.

"Hi," Wes says, and holds up one finger as if he's about to ask an important question. "I'm sorry if this was already covered while I was gone, but I was just wondering"—he grabs the assessment—"what the fuck is this, and what does it have to do with anything?"

Garcia Bobadilla bursts out laughing and quickly covers his

mouth. Lynn Mosiac snorts. Behind me, Nathan shifts in his seat, and his desk presses against the back of my chair.

I quickly look at Dr. Wyatt, wondering how she'll respond. Wondering what she's thinking. Does she know about the Adjustment or that Wes had it done? Does she know he's been erased again? She doesn't give anything away, though, as she motions to the classroom door.

"In my office, Mr. Ambrose," she says curtly, and starts in that direction.

Wes stands, gathering his notebook. "Is it because I said 'fuck'?" he asks loudly, making more people laugh. I smile—mostly in shock—as he follows Dr. Wyatt. At the door, he glances back over his shoulder at me before walking out.

It's a jolt to my heart—the familiar way he looked at me. Is it possible he did that to save me from her scrutiny? Could he . . . remember me?

The Adjustment—a procedure where I donated memories of our relationship to help trigger a controlled crashback—was supposed to help Wes remember everything The Program had erased. But the memories I donated were corrupted, and because of it, Wes became unwell.

He fell apart, and the only cure was to erase him completely and start over. I'd say I've lost him twice, but it's hard to know what's true anymore. All I do know is that Weston Ambrose and I weren't everything to each other like I'd thought. We were just a couple, and he fell out of love with me. We continued in an unhealthy way while he began dating someone else. Of course, none of us were right at the time. The threat of The Program had us all terrified and irrational.

But when Wes broke down after the Adjustment, I blamed myself. I had somehow blocked out the end of our relationship and, as a result, gave him false memories during his procedure. His mind rejected them, even though he refused to reject *me*. He loved me. Again.

And that's the most tragic part of all.

Now that Nathan told me I'd been in The Program, that scenario has changed. It means I was erased too. So how— *why*—do I seem to remember Wes, even if those memories are slightly off? None of it makes any sense.

My teacher closes the classroom door, her cheeks flush, her heart probably racing. "Well," she says. "That was . . . How about we hand in our assessments now?"

I turn and grab Nathan's paper off his desk, and he scrunches his nose. "You're not going to say anything?" he asks.

"What do you mean?"

"Uh . . . Wes just got himself thrown out of class. You don't think that's peculiar?"

"No," I lie. "It wouldn't be the first time."

Nathan narrows his eyes and sits forward in his chair. "That's the thing, Tatum—it would be the first time. Dr. McKee said he wouldn't remember anything. Hell, he didn't even know his parents. Would he really—"

"Sure," I interrupt. "But Wes wouldn't remember to be scared, either."

Nathan purses his lips, thinking over my answer. He rests back and folds his hands on his desk. "This should be interesting, then," he murmurs.

I turn around and pass my and Nathan's papers forward. My fingers tremble, dried blood around my knuckle. I'm suddenly riotous, ready to burst. I want to run out of here and find Wes, but I'll have to wait.

It's nearly forty minutes later when the bell mercifully rings. Wes never came back to the room. My headache has faded completely; I'm almost clearheaded again. The crashback forced me into a memory, and maybe that helped my brain to function properly. Or maybe part of me always knew about my time in The Program, and I just needed the confirmation. Regardless of the reason, this is the clearest I've felt in a long time.

I'm the first person out of my seat, and I quickly loop my backpack strap over my shoulder and grab my books. I have to find Wes. He may not remember me, but whoever he is now—at least he didn't betray me.

"You good?" Nathan asks. "You've been weird ever since . . ." He stumbles over the words and shakes his head as he collects his things from the top of his desk. "Since I mentioned The Program," he finishes in a hushed voice.

"Shh . . . ," I say purposely to make him feel uncomfortable. I want him to stop talking. I need time to think—without him. This is such a stark contrast in our relationship, but it will make processing this easier. I need to think without his influence.

"I'll see you later," I tell him, rushing ahead. "I have to go to the bathroom."

"Thanks for oversharing."

I wave a quick good-bye and hurry out, intent on finding Wes. I try not to focus on the fact that I'm a stranger to him. And it's now that I realize I'm a stranger to myself, too.

CHAPTER TWO

I FEED INTO THE CURRENT OF STUDENTS FILING out of their classes and smile when people say hi to me. I keep my eyes downcast, but I can't help wondering who else knows. Do any of these people know I was in The Program? Are they keeping it from me too?

I wrap my arms around myself, feeling exposed. Vulnerable. I want to go home and confront my grandparents—they betrayed me by keeping this secret. But first, I need to make sure Wes is okay.

It's not lost on me that going to find him, seeking him out, is exactly the sort of behavior Dr. McKee warned me about. He told me to stay away from Wes to prevent another breakdown. My and Wes's shared past is a mixture of love, betrayal, and heartache. And the sick part is . . . I want to do it all again, over and over. Even if it hurts him. Even if it hurts me.

But I can't go back to the past. I'm not the same person anymore. So, once I figure out what Wes remembers—*if* he remembers—I'll let him live his life: one where we're not together. Because that's love—not hurting each other. For once we can all finally decide to be better people.

I take a deep breath, telling myself that it's not safe to think right now. One moment of letting my guard down could result in a flood of emotions, and I can't let that happen. Not here.

The bell rings, but I don't rush toward the office. As I pass the science hallway, I glance over absently, surprised to find a dark-haired guy watching me from where he's leaning against his locker. It's Derek, another returner. A few months ago, I noticed him staring at me while I was talking with Jana Simms, Nathan's girlfriend. He made me uncomfortable then, and nothing about the look he gives me now does anything to make me rethink my original assessment. He's creepy.

Out of some sense of politeness, though, I smile a hello to him. He doesn't return it. His dark eyes are in shadows, his lips curved, like there's a joke I don't see. His gaze is cold fingers tracing up my spine, wrapping around my neck. The look is familiar and predatory. I shiver and walk faster, holding my breath until I'm past the hallway and he's out of sight. I nearly run into a freshman, who skirts around me to get to class.

I'm suddenly afraid to be in the hallway alone. It's impossibly quiet. I hurry toward the office and rush inside the lobby. Dr. Wyatt and Wes are nowhere in sight, and the attendance clerk is talking to another student. I take a seat, my heart racing, and remember something Foster mentioned a few weeks ago: embedded handlers.

Foster Linn has been one of my best friends since junior high, and sadly, horrifically, his brother died from complications of Program crashbacks—something that's been happening to returners at an increasingly alarming rate.

Shortly after Sebastian's death, Foster began to tell me and Nathan that there were handlers still watching us, even though The Program was gone. I doubted his theory, attributing it to his grief. Maybe I didn't want to admit that it was possible. But I should have known that in this world, anything is possible.

With that on my mind, I think about the way Derek looked at me. It was like he knew me. Knew about me. The idea that he actually might terrifies me.

I take out my phone and text Foster, my thumbs shaking as they pass over the keys.

Foster won't be happy to hear from me right now; he has the flu, leaving him paler than usual. But I'm glad he isn't here today, because Foster has the ability to see through all of my bullshit—through anyone's bullshit. He would have figured out what Nathan told me, and then he would have figured out that I didn't remember The Program. Who knows what would have happened after that.

Hell, I might have to avoid him until I figure out how to cope better. Or at least become a better liar like the rest of them. Luckily, I can be more evasive over text.

You awake? I write.

No, Foster texts back, and I smile. I check to make sure the clerk is still distracted and respond.

You seem better. Actually, what do you know about Derek Thompson? I ask.

Uh . . . not much, Foster responds. He used to be in The Program. Why?

I can still feel Derek's eyes on me as I start to tell Foster what happened. Just saw him in the hall, I text, and he was staring at me.

Wow, super ego. I'm assuming it's more than that for you to text me on my deathbed, Foster writes.

It was the WAY he stared at me, I clarify. Is it possible . . . My thumbs pause on the keys, and I'm not sure I want to continue with the question. I push forward. Is it possible Derek is a handler? I ask.

A response bubble pops up immediately and then disappears. It does that several more times, no actual words appearing. I glance up and notice the clerk watching me, the student who was there before me now gone.

"May I help you?" she asks.

I quickly stash my phone in my backpack and cross to the desk. The attendance clerk waits for me to speak with a bored expression. I want to come right out and ask if she's seen

Weston Ambrose, but before I can, the inner office door opens, and Dr. Wyatt steps out.

I put my hand on my cheek in an attempt to shield my face, but it doesn't work.

"Miss Masterson," Dr. Wyatt calls suspiciously. "I was just coming to look for you."

Her comment shocks me, and I have to gather myself before turning to her. "I'm not feeling well," I say, trying to add exhaustion into my voice. "I came in to call my pop."

Dr. Wyatt watches me carefully and then takes a step closer. Examining me. "Headache?" she asks. And the question is loaded with assumptions, the beginning of a cross-examination.

She must know that returners suffer from headaches. Being a monitor, she probably knows more about aftereffects than I do.

"No," I say, and place my hand over my stomach. "Cramps."

She smiles, but I get the feeling that she can see straight through my lie. "I'm sorry to hear that," she says, pushing open her office door. "This won't take long."

My lips part, and I see Wes sitting on the chair in front her desk, seeming deeply annoyed. I'm about to make an excuse, but the expression on Dr. Wyatt's face leaves no room for argument. I walk toward her office.

The phone on the clerk's desk rings, and after she answers it, she calls to Dr. Wyatt. Irritated, the monitor tells me to have a seat in her office. I go inside, and when he sees me, Wes smiles broadly like we're old friends. It's an arrow into my heart, throwing off my balance. Although I came looking for Wes, now that he's here, I can't find the right words. I don't know if there are any.

"This Dr. Wyatt is really infringing on my education," Wes says. "I hope she's going to provide private tutoring." He acts like this is all a big joke, but the expression on my face must alarm him, because his smile fades.

"Don't worry," he says. "They can't expel us for sitting in English class."

I'm reminded that he has no idea the gravity of this world, how quickly things can go very wrong. I can't believe he's talking to me; I can't believe I have to act like I don't know him. It's unnatural. And it's painful.

I don't respond as I take a seat in the chair next to him, awkward and silent. I keep my eyes on Dr. Wyatt's impeccably neat desk, afraid to look at Wes. Afraid I'll blurt out our entire past with another flash of his dimples and easy smile. My phone buzzes, and I check the open doorway to make sure Dr. Wyatt's still occupied.

It all hits me: The Program, the handlers, it's like being submerged in ice water—the fact that my life is no longer my own. Someone has tampered with my past. Heartbreak and fear combine to make my head spin. Again.

I take out my phone and see that Foster sent me a response to my question about Derek being an embedded handler. The reply is only one word, and my stomach sinks as I read it.

Yes.

"Thank you for waiting," Dr. Wyatt announces, making me jump. I quickly shove my phone into my pocket, blinking away my shock at Foster's answer, what it means.

Yes, there are embedded handlers. Yes, they could be watching me.

Dr. Wyatt closes the door, but she doesn't go to her desk. Instead, she comes to stand directly behind our chairs. I look over my shoulder at her, lip curled and brows pulled together.

"What's this about?" I ask, finally finding my voice. "You can't just . . ." I look at Wes, who's waiting to hear what I have to say. I temper my annoyance. "You can't just make me miss class," I tell her. "I didn't do anything."

Truth is, I'm sure Dr. Wyatt has noticed the change in Wes. Notices that he's different than he was a few weeks ago. I don't even know what excuse his family gave as to why he was gone this time. Dr. Wyatt has no real idea about the Adjustment. She doesn't know what it does or who runs it. I'm no longer protecting Dr. McKee and Marie, but I also don't want Wes, or possibly me, to become lab rats for Dr. Wyatt and whoever she's working for.

Dr. Wyatt walks around to lean on her desk, leveling her gaze at me. "I can pull you out of class if I deem you to be dangerous," she says simply.

"I thought this was all because I said 'fuck,'" Wes says to me conversationally. "But now I'm really starting to wonder." He turns back to Dr. Wyatt. "Is it because we were reading a book in class? Are you . . . are you afraid of original thought?

SUZANNE YOUNG

Creativity?" He tilts his head like he's trying to decide which it is. Dr. Wyatt takes his attitude in stride, letting him continue.

"Definitely autonomy," Wes continues. "Look at us, making our own decisions. Thinking for ourselves. That must burn you up."

As I watch him, I realize Wes's natural state is defiance. No amount of memory manipulation can erase that part of him.

"Don't play games with me, Weston," Dr. Wyatt says. "You're not clever. You—"

"Well . . ." He holds up his finger, scrunching his nose like he hates to argue the point. "I am in the gifted program. But if your measure of intelligence is test scores, then . . . no, wait," he says, as if confused. "Those say I'm a genius too."

Dr. Wyatt looks at me accusingly. I shrug, emboldened by Wes's jokes, and it's then, in a sudden movement, that Dr. Wyatt jumps forward. She gets right up in Wes's face—a drill sergeant shouting commands. It's unexpected, and it throws both me and Wes off balance.

"I want answers," she calls out sharply, her hands on the armrests of his chair as she faces him. "You were in The Program, Mr. Ambrose. I saw you there myself."

Wes flinches away from Dr. Wyatt, blinking quickly.

"Stop it," I tell her immediately. She doesn't know that he's been reset. She doesn't know that she can cause a meltdown by bringing up his past.

Dr. Wyatt ignores me and continues her interrogation.

"You were in The Program, and they erased your memory,"

she says. "You came back, but whatever has happened to you since . . . this isn't The Program."

She reaches to tap his temple, and Wes lifts his face to stare at her, his eyes wide. His skin pale.

"What have you done?" she demands.

"I don't know what you're talking about," he replies, teeth clenched.

"Yes, you do," she says. "Who did this to you, Weston?" Dr. Wyatt is beginning to lose her cool, and I'm half out of my chair, ready to push her away from him if I have to.

"They tampered with your memories," she continues. "Erased them. It's against the law to manipulate memories. Why did they do it? What do you know?"

"I said I have no fucking idea what you're talking about," Wes snaps at her.

"Tell me," she growls, leaning down. Her behavior is erratic, alarming.

"Leave him alone," I say, taking her by the elbow to pull her back. "He doesn't remember."

Dr. Wyatt turns on me fiercely. "Do you?" she demands. "Are you the reason—"

"No," I say quickly. "We don't know anything!" The words echo around the room, and I lower my hand from her elbow, wrapping my arms around myself. I'm scared, and I don't know what to do. I don't know how far this will go.

"Can we please leave?" I ask, trying to sound brave.

Dr. Wyatt stares me down, and for a second I'm afraid she'll say no. That she'll imprison us in her office for life. Instead, she takes a step closer to me.

"I'm trying to save him," she says in a low voice. Pleading.

"Then I guess you should have saved him from The Program in the first place," I reply coldly. "Because right now he wants you to leave him alone." I turn back to Wes, willing him to get up. "Come on," I say to him, hoping he's all right.

For his part, Wes looks confused, his easygoing attitude troubled. I watch the clouds gather on his face. I say his name, and he stands up, avoiding my eyes. Avoiding Dr. Wyatt's glare.

He walks to open the door and leaves without even a backward glance. When I go to follow him, Dr. Wyatt calls my name.

"I hope you feel better," she says disingenuously, knowing I was lying in the first place. I narrow my eyes and turn around.

"I already do," I respond. "But thanks for your concern."

She smiles, motioning that I can leave. I walk out hurriedly, but when I get into the main hall, Wes is already gone.

CHAPTER THREE

I GO THROUGH THE REST OF MY MORNING HAUNTED by the expression on Wes's face after Dr. Wyatt confronted him. I shouldn't have gone searching for him—rationally, I know that. But if I hadn't been there, how far would Dr. Wyatt's interrogation have gone?

Unless . . . I made it worse by showing up. Maybe I always make it worse for him.

When it's nearly lunch, I walk down the hall as text messages from Nathan blow up my phone. I'm filled with dread. I don't want to see Nathan right now, but I'll have to make an excuse to get away from him. And I'll have to be convincing.

I take a cautious look around, expecting to find strangers watching me—*handlers everywhere*. My attempt at normalcy is hanging on by a thread.

The hall is filled with students rushing for the parking lot. Lunch recently became open campus, despite the best efforts of a handful of overprotective parents. Even though the school has instituted a monitor, all the newspapers have claimed the epidemic is over. A new board member even suggested that keeping us locked in school could cause further damage. The tide seems to be turning in our favor—at least in public.

But with returners getting sick, I'm not sure how long that good faith will last.

My stomach knots when I see Nathan waiting at my locker, looking down at his phone. For the past few weeks, we've been going to Campus Inn for lunch, but I won't eat with him today. I'll have to find a way to convince him it's not because he destroyed my world this morning—even though that much should be obvious.

"Hey," he says when he sees me. He holds up his phone. "I've been texting you."

"Sorry," I reply. "What's up?"

"*What's up?*" he repeats, studying me. "You took off after class. You didn't answer my texts. I'm assuming you went looking for Wes. Did you find him?"

"Oh, no. I didn't," I lie. "He must have left for the day." I don't tell him about Dr. Wyatt, even though Nathan should be the first person I discuss it with. But I don't trust him; it's horrible to say. It's unthinkable. Right now, I don't trust him, so I don't tell him that the monitor scared the shit out of me.

Or that she might have hurt Wes by bringing up The Program.

Nathan shakes his head. "Nah, I saw Wes walking to class last hour," he says. "He didn't even look at me. He really must not remember anything."

His words sting me—part of that "anything" is my long-term relationship with Wes—and I move past Nathan to spin the combination on my locker.

"I'm sorry," he says, reaching to touch my forearm in apology. Normally it would be comforting, but after everything it feels more like emotional manipulation.

"I'm fine," I say, turning so that his hand falls away. I'm still trying to figure out how to be on my own for lunch, when Nathan sighs.

"This is really bad timing," he says. "But would you hate me if missed lunch today? Jana's not feeling well and asked for a ride home." He nods down the hall, and I see Jana at her locker, waiting for him.

I nearly sway with relief but quickly catch myself. "Of course not," I say. "I hope she feels better."

Nathan waits a beat. "That's it?" he asks. "You're not going to give me a hard time about ditching you?" He narrows his eyes. "You're not even going to call me an asshole?"

"We need something to do later, right?" I say, and try to smile. When he doesn't buy the act, I shift tactics. "Your girlfriend is sick—I get it. You don't owe me an explanation. But if it helps, I really do think you're an asshole." I smile winningly.

"There it is," he says. "But if you need me, I'll stay. Today has been . . ." He pauses. "It's been a weird day for you. I don't want to just—"

"Nathan," I say, putting my palm on his chest and pushing him back a step toward Jana. "I'll be fine. Between Wes, The Program, and those damn assessments . . . I might just lose my mind. I'm tired of talking about it, thinking about it. So I'm going to work on my and Foster's missing labs this hour. It'll be a nice distraction. Just call me when you get back, okay?"

Nathan waits a moment, trying to discern my behavior. But at the same time, he must accept my explanation, because he gives me a quick hug. "I'll check in soon," he says before heading in Jana's direction.

I look past him to where Jana is standing, watching us curiously. I wave politely, and she smiles—quick and impersonal.

As they walk away, the tension in my body lessens, but it also leaves more room for my fear, my misery. I dart my eyes around the hall, feeling like I'm being watched.

It's a fact that everyone I love betrayed me. How can I square that? How can I feel okay when there's no one left to trust? When I'm so fucking alone? When I'm forgotten?

I slam my locker shut and rush for the back exit, desperate to escape the confines of the school. To breathe. I can't stay here anymore. I have to figure out what the hell is going on.

The moment I exit the double doors to the parking lot, I take a big gulp of air. The sun shines brightly, blurring everything in a haze of yellow. I take another breath, but the panic floods in, overwhelming me like an ocean wave crashing over my head. My chest constricts and I'm drowning.

My life is a lie.

I walk faster, my heart beating rapidly, pins and needles prickling over my skin. I need to get to my Jeep. Several people are hanging around, laughing, and making plans for lunch, but my singular mission is to get to my Jeep without collapsing.

I've made a mistake; I've let myself think—feel—too much. I should have gone home with fake cramps hours ago. Now I'm walking devastation.

My Jeep comes into focus, and the relief is immediate. I pull my backpack off my shoulders and jog to the door, opening it and tossing my bag across to the passenger seat. My hands shake as I climb in and grip the steering wheel.

I turn the ignition, but instead of starting, my Jeep revs, never catching. I turn it again, slamming my foot on the gas, but the engine only sputters, and I let it die.

It's a karmic pile-on, and I can no longer hold back. The quiet in my Jeep is deafening, the air warm and thick. I scream, the shriek cutting through the small space, and I smack the heel of my palm against the steering wheel. It hurts, but I do it again, harder—letting the anger take over.

The image of my grandparents, trying to pull me away from the handlers—crying and helpless. They didn't save me. They couldn't. No matter fault, they still failed me.

SUZANNE YOUNG

And then, even more unforgivable, my grandparents lied to me—both indirectly and to my face. Those pills they gave me . . . I realize now they were probably to keep me well-behaved. Keep me in line. What else have they done to cover this up? I don't know how deep this all goes, but I know that life as I know it is over.

I choke on the start of a sob and use my other hand to slap the steering wheel, accidentally blasting the horn. I'm losing it right now, dissolving into ashes and ready to blow away. People may be watching. Gossiping. But I don't care.

I'm about to hit the wheel again when there's a sharp knock on my driver's-side window. Startled, I spin to look, and my entire body freezes.

"Hey," Wes says, his voice muffled behind the glass. My lips part; my heart registers shock. When I don't move, he mimes rolling down the window, exaggerated and funny.

I've barely caught my breath when I lower the window, and I quickly wipe away the tears on my cheeks. For his part, Wes is disheveled, as if his first day back to school was more traumatic than he thought it would be. I search his expression to see if our meeting with Dr. Wyatt has hurt him. But there's no bloody nose, no flinching. He just looks tired.

"What are you doing?" I ask, still half in my head. This is the second time he's seen me cry today.

Wes smiles sheepishly, like he's wondering if he should leave. But he must overrule his instincts. "I saw you trying to start the Jeep. You know, before you started beating the shit out of it. I'm pretty good with engines—want me to take a look?"

"Why would you do that?" I ask, unsure of what he's thinking. Why he's here at all.

"Because I'm a nice guy," he offers with a smirk. He's flirting despite the clearly shitty day we're both having. Doesn't he wonder why Dr. Wyatt pulled me into his meeting? Or maybe he just wants to forget about it.

Despite my reservations, I pop the hood of the Jeep. "All right," I say, a little shaky. "Have at it."

Wes drops his backpack on the pavement, rounds the Jeep, and props up the hood. I lean down so I can see him through the opening near the windshield. He presses his lips together and stares at the engine, making his dimples deepen. The sun beats down on his cheeks, and they're slightly red, freckles dotting his nose.

What starts as admiration quickly turns into longing. It hits me how much I need him to know me. Love me again— the way he did in the beginning of us. I want him to confirm that I'm real—that some things were real.

"Well," Wes says, looking up from under the hood. I quell the rising panic in my chest, not wanting to alarm him. "It could be your battery," Wes says. "Can you try starting it again?"

I do just that, and, to my surprise, the engine turns over. Wes closes the hood, grinning at me. I leave the engine running and get out of the driver's seat.

"I swear it wouldn't start," I say, temporarily stunned out of my misery.

"You sure you weren't just trying to get me to come over?" Wes asks, leaning against the Jeep.

Suddenly the engine sputters and dies out. Wes laughs loudly, staring at me wide-eyed like he caused it to stall by making a bad joke. He tells me to pop the hood again, and we try, unsuccessfully, to get the engine running.

After a few minutes, I give up and climb out from behind the wheel. Wes still stands in front of the Jeep, his hands folded on top of his head as he stares at the engine.

"Well, shit," he says. "Do you have jumper cables?"

"I don't," I say.

Wes scans the parking lot. "I can ask around," he says. "Someone should—"

"It's fine," I say, not wanting him to worry about it. "I'll call my grandfather. Thanks for trying, though."

Wes closes the hood and comes over to where I'm standing next to the Jeep. He picks up his backpack from the concrete, pulling one strap over his right shoulder. He doesn't walk away immediately, and I don't want him to. There are so many questions burning in my mind. In my heart.

Do you love me?

Did you know I was in The Program?

Can I ever let you go?

I finally gather some nerve and open my mouth to ask about our meeting with Dr. Wyatt. A simple start. But before I can, Wes peeks around the open driver's door and motions inside the Jeep.

"Mind if I check it out?" he asks, his eyes flashing with anticipation.

"Oh," I say. My question falls away, and I wonder if that was his intention. "Sure. All yours."

Wes has always loved my Jeep. He'd change the oil and get it washed for me. Every so often I'd let him drive and gaze at him as he drove too fast. The fact he wants to see it now strums my heart, and I don't want to ruin the moment. It's too familiar, too right.

Wes climbs inside the Jeep, making himself comfortable in the seat as he inspects the dash and the gearshift. He looks over at me.

"What year is this?" he asks as if he can't tell. He probably can't. It's been rebuilt a bunch of times, something Wes no longer remembers.

"She's about ten years past her prime," I say, studying his every movement. Looking for flashes of him.

"Nonsense," Wes replies, running his hand lovingly across the steering wheel. "She's perfect."

Just then I catch something out of the corner of my eye. I turn and see a guy, slightly hidden by his car, across the parking lot. He looks away, pretending he hasn't been watching us, but I recognize him. I saw him in the Adjustment office; he knows Marie Devoroux. What was his name? It was unusual. Realm. Michael Realm, I think.

"Hey," I say to Wes, tapping his arm. He looks down at where I touched him before lifting his eyes to mine. "Do you know that guy?" I ask, nodding toward Michael Realm.

Wes leans out, but I stop him.

"Covertly," I say.

He sniffs a laugh and then ducks down to look in the side-view mirror. He narrows his eyes. "The tall guy?"

"Yeah."

"Is he your boyfriend?" Wes asks. "I'm jealous."

His comment catches me off guard, makes me blush. I stare at him for a moment, surprised by how easily he flirts with me, and hoping it means more than it probably does.

"No," I say quietly. "He's not my boyfriend." Wes puts his fingers over his lips like he's trying not to smile at my answer. I turn back to Michael Realm. "I met him once," I say, growing distracted as I search my memory. "I'm sure it's him."

"Well, I've never seen him before in my life," Wes says. In reality, Wes was with me when I met him.

I watch Michael Realm a little longer, knowing it's too much of a coincidence that he's here the same day Wes came back. Same day Dr. Wyatt questioned us. I just don't know how he plays into all of this.

"What is he doing here?" I say more to myself than Wes.

"Did you want to go talk to him, or . . . ?"

"No," I say. "That wasn't what I . . . I'm not interested in him."

"Good," Wes responds. "I was worried I'd have to be more obvious."

I laugh, and the sound of it—the lightness of it—is startling. Surreal and free of consequence. "I'm not sure you're being that subtle," I say, making him smile. The truth is, I *like* how he's flirting with me. I like how it makes me feel, how it overshadows the absolute wreckage of my reality.

Wes leans back in the seat, carefree. He doesn't have the weight of his memories, his past. He's not a tortured soul. At least, not anymore. I barely remember this version of him. In fact, I'm not sure I *ever* knew this version of him.

I throw an incautious glance in Michael Realm's direction, and he hurriedly gets into his black car. He could be here to remind me of Dr. McKee's warning to stay away from Wes—to keep his past from him. I promised I would. I begged the doctor to save Wes's life, and he did.

This is the cost.

I look at Wes and know that I can't ask him the questions I want. I can't tell him who he is to me, who we are to each other. Even though he's right here in front of me, he's never felt so far away.

"Do you want to grab lunch with me?" Wes asks, climbing out of the Jeep. "There's a pizza place—"

"No," I say too quickly. Rejecting him doesn't come naturally to me, and we both shift uncomfortably. I avoid his eyes when he turns to me.

"Do you . . . I mean, your Jeep won't start," he says, a slight insecurity in his voice. "And it's lunchtime. What are you going to eat?"

I look over at him, standing close enough to touch. Knowing how easy it would be to fall into a relationship with him again.

"And not to sound pathetic," he adds, "but I don't have any friends. So if you're feeling charitable—"

"Do you like pancakes?" I ask.

"I happen to fucking love pancakes," he responds immediately. "Why do you ask?"

"There's a place that serves breakfast all day. None of that IHOP shit either. You know Lulu's?" Wes and I had only been there once before.

"I don't know it," he says. "But it sounds perfect. I hope you're inviting me and not just taunting me with your talk of all-day pancakes."

I laugh. "We can probably get there and back before next hour," I say.

"Or . . . ," he offers, shrugging one shoulder. "We don't come back."

"Huh," I say like he's got a novel idea. "I'll think about it. But do you mind . . . ?" I motion to my nonstarting Jeep. "I doubt it'll start a second time."

"It would be my absolute pleasure to drive you to brunch," he replies. Wes smiles, and it's the purity in his expression that reminds me of how Wes makes me feel like the most important person in the world. Like he can see me. Like he can make it all real again.

Sharing a stack of pancakes together can't hurt. In fact, being near him is the only thing that doesn't hurt right now. We're in our own private universe.

Wes closes the door of my Jeep, and we start toward his parking space.

"Hope you don't mind the open air," he says, pointing to his motorcycle. "I have an extra helmet."

"I don't mind," I tell him, not wanting to give away that I know what he rides, and I know he always has an extra helmet—a habit he started when we got together.

We get to his bike, and Wes pulls my helmet from the pack and holds it out to me. As I take it, he runs his eyes over me. He seems to debate what he's going to say next. "It was Tatum, right?" he asks.

I nod, and neither of us acknowledges that it was Dr. Wyatt who mentioned my name in the first place. Wes climbs onto the bike, moving up on the seat so I can get on behind him.

"And do we know each other, Tatum?" he asks, snapping the chin strap on his helmet. He doesn't look back at me, but something in his voice tells me he's been waiting to ask that question from the first moment he saw me in class. I must be familiar to him.

My entire body warms with the depth of the answer, the love between us, but I can't explain it to him; I won't put him in danger. But I can't outright deny it either.

"Yeah," I say quietly, putting on my helmet. "We do."

Wes kicks the bike to life, and it sends a vibration over my entire body. I put my hands on either side of his waist, a familiar movement that is suddenly anything but. He doesn't follow up on the question, and I'm grateful. I don't want to lie to him. And I don't want to tell him the truth.

I'll have to figure out exactly what I can say, but for now, we're going for a ride on his motorcycle, wind in our faces, free.

And as Wes revs the engine and drives us toward the parking lot exit, I glance back at Michael Realm and find him watching us leave. His expression deadly serious.

CHAPTER FOUR

WES AND I DON'T TALK AS WE RIDE TOWARD THE restaurant. Normally, Wes would turn back to me at every stoplight, continuing a conversation the entire way. We have less to say to each other now—odd, considering we have so much more to talk about. But there's intimacy in conversation. An intimacy based on shared experiences. He doesn't remember those.

Lulu's is a house-turned-café with overflowing flower beds, pale yellow siding, and a white picket fence. Their pancakes are legendary, as is the usual wait time to get a table.

As we pull up, Wes glances around and then smiles at me. "Now, this place is goddamn delightful," he says emphatically.

"It is," I agree. "It's usually really busy, but it doesn't look too bad today."

We stash our helmets and go inside. Even though there's

not a wait, it's a little hectic, nearly every table taken. The café smells like hazelnut coffee and maple syrup, the air warm from all the bodies in here. The music is on, but it's not loud enough to make out what's playing. Right now it sounds like moaning whales.

It's a seat-yourself situation, and Wes and I go stand at a table near the window just as the guy sitting there packs up his laptop. When he's gone, Wes and I sit across from each other, perusing the menu. The server comes by, and we order coffees and two stacks of pancakes.

Wes puts his elbows on the table and leans in. "Before we address the psychotic school administrator with the out-of-line interview tactics," he says, "I feel like we should talk about your fists of fury in the Jeep. I mean, I wasn't going to bring it up . . . but you . . ." He scrunches his nose as if making sure it's a topic he can mention. "You were crying during first hour too. I was worried."

I study him to see if this is all a ruse somehow, like he might remember. Otherwise, why would he worry? Why would he ask me to lunch? I'm probably projecting, but then again, maybe it's still there—our love. But the way his soft brown eyes study me, trying to figure me out, confirms he's not the old Wes. Not the one I knew.

"This morning, when you saw me," I say, lowering my gaze to the table, "my best friend had just told me something devastating. Life altering. And I . . . I'm not handling it all that well."

There's a sudden and aching fear creeping into my lungs, squeezing. Grief surrounds me. I'm scared because it feels like

I'm all alone in this. In my whole life, I've never been truly alone until now.

"You can tell me," Wes says, and I look up at him. "I know I'm sort of a stranger," he adds, "but I don't have any ulterior motives. At least none that I can remember." He offers me a small smile.

The server appears and drops off our coffees. I nod a thank-you and wrap my hands around my hot mug.

"To be honest," I tell Wes. "That's why you might be the only person I can trust right now."

"Exactly."

I watch him, his concern, and imagine things are different between us. The way they used to be. But that only lasts a moment because there is no "used to be." Wes and I were just as big a lie as the rest of it. The only real thing is now. This moment.

"What did your friend tell you, Tatum?" he asks. "What could be so bad?"

"I was in The Program," I murmur, the words breaking my heart. "I was in The Program, and I don't remember any of it."

Wes tilts his head, seeming confused. "Isn't that the point?"

"No. I was supposed to forget my problems, or at least what they considered problems. But I remember the bad stuff. I mean, some of my memories are wrong, but overall, I have them. It's The Program that's gone. They made me forget the wrong stuff. They've done something. They changed me."

"You're not who you used to be," Wes says, grabbing sugar

to pour into his coffee. "Funny story, neither am I. Seems we have that in common, Tate. Two lost souls."

He called me Tate—he must remember that. Or maybe it's proof that, given the chance, most of us would make the same decisions, same mistakes, even if we don't realize we're making them. Maybe that's what fate really is.

"I don't know what to do now," I confide. "Because it's not just that I forgot. No one *told* me. My family, my friends, they kept it a secret. How can I face them, knowing they kept something so huge from me?"

"I can relate," Wes says, stirring his coffee, the metal spoon clinking on the ceramic. "My parents act like I've been away at summer camp. None of us has said a word about my past. So I can tell you that eventually, you'll accept it. And you'll forgive your family because you have to."

I'm not sure if Wes is right, but the level of sadness in his voice bothers me. Forgiveness is voluntary. There should be no "have to" about it.

"Besides," Wes adds. "I'm starting to believe that our memories can be a dangerous place. Part of why I'm so damn charming is because I don't remember how royally fucked my life has been. So I refuse to look back," he continues. "I'm afraid it will kill me. You're welcome to join me in my blissful ignorance if you'd like." He smiles, hopeful.

That's why he didn't immediately bring up my inexplicable presence at his meeting with Dr. Wyatt. Blissful ignorance—it can have its advantages in this world. And honestly, I want to say that I'll join him. But I can't let this go so easily. It's not fair—it's not fair to me. To be lied to. Betrayed. I have to know how deep it goes before I can put it behind me.

"You're not going to take my offer," Wes says, sounding disappointed.

"Not yet. But . . . maybe I can once I have answers."

Wes lifts one eyebrow like he doesn't believe me, sets his spoon aside, and takes a sip of his coffee. He hums out that it's good.

"Well," he says. "Speaking of answers, we should get back to that psychotic administrator. Dr. Wyatt, was it? She's kind of weird. Why does she care if I was in The Program?"

"She's obsessed with returners," I say. "Monitoring them and looking for signs of another outbreak, I guess."

"Outbreak?"

I stare at him blankly, not sure how to begin explaining an epidemic that killed so many of our friends. I could never illustrate the gravity of it. What it did to us.

"Oh," Wes says. "You mean the suicides? I read about that," he adds quietly. Which means he knows the reason both of us ended up in The Program—they thought we were a danger to ourselves. True or not, that was the excuse they used to erase our pasts.

"Dr. Wyatt is acting like they did something *else* to me," Wes says, lifting his eyes to mine. "Do you know what she was talking about?"

I swallow hard, but before I can figure out what to say, the server drops off our pancakes. They smell both sweet and buttery, and Wes lets the question drop as he digs into his food.

We're quiet for a while, and when we're nearly done eating, I absently look over to the counter. My stomach sinks when I see Kyle Mahoney there, picking up two coffees to go. Her white-blond cascade of hair, her tan legs and bare shoulders—I'm not imagining that Wes's eyes drift toward her.

It's a stab in my heart, and I want to tell him to stop. Stop looking at her. Stop noticing her. But Wes once told me that the heart has muscle memory . . . and that would apply to her, too. I wasn't the only one who took up space in his life.

I push away the unfinished pancakes and grip my hot coffee cup. When I lift my head, Wes is watching me.

"What's wrong?" he asks.

"Nothing," I say unconvincingly.

"Is it her?" he asks, nodding at Kyle's back. "Do you know her? Wait, do I know her? Never mind. Don't tell me. It doesn't matter."

"But maybe it does," I say quietly. "Not just her—but maybe it all matters." I want to believe his past matters—that *I* matter to him. But my conscience screams at me. *Don't tell him. Don't hurt him.*

"You think I should know everything," Wes begins, "but I don't see it that way. It's deciding between my past and my future. Which would you choose, Tate? Would you think your old self, your old life—one you don't even remember—would be worth dying for?"

"I don't know. Do you?"

He watches me for a long moment. "No. I just want to be a normal guy. I want to start over. I want . . ." He furrows his brow and lowers his eyes. "Forget it," he says, not finishing his thought.

Kyle leaves the coffee shop without even noticing us, and the intensity of the moment seems to fade without her presence. What would Wes think if I told him he'd left me and started dating her? That he broke my heart utterly and completely?

"No offense," Wes adds. "But you don't really remember either, not if you were in The Program, right? So let's accept that we're different people now and move on. Why spend our lives chasing the past?"

He's right. We could start over and be whoever we want. Leave this place, leave the past. But almost as a cosmic answer, I see another figure step up to the coffee counter. My heart trips.

Michael Realm glances over his shoulder at me and Wes, and then quickly darts his eyes away when he finds me already watching him. He followed us here.

"We should go," I say to Wes. I don't have time to wait for the bill, so I throw down some cash and stand up. I'm truly frightened.

Wes laughs like I'm acting strangely, and he motions to the money. "You don't have to pay. I'll—"

"We have to go," I say in a low voice, more forcefully.

Wes stands up and pushes in his chair. "Fine," he says,

taking one last sip of his coffee. "But buying me brunch doesn't mean I owe you anything, if that's what you're—" He stops joking when he sees I'm not playing around. He swallows hard and holds out his hand for me to take. I almost do, but that would be a signal—proof that Wes and I are building something.

And I don't want Michael to see that. I don't want to give him any ammunition against us. I walk past Wes, my arm brushing against his, his hand left hanging out. I swear I can feel him wilt slightly, but then he shoves his hands in his pockets and walks with me out the door and into the afternoon.

I quickly grab my helmet and put it on, watching the door of Lulu's. I'm on the bike before I realize Wes is standing there, staring at me.

"I don't mean to be nosy," he says, "but are you on the run from the cops or something?"

"What?" I ask, surprised. He smiles.

"I'm kidding," he says. "*Mostly*. But the fact that wasn't immediately obvious is worrisome." He puts on his helmet and gets in front of me on the bike. I slip my arms around him and lean in closer, my heart racing as I wait for Michael Realm to appear.

"Sorry," I say. "I'm just a little freaked out right now."

"Why? Because I—"

"No, nothing about you," I say. "It was this guy."

"Huh," Wes says, kicking the bike to life and revving it loudly. "Another promising development."

"It was the guy I saw earlier—the one I pointed out in the parking lot?"

Wes turns to me, his eyes concerned. "He's following you?"

"Us." I pause. "Or me, I don't know."

"And why would he be doing that?" Wes asks, his voice ticking up.

"I'm not exactly sure," I say. "At first, I thought it was because you just returned, you know? But now I'm thinking it might be me. I don't know. Let's just get out of here."

"Done," Wes says, telling me to hang on. We ride out of the parking lot, on our way back to school, when I lean forward, my lips near his ear.

"Would you take me home instead?" I ask. Despite everything going on, home seems the safest place to be.

"Of course," Wes says, and I give him my address.

I glance back and make sure that no one is following us. I notice the first return of clouds clinging to the sky and immediately miss the sun. Wind blows through the trees, and Wes has to tighten his grip against it.

At the next stoplight, Wes turns slightly to talk to me. I love this angle of him, so familiar. I lean in closer.

"So who is this guy?" Wes asks as if he's just curious. "What's his name?"

"Michael Realm," I say. The light turns green.

"Stupid name," Wes says under his breath, and continues toward my house.

CHAPTER FIVE

MY STREET IS QUIET FROM THE ABSENCE OF CHIL-
dren, cars gone from driveways. It's like we have the entire
block to ourselves. And as far as I can tell, no one followed us
from the café.

Wes pulls his bike up on the side of my house, off the road
and hidden. It's the same place he'd always park, and I wonder
if it just makes sense or if it's a memory. Wes looks at my mod-
est house—not nearly as nice as his. I don't have an entire basement apartment to myself like he does.

"You mentioned your grandfather," he says, both of us
climbing off his motorcycle. "Do you live with him?"

"Yeah. Him and my gram." I unsnap my helmet and set it
on the seat.

"Your parents, too?" he asks.

"Nope. My mom's remarried, and I see her on holidays sometimes. We're not close. And my dad—I don't know where my dad is. New York, maybe."

"I'm sorry."

"Why?" I ask. "My grandparents are great. They—" But the words, the ones I've said over and over through the years, fall silent on my lips. I was going to say my grandparents are great—they never let me down. They've always had my back.

But they did let me down. And they lied about it.

Wes's expression grows serious for a moment, but then it clears and he points to the house. "Mind if I come in for a bit?" he asks. "I don't really want to go back to school yet."

It makes me smile, the way he invites himself—always inquisitive. He wants to know more, wants to explore. It's not expectant or pushy. It's a quality I've always found endearing. Still do.

Even so, I debate continuing our conversation. A large part of me has missed him desperately, madly. But am I putting him in danger just by being near him? Can that trigger a crashback?

I decide that as long as I keep control of the situation, control the narrative, Wes and I will be better for it. We'll each have someone to talk to. Someone to confide in. Or, at least, that's what I rationalize as I lead him toward the back door of my house to enter through the kitchen.

As I unlock the door, Wes peeks over the fence, checking out Pop's vegetable garden. Insatiably curious.

When we get inside, my house still smells slightly of the roast beef Gram cooked last night. Wes looks around, seeming comfortable within the space. When he catches me staring at him, he smiles.

We walk into the living room, and he immediately goes to where my family pictures are hanging on the wall. He points to one of me at my first Communion, decked out in white.

"Adorable," Wes says. I smile. "Are you an only child?" he asks, continuing down the line to inspect each picture.

"Yep," I say.

"When I first came back," Wes says, stopping at a picture of me in eighth grade, riding a horse in Washington, "I thought I was an only child. Turns out I had a sister." He swallows hard and turns to me.

Of course, I already know this. Weston's sister died several years ago in a suicide pact with her boyfriend, Mackey. They drove a car off a bridge and into the water, causing Mackey to die on impact. Cheyenne drowned in the car. It was during the height of the epidemic, when one in three teens died. With so many deaths, theirs could have been lost among the rest, but Mackey's friends started a memorial by the river. And it was at that memorial when I met Wes almost three years ago.

He'd been so lost, watching the water, trying to be close to his sister. He was tormented. I should have known how badly, but I wasn't paying enough attention. I regret that. I regret that I let him suffer.

His sister's gone now. And even though I didn't know her,

Cheyenne was a part of my life too. She was the ghost who haunted him. Her death a wound I couldn't heal.

I loved Wes deeply and truly—but I missed the signs of his complicated, life-altering grief. Despite what I wanted to believe, love wasn't enough.

And just like that, Dr. McKee's warning rings truer in my ears. I have to be careful with Wes. I couldn't live with myself if I hurt him again.

"Did you know her?" Wes asks, furrowing his brow. "Did you know Cheyenne?"

"No," I admit. "But I sort of knew her boyfriend, Mackey. It was awful what happened to them. I'm so sorry."

"I don't remember her," he admits. "I saw her picture and read up on the accident." He looks sideways at me. "Can I call it an accident?"

"Yes," I answer immediately.

The corners of Wes's mouth turn up in a soft smile. "I have to say, you seem like a really good person."

"Sometimes," I respond, although the simple fact that he's here right now might disprove his assumption.

Wes seems to consider my response and walks over to sit on the couch. When I sit next to him, dropping my car keys on the coffee table, he turns to me.

"So how did things get so messed up that both of us—really good people," he adds, "ended up in The Program?"

And I don't have to lie when I respond. "I'm not sure. But I intend to find out."

SUZANNE YOUNG

A car pulls into my driveway, and I go over to the window, surprised to see my grandfather park his car next to Wes's bike. He climbs out, his phone pressed to his ear.

"My pop's home," I say, looking back at Wes worriedly. My grandfather usually works until four or five, and he has no idea that Wes came back to school today. He has no idea that I know the truth about The Program.

"Are you not allowed to have company?" Wes asks, seeming confused by my alarm.

"Get to the table," I say, and point toward the kitchen. Wes is apprehensive, but he does what I ask while I run to the fridge to grab two sodas. The outer door opens, and I quickly set one can in front of Wes. I open mine, drop down in the chair, and look up just as Pop walks into the kitchen. He stops dead when he sees us and lowers the phone from his ear, clicking it off.

His glasses are askew, and he straightens them before darting his eyes from Wes to me. "Tatum," he says in a tight voice. "What are you—?"

I cross in front of him to stop my grandfather from questioning Wes. "Pop, this is Weston," I say, like I'm introducing them for the first time. Pop turns his eyes to mine questioningly, but when Wes stands and offers his hand, Pop shakes it and forces a smile.

"Hello, son," he says to him, a touch of grief in his voice that I don't think Wes notices. For the most part, Pop plays along. Wes sits down and takes a drink from his soda, oblivious to the glare my grandfather sends in my direction.

"Tatum," Pop says. "Why aren't you at school?"

"Lunch," I say easily.

He glances at his watch. "Lunch ended nearly a half hour ago."

I fake a look of surprise. "We lost track of time," I say. "It's been a stressful day. My Jeep wouldn't start, and Wes offered me a ride to lunch. We ate, but then came back here because I had a headache."

Wes doesn't acknowledge the lie I'm dealing my grandfather. He quietly sips his drink.

"Headache?" Pop asks with concern, putting his hand gently on my back. "Are you okay?"

"It's gone now," I say. "Wasn't a huge deal. I think it was too warm today. Or I could be dehydrated. Who knows." I wave away the concern. "I'm feeling better, so we're heading back to school now."

Wes looks at me as if asking if we're really going back. I nod that he should get up, my expression telling him *We're* definitely *not going back to school.* He stands and pushes in his chair.

"Why don't you go ahead, Weston," my grandfather tells him. "I'll give Tatum a ride. We'll look at her Jeep, too."

In his hand, Pop's phone begins to ring, and he glances at the number. "I have to take this," he says, backing away from me. "Stay here. I'll be right back." He answers the phone with a curt "Yes?" and walks through the living room to hurry up the stairs toward his bedroom. The moment he's gone, Wes breathes out a heavy sigh.

"Do you want me to stay while you ask him about The Program?" he offers. And I'm surprised by the question, a little embarrassed. Because even though I want to find out the truth, now that my grandfather's here, I've lost my nerve.

Is it possible to both want the truth and be scared of it?

"Thank you," I tell Wes. "But I've got it."

He looks a little doubtful at first, but then he says that it's up to me. I walk him to the door and hold it open, resting my cheek against the side as I regard him. Wes smiles, not seeming to mind my attention.

"Hey," he says. "Since you and Dr. Wyatt are the only people who talked to me today, I was wondering . . . want to have lunch tomorrow? If not, I can see if Wyatt's available."

There's a pang of butterflies in my stomach, but I'm not sure how to answer. At what point will I know for sure when I'm doing something wrong? Will I even see it? Or will I keep going until it's too late?

"I'll take you anywhere you want," Wes adds, reading my hesitation.

Although I know I shouldn't, the temptation is too great. "Maybe," I say, insinuating that I most certainly will. Wes smiles, triumphant, and backs out of the doorway.

"Well then, I'll see you tomorrow," he whispers.

And when he leaves, I watch him ride away, my heart fuller than it's been in weeks.

CHAPTER SIX

MY GRANDFATHER COMES BACK INTO THE KITCHEN with a manila folder in his hand, and I get a chance to examine him. His face is pale, his breathing a little too fast. He's obviously worried about something, probably me.

"Who called?" I ask.

"A source for a story I'm working on," he says, and briefly looks around. "Did Weston leave?" he asks. When I tell him he has, my grandfather shakes his head, letting his politeness fade.

"What were you thinking?" he demands. "Why would you bring him here?"

"He doesn't remember anything," I say. "He offered me a ride home, and I took it."

I leave out the part about Dr. Wyatt interrogating us, the

part where Nathan told me I was in The Program. My grandfather doesn't exactly have my trust right now.

"And what about you, Pop?" I ask. "Why are *you* home?"

"I needed a file," he says, holding up the folder. He darts his gaze away, and his file seems more like an afterthought. A prop. I suspect it's more likely that he knew I was here somehow.

Michael Realm was following me and Wes today. Maybe he wasn't the only one watching us.

Pop and I are clearly lying to each other about our intentions, but neither of us calls the other out. I can't believe I'm okay with this level of deceit. We've never done this before. At least, not that I can remember.

This is the same person who would slay the monsters under my bed when I was kid. Who would bandage my scraped knee. Who would take up my cause whenever I had a problem. How can he be the same man who would lie about something so awful?

I've lived with my grandparents for as long as I can remember. My mother was seventeen when she got pregnant with me, and my grandparents promised to stand by whatever she wanted to do. Athena—my mother—decided to have the baby and get married.

Unfortunately, a few weeks before I arrived, my father announced that teenage parenthood wasn't really for him. He had plans to go to college in New York the next year, and I guess my mother and I didn't work into that plan. He left.

I was born, and my mother dressed me up like a doll, a

showpiece. I've seen pictures. But she had a hard time with the essentials. She'd leave the house without feeding me. Or forget to change my diaper. Frustrated, my grandmother told her she had to do better. My mother promised she would.

The next day, my mother went out and didn't come home. She called from the road and told my grandparents she was moving to California. That it was best for me to stay with them. That this was her doing better.

My grandparents never really told me about those days, the first days. And I don't remember them. I'm not even sure how I know the whole story. I guess I put the pieces together over time through scrapbooks and overheard conversations.

In all this time, my mother has never offered any sort of apology for abandoning me. I'm not sure she even feels guilty. She's never once mentioned it. She's never once said she loves me.

But she was right—it *was* better. Leaving me was the best thing she's ever done for me, will ever do for me. My grandparents *are* my parents. They've raised me. We don't deceive each other; we're not supposed to. And yet . . . here we are.

"We should head out," my grandfather says, startling me from my thoughts. "I have to get back to the office."

"Yeah," I say with a quick nod. "Let me just grab my keys."

I walk into the living room, and as I pick up the key ring from the coffee table, I see that Pop left his phone on the side table. Without thinking, I grab it for him. But when I do, a new text pops up—a preview on his screen. I look down at it, and a chill settles in my bones.

SUZANNE YOUNG

Just keep them apart.

I recognize the phone number. It's the Adjustment office.

My stomach sickens, and I set the phone facedown on the table, pretending not to have seen it. Now I know who sent my grandfather here. And I guess that means Michael Realm really was there to remind me to stay away from Wes.

The level of interference, spying, and deception is suffocating. It's clear the people around me are trying to control me.

Inside, my anger builds. I'm tired of everyone meddling in my life. Everyone lying. I was stupid to even come here in the first place. The moment Nathan told me about The Program, I should have left school and gone directly to the Adjustment office. Dr. McKee and Marie Devoroux have a lot to explain.

I keep my breathing steady as I walk into the kitchen and find my grandfather standing by the door with his car keys.

"Ready to go?" he asks, and smiles warmly.

And I can barely hold it together when I smile back and say, "Yes."

At the last minute, Pop remembered to grab his phone before we left the house. He doesn't mention the text he received, and I certainly don't bring it up. But the minute we're done, I'm going to the Adjustment office. I'll demand answers.

Our drive to school is quiet, and my grandfather doesn't bring up Wes once. I wonder if he's waiting for my grandmother—she's the better interrogator in our house. Not that either of them have room to judge my behavior at this point. But it would almost be comforting for them to act normal. Concerned. Instead, I'm getting the silent treatment with an undercurrent of surveillance mixed in.

I think about The Program—their tactics. When handlers would come for people who'd been flagged, it wasn't just the person they'd take. They'd finish the erasure by confiscating personal belongings. Replacing clothes. Removing pictures.

But I still have pictures of Wes. My clothes were all the same. How? The only explanation is that my grandparents saved my memories from The Program—even though they couldn't save me.

So why keep The Program a secret? Why can't I remember?

The lack of conversation in the car is starting to become obvious, and at one point, Pop looks sideways at me.

"About that headache," he starts. "Did it happen after seeing Wes?"

It got worse after Nathan told me I was in The Program, but to get out of the conversation, I say, "No. Just a steady headache since this morning."

Pop nods and tells me he's worried. "We should let the doctor know," he adds. I wonder which doctor he means. The nice older pediatrician I've seen since childhood—the one who gives me shots and physicals? Or the doctors who've manipulated my memories?

The school parking lot is full as we pull in, and I quickly scan for Wes's motorcycle. I don't see it. The students are back in the building now, but I'm not going to join them. My grandfather pulls up in front of my Jeep and parks.

The day has only gotten more humid, and the air in my Jeep is practically steam when I climb inside. My grandfather walks around, taking a handkerchief out of his pocket to mop the sweat that's gathered on his brow. He tells me to fire up the engine, and when it doesn't start, he tells me to turn it off.

I do, and then get out of the Jeep while he props up the hood and looks around.

Even though we're only a few feet apart, it feels like miles. I'm suddenly struck with the most intense loneliness I've ever known—like I'm lost. Adrift at sea. My earlier anger begins to feel like desperation.

"Pop," I say, and take a gulp of air. He raises his head from the other side of the hood and looks at me. His gaze is steady, his expression unreadable. I hesitate, afraid to confront him. Afraid of what he might say. I lower my eyes.

"Have you checked the battery?" I ask instead. I hate myself for not challenging him here and now. I'm a coward.

Pop furrows his brow and looks at the battery. "Let's try and jump it, but we'll definitely want to replace it tonight," he adds. "Even if we get it started, it won't last too much longer."

"Good idea," I say.

Pop gets jumper cables out of his trunk, and I help him set them up. I go back to the Jeep, and when I get inside, trickles of sweat slide down my back. I turn the ignition, and although the engine takes a minute to catch, it starts. I give my pop a thumbs-up, and he tells me to keep her running.

He walks around, drying his brow again, and opens the passenger door to heave himself onto the seat. He adjusts the air vent to blow on his face and asks me to rev the engine while he leans over to fiddle with the loose knob on my gearshift. I stare at the side of his face.

"Who told you to come home, Pop?" I ask suddenly. My grandfather pauses but doesn't look up.

"Someone saw you leaving with Wes," he replies. "They were concerned. They asked me to check."

"Who?" I ask, my heart pounding. Pop turns to me.

"Someone who works for Dr. McKee," he admits. "The doctor was concerned you'd trigger a crashback in Wes. Undo the work he'd done to save him. The doctor asked you to stay away from him, Tatum. It appears you don't intend to listen. Think about what happened last time. You both landed in the Adjustment, and that didn't end well for either of you." His voice hitches on this last statement, and he turns to look out the window, hiding his face.

He's hurting me, and part of it is because he's right. But he's also misrepresenting what happened. My grandfather knows I went into The Program, and yet he still doesn't say it. Doesn't acknowledge the effect it had on me, on my memories. He lets me think this is entirely my fault for not letting go. And it really pisses me off.

"It was just a ride home," I say. The lie is obvious, but the truth is evading us both, it seems.

SUZANNE YOUNG

"It was unethical," Pop says. "And I expected better from you." He opens the passenger door to climb out. His words are a slap in the face, and I physically recoil from them.

"The Jeep is running now," he adds. "I'll pick up a new battery and swap it out when you get home. You going back in?" he asks, motioning toward the building.

I look in that direction and then shake my head. "No," I say, my jaw tight. "I decided I still have a headache."

He watches me. "I can have your grandmother call in a prescription," he offers.

Yeah, right. Last time she gave me meds they nearly put me in a coma. "I think I'll just take some Tylenol," I say, my voice a little bitter. "Maybe a nap."

"Okay," he agrees, and presses his lips into a smile. I wonder if he regrets how he talked to me, so in return, he's rolling over on this. "Let me know if you need anything," he adds.

I nod that I will, and he closes the door. I'm angry that he hurt me, lied to me. I'm angry that I was a coward and didn't ask him about The Program. His loyalty should be with me—not Dr. McKee.

And the minute my grandfather pulls out of the parking lot, I shift gears and head toward the Adjustment office.

CHAPTER SEVEN

AS I SPEED TOWARD THE ADJUSTMENT OFFICE, MY anger ticks up. Dr. McKee called my grandfather to warn him that I left school with Wes. But Dr. McKee isn't my doctor; he isn't treating Wes anymore. So what gives him the right to contact my family? Clearly, Michael Realm was there to watch us, after all. Bastard.

I check my phone at the stoplight and see I've missed a message from Nathan. He's another story, one I can't deal with just yet, so I turn off the power on my phone and drop it into the cup holder.

I pull into the strip mall parking lot where the Adjustment office is located. There is a FOR LEASE sign unceremoniously taped to the frosted-glass door, like it had just been some pizza shop and not an experimental treatment center that resulted in multiple deaths.

It makes me ill to be this close again. Ever since I met the doctors of the Adjustment, my life has been steadily falling apart. Headaches and nosebleeds, long-held secrets and scandals coming out. Losing Wes to a reset.

I regret ever coming here. And the more I try to fix that mistake, the deeper my problems get. At what point do I walk away and cut my losses? Which losses are acceptable to take? I don't think I know the answer to that yet.

The door to the nearby deli opens, and I'm surprised to see Dr. Marie Devoroux walk out with a brown paper bag, two ends of subs poking out. Her presence shocks me, even though I was coming here to see her. She looks different.

Her dark skin has dulled, her hair cropped close to the scalp. She is stunningly beautiful—her red lipstick flawless—but her presence has diminished slightly. She's troubled. I swallow hard and climb out of my Jeep.

When I close the door, Marie looks over and stops dead when she realizes it's me. She hugs the bag closer to her chest and forces a smile.

"Tatum," she says, glancing around the empty lot. "What are you doing here?"

"We need to talk," I say. I can't even pretend to not be angry.

"I don't think that's a good idea," she responds curtly.

Although her voice is steady, always professional, her posture gives way to concern. "Dr. McKee said—"

"Did you know I was in The Program?" I interrupt. Her lips part, and she falters a moment with her answer.

"I don't—where did you hear that?" she asks. "That's outrageous. Not to mention dangerous thinking, especially with everything that's happened to—"

"You're going to *lie*?" I ask, incredulous. "Stand there and lie to my face?"

"Why would I lie?" Marie responds convincingly. "Isn't it more likely that whoever told you was lying? Or mistaken?"

Even though I don't believe that, her tone is earnest. Honest. Is it possible she didn't know? It only takes me a second to decide it's not. Marie tilts her head, inspecting me. She takes a step closer and holds out her hand to me in a comforting gesture. When I don't take it, she sighs.

"I'm worried about you, Tatum," Marie says, her tone motherly. "You were part of the Adjustment. You've been through a lot. I'd hoped after everything that happened, you'd want to take care of yourself. Please, go home and rest."

I shake my head, enraged that she won't be honest with me. "And my grandfather?" I ask. "Dr. McKee called him. Why?"

Marie blinks quickly, and I'm guessing she didn't think my grandfather would pass along that information to me. She shifts the brown bag in her arms, and looks impatiently at the Adjustment office door.

"That was for Weston's benefit, not yours." Her words are

SUZANNE YOUNG

cold, cutting, and I think she intended them to hurt me.

"I don't believe you," I say. "In fact, I don't believe *anything* you've said."

Marie straightens her back, pulling herself up to her full height. "Rest," Marie says again, this time more forcefully. "Weston's return was surely a shock to your system. But please, don't repeat past mistakes. Just . . . let it go." She says it emphatically, as if she wants nothing more. I bet.

Marie doesn't wait for my reply. She walks over to the Adjustment door and rings the bell on the side. The lock clicks, and she pulls the door open and slips inside.

I'm furious; my hands are actually shaking. Marie lied to me about The Program—I'm sure of it. And she fully intended to leave out the fact that Dr. McKee called my grandfather, but I caught her. It proves that if I'm going to make accusations going forward, I'll need proof. Something to force them to tell the truth. And that includes my grandparents.

I stomp toward my Jeep and yank open the door to get in. Just as I start the engine, the passenger door suddenly opens and Michael Realm climbs inside. He closes the door and turns to me.

"We need to talk," he says calmly.

My eyes widen, and I press my shoulder against my door, ready to bolt. "What the hell are you doing?" I demand, my voice high pitched with shock.

"I'm not supposed to make contact," he says, holding up his hands apologetically, "but I want to help you."

I stare at him. "Help me with what?" I ask, slowly easing myself off the door. Despite my barely knowing who he is, there is something familiar about him now that he's up close. Something I don't immediately distrust—although I obviously should.

"I'm sorry," he says, his eyebrows pulled together with worry. "I'm not sure if you remember me. My name's Michael Realm."

"I met you in the Adjustment office, right?" I ask.

"Yeah." He smiles, seeming relieved.

"Great," I reply. "Now, why are you following me? Why are you in my Jeep, Michael?"

"Please, call me Realm," he says, like his first name is too formal. "And I was at the school because I knew Wes would be back today. I wanted . . . I wanted to make sure he was okay." He pauses. "Make sure you were okay."

"And what business is it of yours?" I ask.

Realm lowers his eyes. "None, I suppose. But I was concerned anyway."

I watch him a moment, trying to figure out his game. I'm honestly baffled. "Wes doesn't remember me, if that's what you were checking for," I say. "I haven't told him anything about our past, so you can stop spying on us."

"I wasn't—" Realm winces, seeming embarrassed by the accusation. "I guess it was spying, but I didn't mean it that way. I swear."

His brown eyes have some sincerity to them, although the

shading under them is dark, like he hasn't slept. And although I don't know his larger role in the Adjustment—his role with Marie and Dr. McKee—he acts like he's telling the truth. Not that I'm the best judge of that.

"You said you want to help me," I start. "What exactly did you mean? What can you do?"

"Personally?" he says. "Not much. But I wanted to talk to you, let you know just how dangerous it is for you to be around Wes right now."

A wave of sickness rolls over me. "That's your story too?" I ask. "Does everyone think I have amnesia—like I'd forget what Dr. McKee warned?"

Realm chews on his inner lip. "Depends," he says. "Do you? Because you left with Wes. And I saw you at lunch, Tatum. Saw you in your Jeep, losing your shit. Maybe . . . maybe we have a reason to be worried."

"You don't even know me," I shoot back, realizing how unbalanced I must have looked in those moments in my Jeep. My cheeks heat with shame.

"Look," Realm says, leaning closer. "I'm not trying to make you more upset. I'm just . . . Give it all some time to settle. I've known a lot of returners, and I've seen what happens when they get too much stimulus too soon."

"And how much time?" I ask. "When would be an appropriate time for me to live my own life? Or do I need permission?"

Realm smiles at my question, and I notice the nasty red scar on his neck. It proves he has a past, a pretty gnarly one judging by the wound. Despite this, he's charming. Sweet, even. Then again, he could be a really skilled liar. I tend to draw them to me.

"We all want you to live your life, Tatum," Realm says. "An amazing, happy life. But it's hard for you to do that when you're living half in the past. Now, I'm not saying that you and Wes aren't meant to be, or whatever romantic notion has been built up. But you're not meant to be right now. That I can promise. So all I'm asking is for you to—"

"Stay away from him," I finish. Realm nods, looking apologetic.

"We need you to be well," he says in an exhausted breath.

"You said 'we,'" I point out. "Does that include my grandparents?" Realm shifts uncomfortably. "Are you . . . are my grandparents working with the Adjustment office?" I ask, my heart beginning to race at the idea.

"It's not like that," Realm says, shaking his head. "Your grandparents want what's best for you."

His words aren't a denial, and I realize I need to get away from here. I need to figure out exactly how and why my grandparents would be a part of this. It's bigger than just them knowing I was in The Program. This is more involved.

"I have a better idea," I tell Realm. "How about if everyone stops trying to help so fucking much? Now get out."

Realm reaches for the door handle and looks back, sizing me up. "Please be careful," he says simply. "And know that however misguided our help may seem . . . we care."

"Yeah, right."

He smiles like he kind of enjoys my bad attitude, but my expression shares none of his amusement, and he straightens his face.

"Fine," he says. "But until the doctors figure out what's causing the crashbacks in returners, you and Wes should . . ." He stops himself. "Like I said, just be careful."

"Bye," I say, running my hand roughly through my hair as a headache pulses in my temples. "And stop following me," I add as an afterthought.

Realm pushes open the door and gets out. I expect him to try to explain, but he closes the door gently. And just as easily as he appeared, he's gone. I catch sight of him across the road, going into the 7-Eleven.

I have no idea what to make of him. Why would he care what happens to me or Wes? He met us for five seconds months ago. Sure, he probably works for the Adjustment, but that doesn't mean he actually cares about the patients. I made the mistake of thinking Dr. McKee and Marie cared, and look— Wes has been reset and I'm sitting in the parking lot watching a stranger buy a Big Gulp.

Obviously my problems are much bigger than that, but I'm learning to compartmentalize. One problem at a time. And now that I know my grandparents have a lot more to do with my condition than they let on, I'm determined to figure out what role they've played.

How deep does their betrayal go?

I shift into gear and race toward home.

CHAPTER EIGHT

NEITHER OF MY GRANDPARENTS IS HOME WHEN I arrive, and I immediately rush inside. I pause in the foyer at the bottom of the stairs, and it's like walking over my own grave—an incredible sense of dread. A part of me died here—the part The Program erased. It's a horrific feeling, and I practically run up the stairs as if handlers are still chasing me.

At the top, I grip the railing. My heart is racing, sweat gathering in my hairline. I'm suddenly struck with grief, loss. I wish Nathan never told me about The Program. But then again, it would have come out. It had to. Besides, I deserve to know the truth. This is *my* life.

I open the door to my grandparents' bedroom and peer inside. I've obviously been in here hundreds of times before, but everything takes on a new meaning now. Their room is part of their deception. Strangers live here.

I walk past the bed and immediately go to the armoire. One half is filled with drawers while the other has a stack of wool sweaters stashed away for the upcoming summer. The space smells like wood mixed with a light scent of Gram's perfume. It makes me nostalgic, lonely. I push away the feeling and begin to go through the drawers.

There are envelopes with receipts going back to Christmas nearly ten years ago. I scan them quickly and pull open the bottom drawer. My grandfather has saved newspaper clippings, yellowed now with age. They're his first stories, and I have a swell of pride as I look through them.

My grandfather had retired from the paper, but a few months ago, he decided to go back to work to help conduct research on the Adjustment. I thought it seemed like a good idea, but it only resulted in him warning me to stay away. I should have listened.

When I find nothing useful in the armoire, I go to the closet and open the bifold doors. There are rows of boxes on the top shelf, just out of my reach. One in particular stands out—an old moving box, wilted with age. I get on the tiptoes of my sneakers, and as I reach up, my phone slips out of my back pocket and hits the floor. I grab it and set it on the dresser.

I stretch again, getting my fingertips under the box and slowly working it off the shelf. When I get it down, I set it on the bed. There's a coating of dust on the lid, and I run my palm through it to read the label on the box.

My heart beats faster. A date, a few months off from my birthday, is scrawled across in faded black marker.

I carefully take the lid off the box. This could be it. This could be everything. I'm surprised to find a small stuffed dog. I take it out, my fingers shaking. Something about it is intensely familiar, and I bring it to my nose, expecting a certain scent. But it only smells like old cardboard.

Longing begins to nag at me, a shadow in the back of my mind, and I clutch the stuffed dog to my chest. Comforted by it, but wondering why it's in a box with the wrong birthday written on the top.

The doorbell rings downstairs, and I nearly jump out of my skin. I glance at the clock on the nightstand and see it's not even two. Everyone should still be at school.

I quickly put the dog back in the box and stash it in the closet. I walk down the stairs as whoever is at the door begins to knock. Fear claws at my throat. It could be someone to collect me. Collect me like a box of memories.

My breathing becomes erratic. I press my palm against the door and lean in to look through the peephole. My relief is immediate. I pull open the door and find Foster standing there, looking impatient.

"What the hell, Tatum?" he says, and then immediately starts coughing—the sound deep in his throat. He hits his chest to clear it up. "I've been calling you," he adds wearily.

"You should probably be in bed," I tell him, opening the door wider and ushering him inside. Foster looks awful— swollen eyes, a hunched walk that makes me think he's probably still feverish.

"Then you should have called me back," he says. He rounds the couch and collapses. He throws his arm over the side and rests his head back against the cushion. "I was worried," he adds.

"I'm sorry," I say, coming over to sit next to him. I debate telling him what Nathan told me during class. Nathan said Foster didn't know I was in The Program—he'd been out of town. But . . . when he came back, did he at least notice something different about me? It's horrifying to think he wouldn't. Like no one really knows me at all.

"It's fine," Foster says. "I went to school looking for you during lunch. Did you know Wes came back today?"

I smile. "Obviously."

He laughs. "I guess you would. Anyway, I talked to Arturo while I was mostly coherent, and he mentioned that he saw you in the office with Dr. Wyatt. Wanted to know if you were okay." He coughs and waits a beat before continuing. "You didn't mention over text that you'd been in to see that witch," he adds. "What was Wyatt about today?"

I shouldn't be upset that he's asking, but I don't like being watched, seemingly by everyone. "Wes was in there with her," I explain, "and when I went to check on him, Dr. Wyatt dragged me into the meeting. She's seriously unhinged."

"What do you mean?" he asks.

"She demanded to know what was wrong with Wes. I couldn't tell her about the Adjustment, but I also couldn't say anything that would affect Wes's memory. Dr. McKee warned me not to bring up the past, but that monitor . . ." I shake my head. "She was getting worked up."

"So what did you do?"

"I told her to stop, grabbed her arm when she got in his face."

"Damn," Foster says, proud.

"Yeah, well, she scared the shit out of me. It was either that or run for it."

"I'm glad you were there," Foster says. "What did Nathan say about all this?"

Tension settles in my neck, and I pretend to pick at my fingernails. "I, um . . . I haven't talked to him about it. Did you see him when you were at school?"

Foster watches me suspiciously and sits up a little straighter. "I did, in fact. And he was acting like a weirdo too. Especially when I told him you thought you were being watched by handlers."

My stomach drops. Nathan definitely knows something's up now. I wish Foster had stayed home, sick in bed.

"Nathan said he hadn't seen you since lunch," Foster continues, studying my reaction. "In fact, he said he didn't even have lunch with you. Which, of course, set off my 'Tatum is doing something dangerous' alarm. Nathan promised to find you, but turns out, I found you first. Now," he says. "You want to tell me why you're avoiding him?"

I should tell Foster the truth. I can trust him. I *have* to trust

SUZANNE YOUNG

him. "I'm scared to tell you," I say. And immediately my eyes fill with tears. I'm embarrassed, afraid of how he'll react to the fact that I might not really be me anymore. Not the Tatum he knew last summer. I could be someone else entirely.

Foster reaches to put his clammy hand over mine where it rests on the couch. "We don't keep secrets, Tatum," he says seriously. "Look what it did to Wes. I can't have that happen to you. Just tell me what's going on."

I swallow hard, my words filled with grief. "I was in The Program," I whisper.

Foster continues watching me, seeming confused by my statement. "What do you mean?" he asks.

"Nathan told me this morning," I say. "He said it happened last summer, and at first, I didn't entirely believe him. But then . . . I had a memory. A crashback. There were *handlers*"— my voice chokes up, and I point toward the entryway—"and they dragged me out of my house. This house. And I realized Nathan was right—it was true." I sniffle and wipe away the tears that spilled onto my cheek with the back of my hand. "I was in The Program," I repeat.

Foster stares down at his lap like he's thinking over my words. His face flinches a few times, his horror at the revelation clear.

"You didn't know?" I ask him.

"Of course I didn't know," he snaps, and then looks over apologetically. "What's bothering me is that if Nathan knew, why didn't he say something sooner? Why didn't he tell either of us?"

"He said my grandparents begged him not to," I explain. "They warned him that it could make me break down, even kill me. Nathan only now decided he didn't want to hide it anymore. But that doesn't change the fact that he kept it from me all this time. And my grandparents . . . they haven't told me shit. They've all been lying to me."

"It doesn't make any sense," Foster says. "If you were in The Program, why were you allowed to hang out with us again? Why aren't you labeled a returner?"

"I don't know. But it proves Wes's Adjustment failure wasn't my fault—not on purpose. The Program did something to my memories, and I'd bet that Marie and Dr. McKee knew that. My grandparents, too. And yet, they're all still trying to make me feel guilty about it."

"Why would they do that?" Foster asks.

"Because they want me to stay away from Wes."

Foster lifts one eyebrow. "Not a terrible idea," he allows. But when he looks over at me, he smiles. "So did you tell him about your relationship anyway?"

"No," I say. "I didn't. Although he knows something's up thanks to the monitor. And then he came by my Jeep and asked me to lunch. I couldn't say no."

"Definitely not."

"I didn't tell him that we were together before," I say again. "But I needed someone to talk to; I was freaking out. We came back here, and—"

"And you had sex," Foster says like he's finishing my sentence.

"What? No," I say. "We talked a little. Then my grand-father came home. Dr. McKee called him. Like, what the fuck, right?"

"How did Dr. McKee know you were with Wes?" Foster asks.

"He had someone watching me. For real," I say, shaking my head. "There's seriously too much to tell you."

"Seems so," Foster agrees. "Well . . . let's start with Wes at your house. What did Dr. McKee tell Pop?"

"I'm assuming he told Pop to make sure I don't tell Wes about our past. But I wasn't going to." I pause. "Okay, I *wanted* to. But I didn't. I don't need to be micromanaged. I mean . . . he's not even my doctor."

"That was very selfless of you," Foster says encouragingly. "Not telling him." I appreciate that he understands how hard it was for me to restrain myself from professing my love to Wes. "What else happened?" he asks.

I tell Foster about going to see Marie, about her dodging my questions. I tell him about Michael Realm, and how, in the end, I've realized my grandparents might be more deeply involved than I first imagined.

"I searched their bedroom," I say. Foster scrunches his nose like maybe I've crossed the line, but he seems to internally fight his reaction as he weighs all that I've told him so far.

"And I found a box in there," I continue. "Dated a few months before my birthday, and the contents seemed familiar. But at the same time, it was kind of creepy. It was packed away in the closet like I was . . . gone." I swallow hard. "I'm not entirely sure it's mine, but it has to be, right? Unless it was my mother's or . . . I don't know," I say, exasperated.

"Tatum," Foster says, his voice hoarse. "Not to alarm you, but this is all really fucked. We need to tell Nathan."

"But Nathan *knew*," I say, still unsure. "He kept this from me. How can I—"

"Hey," Foster responds, leaning in. "Don't ever doubt him. Sure, Nathan messes up sometimes, but if you think about it, he was the only one being honest with you. Don't punish him for that."

I consider his statement, and ultimately, I know Foster's right—Nathan would never hurt me, not on purpose. And he doesn't lie. At least, he tries not to, I guess. The minute he told me about The Program, I should have questioned it. We could have figured it out together.

Foster takes out his phone but gives me the courtesy of pausing in case I want to reject the idea. I nod for him to call Nathan, a bit concerned about how it'll play out. I'm sure Nathan will be offended that I confided in Foster first, but eventually, after a little brooding, he'll get why. And then he'll help. I hope he can help.

Foster tells Nathan to come to the house, and after he hangs up, he says that Nathan was already on his way. "He'll be here in about two minutes." He coughs a laugh and leans back against the sofa again, closing his eyes like his head hurts.

"Do you want something for your headache?" I ask.

"A guillotine," he suggests.

I laugh, and with effort he lifts his head and looks at me. "So tell me about your afternoon with Wes," he says. "I need the distraction from my pain."

"He still looks good, shockingly good," I say, knowing Foster will find that tidbit especially interesting. He smiles.

"Not sure it's much of a shock," he replies. "And how was he acting? You said he got kicked out of class?"

I nod and pull my legs underneath me. It feels good to talk about Wes, talk about him in a way that's normal. Not focusing on our past or our mistakes.

"He was in a really good mood," I say with a smile. "They erased all of his problems, and I got a glimpse of a different version of him. A happy one. It was . . . refreshing." My smile fades as I stare at my reflection in the blank TV set.

"But?" Foster says, furrowing his brow.

"But they erased me, too," I say, turning to him. "That's why he was happy. Because I was never part of his life."

Foster scoffs and leans forward. "That's bullshit," he says, but pauses. "Okay, not total bullshit, but *you* weren't the problem, Tatum. It was the situation. Either way," Foster says, waving his hand to get past this emotional turn, "Wes ended up at your house. How'd that happen?"

I tell him about the Jeep not starting, about the ride home. As I talk, the corners of Foster's lips upturn.

"That's awfully nice of him," Foster observes. "You know, seeing that you're strangers and all. Does he like you?"

The pure innocence of the question makes me smile. "I think he might," I say. "I think he does."

"Promising."

"Is it, though?" I ask.

We fall silent, both of us knowing that Wes and me getting back together would be tempting fate to rip us apart again. Maybe this time for good. It's dangerous. And it's stupid.

"Yeah, well. At least hook up," Foster offers casually, making me laugh.

CHAPTER NINE

THERE'S A SWIFT KNOCK AT THE FRONT DOOR before it opens and Nathan rushes inside. He looks around until he spots me and Foster on the couch. His eyes are wild, worried. Behind him, Jana slips inside and closes the door quietly. She went home sick, but I guess she's feeling better. She hangs back, as if knowing she wasn't invited to this party.

Next to me, Foster shifts on the couch. "Hey," he says to Nathan. "We need to talk." He tilts his head to look at Jana. "Hi, Jana," he says a bit coldly. "Would you mind excusing us for a while?"

She opens her mouth to answer, but Nathan steps in front of her. "No, she's fine," he says defensively. Behind him, Jana lowers her eyes.

Foster sits up to turn around fully. "It's not fine," Foster says. "There's something we need to discuss. It doesn't involve her."

"Foster—" I start, but he holds up his hand to stop me.

"Sorry, but this isn't for her," Foster says, trying to convey the importance of the conversation he wants to have.

Nathan puts his arm around Jana, bringing her forward to prove a point. It annoys me, although not quite as much as it annoys Foster. I don't dislike Jana as a person, but something about her and Nathan together . . . it doesn't feel right.

"She's my girlfriend," Nathan states.

"Cool," Foster says like it's an interesting fact. "And I have a boyfriend, but you don't see me dragging him into every private conversation."

Nathan scoffs, settling in for a longer argument, but Jana slides out from under his arm.

"It's okay," she says to him. "I have to get home anyway." She gets on her tiptoes and kisses Nathan on the lips, pausing before doing it again. It's grossly intimate, and Foster sighs heavily and turns back around to give them privacy. "Call me later," she whispers.

Nathan says he will, and then Jana walks out the front door. When she's gone, Nathan rounds the couch, glaring at Foster.

"Just because you have mono or some shit doesn't mean you get to be an asshole," he tells him.

"It's the flu," Foster corrects, not matching the hostility in Nathan's voice now that Jana is gone. "And I'm sorry if I came off that way," he adds. "We just really need to talk. It's important. It's about what happened with the Adjustment, Wes coming back . . ." He looks at me, unsure if he should bring up The Program yet.

"You know," Nathan interrupts, "Jana was part of that too. She lost her best friend."

"And I lost my brother," Foster shoots back. "This isn't a grief competition. And she's not part of our little crew, is she? I don't remember her in middle school."

"We're allowed to make new friends," Nathan says, still sore, but warming up slightly. Mentioning our time as kids is usually his go-to move, a history that supersedes all arguments. He probably hates Foster using it against him now, but he respects it.

Like he's just realizing I'm here, Nathan looks over at me. "And what the hell happened to you?" he asks. "You skip school, and then Foster calls, saying you thought there were handlers? Are you trying to give me a heart attack?" He shakes his head, and the depth of his concern becomes obvious. "They were right, weren't they?" he asks, sitting in the chair across from me. "I shouldn't have told you."

My heart sinks again, the heaviness of the revelations continuing to pull me down. "No," I say. "They were wrong." I look at Foster, who nods for me to continue. Nathan notices and turns to him.

"She told you about The Program?" Nathan asks.

"Yep," Foster says. "Now I'm here for the explanation. From both of you, if I'm honest."

"Nathan," I say, drawing his attention. "I don't remember being in The Program. All this time, it wasn't that I was trying not to talk about it. It's been . . . erased."

"What do you mean?" Nathan asks.

"I have my memories, or at least my corrupted version of them—idealized version. But I don't remember The Program. In fact, I had no idea until you told me. And then in class . . . I had a crashback. I suddenly relived the moment the handlers took me, and it was fucking awful." My voice hitches with emotion.

"And now . . . ," I continue, "I don't know what's true. Why did Gram and Pop keep all my stuff to give me when I came home, but not tell me I'd been in The Program? Why would they have you keep it from me? Did they say *anything* else?"

Nathan runs his hand roughly through his hair, looking perplexed. "They just said that you had a hard time in The Program, but that they got to you fast enough so you could keep your memories. I didn't question them. They asked me not to talk about it because the doctor warned it would bring on a crashback." He purses his lips. "Seems they were right about that part."

"You should have told me," I whisper.

Nathan mouths that he's sorry, his silent words heartfelt. I nod that I accept his apology, and after a moment, he furrows his brow.

"Wait," he says. "So if you don't remember The Program, how do you remember Wes? Me?" he asks.

"Exactly," Foster interjects.

"And why would they take The Program memories, but leave the stuff that was breaking my heart?" I ask.

"Unless they didn't know about you and Wes breaking up," Nathan offers. "Hell, I didn't know. And if your grandparents kept your mementos from the handlers, they might not have had much to go off of. They would have had no chance to figure out what was going wrong for you."

"The Adjustment," Foster says suddenly, sitting up. He looks from Nathan to me. "Tatum, they gave you the Adjustment—that's why you remember Wes."

My lips part, and I almost argue—but suddenly it makes sense. The memories, the pills with the Adjustment office's phone number on the bottle. I can't believe I didn't realize it sooner. I'm an idiot; it was so obvious.

The Program erased my memories. The Adjustment put them back. I've been manipulated twice.

I meet Nathan's eyes, his shining with the same realization. "Why did Dr. McKee act like he was meeting me for the first time?" I ask. "Why doesn't anyone know I had an Adjustment? And . . ." I pause, fixing my stare accusingly on Nathan. "And how did they get my memories?" I ask.

"Not me," he says quickly, hand on his heart. "I didn't donate anything, so if that's what happened, they lied to me, too."

Nathan, Foster, and I sit quietly, digesting this information. I think back to when Nathan and I went to the Adjustment office for the first time, how familiar Dr. McKee seemed. Now I know why.

"Do you think Marie knows?" I ask, trying to figure out her angle.

"Definitely," Nathan says. "They all know, Tatum. Including Pop and Gram."

As if he summoned them, there's the sound of a car pulling into the driveway. It's too early for either of my grandparents to be home from work, but when I get up and peek out the window, I see it's my grandfather again. Guess he cut his day short. Unless, of course, I'm still being watched, and someone let him know I have company. I wrap my arms around myself.

I ask Nathan and Foster if I should mention the box I found in the closet, and they both shake their heads no as the front door opens.

"Play dumb," Foster murmurs.

My grandfather smiles widely when he sees them, welcoming and warm. "Hello, boys. I didn't know we were having a party." He grins at me like today never happened. It's unsettling.

"Hey," Foster says, holding out his hand. But Pop pauses before shaking it.

"Don't you have mono?" he asks, making Nathan snort a laugh.

"It's the flu," Foster says. "But just in case, we shouldn't kiss."

"That's probably for the best," Pop says, and slaps him on the shoulder. "Nathan," he says, in a slightly different tone. "Where were you at lunch today? Tatum's Jeep wouldn't start."

Nathan swallows hard, and I see he's having trouble playing along with my and Foster's dumb act. "Jana wasn't feeling well, so I took her home. Plus . . . we had to talk."

"Oh?" my grandfather asks, as if it's completely normal that Nathan would tell him about his love life. It's not. Nathan never had a love life. "Sounds serious."

"We're working on some things," Nathan adds, diverting his eyes.

I exchange a look with Foster, and we both must be wondering if Nathan is laying it on thick, or if he and Jana really had a "talk." What about? Are they having problems?

Foster swallows, about to say something, but instead he starts coughing and doubles over, gripping the side of the couch. I go over to help him, and he tries to catch his breath.

"I should get home," he says between gasps.

"Same," Nathan adds apologetically.

"I'll walk you guys out," I offer, rubbing Foster's back until he can straighten.

"Well, I'm sorry neither of you could stay for dinner," my grandfather says, folding his arms across his chest. "Next time."

"Absolutely," Nathan says for both of them, and takes his house key out of his pocket. He nods good-bye to my grandfather before following behind me and Foster. When the three of us get onto the porch, I close the door and Nathan leans in.

"I'm not imagining—"

"No, it was weird," I say, glancing back at the house. "He's acting too normal. We should have confronted him, but . . ."

I trail off. "Maybe when Gram comes home?" I say it even though I know I probably won't have the guts to confront her yet either.

"Listen," Foster says to me. "Leave them out of it for now. We have bigger problems." He winces. "More immediate problems," he corrects. "You need to watch out for Derek. We have to worry about your past, but we also have to worry about our futures. I told you before and I mean it now—I think there are handlers everywhere. We need to be careful."

"You really think he's a handler?" Nathan asks, scrunching up his face.

"We'll talk about it on the way to your house," Foster says, and then makes a kiss face to say good-bye to me. Nathan pulls me into a quick hug, whispering again that he's sorry in my ear.

Foster and Nathan head down the steps and walk across the driveway to Nathan's house next door. Thick clouds have gathered in the sky, gray and angry, as Foster and Nathan talk in hushed voices. I can see how much the idea of handlers worries Nathan. It worries all of us. Because handlers mean The Program isn't dead at all. Maybe it never was.

I reach instinctively into my pocket and realize . . . my phone is gone. And then it occurs to me where I left it. On my grandparents' dresser.

CHAPTER TEN

WHEN I COME BACK INSIDE THE HOUSE, MY GRAND-
father is in the laundry room, where the sound of flowing water
can be heard from the machine. I use that moment to head
toward the bedrooms. I pause at the top of the stairs, listening
to make sure Pop's not following me, and then I quickly dart
into his room and scan the top of the dresser.

My phone is gone.

Disoriented, I spin around to see if I placed it somewhere
else. But it's nowhere to be found. "Shit," I whisper. I hear my
grandfather's phone ringing downstairs, but it sounds closer
than the kitchen. Bottom of the stairs, maybe.

I slip out of his room and walk swiftly toward my room. I
stop dead when I notice my door is ajar. It was definitely closed
earlier.

I hold my breath as I push open the door. The room looks the same, the bed a mess, a few pictures stuck to the frame of my mirror. A half-filled glass of water on the nightstand.

I'm about to walk out when I notice my phone sitting next to the glass, the screen unlocked. My stomach twists into anxious knots as I pick it up. My texts are open, and I assume that they've all been read.

I can barely keep my breathing under control as I sit on my bed, double-checking everything I'd sent today. The only notable exchange is with Foster. If my grandfather saw that . . . what did he think? Will he bring it up, knowing that I'm scared of handlers?

I set my phone aside, my heart racing. I look at the shared wall between my and my grandparents' room. What else was in that box? I can't search it now, not with my grandfather here. There has to be more; there has to be a good reason they kept it in the first place.

I measure my breathing, preparing to go downstairs. Surprisingly, the most shocking part of the day has faded—I've come to accept that I was in The Program. "Accept" is too strong a word, really. I'm not that far along. I've compartmentalized, but my mental catalogue is beginning to reach maximum capacity.

Right now, the biggest struggle for me is that I've always trusted my grandparents unwaveringly. They've always been there for me. I can still see them in the memory, how broken-hearted they were when I was taken away. How does that compare to now—where I know they've actively kept things from me? There has to be a bigger reason.

I'm scared to face them, acknowledge their betrayal. And I can't accuse them without having some way to check their story. It would be careless on my part. I have to get more information first—it's the most logical approach. I've made too many mistakes in the past. I have to do this right.

I'm considering my next move when my phone buzzes next to my hand. Startled, I answer it without looking at the number. "Hello?"

"Tatum?" a woman says. "Hi, it's Dr. Warren. Have I caught you at a bad time?"

Dr. Warren's voice is soft, yet professional, just like it is during our therapy appointments. The kind of lulling sound that makes you want to tell her your secrets, as if she truly understands. I wonder if that was part of her therapist training or why she became a therapist. We've been meeting for the past year, ever since Wes was taken to The Program. She honestly seems to get me, and I like her.

"Hi, Dr. Warren," I respond politely, confused as to why she's calling me. "And now is fine."

"Good," she says. "Well, I just wanted to check in. You haven't been seen in a few weeks, and I wanted to see how you were feeling."

There's a twist in my gut, prickles of realization. How did she know I was having a hard day? That I'd need to talk about it?

"Did . . . did my grandparents call you?" I ask.

Dr. Warren laughs, a soft lilt that's almost infectious. "Is the timing that obvious?" she asks.

"Yes."

"I didn't get the details," she says. "But yes, they're worried. Your grandfather told me Weston came back to school today. And that you left campus with him," she adds gently. "We talked about this, Tatum."

"He was just giving me a ride home," I say. "My Jeep wouldn't start."

"I understand," she says. "But it must have been jarring to see him. Does he remember you?" Dr. Warren has always been invested in my and Wes's relationship. Always asks about him. In fact, I daresay she was rooting for us.

But after his reset, she advised me to keep my distance from him, for both our sakes. She's worried that if I cause a crashback in Wes, it'll destroy me, bury me in guilt. She's right—it would. So I promised to be careful. And I promised to let her know if that changed.

Still, I'm uncomfortable. I have no idea what my grandparents might have said to her, and that thought suddenly leaves me hesitant. Exactly how much does Dr. Warren already know? Can I trust her? I decide to test it.

"Wes doesn't remember," I confess. "And I didn't tell him anything. He hung out for a few minutes, and then Pop came home. Wes didn't even know my name, Dr. Warren. I kept my promise."

She's quiet for a moment, and I hear her sigh. "I'm so sorry, Tatum," she says. "I know how hard that must have been for you."

The compassion in her voice makes my eyes tear up, and I decide I *do* need to talk to her. Talk to someone who knows me. I settle back against my pillows and close my eyes, the phone cradled to my ear.

"He looks really healthy," I say.

"Then it seems the procedure was successful," she offers. "That's good news."

"It is." I wait a moment, my eyes still closed, and try to decide how much more I should tell her about my fucked-up day. I have to wonder if she'll have insight. A way for me to reconcile how I feel about my grandparents. Isn't that her job?

"Dr. Warren?" I start, my voice low. "You aren't allowed to tell my grandparents anything I say, right?"

"Not without your permission," she says cautiously. "After all, you're my patient—not them. However, if you're a danger to yourself—"

"It's not that," I say. "It's something I was told today. A secret." I open my eyes then, check that I'm alone in the room. It all feels a bit surreal, waiting to confess that my grandparents aren't who I thought they were.

"I'm listening, Tatum," she says.

"Did you . . . ?" I falter with my words, but then sit up straighter and force them out. "Did you know I was in The Program?" I whisper.

"No," Dr. Warren says with finality. "No, you were not in The Program. Weston was."

"And so was I," I say. "I heard it today, and then . . . I remembered." My eyes tear up as I go through the moment the handlers took me in painstaking detail, reliving it. For her part, Dr. Warren stays very quiet. I wonder if she's writing any of this down.

Dr. Warren clears her throat. "I'm not disputing your memory," Dr. Warren says. "But . . . that's just not how The Program worked. And your grandparents certainly never mentioned it to me. I doubt they could keep a secret that big from you."

"There's a box," I say. "One in their closet. It has some of my baby stuff in it, but I don't remember it. Is it possible there's more they're not telling me? I don't know what to do."

"I think you should come in tomorrow," Dr. Warren says, a rustling of papers in the background. "I'll clear my schedule, and we can talk this through. I'm worried, Tatum. You don't sound like yourself. Did something else happen with Wes?"

I have a flash of annoyance. "No," I say. "Not everything has to do with Wes. This is about my grandparents." I look at the door again. "This is about The Program," I add in a quieter voice.

"I understand," Dr. Warren says. "Well, then I'll help you. We can research together, formulate questions for your grandparents so you can confront them. This is a big deal, Tatum. And you don't have to go through it alone."

I consider telling her about seeing Marie today, about Michael Realm watching me, but I decide it might be better to talk in person. I feel too vulnerable here. Too exposed.

"Tatum?" Dr. Warren asks, waiting for an answer.

"I'll come by tomorrow after school," I say.

"Great," Dr. Warren responds quickly. "I look forward to seeing you."

"Same here," I say. But before we hang up, I furrow my brow. "You're not going to tell them, right?" I ask. "My grandparents?"

"I won't," Dr. Warren assures me. "I promise."

Once the call is over, I set the phone down on the bed, feeling worse than I did before I talked to my therapist. I've stirred up emotions. Reignited them. Right now, Dr. Warren is my best option for help. She'll know what to do about my grandparents. Help me sort the lies from the truth.

"Tatum," my grandfather calls from downstairs, and I gasp at the sound of his voice. Even though he can't see me, I quickly brush back my hair, straighten my expression.

"Yes?" I yell back.

"Can you come down, please?" There's a hint of hostility to the question, and panic begins to build. Does he know what I just told Dr. Warren?

When I don't answer right away, Pop calls my name again.

"Coming," I say, my voice lower than before. I stand up, leaving my phone on the bed, and walk out of the room.

My heart pounds in my ears as I descend the stairs, scared of the impending confrontation. This might be about my phone. He's probably going to ask why it was in his room. Ask about seeing handlers.

Pop appears in the entryway, his forehead creased with concern, and before I can ask if he's okay, he swallows hard.

"There's someone here to see you," he says, and motions toward the couch.

My legs weaken when I find Weston's mom waiting there. She spins to face me, and her expression is intense and, if I'm honest, a bit rage filled.

I flip my eyes to my grandfather, but he crosses his arms over his chest and goes to stand near the window, his back to us. He's punishing me. I look at Dorothy Ambrose.

"Hello," I say meekly.

She scoffs and gets to her feet. I brace myself for her verbal assault, which seems to be the only sort of communication we've had since the night Wes was taken to The Program.

"Dr. McKee warned you about the consequences," she says. "But you didn't listen. You never listen." Her eyes, so much like Wes's, are watering with anger.

Well, I'm not just going to admit that I did anything wrong. "What are you talking about?" I ask. My grandfather looks over his shoulder at me, disappointed.

Dorothy tightens her jaw. "Weston came home and told me about this 'pretty girl' he met. Said you went for a ride on his motorcycle. Skipped school. I could guess who it was."

First, I have no idea why Wes would tell his mother *any-*

thing. They weren't even close. Unless . . . maybe they are now since he doesn't remember that she can be a serious bitch sometimes.

"We didn't discuss our relationship," I say. "He has no idea. And it was Wes who asked me to lunch. It was Wes who wanted to come back here. So don't put this all on me."

"You should have said no."

I laugh. "That's ridiculous," I say. "I love him, and you know that."

"That's the problem, Tatum," she says. "You never do what's best for him."

"You don't know what's best for him," I snap.

She shakes her head like she can't believe how pathetic I am. It cuts me, and I take a step back from her. My grandfather turns around to look at both of us, ready to intervene in case this breaks out into a physical altercation. "You're a kid," Dorothy says instead.

"I'm eighteen," I remind her—although my birthday isn't for another two weeks.

"Don't you understand?" she asks. "You've ruined his life twice, Tatum. Do you really think I'll let you do it a third time?"

"Twice?" I say. "How did I ruin his life the first time? He left me, remember? He—"

Her face enflames like she's about to tear into me, but my grandfather walks over and takes her by the arm, pulling her toward the door.

"That's enough, Dorothy," he says in a hushed tone.

Wes's mom yanks from his grip and glares at him. "Get ahold of your granddaughter, Charles, or I swear I'll get a restraining order."

He tilts his head, demonstrating that she's being irrational. "The boy came to her," he says. "Have the discussion with him."

"You know I can't," she says. "The doctor advised against it." She leans past him to look at me again. "Leave him alone, Tatum. He needs to get his life back—one without you. One he deserves."

She makes it sound like I'm the problem of his life. Like it wasn't The Program or even the epidemic. Well, fuck her.

"You don't know anything about us, Dorothy," I say simply.

She narrows her eyes. "I know that you're a danger to both him and yourself. Stay away from us." And with that, she turns on her heels and sees herself to the door, slamming it shut after she walks out.

My grandfather and I are left in the living room with the echo of her anger. After a moment, he looks over at me. "You okay?" he asks.

"I guess," I say. Her threat did its job; I'm shaking. "Not sure why Wes decided to tell her about me," I add. "But it must mean I made an impression on him."

My grandfather smiles softly. "I'm sure you did. The two of you have always had a connection." He pauses. "Dorothy isn't wrong, you know?"

"Yeah, I know. But she doesn't have to be such a bitch about it." I shrug an apology for my language.

"You'd be surprised how far a parent would go to protect their child," he murmurs, and darts his eyes away from me.

And as I watch, still trembling, my grandfather walks past me toward the laundry room to finish loading the washer.

CHAPTER ELEVEN

WHEN I GET BACK TO MY ROOM, I CALL NEXT DOOR with unsteady fingers. I bring the phone to my ear. "Hey," I say when it clicks.

"Should I keep apologizing?" Nathan asks sincerely. "Because I'm an idiot for not—"

"You don't have to apologize anymore," I say, relieved that I still have him on my side. It hits me now how alone I felt without him today, even if it was only for an afternoon.

Nathan hadn't intended to hurt me when he told me about The Program; rationally, I know that. Nathan has always tried to be the best friend he could. And when Wes was in the hospital, nearly dying because of the Adjustment, Nathan was there for me. We promised to never lie to each other again. It's part of why he told me about The Program in the first place. He wanted everything out in the open, even if it was something he'd promised my grandparents he'd never talk about.

I can't hold it against him. I won't. If anything, I need to know more.

"Wes's mom just left," I say. "She was . . . cruel."

"You okay?" he asks.

"Yeah. But I'm ready. I want you to tell me everything," I say. "I can't stand not knowing. I feel like I'm losing my mind. I've already lost my grandparents."

"I'm not telling you how to feel," Nathan says, "but please keep in mind that it's *Pop* and *Gram* you're talking about. They love you. Whatever has happened, there's an explanation. You know that." He pauses. "You know that, right?"

I'm pretty sure I do. But right now, it doesn't entirely feel that way. "Will you come over?" I ask. "It . . . it's too weird right now. I need you."

Nathan must hear in my voice how scared I am—he doesn't hesitate. "I'm on my way," he replies.

I hang up and head downstairs. When I get into the living room, Pop walks in from the kitchen.

"Want to help me get dinner ready?" he asks. His voice is tight, but he's acting like it's any other day. Like we can just make meatloaf together.

"Sure," I tell him. Behind me there's a sharp knock on the front door. My grandfather glances at it, and I quickly go answer it before Pop can ask why Nathan didn't just walk in.

Nathan looks nervous, and I elbow him in his side to let

him know he needs to pull himself together. He scowls at me but then notices my grandfather.

"Nathan?" Pop says, sounding surprised. "Didn't you just leave?"

"Uh, yeah," he replies, pushing his hands into the pockets of his jeans. "But then I saw Weston's mom storm out of here like she'd committed double homicide, so I figured I should check on it. Seems you both survived."

"Barely," my grandfather says. "Are you going to stay for dinner, then?" he asks.

"Yep," I answer for him, and Nathan looks down at me. He doesn't argue, though.

"Great. Could use the extra hands," Pop says, and walks into the kitchen. He starts banging around pots, closing cabinets, and Nathan sighs.

"She was awful?" he asks sympathetically. "Wes's mom?"

"Beyond," I say, and tell him what she said. Nathan rolls his eyes a few times and groans when I mention her threat of a restraining order.

"What about Pop?" Nathan continues. "Did he stick up for you?"

"He sort of did," I say, looking in the direction of the kitchen. "Although I don't think he disagrees with her. But now he's acting . . . normal. Am I just paranoid?"

"Uh . . . no," Nathan says like it's a ridiculous question. "I mean, take a look at your day, Tatum. If you weren't suspicious, I'd be worried about you." He falls quiet before looking over at

SUZANNE YOUNG

me. "You said you wanted to know everything, and I can fill in some blanks. At least about the night before."

I stare at him, dread creeping up my spine. "What do you mean 'the night before'?"

"Hey," my grandfather calls to us, poking his head out from the kitchen. "These potatoes aren't going to peel themselves."

"Have you asked them?" Nathan jokes good-naturedly, and rushes ahead of me into the kitchen. I watch after him, clinging to the edge of what feels like devastation.

"You all right?" my grandfather asks, startling me.

I blink quickly. "Yep. Excited to churn the butter and shuck the corn, too."

Pop laughs, tossing the dish towel onto his left shoulder, drying his hands on the bottom of the red fabric.

"Well, then," he says, putting his arm around me when I get to him. "Everything is right with the world."

My gram comes home from her shift at the hospital, and the four of us chat at the kitchen table about our day—although Nathan does most of the talking. He overtalks when he's nervous. I mention Wes briefly, and my grandmother doesn't react, which leads me to believe my grandfather already informed her. Of course he did.

"Oh," my grandfather says when he's done eating, swiping a napkin over his mouth. "I grabbed a new battery for the Jeep. Do you need me to put it in?"

"No, I've got it," I say. I only have the basic idea of how to do it, but it'll give me the perfect excuse to head outside with Nathan. "Want to help?" I ask him, smiling brightly.

"Uh . . . I'm not exactly a car guy, but I can hand you a wrench or something." He pauses. "I'll need a wrench, right?"

Me and my grandparents laugh as Nathan and I get up. I put our dishes in the sink and then go over to kiss my gram on the head since I hadn't gotten the chance to do it when she first came home. It was such a natural response—something I always do; it isn't until I straighten and see Nathan staring at me, his eyes glassy, that I realize the level of affection.

He was right. There will be an explanation. I know my grandparents love me.

"Let me know if you have any trouble," Pop says, going over to start the coffeemaker for his and Gram's after-dinner drink.

"I will," I murmur, although I'm still watching Nathan's reaction. In a world after The Program, we have to have some level of forgiveness for the adults in our lives. Sometimes, though, it's hard to know what's forgivable. Right now, I don't think we know the line yet. We're still learning.

I lower my eyes and walk ahead, plucking my grandfather's fuzzy sweater from the hook before going to the garage to grab the battery that Pop bought me.

"Do you really know how to change a battery?" Nathan asks as he leans his elbow along the edge of the open hood of my Jeep. There's a rumbling of thunder in the distance, the night stars blotted out by clouds.

"Pop showed me how once," I say. "And I've seen Wes do it. Figured I'd give it a shot." I look over at him. He nods and checks to make sure my grandparents aren't watching out the kitchen window before coming closer.

"It was nice in there," he says. "Really had me rethinking the entire sinister plotline that was starting to develop."

"Same." I sigh and leave the battery where it's at for now, wiping my hands on the rag I grabbed from the garage. "Now," I say in a hushed voice. "What were you going to say earlier? What happened the night before I was taken?"

"It was around the time of Casey Jones's party," Nathan begins. "One night, you showed up at my house, I don't know, around midnight. My mom was at a Mary Kay convention in Vegas. You'd been crying, which, let's be honest, was a bit scary during Program times. You asked if you could come inside, and then we went to sit in the living room. You were shivering, and I was terrified for you. When I put my arm around you, your skin was ice-cold."

I don't remember any of this. I don't even remember his mother being out of town. "Why was I crying?" I ask, feeling sorry for that girl—a girl distant from me.

"That, I don't know. At the time, I assumed you and Wes had gotten in a fight, or maybe it was because handlers had taken two people from class that day. It could have been anything. I just knew you were broken, and I didn't know how to help."

"Well, then—what did I say to you?"

"You asked if you could stay awhile," he says like it was the most pathetic request in the world. "But it was late. . . ."

The idea of me at his house, broken down like that, makes me feel vulnerable.

"I told you to go home," he continues. "But you begged me not to send you out into the dark." His face cracks, and tears well up and spill over. "You told me you were scared of the dark and not to send you into it. So I sat back down, and you crawled over to me and cried. I didn't know what to do. I tried to call Wes, but he didn't answer."

Nathan wipes his face and then blinks quickly, as if the emotional moment passed. He reaches to touch a few bolts in the engine, fidgeting.

"So when I couldn't get ahold of anyone else, I walked you to the door. And you looked up at me with those sad brown eyes, and . . ." He stops and turns to me.

"What?" I ask.

"I just realized, that was the last moment," he says. "My last moment with you—the old you."

The idea is heavy between us, and I look away, feeling like an imposter. The wind kicks up, and above, a brilliant flash of lightning electrifies the sky.

I finish installing the battery, and when I'm done, Nathan takes my grease-streaked hand.

"I sent you out into the darkness," Nathan says apologetically. "I told you that I loved you and closed the door. And the next day, I went to your house to check on you. But you were gone. Pop pulled me inside, and then he and Gram told me The Program had taken you. They weren't even sure why. They said you'd been completely fine, which—if I'm being honest— wasn't true."

"None of us were fine," I say.

"Yeah, but you were worse off than most. But that's not all of it," he tells me. "Pop said . . . well, he said he knew who called the handlers. Who turned you in."

I slam the hood of my Jeep, my entire body alert. "Who was it?" I demand. "Who did this to me?"

Nathan swallows hard. "It was Wes's mom."

I stare at him, although I shouldn't be surprised. "Why?" I ask, feeling like I've just been socked in the chest. "Why would she do that? Why would she try to destroy me?"

"I'm not sure what happened," Nathan says, holding up his hands like it proves he's being honest. "But when Wes found out, he went a little nuts. I mean . . . he *hated* his mother after that, Tatum. He went to her work and caused a scene. He said he'd never forgive her." Nathan shrugs. "Wes may have been dating Kyle, or whatever was going on between them, but he still wanted to protect you."

"Wes and I . . . ," I start, not sure how to finish. "Like my pop said, we have a connection. Wes and I have always loved each other. Probably always will. So he would have been angry with his mother. It would have made him sick."

"Clearly it did," Nathan says. "Not that he talked to anyone about it. He'd already withdrawn by then. After you were taken,

I only saw him once. He was sitting in front of your house on his motorcycle, reflective sunglasses hiding his eyes. He looked . . . I don't know, it was like he was shaking even though he was perfectly still. I called out to him, asked if he'd heard anything, but he didn't respond. He just started the engine and took off. And then . . . you came home and I didn't see him again."

"Maybe he felt guilty for what his mom did to me."

"Or what he did with Kyle," Nathan offers, and when I flinch, he quickly apologizes for bringing her up again. "Anyway," he says, trying to cover. "You came home, but I wasn't allowed to see you at first. Then, that Saturday, Pop called and invited me over for dinner, like it was any other Saturday. But he caught me outside the house before I went in."

I watch him, trying to see the memory through his eyes. "Why?"

"He asked me not to mention The Program to you," Nathan says. "He said he'd gotten to you early, and that although they might have taken a few smaller memories, you were completely intact—just like before. I didn't want to tell him I hoped it wasn't *exactly* like before.

"And then," Nathan continues, "Pop made me promise not to bring up The Program because the doctor warned him you were a special case—short-term memory loss, but with the highest potential for danger. He told me a crashback could kill you, so I made a deal to never bring it up. And then I went inside, and we ate enchiladas like nothing had ever happened."

I wonder how Nathan could have gone through the

motions, ignoring something so huge. Was he as awkward as he was tonight with my grandparents? Worse? I'm not sure, because I wasn't paying attention. I didn't know anything was wrong.

"Was that the night I found out Wes was missing?" I ask, piecing it together.

"Yeah," Nathan says. "You called him after dinner and found out he was gone. None of us knew what had happened to him, but privately, I assumed he ran away because you were in The Program. I figured he didn't know you got out. Thought maybe he couldn't live with what happened to you. I'll be honest, Tatum," he says like this pains him. "I thought he'd killed himself."

"So did I," I whisper, laying my hand flat on the cold metal of the hood. "But he didn't. He came home."

"He must have heard you were back," Nathan says. "And that's why he showed up at your door. I was scared when you went to his house to bring him home. I was scared Dorothy would call the handlers again. But she must have seen you were cured."

"It was never a cure," I say immediately.

Nathan allows this, and then looks at the house just as the kitchen light goes out. "That's all I've got," Nathan says, turning back to me. "That's everything I know. I wish I had told you sooner."

"But what if my grandparents were right?" I ask. "What if it had knocked something loose in my head? Caused a crashback? What if that's happening to me now, and I don't even realize it?"

"I won't let you crash," Nathan says like it's something he can stop through sheer will. "Do you trust me?"

I wait an extra second before nodding at him. "Yeah," I say.

"Good."

Nathan and I survey the house for a moment, and then he groans and says he has to study for his math test. He gives me a greasy high five and begins to walk away. Before he crosses onto his front lawn, his hair blowing in the wind, he turns back to me.

"I am curious about something," he says in a low voice. "Did The Program take any of *our* memories? Anything between us?" For the first time, I see vulnerability in Nathan's eyes. The idea that he could be erased from my memory scaring him. Invalidating him.

"I'm sorry," I say, "but I really wouldn't remember."

He smiles sadly at this. "I guess you wouldn't. Still holds true that I'm your healthiest relationship."

I laugh and agree that he probably is.

"Let me know if your Jeep starts in the morning, Dale Earnhardt," he says.

"That honestly doesn't even make sense," I say.

"Told you I'm not a car guy." And he turns around and walks to his house while I test out the new battery.

CHAPTER TWELVE

THE HOUSE IS QUIET WHEN I GO BACK INSIDE FROM the garage. I wash my hands, and when I'm done, I find my grandparents in the living room, the TV volume too low to understand. The picture glitches and pauses.

"How did it go?" Pop asks.

It takes me a second to realize he's talking about the battery. "Oh, good," I say. "I put it in and started her up. Still sounds like crap, but that was expected."

He laughs. Next to him, my gram smiles at me.

"Do you want to sit and watch a show with us?" she asks. "Although with this storm, I'm not sure how long we'll have satellite."

I look out the front window just as another flash and rumble tear through the sky.

"No, thanks," I tell my grandparents. "I have a paper to write for English class." I don't want to stay downstairs—afraid to talk about what's really bothering me. I want to pretend things are normal for just a little longer.

"Okay, honey," my grandmother says, but then pauses like she has something to say. I knew it. "And about Wes coming here today . . . ," she adds gently.

I shift on my feet, and she holds up her hand as if to tell me she's not judging me. "I'm glad he's back," she says. "And I know he came to you. How could he not?"

Her words give me a sense of justice, like someone finally understands. It makes me choke up a bit.

"I didn't tell him anything about our past," I say, wanting her to know.

"That must have been hard," she allows. "But you're doing the right thing. And Dorothy—"

I cringe at her name.

"—is also right," my grandmother says. "About the two of you, although I disagree with her assessment as to *why* it's gone so wrong in the past. The fact remains. . . ." She tries to pour sympathy into her voice. "It's over, honey. You have to let it stay over."

I stare at her and then flick my gaze to my grandfather, who swallows hard. Maybe he chickened out of leading this conversation. Clearly, he echoes her sentiments, though.

Her words now prove she doesn't get it. She doesn't get my relationship, and she obviously doesn't get me. I can't confront

SUZANNE YOUNG

either of my grandparents right now. Hopefully, Dr. Warren will have some thoughts on how best to approach this situation. She must have some kind of therapy she can use.

"I won't stop being Wes's friend," I say to my grandmother, a little raw. "I won't turn my back on him."

"And we're not asking you to," my grandfather says immediately. "Just . . . be careful what you say to him. That's all we're asking. Let him move on. Let yourself move on."

It takes a huge amount of self-control to hide my annoyance. "Sure," I breathe out. "I'll do my best."

The screen on the TV goes dark, the light blinking on the modem. "Well, that's it," Pop says, clicking off the power. "Guess we're going to bed."

As the storm ramps up its rage outside, I tell them both good night and head upstairs.

I lie in my bed, the Internet out on my computer and my phone a little slow. Wind blows against the window with small taps of rain, growing louder.

My grandparents went into their room an hour ago, so they're probably asleep. But I'm not tired. And I sure as hell don't feel like working on homework.

Instead, my mind turns back to the day, to the revelations. I consider contacting Dr. McKee, wondering if it would be smarter to approach him directly and ask if I'd been given an Adjustment. He might have my file from The Program. He might have the key to my life.

But that raises another question: If he did have my file, shouldn't he have known the truth about me and Wes? That we were broken up? Then again, he got it wrong with Wes. It must not have been in his file either.

I wish I knew what that meant, the fact that Wes and I could deny our breakup so thoroughly that even The Program couldn't find out. What did that say about us?

I curl up on my side, and my gaze drifts to the pictures of me and Wes on my mirror, happy. I'm curious about why they're still here. Why let me keep these pictures of him? Why let me mourn him after he was taken?

So many whys, but in the end, it comes down to the simple fact that I was changed. A why I might never understand.

There are other pictures—newer ones. And I smile at one of me and Nathan at Rockstar Pizza, his mouth open to expose his half-chewed food. There's another of us with Foster and Arturo, the two of them kissing while Nathan and I point to someone off camera. It was Jana, and we'd been calling her to jump into the photo, but she hates getting her picture taken.

There's a photo of me with Pop, pretending to bite his balding head while he holds up his hand to stop me from taking the selfie. My grandfather—the man who raised me—pretending that all is fine. Betraying me every day since last summer.

Betraying me even now. And the way Marie lied to my face, I have to believe I'll get the same response at home without proof. All I want is the truth. It's inexplicable how evasive it is.

My phone vibrates on the side table, and I reach over to

grab it, absently looking at the caller ID. My heart skips, and I sit up in bed. It's Wes. I have no idea how he got my number.

"Hello?" I ask in a hushed voice.

"Shit," he replies immediately. "Did I wake you up?" He matches my volume even though I'm sure there's no need for him to whisper in his basement bedroom.

I smile. "No," I say. "I was just lying here listlessly, rethinking my entire life. You?"

"Same," he says dramatically, like it's an entirely normal thing to do. "And I hope you don't mind that I tracked down your number through social media and well-placed inquiries. It's kind of lonely here."

I'm quiet, not sure what response his comment warrants. "I bet there's homework you can catch up on," I offer.

"Good suggestion," he says. "But I was thinking that maybe you'd want to come over. Our cable's out, but I downloaded a movie. And before I called you, I checked with my parents."

"You told your parents you were going to invite me over?" I ask, my stomach clenching.

"God, no." He laughs. "I told them I was going to bed and that I'd see them in the morning. They won't bother us, so, you know, if you want to come hang out, I'm just a loser new kid with no friends. I already asked Dr. Wyatt, but she said no. Not to put any pressure on you . . ."

I cradle the phone to my ear, looking out the window as the tree branches bend in the wind, the leaves rustling violently. I take it as a warning and lower my eyes.

"I shouldn't," I say quietly.

"'Shouldn't' sounds like you kind of want to, though," he says. "Is it me?"

"No," I whisper.

And it's not him. He's being perfectly normal—adorable, even. I've promised people—including myself—that I wouldn't start up this relationship again. It would be dangerous to be alone at his house with him. Selfish.

That doesn't mean I don't want to, though. I want to suggest I come over, spend the night, and that we don't tell anybody—our secret. But that's the sort of behavior that got him erased. That's how fucking horrible I am, that I would do the same thing to him again.

Tears well up in my eyes, and I turn away from the window. "Maybe another time," I suggest, trying to sound light. "You know, with adult supervision."

He laughs. "That sounds . . . horrible, actually."

"Yeah, well. You should probably work on your English paper, anyway."

"Thanks, Mom," he says. We both pause.

"Ew—"

"Yep, sorry," he says immediately. "I didn't mean to go there."

We laugh, and I tell him I'll talk to him tomorrow. Wes sounds reluctant when he says good-bye, and I close my eyes when I hear the click.

I set my phone back on the side table and go to my mirror,

gathering all the pictures. I sit down on my bed with them, my heart aching, as the storm intensifies outside. I trace my finger over a picture of Wes.

Why is it so easy for us to fall back in love? It shouldn't be allowed. I should hate him, or he should hate me. Or better yet, not care at all. The opposite of love is indifference. Why can't we be indifferent?

He's not. His heart remembers me—it's obvious. And I can't turn away from him. It'd be like refusing to breathe.

I set the first picture aside, looking through the others, trying to date them to find the ones around the time when The Program took me. I put the photos in chronological order, starting with middle school.

I snap down the corners of the pictures as I lay them out in a line. And as I get into what I'll call the Weston Years, I see myself grow up. The subtle changes of a person falling in love. It hurts. God, it hurts. But it's also beautiful to see happiness.

I pick up a picture of me and Wes and examine his face. He looked calm, the reserved happiness that was allowed during a suicide epidemic. Something changed shortly after this. Something in him. In me. And between us.

But for a moment, I allow myself to remember what it was like to feel loved and to love in return. It was the happiest I've ever been. What changed that? A dull ache begins behind my eyes, and I'm the verge of tears.

I don't want to be alone anymore. I don't want to be forgotten.

The weight of the day is heavy, and the wind howls against the window, rattling it, making me feel small and vulnerable. I just want to feel loved again.

I look over at my phone, thinking it's a terrible idea, but finding myself unable to resist the temptation. I dial.

"Hi," Wes says, and I can hear the smile in his voice. "I was really hoping you'd change your mind."

"You think you can get me inside without detection?" I ask.

"Absolutely." He sounds thrilled as he rattles off his address. His excitement encourages me. Why wouldn't I want him to be this happy? Why wouldn't I want to be? I'm not to blame for The Program, and neither is Wes.

"I'm on my way," I tell him.

After we hang up, I ease my door open, listening for my grandparents. I hear the soft sound of my grandfather's snore, and I sneak quietly down the stairs.

I go into the bathroom and brush my hair and teeth. When I'm done, I examine my appearance. My eyes are a little red, and I still have on today's clothes, but I can't chance going back upstairs and waking my grandparents. Besides, this isn't a hookup date. Not like the last time Wes returned. I just want to hang out with someone. With him. I'm feeling vulnerable. And yeah, lonely.

I walk out of the bathroom, the sound of thunder rumbling the dishes in the kitchen. I survey the house, everything dark until lightning flashes. I stand there a minute, listening for any movement upstairs. There's nothing.

SUZANNE YOUNG

I grab my keys and head out the kitchen door, glad my grandparents won't be able to hear my Jeep start over the sound of rain.

And it is *pouring* out, soaking me through before I get to my Jeep. It's coming down so fast that my windshield wipers can hardly keep up. The streets are quiet, even though it's not that late. Bad weather has a way of clearing the roads.

I drive carefully, avoiding the flooded parts of the streets that can possibly stall my engine. I lean forward, trying to see through the steady stream of water rushing down my windshield.

When I finally get to Wes's street, I park in my usual spot, obscured from view by low-hanging branches. I get out, and a gust of wind pushes back against my door, nearly closing it on me. The branches rustle heavily above me, sending down fat droplets of water. I get the door closed and face the wind as I hurry along the sidewalk until I'm at the basement entrance of Wes's room.

I shake my arms, realizing my clothes are soaked through to the skin. I blow water off my lips as rain runs down my face. The door swings open, and Wes actually laughs out loud when he sees me—my hair stuck to my forehead, my lips probably blue from the chill.

"Holy shit, Tate. You look like you just crawled out of a watery grave. Get in here." He holds the door open wider, and I walk inside, immediately comforted by the heat. I stand there, dripping on his carpet. Wes shuts the door and then turns to survey me.

"I guess it's still raining," he says casually, and then we both burst out laughing.

"I'll get you a towel and something to wear. The dryer is down here if you want to toss your clothes in."

I tell him that I will, but I already knew the dryer was down here. I've used it before. That little detail is a knot in my stomach as I follow behind him. He points me to the bathroom as he goes in search of clothes.

When inside the small room, I strip down to my underwear. My bra is soaked, and I toss it on top of my other clothes and wrap myself in a large beach towel. I find my reflection in the mirror above the sink. My hair hangs in stringy waves just under my chin, and my cheeks are red from being outside. There's a knock at the door, and I open it.

Wes keeps his gaze turned away and thrusts out his hand with a pile of clothes in it. I tell him I'll trade him and give him my wet ones in exchange. While he goes to put them in the dryer, I put on his clothes.

They're oversize—a pair of black basketball shorts and a Nike T-shirt. He even gave me a pair of bright white athletic socks, and I pull them up to my knees. When I come out of the bathroom, Wes is sitting on the couch, and he smiles broadly.

"Okay, that is the cutest thing I've ever seen."

"What?" I ask, looking down at my outfit.

"You," he replies. "I'd say you should wear that to school, but on second thought—please don't." He pats the couch next to him, and I almost don't sit there, remembering what happened last time I did. But it's different now. I may be weak willed, but I'm not actively trying to get him back. I just . . . want to spend time with him. It's different. At least I tell myself it's different.

"I'm glad you came over," Wes says as I sit next to him. We're on opposite ends of the couch, and when I settle in, I put a pillow between us, leaning my arm on it.

"Me too," I say. "I wanted to hang out with you. I wanted to hang out here." I glance up at the ceiling, where his family's living room would be. "With you and your parents," I whisper jokingly.

He snorts. "They're watching TV in their room, otherwise I'd totally ask them. Although I did lock the door."

"You don't think that'll seem suspicious if your mom tries to come downstairs?"

"Why would she try to come downstairs?"

"I don't know, if she hears something?"

"What would she hear, Tate?" he asks.

My cheeks warm with his innuendo. "The dryer," I say.

He smiles. "It's okay," he says, waving off my concern. "I lock that door every night. I don't want anyone sneaking up on me."

I stare at him, even as he turns away to grab the laptop. It's an odd statement. That he locks his door every night. He didn't use to do that. I wonder why that changed.

CHAPTER THIRTEEN

IT'S ABOUT AN ALIEN INVASION. THE MOVIE IS KIND of scary—okay, it's pretty damn scary—and the wind and rain blowing against the high-set basement windows isn't helping matters much. I'm curled up on the couch, my elbow on the pillow between me and Wes. He's also leaning on the pillow, but we're not touching—like an invisible barrier is keeping our arms apart.

Wes jumps, and then laughs and looks at me sheepishly. Wes has always done that—jumped at the scary parts in movies. I find it incredibly endearing.

There's a thump upstairs, and Wes and I sit perfectly still and lift our eyes to stare at the ceiling. The last thing I need is for Wes's mom to find me here. She might literally kick me out. The toilet flushes. And then the thumps cross the ceiling and the sounds are gone.

Wes and I exchange a look of relief and then go back to watching the movie.

When it's over, Wes sits up and stretches his arms over his head. He's thinner than he used to be, leaner. I admire him for a moment before I excuse myself to the bathroom. While I'm in there, still wearing his clothes, I take a peek at myself. I look sleepy, like I've just woken up.

In a way, it's like I have. Being here with him, comfortable and quiet—it's my favorite part of us. Sure, I love the other stuff, but it's how easily we fit into each other's space—that's what I loved. Being here reaffirms that.

When I get out of the bathroom, Wes is standing by his stairs, watching the credits roll down the laptop screen, holding my clothes from the dryer. He glances over at me, smiling when he sees his oversize basketball shorts. He tosses my clothes onto the couch.

"Want to sleep over?" he asks. I laugh because he doesn't realize he asks me that every time I come over. Sometimes I say yes.

"Your mom would hate that," I tell him.

"Kind of makes you want to do it more, right?"

I laugh. "Yeah, it does," I admit. I walk over to the couch and sit next to my clothes, not really wanting to put them on.

"What if I say please really sweetly?" he offers.

I lift my eyes to his. "It's not a good idea."

"Are you kidding?" he asks. "It's a fantastic idea. And besides, look outside. It's a torrential downpour. In fact, staying the night is the mature, responsible thing to do."

"Hm . . . ," I say, leaning back on the couch and enjoying his rationalization. "I'm sure my grandparents will assume me staying in your bed is due to inclement weather."

Wes raises his eyebrows. "You want to stay in my bed?" he asks, seeming a little surprised. My thoughts stumble, and I shake my head like I was only just kidding. That was stupid of me.

"Not what I meant," I say. I grab my clothes and stand, and Wes's face sags with disappointment. "I should get changed."

"You can have the bed," he offers as I walk past him toward the bathroom. "I'll sleep on the floor. It's a great carpet. That way we can talk, or . . . whatever."

"It's the whatever that I'm worried about," I say. I'm about to expand on my refusal, when I turn around and look at him. I'm struck by the vulnerability in Wes's expression.

"I don't want to be alone," he blurts out, and then lowers his eyes, embarrassed. "I'm having a hard time being alone, Tate."

Chills run up my arms, and I step a little closer to him. "Why didn't you say something earlier?" I ask.

He presses his lips into a sad smile, his dimples flashing. "I did. I called you, remember?"

I shrug. "Yeah," I say. "But I thought it was just the typical loneliness."

Wes rubs his hand roughly through his hair, admonishing himself. "I've probably made you want to run out of here twice as fast," he says.

I turn toward the window. I can't see outside from here, but I hear the wind howl against the glass and the steady beat of rain. The clicking of debris and pebbles. It's shitty outside.

"I can stay for a while," I offer. "Wake up before dawn and drive home. My grandparents can't think this is a terrible idea if they don't know about it."

Wes looks over at me. "I still think they'd consider it a responsible, mature idea, but whatever you want."

What I want isn't a possibility right now, but I won't leave him here if he's feeling lonely like this. If I keep it platonic, there's no harm. We can be friends. It's what he wanted the first time he came back, but I kept pressing the issue. Now I know better. Now I know better for both of us.

"You'll really sleep on the floor?" I ask.

"Yep," he says, putting his hand over his heart like it's a solemn oath. "But are you tired now? We can watch another movie. I'll even get us some chips and sodas. I had my mom put a fridge down here." He grins as if acknowledging he's outrageously spoiled, and I roll my eyes.

"Fine," I say, tossing my clothes onto the closest chair. "But no more aliens."

"Romance?" Wes asks with a smile.

"Thriller," I suggest instead. He nods that it's a good plan and goes over to the computer. He clicks through his movies, searching for an appropriately scary one that will allow us to forget the real horrors outside his basement bedroom. And this time, as we watch, his hand gently grazes mine, resting there.

But he never holds it.

It's just after midnight when we go into his room, not really talking. My heart is beating fast, like the plan will change somehow. But it doesn't. Wes takes one of the pillows off his bed and tosses it onto the floor. He opens his closet and takes out a sleeping bag. He unzips it and lays it out, then grabs a folded blanket from the edge of his bed and puts that on top. It doesn't look too awesome, and I'm about to suggest the couch, when he points to the bed as if he's telling me not to argue.

I smile and climb onto his oversize bed, slipping my bare legs under the covers. His bed has always been ridiculously plush and comfortable. I hear Wes's knee crack as he climbs down, a little groan, and then he takes a deep breath.

The room is dark with just a small light on his dresser and the clock on his nightstand. Outside the window, the wind still blows—although admittedly not as hard.

"So . . . ," Wes says from the floor. "How's that bed?"

I smile, knowing Wes can't see me up here, and I turn on my side. "It's way too soft," I tell him. "Like lying on a cloud."

"Ugh, I hate that," Wes says in an equally serious voice. "If you want, you can try out the floor with me. It has the perfect buoyancy." He reaches over and knocks on the floor, a hollow echo of concrete under the carpet.

"Wow, that does sound comfy," I say.

SUZANNE YOUNG

"You should come down. There's plenty of room."

I peek over the side of the bed to where Wes is lying on his back, staring up at the ceiling. The little bit of light cast perfectly across his face.

"Okay," I say, and see him instantly smile.

I climb down from the bed, taking my pillow with me, and lie next to him on the unfolded sleeping bag. I curl on my side, and my hip and shoulder ache from the pressure of the hard floor. I tuck my hands under my chin, and across from me, Wes mimics the movement. We're a pillow away, but curved in, our knees nearly touching.

"I'm curious about something," he says, his voice barely above a whisper. "Have I ever asked you out before?"

I smile softly, not willing to lie. I like how he flirts with me. I don't really want him to stop. "Maybe once or twice," I offer.

"Twice?" he repeats. "I bet it was more."

"And why do you think that?"

He shrugs one shoulder. "Because I'm persistent. And it helps me understand."

"Understand what?"

"Why I feel this way," he replies.

A wave rolls over me, and I'm breathless when I ask, "And how do you feel?"

"Like I know you," he whispers. "Know everything about you, but just can't remember."

I realize that I want him to guess our relationship—say it out loud so I can't deny it. Make me tell the truth. Make me hurt us both with it, but at the same time, set us both free.

"And I feel . . ." Wes pauses like this is the most important part. "I feel like lying on this hard-ass cement carpet floor is almost bearable because I'm close to you."

Silence falls over the room, and I see the first twitch of a smile on his lips.

"You want to move to the bed, don't you?" I ask.

"Definitely," he responds immediately, like that was the point all along.

"Fine. But only because this floor sucks."

Wes laughs, and we grab our pillows. We head to opposite sides of the mattress. I watch him, unsure of how serious he was about knowing me. Where does his joking end? Where do my lies end?

We climb onto the bed, me under the covers, him above. I murmur good night, and he says it back. But the lightness is gone from his voice, and I wish we hadn't moved from the floor. There we could play off the conversation. We could pretend.

I turn on my side, facing the door. I feel Wes do the same in the opposite direction.

We're quiet, and I may have dozed off at one point. It's still dark outside, and Wes's breathing is calm. I can't believe he's next to me. I can't believe I'm in his bed again. The way I've missed him is torturous. I shouldn't have come here. I should have known it would be too difficult.

I can't live in this constant state of dishonesty. I can't keep things from him, not if I love him.

"Do you want to know the truth?" I whisper softly, and turn to look at the back of his head.

I don't expect him to answer, but almost like he was waiting, he whispers back, "Yes."

Wes turns over in the bed, facing me. His eyes are questioning, a little unsure. I'm beginning to shake, scared of what I'll say. Scared of what it will do to him, to us.

"But I'm more interested in now," he adds. "If I asked you how you felt about me *right now*, would you answer?"

My senses try to flood in, keep me from making a mistake. The past is one thing, but Wes wants *now*. And it's the one thing I can't give him. I'm trying to be a better person. I'm trying fucking really hard.

"No," I reply.

"If I asked you to kiss me anyway, would you?" he whispers.

I watch the openness in his expression. That simple way Wes always had about him—this raw honesty. His fearlessness.

And despite how my heart aches for him, the word sounds like it comes from someone else when I whisper, "No."

Wes seems shocked by my answer, but he quickly recovers and smiles.

"I bet I asked you out at least three times," he says.

"Maybe even four," I answer immediately, wishing I was the person who could make him happy. But knowing that I'm not.

Wes's smile softens, and he sighs heavily, gazing at me. "Just friends, then," he whispers.

"Just friends," I reply.

The little bit of light reflects in his eyes. "Good night, Tate," he says.

"Night." We watch each other a moment longer, never touching, even though I can feel the heat from his body being so close to mine.

And when I close my eyes, I focus on being next to him. Just as I drift off, a tunnel opens into my memory, and I fall in.

"Don't make me go home," I whimpered, standing on my doorstep with Nathan. He stared down at me—worried, a little scared. I needed someone to love me, especially now that Wes didn't. And I couldn't tell Nathan the truth. I wouldn't acknowledge it.

"Go in and sleep this off, Tatum," Nathan said. "I'll see you in the morning."

He was scared of The Program, and it overruled his worry for me. He turned and went to his house. The minute he disappeared inside, I jogged to my Jeep and got in.

My body shook, cold running up and down my arms. It was summer, but I was so cold. I was so fucking empty. For weeks I've been slowly draining away.

Tonight I saw Wes with another girl. I saw him smile at her, touch her arm. I couldn't wrap my brain around the kind of hurt that created. I wasn't just losing Wes—I was losing me. The person I was with him. The person I'd been for the past few years. Since meeting, we'd grown so much together, had so many firsts—and even more than that, we'd been surviving The Program together. I depended on him. I needed him. And, yes, I loved him.

But he didn't love me anymore. Not in that way. And to me, it felt the same as if he hated me. As if he wished I were dead. As if he wished I would evaporate and leave him alone.

I was nothing anymore. I was no one.

I sputtered out a cry and put my fingers to my lips. I shoved my keys in the ignition and started the engine. I had to see him. Beg him to come back, work this out. He had to forgive me. He couldn't just leave me like this. He never could before.

Tonight felt different, though. It felt final.

I wish I were dead.

I drove fast, speeding toward Wes's house. He should be home by now, and if I could just talk to him—

"I love you," I said out loud in the small space of my Jeep. "I love you, so you can't do this to me." My voice cracked, but I believed it was true. I could convince him to stay. I didn't care why.

There were cars in the driveway of Wes's house, so I pulled in behind them and rushed ahead to his basement entrance. I knocked, shivering.

Was I acting erratic? Was this how lives were ended, how The Program flagged people? My eyes began to tear up, and I thought about Suzie McColm, who was pulled from math class. She had been crying, but she didn't fight. She let them lift her out of her seat, lead her to the door. Before she left, I heard her whisper: "Just let me die already."

The Program was our collective nightmare. Our bogey-man. Our death sentence.

I knocked again on Wes's door, harder. It occurred to me then that he wasn't here. He was still out with her.

I put my hand over my eyes and leaned against the frame. I didn't want to picture them together, but my mind went there anyway. Wes holding her cheek, kissing her with his eyes open. She was prettier than me—I knew that. He probably enjoyed looking at her. Touching her.

My cries intensified, and I slumped against the door. I pictured them in bed together. I pictured him murmuring her name. It was a spiral, a dark black spiral spinning me deeper and deeper into my grief.

I screamed and hit the door with my closed fist. There was a sharp sting as a cut opened across my knuckles, a bloody smear on his door. The shaking in my limbs grew, but my eyes were wide, my lips tight around my bared teeth. Maybe they were inside.

"Open the door," I called. There was no answer, and I punched it again. "Open the door!" I screamed, and heard my voice echo three times down the road.

I was out of control—out of body, almost. I was mad—this was what it felt like to lose yourself. I sobbed and wrapped my arms around my waist.

I couldn't stop it. I couldn't stop the shadow taking me over. The darkness. I just wanted to talk to him, and then I would be fine. I told myself I would be fine. I didn't really believe it, though.

It was like I'd just stepped off a cliff. My heart in my throat, falling toward an impact I couldn't stop.

"Tatum?" a groggy female voice called, and I spun to find Mr. and Mrs. Ambrose coming down the walkway from the front door. "What are you doing?" Mrs. Ambrose added, tightening her robe around her.

But as she saw me under the lights, her mouth fell open. Her husband took her by the arm, and both of them stared at me.

"Tatum," she said softly, like I was about to jump off a building. She had no idea how close she was to the truth. "Come inside, honey. We'll call your grandmother."

"Is he in there?" I asked. And my voice was different, hoarse. Raw. My throat burned, and I wondered if I'd been screaming the entire time.

Mrs. Ambrose gave a quick shake of her head to let me know her son wasn't home. I flinched, and then groaned like I'd been punched in the chest. It felt like it.

I wanted the spiral to take me. Death was scary, but the pain—the pain was a distraction. It pulled me deeper, and I squeezed my eyes shut, and I ground my teeth, my fists clenched.

"Tatum?" Mrs. Ambrose called, and she sounded scared. "Please, you're bleeding."

He did this to me, I thought wildly. Wes did this by continuing to hook up with me. Giving me hope when there was none. I was a pathetic creature he felt sorry for. One he used. I was worthless. I was a joke.

I hate myself.

"You're scaring me," Mrs. Ambrose said, and took a step closer to me. "I think you should go now."

I looked at her fiercely. She was the second person to turn me away tonight. First Nathan, now her. No one wanted me. Only The Program wanted me, and they couldn't have me.

"Don't tell me what to do," I growled.

Mrs. Ambrose shot a concerned glance at her husband, then turned back to me. "Go home, Tatum. You're not well."

Her words struck me like a slap. A warning. "A threat." I said the last part of my thoughts out loud. "You're going to call them?" I asked. I flinched again, this time half of my face scrunching up. I couldn't control it.

"You need help," she whispered, almost desperately. "Now go. I don't want Wes seeing you. Stay away from him."

"Fuck you," I said instantly. She was worried I'd taint her son, ruin him. Maybe I would. Maybe he deserved it.

I closed my eyes for a moment, sudden clarity coming through. I'd scared myself. I understood that this wasn't me; this wasn't how I really felt. I loved Wes, and I would never hurt him. I wouldn't hurt myself.

I looked at Mrs. Ambrose again, swaying on my feet. I was ready to apologize, but her face was a growing storm of rage. "I think I need help," I murmured.

She scoffed, clearly not forgiving my outburst. "Leave," she said coldly. "Before I call the police."

The police would haul me off to The Program without hesitation. She might call them anyway. I wanted to plead with her to forget I was here, and fear crawled over me, replacing my misery. I looked at Mr. Ambrose, and his brows were pulled together sympathetically. He nodded his chin as if telling me to leave.

I started to back up, my steps unsteady. My lips parted to tell her I was sorry, but Mrs. Ambrose turned her back on me and took a step toward the house.

She was going to turn me in. She was going to send me away and have them destroy me. She was going to kill me.

"Pop," I whispered, running my hand roughly through my hair as I rushed toward my Jeep. I needed my grandparents to save me.

I ruined everything.

The alarm on my phone goes off, and I sit up with a gasp. I stare straight ahead in the darkness of Wes's room, sweat on my skin, heart banging against my chest. I click off my phone alarm, momentarily disoriented as the fear that I felt in the memory begins to slowly dissipate.

I know why Wes's mother called The Program on me. I don't even really blame her. I was out of control. I needed help.

The wind is quiet outside, and even though I was quick to cut the ringing on my phone, Wes groans and turns over, slapping the pillow on his head.

I stare at his back, stunned that I'm here. The memory is still with me, and I can feel the devastating loss of him. What it did to me. How it hurt me.

Wes hurt me, I think weakly. He may not have meant to, but it was wrong. And how I reacted to it was wrong. And sitting here in his bed, I'm truly convinced for the first time . . . that *we're* wrong. We are wrong together.

I get up from the bed, quiet as I slip off his shorts and pull on my jeans, change my top, and stuff my bra into my pocket. Once my shoes are on, I grab my car keys and go to the door. I pause there a moment and look back at the bed, Wes sleeping soundly. I'll be gone when he wakes up, and he'll wonder why I didn't say good-bye.

We never were good with good-byes.

I open the door and go outside; the smell of rain—damp earth and grass—is thick in the air. It's cold, and I wrap my arms around myself. The wind and rain are gone, leaving the street a mess. Branches on the road, a buzzing powerline above me. I open and close my fist, as if my knuckles are still injured from the memory.

I get to my Jeep, relieved to see there's no note or anything to say that I've been found out. As if I'm under surveillance. Which doesn't feel that far off, if I'm honest.

Once inside the Jeep, I pump the heat, shivering all over. When I start toward home, I go over the memory in my head, tears dripping onto my cheeks as I see the girl I used to be. See that version of me so broken. It's horrific—humiliating, devastating, and ugly. My thoughts were so skewed, my emotions twisted. I don't even know her. And I don't ever want to be her again.

I turn up the radio to drown out my thoughts. I know what I have to do, but I allow myself one more moment with him.

SUZANNE YOUNG

I can still smell his sheets. Feel his warmth.

Wes said he didn't want to be alone, and I get that. Lately, I feel more alone than ever. Part of me wishes we could just pack up and run away from all of this. Start over where no one knows us, or our pasts. No one to judge or warn us.

No one to protect us.

I click off the Jeep's lights as I pull into the driveway of my house. The street is completely desolate, and none of the houses are lit up. I'm careful with how loudly I close my door now that the rain has stopped, and then I make my way inside the kitchen, half expecting my grandparents to jump out and scare me.

The house is soundless. I slip off my wet shoes and walk through the living room and up the stairs toward the bedrooms, carefully avoiding the creaky floorboards.

When I go past my grandparents' room, I pause and listen. It's silent, and I know I've gotten away with it. I should feel guilty, but instead it feels kind of justified. Like it was meant to happen. I was meant to remember the truth of what happened with me and Wes. Why I ended up in The Program.

I get into my room, close the door, strip off my clothes, and put on an old T-shirt. And after I climb into bed, I stare up at the ceiling in the dark.

"I've always loved you," I whisper in the dark.

And then I take out my phone, click his name, and send Wes one last text. Knowing that I mean it this time.

Good-bye.

PART II
THE COMPLICATION

CHAPTER ONE

I WAKE TO THE SMELL OF BACON FRYING, AND WHEN I go downstairs, I find my grandparents in the kitchen. Gram is scraping eggs onto three plates, strips of bacon lined up along the side. She's already dressed for work, but my grandfather is still wearing his pajamas. He tells me he's going in later today.

"Did the storm keep you up last night?" Gram asks, giving me a morning kiss on the head as she sets a plate in front of me. "You look exhausted."

"It was fine," I say, the first hint of guilt attacking my conscience. I quickly change the subject. "I have an appointment with Dr. Warren after school today," I add.

My grandparents exchange a glance, and something about it catches on my consciousness.

"Oh?" Pop asks, pretending (badly) that he didn't know.

"Yep," I say, stabbing some scrambled eggs. "And she already told me you called her, so maybe just give me a heads-up next time."

"Sorry, honey," Pop says. "I was just—"

"Worried," I finish for him. "I know. Well, I'm going to see her, and we'll talk about Wes and whatever else it is you've been stressing about." I smile at my grandparents; part of my graciousness is because I snuck out last night and have my own shit to feel bad about.

Even so, they've given me yet another reason not to trust them.

"Thanks for letting us know," Gram says pleasantly, and takes a sip of her coffee.

We continue eating breakfast, completely normal in every way, and after I clean my plate, I grab my bag and head to school.

Nathan is waiting with coffees when I arrive at school, begrudgingly fulfilling his portion of our coffee-fetching arrangement. Jana doesn't take part, typically. Most days she arrives at school late. Nathan says she's late to everything they do, although it doesn't bother him that much.

I stop at the top of the stone staircase at the entrance of the building, surveying the front yard of the school, and hold out my hand. Nathan places a vanilla latte in it.

"Did you see Miller Ave. was flooded?" he asks casually. "Because I nearly died."

I look sideways at him. "I noticed it last night," I say.

"I wondered where you were going," he says, taking a sip of his steaming coffee. He meets my eyes, acknowledging that he knows I snuck out. "Probably wasn't wise to go out into a thunderstorm," he adds.

"It definitely wasn't," I agree. "But you know me, queen of bad decisions." I blow on my latte, testing a sip.

"I'm assuming it had to do with Wes?"

"You assume correctly. We watched a few movies together."

"Sounds sweet. Was it a date? Did you tell him that you used to date?" Nathan questions me like it's any other conversation, even though we both know it's not. I was stupid. But at least I'm acknowledging it, which I'm sure comforts him.

"No," I say. "We agreed to be friends. Besides, Dr. McKee warned me not to get involved romantically, remember? I'm sure he has my best interests in mind." We exchange a pointed look, and a cool breeze blows open my jacket. I pull it closed around me.

Nathan takes his time as he drinks his coffee. "In theory," he says, "I support the doctor's decision, but, in actuality, he either didn't know or didn't tell you about your time in The Program. One makes him incompetent. The other makes him a monster."

"Wait, are you saying I shouldn't take his advice?" I ask.

"I'm saying I don't know," Nathan responds. "I'm not going to rely on his word. And you know how hard it is for me to admit that you might *actually* belong with Wes."

He laughs, but I don't join him. He turns to see why, and I feel tears sting my eyes. I quickly blink them away. "I remembered," I say.

"Remembered what?"

"What happened that night," I say. "After I left your house, I went to Wes's, and I cussed at his mother."

Nathan takes a casual sip of his drink, then, as if he misheard: "I'm sorry. What?"

"I remember going there," I say. "I knew about Wes and Kyle, and I went there to beg him . . ." I stop, too embarrassed to explain it. I wish I had been stronger. Braver. But I can't change the past. Apparently, it can be rewritten, though.

"I went there to talk to him," I say self-consciously, "but Mrs. Ambrose called The Program on me because I was unwell. She told me to stay away from Wes. And now that I know, now that I've relived it . . . I think she's right about us not belonging together." I shrug one shoulder, miserable. "So I've let him go, Nathan. Wes and I are over."

Nathan swallows hard. "That's probably the biggest lie you've ever said to my face."

"Not true," I say, sniffling. "There was also the Adjustment."

"Shit, you're right," he says with a sad smile, and when the moment goes on too long, he pulls me into a fierce hug. "I'm sorry, honey," he says, finally acknowledging the gravity of my statement.

"So, that was my night," I add when I pull back. He whispers again that he's sorry.

SUZANNE YOUNG

"Will you come with me to the Adjustment office later?" I ask. "I need to confront Dr. McKee."

I expect Nathan to point out this is a dangerous idea, but he doesn't. "Yeah," he says. "Of course I'll go with you."

I thank him, and we turn to stare across the front lawn of the school. On the grass, there are a few guys playing Frisbee, flinging it with full force, even this early in the morning. Nathan says he admires their commitment to looking douchey despite the hour.

"Not to change the subject," Nathan says, drawing my attention. "Did you finish your essay?"

"Essay?"

"Damn," he says. "I was planning on copying yours." He hikes his backpack higher up on his shoulder. "First hour. We should get in there and write it before Miss Soto arrives. At least tell me you read the book."

To this, I smile. "I always read the book."

"Excellent," Nathan replies. "And I have a pencil. Together we're like one full brain."

I loop my arm through his with a laugh, and we head toward the building to go work on our papers.

Nathan and I make a plan for later. I'll go to my appointment with Dr. Warren at two thirty, and then Nathan will meet me at the Adjustment office at four. We're going to demand answers. I'm glad Nathan's coming with me. He's my magic feather—my confidence booster.

Wes isn't in class when I arrive, so we don't have the awkward "Hi. I slept in your bed last night, and it was a huge mistake" conversation, but he does show up near the end. He smiles at me before sitting down, and I hear Nathan groan behind me. This isn't going to be easy to untangle.

There are no class interruptions today, no sign of Dr. Wyatt. There is one kid absent, Robert Rodrigo. I heard a rumor that he's in the hospital, but when I asked about it, his friend quickly brushed me off.

What's concerning about that piece of information is that Robert is a returner. And the past few weeks have returners dropping like flies—whether by a meltdown, an aneurysm, or . . . self-inflicted trauma. Two or three just opted out of school altogether. The assessments are dredging up bad memories for all of us.

I realize that I'm part of this high-risk pool now. I'm in danger because I'm a returner too. And I guess that's something I'll have to bring up to Dr. McKee, among my other questions. Why exactly are the returners crashing back?

I'm not sure he'll answer. And even if he does, I don't know if he'll tell me the truth.

Wes doesn't wait for me after class, and I check my messages to see if he replied to my somewhat dramatic good-bye this morning. But he didn't. I can't help but wonder what he's thinking. At some point, he'll want to talk about it. Then again, he might realize we shouldn't—not if he wants to keep his blissful ignorance.

The morning passes quickly, and I'm surprised when Foster asks us to stay in for lunch with him, claiming that in just a few weeks, we've lost the "purity of recess" by spending half the time driving. He said he wants us to get back to our roots.

We agree to this plan over group text, and Nathan tells us Jana won't be there. Neither Foster nor I ask why, and Nathan doesn't offer an explanation.

Wes doesn't contact me, so either he changed his mind about lunch, or he's honoring my good-bye text.

I push through the doors to the courtyard and find Nathan is already at the half wall, our old spot, and he has an array of snacks from the cafeteria laid out for us. None of us had packed a lunch, so he told us he'd take care of it.

I smile when I sit next to him, grabbing an apple first and taking a bite. I scan the courtyard, noting that it's a lot less busy than it used to be. I don't mind; it's kind of peaceful.

"Hello, my dudes," Foster says as he comes over. He sits on the other side of the food, and we all settle in. Foster isn't fully recovered from the flu—the tip of his nose is still red, and his eyes are a little puffy—but he's moving a lot better than he did yesterday. He's no longer hunched over with body aches, at least.

"If I'd have known about this date sooner, I would have brought you soup," Nathan says, studying him. "God, you look like shit."

I slash out my hand and slap Nathan in the chest with a thud. He cough-laughs and pushes my arm away.

"Thank you," Foster says. "And just in case that doesn't add to my insecurity, Arturo decided to go have lunch with Jana and company. Why isn't your girlfriend eating with us?" he asks Nathan.

"Because I didn't ask her," Nathan says simply, and opens a snack bag of chips. "Plus, I wanted to eat with you guys."

"Aw . . . ," Foster says. "I love when it's just the three of us." He beams, his eyes glassy from after-flu, his skin sickly. Regardless, he's still adorable.

"Love you," I murmur to him, and pass him a cookie.

"So . . . ," Foster says, taking a bite of the cookie. "Nathan told me you were with Wes last night. Is he your boyfriend again, or are we trying something less conventional?"

Nathan tsks, annoyed that Foster brought it up.

"We're friends . . . ish," I say. "I don't want his brain to melt down because of me."

"You do have that effect on men," Foster jokes, and I laugh.

"Besides," I tell him, trying not to the let the emotions of the story take over, "I remembered some things." I recount the crashback calmly, detached, and watch as Foster wilts. Feeling sorry for me, I'm sure.

"How about handlers?" Foster asks, changing the subject. "Notice anything?"

"No," I say, and Nathan agrees. "I haven't seen Derek." I pause. "You really think he's a handler?" I ask.

"Anyone can be," Foster says, examining the cookie I gave him. "Even those close to us."

"I don't know if I'd say *anyone*," Nathan argues. His voice has a hitch in it, and Foster smiles, shaking off the moment.

"Right," he says. "Only the really creepy people."

"Well," I say. "Nathan and I are going to the Adjustment office later today. We're going to confront Dr. McKee in person. He'll probably lie, but at least he'll have to do it to my face. And I'll be able to tell."

Nathan scrunches up his nose and looks sideways at me. "*Really*, though?" he says. "You're not the best judge of character."

"What?" I say. "I'm a great judge."

"I agree with Tatum," Foster says. "I mean . . . she is here with us."

Nathan smiles to himself, and then he picks up a can of soda, pops the top, and hands it to me. "She's making better decisions every day."

CHAPTER TWO

I SORT OF FLOAT THROUGH THE REST OF THE DAY,
nervous about going to the Adjustment office after school,
but comforted by my low-stress lunch. Having friends is
powerful—knowing you have people to watch out for you. In
the days of The Program, it was the best defense a person could
have. Obviously, it didn't always work (I'm the perfect example
of that), but it kept the dark hours at bay. I'm lucky that I have
both Nathan and Foster. Right now, it makes me feel a little
invincible.

When I get to my last class of the day, the teacher tells us
we're going to the library. A few people boo, not wanting to
do any research, but I don't mind. I grab my stuff and head
over there.

The library is quiet today, even with my entire class there.

The librarian is hanging in her office, occasionally looking out at us. She seems worried, and I wonder if she's having personal problems.

I take a spot at the table and run my gaze down the assignment sheet. We're supposed to collect firsthand stories throughout history and write a paper about how historical events were viewed from different perspectives. It's interesting—and, dare I say, educational.

I leave my backpack at my chair and walk into the stacks, trying to find a nonfiction book from World War II. I locate the section, and when I pull the book off the shelf, I notice someone in the row with me. I look up, surprised when I find it's Wes.

"Hey," I say, swallowing hard. "What are you doing here?"

"Apparently, I have four term papers to make up, so they gave me a pass out of my last class to work in here. You?"

"Research report."

Wes comes to stand next to me, examining the section of books that I'm picking through. "Look at us," he says. "A couple of smarties." He glances over and smiles, his dimples flashing adorably.

"Ha. Yeah, I guess." I put back the first book I grabbed and select another. Wes shifts, and his arm grazes mine.

"What was up with the cryptic good-bye text?" he mentions casually, and runs his finger down the spine of a book on the shelf. "You could have woken me up when you left."

My heartbeat quickens. "You looked tired," I say. We're

quiet for a moment, and I'm afraid to turn to him. The silence between us feels intimate, much like it did last night.

"I was worried," he says, taking a book and flipping through the pages to examine the pictures, fidgeting. "Thought maybe I came on too strong."

"No," I say. "It's not that."

He clears his throat and puts the book back on the shelf. He moves down a little bit, and the sudden absence of his body heat sends a chill over my arm. "You meant what you said about being friends," he murmurs. "Is that it?"

Of course that's not it, but it's the way it has to be. Anything more is cruel to both of us.

Be better, I tell myself.

"Last night was a mistake," I say, clutching the book I was holding to my chest. "Friends don't really . . . share a bed."

"They probably shouldn't," he agrees.

I start to explain that I still think he's great (not the best answer), when Wes cuts me off, sounding unbothered.

"I want you to like me," he says.

The sentence catches me completely off guard. "I do like you," I whisper.

"I'm not stupid, you know," he says. "You think because you're not telling me that we were together that I can't still figure it out? I mean, you should have seen your face when I walked into class yesterday, like I was back from the dead. Not to mention Dr. Wyatt asking *you* about my life."

I lean in closer, drawn to him. Drawn to the truth.

"I can tell by the way you talk to me," Wes adds in a low voice. "The way you look at me. The way I wanted you to kiss me."

And I'm gazing at him now, willing myself to not profess my love. To keep my emotions in check before I ruin everything. Ruin us.

"I want you to like me, Tate," he repeats. "Not because you used to, or whatever went on between us, but because you just do. I want you to be crazy about me." His mouth flinches with an embarrassed smile.

But it's not that easy, not with our history. Not with the promise I made to Dr. McKee to stay away from him. And I have to decide if I'm going to lie—boldly lie—despite everything.

I feel sick when I utter, "We weren't like that." I force myself to hold Wes's gaze, see the flash of uncertainty, and then disappointment. "We were just friends, Wes. And it's all we'll ever be."

His throat clicks as he swallows hard, turning to the books. "Then I guess I'm an idiot," he says. He looks sideways at me and smiles. "I must have been the 'secretly in love with you' best friend."

"I don't think that was the case," I say, not wanting him to feel worse than he already does. I'm trying to let him down easy, destroy years of our relationship with lies and smiles. By trying to be better, I'm starting to despise myself.

Neither Wes nor I leaves the stacks, and I help him find a book for his class. At one point, he chews on the inside of his lip like he's waiting to say something.

"What?" I ask, pushing his shoulder. He laughs.

"I'm just wondering if you want to go out tonight," he says, checking my reaction.

I tilt my head. "Didn't we just agree—"

"To not share a bed again," he finishes the sentence. "And we won't. But I'm pretty sure friends share meals—especially friends like us. We might even share ice cream."

"Sorry," I say. "But I'm lactose intolerant."

"Ah . . . ," Wes replies like it explains so much about me. "We can go anyway," he offers. "Get a burger or something."

And the truth is, this hurts—rejecting him hurts me. But I saw what our relationship did to us. If I lead him on, it would mean his mother was right—I'm bad for him. I never do what's best for him. This is our real test, I guess.

I've already lied to him, and now I have to let him live. I can't hold on to our ghosts.

I grab another book off the shelf without reading the title and press it to my chest with the other, my movements careful so as not to give away my thoughts.

"I can't," I say with a quick shake of my head. "I have plans tonight. And that research paper to write." I motion over to the tables where the other students are working. "Look, I have to go," I say. "Maybe I'll see you tomorrow."

I start to walk away, and Wes laughs. "Maybe?" he repeats. "We have class together."

I look back over my shoulder at him, and I can see he'll take friendship over nothing because he's drawn to me the same way

I'm always drawn to him. But I can't play this anymore. Being Wes's friend will be impossible because it means watching him carry on with his life. Eventually loving someone else. And that just might kill me. I have to break with him completely.

"Bye," I say with a soft smile, and turn around and start walking toward the tables.

And when I sit down, all alone, a wave of grief hits me. It's like the air has been sucked from my chest, my soul being torn from my body.

I squeeze my eyes shut and shield the side of my face with my hand. And I accept that it's really over.

When class ends forty minutes later, I don't see Wes in the library. I make my way to my locker to grab my things, partially dazed as I force myself not to think. *Not here.*

Nathan texts me as I exchange some books at my locker and says he'll meet me at the Adjustment office later. I tell him it's a plan, and I leave it at that. I don't tell him about seeing Wes. About ending things. I don't want to make it real by telling anybody yet.

I slam my locker shut and hike my backpack onto my shoulders. I turn, and I'm startled when I glance across the hall and notice Jana, talking in a doorway with Derek Thompson. She has her finger in his face, snarling a response.

I watch a moment longer, watch as Derek laughs and reaches over to touch her hand before she rips it away. I didn't think they knew each other, and certainly not enough to be arguing.

"Stay out of it," she tells him. Jana storms past him down the hall, never noticing me.

I stare after her, and when she turns the corner and disappears, I look at Derek. He seems pissed, emasculated. Well, then good for her. I have no idea what that was about, but I reach for my phone to call Nathan. I don't want Derek harassing Jana either.

Before I can call, Derek turns to me, his eyes widening before he narrows them. He laughs to himself and saunters in my direction.

I'm already feeling vulnerable, but rather than fear, I'm suddenly emboldened because I have nothing left to lose. I cross my arms over my chest defiantly, chin raised. He comes to a stop in front of me, his lips turned up with a sinister smile.

"What is your problem?" I ask. To this, he actually snorts a laugh.

"You're a brave little toaster today," he says mockingly. "Have your friends toughened you up? I know you told them about me."

There's a sharp turn in my gut. "Have you been following me?" I ask. "What do you want?"

"I'm just keeping an eye on things," Derek says, looking me up and down.

"Why me?" I ask.

He's still for a moment, and then he leans down to whisper in my ear. I'm struck by the smell of him, a combination of musty clothes and rubbing alcohol. It stings my nose.

"Because I know your secret," he whispers. His words send a chill down my spine, and I quickly pull myself to my full height and push him backward into the middle of the hall. He laughs, and a few people look at us.

"Keep control of that temper," he replies condescendingly, and fixes the collar of his shirt. "You wouldn't want to get flagged."

Derek reaches to touch my waist, but I punch him in the chest, making him cough and stagger back. He rubs the spot, still smiling.

The idea of his hands on me sends me reeling, sickens me. He's not allowed to touch me *ever*.

"Haven't changed a bit. I'll see you around, troublemaker," he says like we're friends, and walks down the hall.

I'm confused on all fronts. First, why would he act so familiar, friendly—we're definitely not. How does he know I'm a returner? About telling Foster and Nathan about him? And a new fear starts, one I don't want to put into words yet. Why was Jana talking to him?

I glance around the hallways and see a few people noticed our interaction and are whispering about it. I tighten my grip on my backpack and head to my car.

Nathan doesn't answer when I call, so I text him and tell him we need to talk. And then I put away my phone and drive to meet with my therapist.

CHAPTER THREE

DR. WARREN'S OFFICE IS A CUTE, WOOD-SHINGLED building. The lawn is bright green and well-manicured, and there's a cherry tree along the stone pathway. I remember the first time I came here, by my grandparents' suggestion, and I thought a place this adorable would have a pretty cool therapist.

And so far, I haven't been disappointed. Dr. Warren has been amazing to work with. She's kind and patient. And honestly, just really likable. I feel as if I can tell her anything. Right now, I need that more than ever.

As I step onto the porch, I keep the confrontation with Derek close; something about his words has struck me in a way that feels honest. Scary, but honest. Yet another mystery piled on.

I try not to let my mind wander to Wes, either—at least, not until I can get some support. I'm going to tell Dr. Warren about the memory I had of Wes, and I'm hoping she'll say that I was right—that I am being a better person by keeping it platonic.

But the main point here is my grandparents. How do I talk to them about The Program? I need Dr. Warren's help with that most of all.

The waiting room for the offices is small and tastefully decorated with live plants and abstract paintings that mimic inkblot tests. I asked the doctor about them once, and she laughed.

"They were supposed to be ironic," she said. "But I ended up loving the color scheme. Now they're a conversation piece. Every patient asks about them."

I like the paintings. They're on white canvas with splashes of bright colors, bleeding into shapes. What exactly they form is up to the viewer. Sort of like finding shapes in the clouds. I almost always see hearts.

Dr. Warren's receptionist smiles warmly from behind her desk, and she asks me to take a seat. I grab a chair nearest the door and look around the waiting area. I think this used to be a living room, and on either side is an office.

On one side is Dr. Warren's, and on the other is the office of a therapist I've never seen in person, although I've noticed a few patients go in that door. A plaque on the wall reads MR. CASTLE—LICENSED THERAPIST.

I'm the only person in the waiting room now, and I take out my phone to check for missed messages. There is one from Wes, and my heart sinks when I see his name. I click it open.

Good luck on your paper.

I don't know how to answer, so I turn off the phone and put it away. He's trying to get to know me. And honestly, if I hadn't remembered, I would have fallen right back into a relationship with him. But the self-hatred I felt that night at his house . . . I'll never forget it again. That kind of pain is forever.

I needed help, and instead I got The Program. I won't put either of us in that position again.

"There she is," Dr. Warren announces, startling me. I look up and see her standing at the door of her office. She's wearing a denim dress with a red belt and tall brown leather boots. "Come on in." She waves me forward and walks into her office ahead of me.

I follow her and go sit in my usual spot—an oversize leather chair with high arms and worn soft cushions—as she closes the door. Dr. Warren picks up a clipboard from her desk and takes a seat on the couch opposite me.

Dr. Warren is slight with cropped short hair and stylish glasses. She seems like she'd be somebody's favorite aunt.

"Thank you for making time for me today," she says. "I was worried."

"My grandparents shouldn't have done that," I respond. "I would have called you if I needed you."

"Would you have?" she asks, taking a pen out of the breast pocket of her dress. She clicks it and then steadies her gaze on me. "What's going on, Tatum?" she asks. "I can see you're upset."

She has such a soothing voice, and I want to tell her my

problems, get her advice. "I'm not sure where to start," I say.

"Well," she says. "We've covered the Adjustment and what it did to both you and Weston, so perhaps it's best to start with his latest return. Your grandparents were greatly concerned. Mentioned headaches?"

"My headaches have nothing to do with Wes," I tell her. "And I'm not here about them. I'm here about The Program."

Dr. Warren presses her lips into a concerned smile. "I told you, Tatum. You were never in The Program. Where did you hear that?"

She gives nothing away—exhibiting the same demeanor I've trusted for over a year. But I'm not going to throw Nathan under the bus. "Someone at school," I say like it doesn't matter. "But how can you be sure it's not true?" I ask, leaning forward. "You wouldn't really know. . . ."

"I've worked with a lot of returners," she says, jotting down a note. "You have zero markers, no symptoms—"

"The headaches?" I point out. She smiles.

"Stress," she says. "And I don't think we'll have to look hard to find the cause."

Back to Wes again. I huff out an annoyed breath and lean my head against the chair. "It's not Wes," I say. I'm being defensive, even though I know she has a point. We're quiet for a minute, and I relent.

"Okay," I admit. "He might have a little bit to do with this. But it's over. Wes and I are over. I lied to him today—told him we were never a couple and that we were just friends."

Dr. Warren's lips part in surprise. "That . . . that must have been difficult. I'm sorry you had to lie."

"So am I," I say. "But I wanted to be better. His mother said some pretty hurtful things. They hurt because they weren't wrong."

I want to get back to discussing The Program, but Dr. Warren seems pretty certain I wasn't there. She'll need proof. I guess it's possible my grandparents never admitted it to her; it's possible they never told anybody.

Dr. Warren leans forward and pats my knee. "I'm so proud of you for breaking things off," she says. "It was selfless."

"My friend said the same thing," I tell her. "But I'm not sure the opposite of selfish is selfless. I just stopped hurting him. Hurting both of us."

She sits back, making another note. "I have to say, Tatum," she begins. "This is the most mature I've ever seen you. I'm encouraged, and with your permission, I'd love to tell your grandparents that you've made huge strides toward wellness."

"Sure," I murmur. But there's a tingle up my arms as I take slight offense at her words. First, my life is pretty fucked—it's not fair to say I was immature before. Second . . . I'm not sure what she means about wellness. Wasn't I well before?

No, I realize. I wasn't well—not if I was flagged for The Program. She might have seen that during therapy, the remnants of my spiral. But again, wouldn't that have clued her in? I'm starting to doubt her effectiveness as a therapist. I'm starting to doubt her.

SUZANNE YOUNG

Almost in response to my thoughts, Dr. Warren smiles warmly.

"Can you tell me what made you decide to finally break off ties with Wes?" she asks. "Was there an epiphany of some sort?"

"Sort of," I say. "I remembered something."

"Something negative?" she asks. And I'm not imagining that she scoots closer, riveted. I like her attention. It might be a little needy, but I miss my grandparents. I need them, so I'm letting Dr. Warren fill in—act the role of the concerned adult.

Besides, I'm still sore from earlier. Still broken from the memory.

I tell Dr. Warren all about going to Wes's house and spending the night. I recount the painful memory I had, including telling off his mother. Including wishing I was dead. I don't mention the handlers at my house or even The Program. I want her to know that I mean what I say about ending things with Wes. But rather than appearing encouraged, Dr. Warren flares her nostrils and tightens her jaw.

"I don't understand," she says, adjusting her glasses. "You *knew* Wes was dating someone else? You were suicidal?"

"I put together that he was seeing someone," I say, "but I don't believe I would have hurt myself. Okay, I admit there was a decline in my health, but when it came down to it, I knew I didn't want to die. I didn't want to hurt anybody. I just needed help."

"And you never got it," she says, mostly to herself. Her pen presses into her paper, scraping the clipboard underneath.

"The Program—" I start to say, and she slaps her clipboard onto the couch.

"You were never in The Program, Tatum," she says forcefully, startling me. My eyes start to tear up, feeling scolded, and Dr. Warren smiles an apology.

"I'm sorry," she says in that same soothing voice she's used for over a year. "I'm . . . unnerved by these revelations. Despite what you told me about wanting to be better, you slept over at Wes's house last night. That was unethical."

I lower my eyes. "Yeah, but nothing happened. I didn't—"

"I'm sure your grandparents don't know?"

I lift my eyes to hers because the tone of her voice . . . it feels kind of like a threat.

"No," I say. "But they're not your patients, remember?"

We stare at each other, and then Dr. Warren nods and smiles. "That is true," she says lightly, like we're gal pals again.

But now I'm the one unsettled. She can't really be that mad that I went to Wes's house. Is she secretly working for his mother or something?

"Tell me more about your memory," she says casually, picking up her clipboard again. "Was there anything else you suddenly remembered? It's highly unusual, but we've established that you were traumatized by the ending of your relationship with Weston. If this flashback is indeed true, it could be why. I'm sorry you didn't realize sooner. Probably would have saved you both from the Adjustment."

It's a dig, once again putting the blame on me. And I feel

myself close up. I'm not going to tell her any more about The Program or that I think I had an Adjustment to fix it. I'm not telling her shit.

"That's it," I say with a shrug. "Seemed like a good enough reason to make sure Wes and I didn't make the same mistake."

"Sure does," she agrees.

I'm doing my best not to fidget, ready to leave her office. When she asks if I'd like to formulate questions for my grandparents, I tell her maybe next time. Whatever Dr. Warren's motive is, I no longer think it's in my best interest. Whether on purpose or as the "concerned adult," she's overlooking my actual problems in hopes of treating the symptoms.

And for now, we're done.

"I should go," I say, checking the time on my phone. I've only been here twenty minutes, but I make a quick excuse about meeting Nathan.

"And how is Nathan?" she asks. "How did he feel about Wes coming back today?"

"Oh, uh . . . he told me to be careful," I say, surprised she's asking about him. "You know Nathan—made some jokes and whatnot."

There's a buzzing on her desk, and Dr. Warren flinches, looking in that direction. "I'm sorry," she says, standing up. "I have to answer that." She sets her clipboard on the seat and goes over to her desk. I watch as she picks up her phone, not even checking the ID as she says, "Yes?" in a hushed voice.

She turns toward the window, and I wait for her, not

wanting to be rude by walking out. My eyes drift to the couch and eventually the clipboard resting on the cushion. I don't mean to, but I read the words, able to decipher them upside down.

Evasive

Falsified history

I quickly lower my eyes before turning slightly to look at Dr. Warren. She still has her back to me.

Evasive? Okay, she might not be totally wrong about that, but in fairness, it was based on her reaction. But what the hell does she mean about *falsified history?*

But, of course, it's the words near the bottom of the paper that send a cool breeze over my soul, a warning shot.

Possible flag

It seems a direct relation to The Program, and that means she knows I was there. She's been lying to me. How much more does she know about my situation? I have to wonder, especially if she's involved with my grandparents.

And it hits me: My grandparents called her, I knew that, but they're also the ones who set up these sessions last summer. Whatever they're involved in, it's likely Dr. Warren's involved too. I turn to look at the door and decide I have to get out of here. Get the proof I need to confront them all.

While Dr. Warren's back is turned, I get to my feet and creep toward the door. I open it slightly and then call her name. When she looks at me, I smile apologetically.

Got to go, I mouth like I'm really sorry about it. She puts

SUZANNE YOUNG

her hand over the receiver to say something, but I duck my head and slip outside.

Once I'm back in the lobby, the receptionist glances up from her computer. She asks if I want to schedule my next appointment, but I tell her I'll call and hurry past before Dr. Warren can chase me down and tell me not to leave.

CHAPTER FOUR

THE AIR OUTSIDE HAS WARMED AND BECOME HUMID as I walk out of the office and head to my Jeep. I'm keyed up, agitated that I can't seem to find one damn person who'll tell me the truth. I'm immediately struck by the fact that I lied to Wes today, placing me in that same category. I straight-up lied to his face, and although it may have been the *right* thing to do in our situation, it doesn't feel very right. It feels as morally overreaching as The Program.

I start the engine of my Jeep, when suddenly someone appears outside the passenger door, and I yelp, clutching my chest. It's Michael Realm, and I consider driving off, possibly over his foot. But he shrugs like he knows it's outrageous for him to ask as he points at the door.

I curse myself, far too curious to not see what he wants, and unlock the door. He gets in.

"I can explain," he begins, and when he turns to me, he can't help but smile. "For the record, you should definitely not open the door to strangers."

We're quiet for a moment, and then we both laugh.

"Okay," I tell him. "Any reason why I shouldn't kick you out? Considering you're still following me after telling me you wouldn't."

"Not sure I said that," he points out, "but yes. I have several great reasons to talk to you. I've worked with Marie and Dr. McKee in the past, and—"

I scoff. "When, like *yesterday?*"

"Yes, actually," he says with a self-conscious laugh. "But not today. Not anymore." He pauses. "Not ever again." I watch him, trying to measure his honesty.

"What happened?" I ask, wondering what could have made him part ways with the Adjustment doctors. Wondering if it brought him here.

Realm glances over to the front door of Dr. Warren's office before turning back to me. "We should go first," he says.

"Yeah, right," I say. "I'm not driving off with a stranger."

He looks at me guiltily, acknowledging that this could be scary for me. "I'm sorry," he says. "Maybe . . . around the corner or something? I can't let Dr. Warren see me. Not with you."

"You know her?" I ask. I don't love that he personally knows my therapist.

He waits a beat and grabs the strap to pull on his seat belt. "She was a doctor in The Program," he murmurs.

The world drops out from under me, and the air within my Jeep turns to concrete. "What?" I ask in a stunned voice. "What—?"

"Tatum, please," Realm says, looking at the building again. "We have to go."

My mind spins, and I can't wrap it around what he just said. My therapist, the person I've told everything to . . . she was part of The Program. Oh my God.

With my hands shaking, I shift into gear and pull onto the road. "That can't be true," I say, searching my memory. The street in front of me is slightly hazy through my blur of tears. "I mean, I thought she was definitely hiding something, but—"

"Everyone's hiding something," Realm says under his breath, and looks out the passenger window.

I don't park around the corner; I drive a few streets over until I find a grocery store parking lot and take a spot near the back, half under sagging tree branches. I turn off the engine and take a steadying breath.

I needed another piece of the puzzle of my life, not to find out my entire picture was wrong. I squeeze my eyes shut and lower my face. This can't be happening. I seriously can't take more mystery. I fight back my emotions.

"Do you want to talk about it?" Realm asks.

SUZANNE YOUNG

I find his dark brown eyes have some sincerity to them. Despite that, they're rimmed in red, slightly bloodshot. He looks exhausted. I don't even know him, and I've already told him more than I've told my grandparents in the last twenty-four hours.

Fuck it.

"Everyone is always lying to me," I say, raw with honesty. "I just found out I was in The Program, and let's just say I'm not handling it well."

Realm blinks quickly and looks down at his lap. He doesn't look shocked, and prickles of realization climb up my arms.

"You already knew that?" I ask.

"I don't want to lie to you, Tatum," he says. "Yes. I already knew."

I can't believe this. The proof I needed sat down in my car, and just like that, I'm both validated and afraid. "And Marie?" I ask. "She denied it yesterday when I asked her."

He laughs to himself. "Sounds about right. And I'll tell you right now, you won't get much from McKee, either."

"But . . . why?" I ask, my heart sinking. "Why keep it a secret?"

"With all the other returners crashing back," he says, "Marie was afraid the same would happen to you."

"And the Adjustment?" I ask, anger starting to tick up in my voice. "Did they give me an Adjustment? Is that why I remember some things?"

"Yeah," Realm says. "But I wasn't there for that."

So it's all true. Dr. McKee adjusted me, and holy shit—it means that I have no idea what's real and what's not. I run my hand through my hair, knotting it in a bun with my fingers as I think.

"And what was your part?" I ask him.

Realm inhales and takes off his seat belt, settling in. "I was brought in as a consultant to keep an eye on you in case you showed any . . . complications," he says. "And when they adjusted Wes, I thought it would all work out. You have a long history." He flashes a pained smile. "Not all of it terrible. But it seems the more people try to fix things, the worse it gets."

"A cure for a cure for a cure," I murmur. "And Dr. Warren?" I ask, motioning vaguely down the road. "She's from The Program? Do you think she knows me from there?"

Realm purses his lips. "Yes," he says. "I imagine she does."

I whine out my disbelief, horrified. Disgusted. "And for a year she's been pretending to help me," I say. "Why? And why isn't she in jail?"

"Few people went to jail for The Program," Realm says. "The powerful rarely pay a price for the damage they inflict on society. In fact," he says, "they keep going. They find new ways to manipulate the masses."

I watch him, seeing the defiance in his posture. The compassion in his expression. "Was Dr. Warren working with Marie and Dr. McKee?" I ask.

He shakes his head no. "As far as I can tell, Dr. Warren is on her own team—one with ties to The Program." His mouth turns down. "I don't want to scare you, but I believe there is a group of people still operating within The Program. Only this time, it's without government involvement. But that's just a hunch."

"Are you usually right?" I ask.

"Yes," he replies.

My heart pounds, and I'm scared to ask my next question. "Are you saying . . . Do you think The Program is coming for me again?"

Realm holds my gaze steady. "Yes," he repeats.

I fall back against my seat. I don't even know what that means or how I'm supposed to react. "What do I do?" I ask.

"I don't know yet," Realm responds. "But I'll keep you posted." He adds the last part casually, and when I look over, we both laugh at how horrifically ridiculous this is. The Program—my nightmare—is still chasing me. And as far as I know, there's nothing I can do about it.

"So . . . ," Realm starts. "Maybe don't make any more appointments with Dr. Warren."

"Yeah, pretty much got that part," I say. "Who else do you think she's working with?"

"Couldn't say," Realm responds, his eyes trailing a person crossing the parking lot with a few grocery bags. I like how observant Realm is, and I assume he's been this way the entire time. Has noticed things I haven't. He might be a good person to have in my corner.

"From what I can tell," he continues, looking at me, "we've

got three groups fighting for control: the Adjustment—the latest cure; Dr. Wyatt, the monitor at the school—who claims to have the moral high ground; and The Program—who wants to burn it all down and control what's left."

"And which group do you fit into?" I ask.

Realm smiles at me. "The rebels, obviously."

I laugh and nod along like that's the right place to be. We fall quiet for a few moments, and I decide that although I don't know him well enough to fully trust him, I don't think he's trying to hurt me either.

"Now that you're no longer in therapy," Realm says, "I can try to help. You know"—he smiles—"the whole consultant thing."

I decide I can tell him all the same stuff I told Dr. Warren, because if he *is* working with her, he'll find out anyway. But I don't think he is; I think he actually wants to help. He coughs, turning his head away, and when he turns back to me, I start talking.

"I'm in love with Weston Ambrose," I say. "And today I boldly lied to him. I told him we were never more than friends. I kind of hate it, even though I'm doing it for him."

Realm seems troubled by the statement. "Why would you do that?" he asks.

"Because I'm trying to be a better person." I furrow my brow. "Dr. McKee told me that if I told Wes about our past, it might kill him. Do you think that?" I ask. "Do you think the truth could kill Wes?"

　　　　　　　　　　　　　　　　　　　　　　　　　　　　　　SUZANNE YOUNG

"Honestly?" he says in a hushed voice. "No. No, I don't think the truth will kill him. But I do think it might confuse him. It might change who he'll become."

It wasn't an answer I expected. "What do you mean?" I ask.

"Well, that's the thing about our past—it shapes our future. And right now, Wes has the luxury of a clean slate. For years, we all wanted our memories back, right? We fought so hard. And for what? Believe me," Realm continues, "remembering doesn't always make it easier."

"Were you in The Program?" I ask, the question suddenly occurring to me.

"Yes. But I . . ." He pauses like maybe he doesn't think he should tell me what he's about to. The struggle plays across his face, until finally, Michael Realm looks at me like he's known me his whole life. But even then, I can tell he's holding back.

"I once knew a guy," he says, his voice drifting off dreamily, "who could never forget anything. He was stuck remembering every word, every place, every emotion. And although that might not seem terrible on the surface, think about how that plays out over time. Think if you had to relive the entire years of The Program scare. Everyone you lost, still right there. Grief is a painful emotion, Tatum, but the gift of it is that it gets better over time. It fades just enough to take the edge off.

"Now imagine if your grief stayed sharp," he continues. "A razor against a fragile heart." He rubs his hand absently over the scar on his neck. "Imagine remembering everything. And what a fucking curse that would be."

"What about you?" I ask. "Would you want to remember?"

Realm lowers his arm to his side, dejected. He takes a moment, and then looks at me and smiles. "I was in The Program," he says. "I wish I didn't know that. There are a lot of things I wish I didn't know."

He's devastation, sitting in the front seat of my Jeep. I'm not sure I've ever met someone so tortured. So raw. I look past him and see the grocery store has an attached café.

"Do you want to grab a coffee?" I ask suddenly. Realm studies me like he doesn't trust my offer, but then his expression softens.

"I would love to," he says.

CHAPTER FIVE

REALM AND I GRAB A TABLE IN THE DESIGNATED café area. There are six tables in this corner of the grocery store, and except for an old man eating a pastry, the place is deserted. Even the barista hangs near the back, where she's cleaning a machine.

Coffees in hand, Realm and I sit across from each other, half-hidden behind a wood beam. Realm leans forward, elbows on the table, and wraps both hands around his coffee cup.

"So you went to Dr. Warren to get guidance on Wes," he starts. "Or did you really want her to tell you that you shouldn't lie to him? That you should get back together with him?"

"I think I wanted validation," I say, staring down at the lip of my cup, running my finger along it. "I wanted her to acknowledge how difficult it was, and yeah . . ." I smile. "Maybe part of me hoped she'd tell me it was unnecessary. I don't want to walk away from him, Realm. I love him. But after seeing how deeply hurt I was in the past, how . . . damaged, I'm scared to go back there. I'm scared for him to end up there."

"But you still love him," Realm says sympathetically, like he's finishing the thought for me.

I pick up my coffee, blow on it, and take a sip. "Doesn't that suck?" I ask, trying to lighten the moment as my tears fade.

"It's . . . it's super shitty—I'm not going to lie."

I sniff a laugh and set my cup down. "It doesn't really matter what I do," I add. "Wes doesn't remember me, so it was stupid for me to assume he would just love me again."

"I don't think it's stupid to assume that," Realm says, and drinks his coffee. "Wouldn't be the first time."

I study him a moment, noting he's smart, attractive. Noting how lonely he seems. "Do you have a girlfriend?" I ask.

"I have an ex that I'm fond of," he offers.

I laugh. "Oh, hey. Me too."

He smiles, but it doesn't reach his eyes. "Dallas was the better part of me," he adds. "Or at least she used to be when we were together. She's exploring the world now—traveling with her friend Cas."

"You miss her," I say.

"I do."

"Is she the love of your life?"

Realm sits thoughtfully for a moment, and then he shakes his head. "No," he says. "Because she always deserved better than me. Most people do."

　　　　　　　　　　　　　　　　　　　　　　　　　　　SUZANNE YOUNG

It's such a miserable thing to say. I'm not sure if he's being self-deprecating or truly feels that low, but his sadness is overwhelming. He hunches down slightly, his thin shoulders jutting out through his T-shirt.

I don't believe for an instant that what he said is true. We all make mistakes, but it doesn't mean we don't deserve to be loved.

However, the realness of him right now cuts me. Worries me in a way I don't quite understand. He coughs again, turning away, and I examine him more closely. He doesn't look well—deeply exhausted. It makes me wonder what type of problems he loses sleep over. I don't want him to dwell on his anguish, though, so I bring the topic back to the really messed-up shit.

"How do you know Dr. Warren?" I ask. Realm's dark eyes flick up to me immediately. He studies me before answering.

"From The Program," he says in a low voice. "And she's treated several of my friends."

"Why are you hiding from her?" I ask. To this he smiles.

"Because she'll never give up. Dr. Warren doesn't let things go. And for the past year, she's been trying to find me. Not going to happen."

"Why does she want to find you?" I ask.

"Several reasons, I'm sure. But the main one? Sloane Barstow. She burned up Dr. Warren pretty good."

My mouth falls open. This time, I'm the one who leans closer. "You know her?" I ask. "You know Sloane Barstow?"

"And James Murphy—yes." He glances around at the

empty tables before taking a big, steadying breath, like this was a long story. "I met Sloane in The Program. Met James after. He's the kind of guy you love to hate, if only he were hateable."

There's affection in his voice, and it draws me to his story. "Why did you want to hate him?" I ask.

Realm glances down at his coffee and lifts one shoulder in a shrug. "Because I was in love with Sloane."

"Oh . . ."

"I know," he says, interpreting my reaction. "Sloane and James forever. Still, I thought I had a chance. But they love each other a maddening amount. Sickening to watch, really."

"And you don't hate James?" I ask.

"He's my best friend."

"Okay . . . that's got to be awkward."

"It is," Realm agrees. "But he knows I love her, and I know she loves him. So he doesn't have much to worry about."

"I'm sorry."

"No reason to be sorry." Realm waves off my apology. "I knew their relationship. I should have adjusted my goals accordingly."

"Yeah, well," I say, picking up my coffee. "The past is over. Sometimes, the only real thing is now."

Realm's lips part as he watches me take a sip of my drink, his dark eyes sweeping over my face. When they meet my gaze, he flinches a smile, a blush rising high on his cheeks.

"Right," he says with a quick nod. "You're damn right, Tatum."

I'm about to commiserate on our similar situations when Realm pulls back and takes out his phone. I see he's getting a call. He groans softly and clicks off the phone before sliding it back into his pocket.

"I'm so sorry to cut this short," he says. "But I'm running late. I was supposed to meet someone an hour ago." He smiles as he stands up from the table. "I got caught up chatting with you."

He's kind of flirtatious. Manipulative? I'm not sure, but I stand up too. "Did you need a ride back?" I ask.

"No, I've got a ride coming," he says, although there's no way that's true. I still can't believe he knows Sloane and James. I have no idea what I'm getting myself into by talking to him.

"What aren't you telling me, Realm?" I ask.

He laughs and slaps the table. "Obviously, *a lot*," he admits, picking up his coffee. "So let's talk again soon, yeah?"

I don't tell him that we will, mostly because I'm not sure what all this means. I'm definitely going to check his story against whatever Marie and Dr. McKee admit.

"Good luck with your rebellion," I tell Realm, making him smile.

I start toward the exit and drop my empty coffee cup into the trash, but before I walk out, Realm gently touches my shoulder. I turn to him, slightly unsettled by being so close.

"If it means anything," he says, "I don't think you should give up on Wes. Having a history with someone . . . although it may not be everything you thought it was, it did help create who you are now. He's part of you. You don't have to forget that."

I'm not sure why, but his words hit me hard, and I instantly feel a lump in my throat.

Realm offers a smile, and there's a long pause like he might hug me. But then he turns and walks through the automatic doors and out into the parking lot.

It's been a weird day. I text Nathan again, telling him I need to talk to him. I don't want to specifically call out Jana in case she sees his phone. And beyond his girlfriend talking with a sketchy guy from school, I have to tell him about my run-in with Realm, the bombshell about Dr. Warren, and my current status with Wes. Once again, Nathan doesn't answer. I text Foster, and he responds that he's with Arturo and asks if he can call me later.

I still have an hour before I'm supposed to meet Nathan at the Adjustment office, and I don't think it'd be smart to go there alone. I can go home to think about everything I learned today, but I'm dreading it. I abruptly left Dr. Warren's office, and she probably already called my grandparents and told them. They might show up, and then how do I explain? I can't.

But I'm going to the Adjustment office in a little while, and by the end of the day . . . I might know everything. And once I do, I will confront *everyone*. No more deceit. No more fucking lying.

I just have to pretend for a bit longer.

SUZANNE YOUNG

I glance at the clock on my dashboard, not wanting to be alone. I have nowhere to go, and few people know about my predicament. Even fewer that I can trust. And even though I was determined to be better, Michael Realm has left me thinking. If I don't have to forget Wes, can I still be his friend? Can I still confide in him?

There was hurt and pain in our relationship, but there was also friendship—true friendship. Maybe I should be building on that, creating something new and positive for both of us. I want to be that strong. I want to be the kind of person who can do that.

I check my reflection in the mirror and think the circles under my eyes look a little darker than usual; I'm slightly drawn. I haven't exactly been taking good care of myself lately. I'll have to focus on that more.

But for now, I begin the drive toward Wes's house.

CHAPTER SIX

WES'S MOM IS HOME, AND I ALMOST DRIVE PAST HIS house to avoid her. I'm surprised she's there, but I'm guessing she's in overprotective mode. Hovering.

I decide to stop anyway because Wes's motorcycle is in the driveway. I'll go to his door, and if he doesn't answer, I'll text him. We've always been good at avoiding his parents.

I go around the block and park in my usual spot under the trees. I slip my hands into my pockets as I walk to his door, my heart beating wildly. We're on the same page now—just friends. It shouldn't be that hard to act on it. At least, that's what I try to tell myself.

I check around the street, and then I knock on Wes's basement door. There's a shadow, so I know he's there. I wait nervously until finally, the door opens.

Wes's eyes widen, and he takes in a sharp breath. "Hi," he says, surprised. He's wearing the same clothes he had on at school, his hair a little messier. He rubs his hand over it to smooth it down, like he's trying to impress me. He's adorable, and I can't help but smile when I see him.

"Can I talk to you?" I ask, expecting him to push the door open wider.

But his lips form an O, and he quickly looks back over his shoulder inside the house. "It's not a good time," he says quietly, edging the door tighter against him.

I don't understand at first, but then I hear his mother's voice from the living room.

"Weston?" she calls. "Who is it? We're not done here."

My heart seizes up, and I take a step back. The last thing I need to cap off this catastrophic day is Dorothy Ambrose filing a restraining order against me.

Would she even be wrong at this point? God, I'm an idiot. I can't believe I keep running back to Wes in the same breath that I'm wishing him away. If I don't stop, I'll cause serious damage. Maybe I already have.

I stand there, unable to articulate why I'm here. Instead, without a word, I spin around and start walking quickly toward my Jeep.

"Be right back," Wes says to his mother. He closes the door behind him and runs after me in his bright white socks. "Wait up!" he calls out, but I don't stop. "Hey," he says more forcefully to get my attention.

I turn, and Wes holds up his hands apologetically as he approaches my Jeep. "I'm sorry," he says. "I wasn't trying to get rid of you, it's just . . . my mom. She's asking questions—an interrogation, really. I didn't want to drag you into it."

He doesn't realize how much she hates me. And I hate me a little too. I hate that I'm lying to him. I hate that I'm hurting and confusing him. My eyes well up because my coming clean now would put a strain on his family. All I ever do is hurt him.

"Tate," Wes says softly, like an invitation.

I can't help it. I step into his arms, and he hugs me fiercely, knowing that I need it—intuitive, even as I try to hide from him.

We don't say anything at first, his hand firm on the back of my neck, my fingers threading lovingly through his hair as I get on my tiptoes to get closer, my cheek on his shoulder. Wes sighs against me, and I absorb the feel of him, the smell of him.

But the scene is far too intimate, and I force myself to pull away, straightening out of his arms like it meant nothing. This desperation feels too similar to my memory of the night I went into The Program. Me, never letting him go. It scares me out of my head.

"Tate," Wes says, shaking his head. "I don't know how you want me to act or what's going on between us. I don't know what you want from me."

And the truth is, I don't know either. When I don't answer, he blows out a frustrated breath.

"I won't chase you when you made it clear that we're friends," he says. "We're still just friends?"

SUZANNE YOUNG

I nod that we are, and Wes takes a step back from me.

"Then don't look so hurt," he says with a bit of an edge to his voice. "Just . . . talk to me. Explain it to me." He wants me to admit how I feel; he wants me to be with him.

But I can't. Michael Realm said our past helped create who I am now, but I don't want it to. I don't want to be hurt and angry. I don't want to make each other miserable.

"I'm sorry I bothered you," I tell Wes. I brush off any show of emotion, standing here and pretending I didn't freak out moments ago.

"You're not bothering me," he says like I should already know that. "Why did you come here anyway?"

"I wanted to talk about something that happened at therapy," I say, "but it can wait until tomorrow."

"You sure?" Wes asks. "I mean, I can grab my shoes, and we can go for a ride."

I force a smile and wave my hand. "No, it's fine. I'll tell you about it tomorrow."

"Okay," Wes says, taking a step back. "But . . . if you want to come back, just let me know. I'll be here."

"I will. Thanks," I say, unlocking my car.

I get in, and as I close my door, I hear him murmur, "Goodbye, Tate," before he jogs back toward his house.

Nathan is sitting on my porch when I arrive home. I texted him, saying I needed to talk before we went to the Adjustment office. Before I say anything, I drop down next to him on the top step, both of us staring toward the street.

"How bad is it?" Nathan asks.

"Bad," I whisper before the floodgates open. I sob and tell him everything. I pour my heart out and listen as he says that one, Dr. Warren is the worst; two, I shouldn't talk to strangers in grocery stores; and three, Wes needs to know about our relationship.

"I can't believe you lied to him," Nathan murmurs, petting my hair back from my wet cheeks. "You shouldn't have done that, Tatum. You didn't have to tell him the whole truth, but you shouldn't have made shit up."

"It seemed like a good idea at the time," I say, my voice scratchy. Nathan smiles and bumps his shoulder into mine.

"Turns out," he says, "life after memory erasure, implantation, and monitoring is a little tough to navigate. Go figure."

I laugh. "Maybe you should be my therapist," I tell him.

"You couldn't afford me," Nathan replies easily. He looks sideways with a smirk. The sun reflects on his face, and I turn toward the sky, wishing it would cloud over. Go away and leave me to grieve in the dark.

"Okay," I say, waving my hands like I'm done with the topic. "Enough about my nonsense. Where were you earlier? I needed to talk to you about Jana. I saw her at school arguing with Derek Thompson in the hallway. Do they know each other? Has he been harassing her, too?"

"What?" Nathan asks, surprised. "She doesn't know Derek."

"She sure seemed like she did," I say. "And then Derek came

over to me and insinuated that he knew I had a secret, and that it was possibly The Program. So please tell me how the fuck Derek Thompson knows more about me than most people, and for the second part of that question, does that mean your girlfriend knows as well?"

Nathan looks troubled, and I wonder if I should have softened my inquiry. "I'm sorry," I start to say, but he holds up his hand to let me know that I don't have to apologize.

"I don't know the deal with Derek," he says. "But I didn't tell Jana anything about you. And definitely nothing about The Program. So . . . I'm not sure what to think anymore." His posture sags.

"Did you really have a talk with her yesterday?" I ask. "What about?"

"Let's not—" he starts.

"No way," I interrupt. "I've told you everything, Nathan. You don't get to spare me your drama. What's going on with her? Is she okay?"

"I like how you're pretending to actually care about Jana," he says, glancing over at me.

"I care about *you*," I say quickly. "And, by extension, that means I care about your sketchy girlfriend, too." I keep a straight face, but when he smiles, we both laugh.

"Fair enough," Nathan says. "But it's going to sound weird."

"I can handle weird. I'm becoming an expert at it."

"I was at her house yesterday," Nathan says, "and she was making food when her mom came home from the store. I was chatting with her mother on the couch, and . . ." Nathan pauses, furrowing his brow. "And her mom leaned closer to me and whispered, 'Be careful of that girl.'"

Chills run up my arm, and my logical side wants me to jump to an easy answer. "Was she saying her daughter will break your heart?" I ask lightly.

"No." He shakes his head. "I don't think that was what she was saying at all. I got the impression . . . it seemed like she was scared of her."

"Scared of Jana?" I ask.

"Yeah. Because then Jana came into the room, saw me sitting with her mother, and there was this slight . . . I don't know, this flash of worry, I guess. Jana told her mother to leave us alone, and . . . she did. Her mom got up, shot me a pointed look, and then walked past Jana into the back of the house. Their body language, their lack of resemblance—it was weird. If I'd seen them together anywhere else, I would have thought they were hostile strangers."

"They might not be close—like me and my mom."

Nathan leans forward, elbows on his knees, seeming to think it over. "Anyway, I asked Jana about it," he says, "and she went off on me. Told me I shouldn't interrogate her mother, as if I was the one to start the conversation. She told me she loved me, and asked why I didn't love her."

There's a twist in my gut, a thought that hadn't occurred to me. "*Do* you love her?" I ask quietly.

Nathan swallows hard. "I think so," he says. "But the whole

SUZANNE YOUNG

situation . . ." He shakes his head. "It's kind of fucked. She told me I was hurting her by never including her with my friends. She said I was an asshole—and not in an endearing way. It's why I brought her to your house with me yesterday, to show her that I care. I promised to include her more."

"And lunch today?" I ask.

"I hadn't done enough, apparently. She texted this morning claiming I didn't love her, because if I did, I'd tell her everything. Like . . . what the fuck is *everything*? I don't even know what she's talking about. And, to be honest, I'm getting a little tired of being called an asshole." He pauses. "With the exception of you," he allows, and I nod.

Nathan sighs. "I'm not going to fight a losing battle," he says, his hazel eyes reflecting the light. "And it's starting to seem pretty obvious that she's . . . well, she's the one not being honest with me. I just don't know what she's lying about."

"Nathan," I say, truly concerned. "I think you should stop dating her. You're right, this is weird. Her mom, Derek, calling you an asshole? That's not . . . normal."

Jana is Nathan's first serious girlfriend, and that worries me. Because he might really love her, and that would give her the opportunity to take advantage of him. Nathan's my best friend, and I want to look out for him. He's done the same for me.

"You know you have other options, right?" I say gently. "You're a cool guy. You can meet another girl."

"Sure," he says like he doesn't believe it.

"For real, Nathan." He looks over at me, and I see the sadness in his eyes. Nathan doesn't want to fail at this relationship, and what Jana said to him, accusing him of basically being a bad boyfriend, was manipulative. I already didn't like her very much; he was right about that. I won't let her break his spirit.

"Listen," I say to Nathan in mock seriousness. "You have options. You are moderately attractive, your sense of humor is slightly above average, and, dude," I say, trying not to smile, "your laundry detergent always smells really nice. Fresh. So don't sell yourself short, kid."

Nathan stares at me a moment, his lips flinching. "I'm also so-so at video games," he adds. "You forgot that part."

"I did," I say regretfully.

Nathan smiles, and then unexpectedly, he reaches over and takes my hand, squeezing it. He rests his head on my shoulder, and I lean my cheek against him. The sadness rolls off of him, and I wish I could make it better.

"I hate liars," he whispers. "I can't date one."

I consider his words, and reluctantly, I have a moment of sympathy for Jana Simms. After all, she lost her best friend recently. Many of us understand to some extent (thanks to the epidemic and The Program) what that means. Erratic behavior is one of the signs that something's wrong. Add Derek and family problems to that . . . and maybe I've jumped to conclusions about her. I don't want her to get hurt, but I also can't let her hurt Nathan. I might just talk to her myself.

"What time is it?" Nathan asks, sitting up and taking out

his phone. My heart starts beating faster, and I swallow hard before looking at him.

"Time for some answers?" I suggest.

He nods solemnly, and then we both stand up and walk quietly to the Jeep. Determined to follow through on our plan. Determined to find Dr. McKee.

CHAPTER SEVEN

WE SIT IN THE PARKING LOT OF THE ADJUSTMENT
office, neither of us speaking. I turn off the engine, and Nathan
unbuckles his seat belt. He puts his hands on the dashboard
and stares ahead at the office before turning to me.

"They're going to lie," he says steadily.

"I know."

"We can't let them get away with any of it," he adds.
"Remember, they manipulate people for a living. We won't give
them a chance to do that to us." He pauses. "Again."

"Thanks," I say, and slap his thigh. "And I'm prepared this
time. I got proof from Michael Realm, remember?"

"I do."

"Realm confirmed my worst suspicions. I'll make Dr. McKee

and Marie freely admit they've lied, and after that . . . I'll dive into all the other shit, I guess."

"There is definitely a lot of it to wade through," Nathan says.

I want to understand what happened in The Program. How did I block the memory of me and Wes? How did Wes? There has to be an answer. And it has to mean something.

"Well," Nathan says with a cleansing breath. "I'm already sick of this Michael Realm guy, but okay—we'll start with the Program questions. Just be prepared for the answers."

I watch Nathan a long moment. "Is that even possible?" I ask.

"No," he murmurs, and grabs the door handle before climbing out of the Jeep.

We both cross to the front of the building just as the sun passes behind the clouds, setting the scene in a weighted gray color—ominous. I'm scared of what comes next.

"They kept me a secret," I say, as if just realizing the madness of all of this. "They adjusted me, and then pretended to have never met me. There must be a reason."

"We'll figure it out," he replies.

"Maybe . . ." I pause. "Or maybe we should just come back at night and go through their files," I offer.

Nathan's face is unreadable for a moment. "That is . . . ," he starts, before creasing his brow, "easily the dumbest idea I've ever heard. I mean—it has exactly zero chance of working."

I laugh, appreciating his sense of humor right now.

"But if you decide to break and enter," he adds, "I'll go with you. You know, just to make sure they don't strap you down and erase your mind."

"You're the best," I say.

He turns to face the frosted-glass door. "Let's do this," he murmurs, and pulls it open, both of us exchanging a surprised glance to find it's not locked.

Nathan and I walk inside and ease the door shut behind us. There's no receptionist like there used to be. No art on the walls. There's only an empty desk and several chairs stacked up beside it. The door to the back offices is closed—the place where they took my false memories and implanted them into Wes's brain, creating a situation we couldn't come back from. It was their fault he had to be reset again. It was their fault because they knew I'd been in The Program, and they adjusted him anyway.

So why did they trust my memories? They should have known better.

"Do we wait for someone to come out?" I ask, looking at Nathan. He snorts a laugh.

"Absolutely not," he says simply, and opens the door to the back offices.

My pulse spikes, and I follow closely behind him. There is a soft murmur of voices coming from the end of the hallway, and Nathan and I continue in that direction.

Dr. McKee's office door is shut, but whatever meeting

is going on is behind a different closed door. It takes me a moment to realize it's the treatment room—where they give the Adjustments. My stomach feels sick. Are they performing an Adjustment right now? After everything that happened, they should be shut down.

Nathan must sense my growing fury, because he reaches out to touch my hand. But I won't let them hurt anyone else—risk any more lives.

I pull away from Nathan and rush forward, grabbing the handle of the treatment room door and busting in. I startle the people inside, and Dr. McKee lets out a little yelp. Marie clutches her chest. And sitting between them, casually swinging her legs over the edge of her chair, is Jana Simms.

There is no procedure happening, although there are files laid out on the table, a scan pulled up on the computer screen that they seem to have been discussing. Jana is the only one who doesn't flinch, but I watch as the color drains from her face. Her eyes drift past me to Nathan. I feel his presence behind me, hanging just inside the door.

"What are you doing here?" he asks in a voice so intimate you would think it was just the two of them. Before Jana can answer, Marie gets to her feet and crosses her arms over her chest.

"No, Nathan," Marie says. "What are *you* doing here? Did you break in?"

"The door was open," he responds, hostile. He looks past her. "Jana," he calls, waiting for an answer.

At first, I'm worried that Jana is here for an Adjustment, and it doesn't make any sense. She doesn't need one. But as I look around the room, I notice the files and notes, pens out. She has a coffee near her, an old sandwich wrapper. She's been here awhile. She . . . belongs here.

Jana isn't here as a patient. It must hit Nathan at the same moment, because he curses under his breath.

"Who are you?" he demands.

"Nathan, calm down," Jana says, keeping her voice steady. But her eyes are too wide. Too innocent. "It's not what you think."

"Oh, you have no idea what I'm thinking," he says coldly. "But the past couple days are starting to make some sense."

I look from Nathan to Jana, the tension ratcheting up. Nathan was suspicious, and it turns out he had a right to be. It also means Jana did know the truth about me. She must have if she's involved with these doctors.

"This is a private facility," Dr. McKee says, as if he's never met us before. I turn on him fiercely, and I watch his pretend professionalism falter.

"Who are you?" Nathan asks Jana again, but this time his voice is pleading.

"Jana," Marie says in warning. But Jana looks over her shoulder at her, her expression miserable, and shakes her head.

"That's not my name," Jana says. Marie closes her eyes, frustrated, and Jana turns back to Nathan. "My name is Melody," she says to him. "I used to . . . I used to be a handler. I used to be a lot of things."

I'm not sure what Nathan thought she was going to say—I don't even know what I thought—but he rocks back on his heels. I put my palm on his back, reminding him that I'm here for him.

"Foster was right," Nathan says. "I should have known; he's always right. He didn't trust you, and he told me you were hiding something. But I defended you." Nathan's voice crackles with hurt. "I fucking defended you."

"That's enough," Dr. McKee says, coming over to put his hand on Jana's shoulder. *Melody.* "You need to leave," he tells us. "This is a private facility." He shifts his eyes over to me, and there is a moment of apology there. I pounce.

"We're not leaving," I say. "You owe me an explanation. And she"—I jab my finger in Melody's direction—"owes Nathan a little clarification."

Marie's hard stance behind Dr. McKee eases. "It's time to tell her, Tom," she says, surprising me. "She already knows anyway."

Dr. McKee turns to her, and after a moment, he nods and motions toward the door.

"Let's go into my office," he says to me in a low voice.

I check with Nathan, and he's a bit torn, not wanting to leave me alone.

"I'll be fine," I say, and look toward Melody. She stares at Nathan desperately, not even acknowledging me.

I'm burning up, ready to scream at her and ask her how she could do this to him. How she could lie to him? Ask her *why*?

But ultimately, this is Nathan's fight. He gets to decide what he forgives—*if* he forgives.

Nathan swallows hard, seeing the anger in my expression, and tells me to go ahead with Dr. McKee. He turns back to Melody, his jaw set hard, pink high on his cheeks like he might cry but is trying to tough it out.

Melody, on the other hand, is dragged down. Devastated. She stares at him intensely like she can explain everything. Well, she'd better have a good excuse, then.

I follow Dr. McKee and Marie out into the hall, the three of us submerged in heavy quiet as we walk. The doctor leads us to his office and goes inside. Marie stays in the doorway, watching me as I move past her and take a seat in the chair in front of the desk. I don't even realize I'm sitting until I look at them, both standing by the file cabinet. It was an automatic response to entering the office.

Dr. McKee presses his lips together, making them go white. Nathan said the doctors manipulate people for a living, but I have to concede that Dr. McKee doesn't seem all that good at it. It's probably a ruse, but he seems defeated. A little regretful. And if I'm being honest, he looks older than he did last time I saw him. Maybe his guilt is aging him.

For her part, Marie studies me from the doorway, giving nothing away.

"Well?" I ask them both, unable to take the suspense anymore. "Are you ready to admit that I was a patient of The Program *and* the Adjustment?"

"Yes," Dr. McKee says immediately, and it's a punch straight to my chest. The easy answer steals my fight, and I blink a few times, trying to solidify my resolve.

"Okay," I say, my voice smaller. "So do you want to start, then? Because I'd really love to know why everyone lied to me."

Dr. McKee slips his hands into the pockets of his lab coat, measuring his words. He comes over to the desk and leans against it, facing me.

"Tatum," he says kindly. "I've known your grandmother for years."

I look at Marie, expecting her to contradict this, but she stands stoically at the side of the room. I worry suddenly that Dr. McKee is a better liar than I've given him credit for. I can't see where this response is leading, though.

"I don't believe you," I tell him.

"I've worked on and off with your grandmother through the hospital," he says. "She used to assist me and my work with the grief department."

"The what?" I ask.

"Grief department. It was a company that helped grieving families. Marie and I used to run it, under the supervision of Arthur Pritchard."

There's a nagging in my brain, something familiar, although I can't quite place the name. Dr. McKee breathes out heavily.

"Arthur went on to create The Program," he adds.

I jump up from my chair. "So you *are* part of The Program?" I ask, taking a step back from him. "And you're saying my grandmother was too?"

"No," Dr. McKee says. "My goal was to *stop* The Program. We"—he motions between him and Marie—"tried to prevent it. But it was beyond our control. Now, as you may have heard, last year Arthur Pritchard died from complications of violating his contract."

I furrow my brow, not understanding what he's getting at.

"But in the beginning, we all had good intentions," he says. "The grief department was a force of good. I would work with hospitals to identify parents and loved ones who had been left behind by tragedy. Your grandmother helped me find those who needed help, those so devastated by grief that they were at risk of dying themselves. We would send in closers—a therapy method where an impersonator filled in for the deceased family members so that others could say good-bye. We would close the loop of grief. For nearly ten years, your grandmother helped our department change lives."

I can't believe my grandmother would have anything to do with a company that manipulated people. Manipulated their feelings. I must have been small when she worked with them, because I don't remember even a hint of this. Then again, it's hard to remember a time before the epidemic.

"When the grief department was shut down," Dr. McKee continues, "your grandmother reached out to me. Even offered me a job within the hospital. But Marie and I were already trying to work on a cure for what The Program was doing. I told her so."

Dr. McKee's gaze grows sympathetic then. "And when

you were taken by The Program, your grandmother called *me*. Begged for my help. I didn't have much influence anymore—Arthur Pritchard was already on the outs with the company he'd created. But there was help from within—there were people there on your side." He smiles like this should make me proud. Instead, it makes me wonder who the hell else was involved.

"So how'd I get out?" I ask, breathless.

He lowers his eyes, folding his hands in front of him. "Dr. Warren was able to facilitate your release after a few weeks, limited erasure."

Realm was right. She did know me from The Program. It's horrifying when I think about it; the idea of her listening to my problems while knowing more about me than I knew about myself. It was the ultimate manipulation.

"So The Program's back?" I ask.

"Tatum," Dr. McKee replies. "The Program never left."

CHAPTER EIGHT

MARIE SHIFTS, SCRAPING THE HEEL OF HER SHOE across the floor. "I'm going to step outside and check on . . . the others." Marie exits, and I run my palm down my face, holding on for the bigger reveals to come.

"After your release from the facility was secured," Dr. McKee continues, "your grandmother brought you to us. She was concerned because you still seemed so deeply sad. Marie and I . . . we felt we had a viable cure with the Adjustment. We thought we could fix you."

"I'm a human being, not a computer virus. And how do I know any of this is true? Nathan told me that my grandfather used his journalist connections to get me out."

"That was part of it," he admits. "The possibility of exposure did aid in your release. But there were side deals. And ultimately, Dr. Warren signed off on a statement saying you weren't a threat to yourself, her position supported by your handler."

"I wasn't a threat," I snap at him automatically.

"But you were," he says sadly. "You most certainly were, Tatum."

I want to deny it, but I remember what I was like the night I was taken into The Program. The way my knuckles bled. The way I hated myself. I needed help. I didn't need The Program, but I did need help. Maybe I *was* a threat.

Dr. McKee continues talking, beginning to pace the room, slightly out of breath. "In the agreement to let you out, Dr. Warren insisted on erasing your time in The Program. Erased the history of you and Wes. We'll never know all that she erased, but we had a good idea because we had your file. Still, this had to be done undercover—without her knowledge. If she knew you'd been adjusted, it would have broken the arrangement. You would have gone back to The Program."

"Give me my file," I say.

"I don't have it. We lost it months ago."

"Of course," I say, not believing him. "So you gave me back memories—wrong ones—and wanted it secret. But you let me keep seeing a Program doctor," I continue. "Putting myself in danger every time I showed up for therapy. She could have flagged me at any point!"

"We couldn't risk her knowing we'd interfered with your care. We erased the Adjustment while we gave it."

"What did my file say?" I ask. "What memories did you put back in, and why are they wrong?"

"Over two days, we implanted all the information we could gather. But we focused on memories that would allow you to resume your life. We had no idea that you and Weston Ambrose had broken up. It wasn't something you admitted to in therapy, even with the help of medication."

"How?" I ask. "Doesn't The Program always find out the truth?"

"Yes," he admits. "They have their ways. And that's also why we've dedicated significant resources into keeping you healthy, both you and Wes. You beat The Program. To some extent, you did. We're hoping your continued health will prove the Adjustment works."

Right now I don't feel like the victor. I feel like a lab rat. "My grandparents let you put memories in my head?" I ask.

"They wanted you to come home, not just physically— fully. They were worried about you."

"Did I fight?" I ask, sitting back in the chair. Dr. McKee comes to lean on his desk, and I notice his right shoulder sags slightly. He swallows hard.

"Yes," he says. "You were not a willing subject, Tatum. And this was . . . this was difficult for everyone involved. But it was for the best. Your grandmother knew she could trust me, so she let us treat you."

I cover my mouth, horrified at the idea of these doctors strapping me down, injecting me with serums, all while my

SUZANNE YOUNG

grandparents stood by. How far will people go to keep their family? At what point is it no longer my life to control?

"Tatum," Dr. McKee says softly, as if he can see I'm struggling with his explanation. "You're safe now," he says.

"But I'm not," I say. "I'm going to fall apart just like the rest of them. I'm a returner too. And in case you missed it, they're crashing back."

"That won't happen to you," he says. "Not the same way. You'll have crashbacks, yes—but you come back. You process these memories differently. Don't you see? You are the only one who has come through the Adjustment without a setback. You are our proof of concept. You are the cure."

"I'm no cure."

"But you are. Our entire case study is built around you. We haven't figured out the difference—why the procedure worked on you and not the others. Why not Wes? Why not Vanessa? We don't know the answer yet, but your existence proves the Adjustment can work. And Marie is close to the answer. You're going to save lives."

"No," I say, horrified. "I've *ruined* lives. Because it worked on me, Vanessa is dead. You wouldn't have replicated it if I hadn't proven it could work. And Wes wouldn't have been reset again. You've turned me into a weapon. It's on my conscience."

"Oh, honey," Dr. McKee says, and reaches for me. I slap his hand away, a sharp sting on my palm. He slides his hands into his pockets.

"Why did you use my memories in Wes's Adjustment?" I ask. "You knew they weren't real."

"We thought they were accurate," he corrects. "In fact, we thought they might be better, clearer than real memories. It was a risk that didn't pan out."

"Didn't pan out," I repeat in disgust. "And what about Jana—Melody? Or whoever she is. What is she doing in all of this?"

"Melody Blackstone is a handler, and she has worked closely with Marie since the beginning. She left The Program and wanted to make things right. She wanted to cure people. So she was assigned to watch Vanessa and, from a distance, you. Unfortunately, Vanessa found out who Melody was, and it caused her breakdown. We'd hoped to avoid that."

"So she's using Nathan?" I ask, my anger rising. "She's using him to watch me?"

"She's trying to protect you."

"I don't want your protection!" I shout. "I want you to leave me alone. Leave all of us alone. I won't be your cure, your case study. Leave me out of it. I won't be your excuse to kill anyone else."

"Tatum," Dr. McKee says like I'm being unreasonable. He stands up and tries to take my arm, but I rip from his grasp.

"Don't touch me," I hiss. "Don't you get it? You stole my life."

"We were trying to give it back to you. We did."

"No." I shake my head. "This was a deal with a doctor who

erased only part of me, a part that you tried to fill in, patching up holes with false memories. Changing my life. Who knows if anything I said in The Program was real. If I could hide one truth, I could hide them all."

I stare at him, and the familiar sense that I know him is back. An awful idea itching at the corners of my mind. I take a step toward him.

"You knew my grandmother for years," I start, my voice hoarse. "Am I supposed to believe that using me as your pet project only occurred *after* I was taken into The Program?"

"Yes."

"Because you say so?" I ask. "How long have you been treating me, Dr. McKee?"

And it's the slight pause, the one second of raw guilt that makes my heart sink. Before he goes on to deny it, I lunge forward and grab him by the collar of his lab coat, fierce and violent. "How long?" I demand.

Dr. McKee meets my gaze head on, and I watch his Adam's apple bob as he swallows hard. "I treated you when I was with the grief department," he says quietly.

Oh my God. He *has* treated me before. "For what?" I ask with barely a breath.

"Your mother," he says. "She neglected you."

"I know—"

"No," Dr. McKee says with a wince. "You don't know, Tatum. Your mother took off with you when you were about five. She left the state."

"Five?" I say, letting go of his jacket. "No, my mother left when I was a baby."

Dr. McKee watches me carefully, and then continues his story despite the discrepancy. "Your grandparents didn't think your mother was well, and they wanted her to get help. But she refused, and she ran off with you. I'd sit with your grandmother at work as she called around to hospitals, searching for unidentified bodies of a mother and her child. There was a stretch—nearly three months—when she was convinced you were both dead."

He looks at the floor, his expression weighted with compassion. His mouth sagging. I don't want to believe this. I have to trust some of my memories, and my childhood is beyond reproach. The manipulation can't go that far back.

"Your grandmother asked me to help her . . . help her cope," Dr. McKee says. "I was going to send in a closer to end the loop of grief—someone to pretend to be you so your grandmother could say how much she loved you. How she'd always protect you. And just before the closer was due to arrive," Dr. McKee continues, "we got a call. Police had found your mother, safe—but malnourished and filthy."

"And me?" I interrupt, growing invested in the story despite my doubts.

Dr. McKee's jaw tightens, but he doesn't look at me when he talks. "You were there," he says. "Same condition. Your mother was set to face charges of neglect, but she agreed to sign over custody of you to your grandparents and be on her way. However," he says, looking at me finally. "You were having trouble with the new arrangement. You wanted to stay with your mother. Your grandmother asked what I could do to help you cope. And I . . ."

Dr. McKee flinches and clears his throat, looking perturbed.

"I brought you to Dr. Arthur Pritchard," he says. "He was renowned for his work with children. He met with you, and through a combination of therapies, you forgot about *before*. Those memories were rewritten—happy ones with your grandparents placed instead. We gave you the gift of contentment." He loosens his tie. "If you saw what you were like when you arrived, you would agree that it was a gift."

"I was *five*. You stole my memories," I say, offended. Horrified. "You and that prick thought that you knew what was best. You decided. At least my grandparents loved me; their complicity in this is somewhat understandable. But you . . . ," I sneer, unable to even find the right word to describe a man who manipulates grief, abuses broken hearts.

I'm about to shout, scream, when Dr. McKee sucks in a wispy breath of air, seeming to choke on it, before taking another. His eyes widen, and he quickly bangs once on his chest, hard enough to make it echo in the room. I take a startled step back, knocking into the chair and sending it to the floor with a loud thud.

He gasps again. "Marie," he chokes out.

I look around the room and remember that she left. The doctor's face is growing red on his cheeks, blue near his lips.

"Marie!" I scream, and it's only a second before she rushes into the room.

I turn back to Dr. McKee, and his expression is twisted in pain. He reaches his arm out to Marie. Before she gets to him, he falls forward, and I do my best to catch him, stumbling back. Marie grabs on to him and carefully lowers him to the floor.

"Call 911," Marie says to me calmly as she brushes the doctor's hair off his forehead.

I take out my phone and dial, holding it to my ear as I watch them. Marie looks down at Dr. McKee.

"Stay calm," she tells him soothingly.

Dr. McKee wraps his hands in her coat, his face pleading. "You have to call my daughter," he begs. "You have to call Nicole."

Marie stares at him, her dark eyes filling with tears. "You know I can't do that, Tom," she whispers back miserably. They hold each other's gaze—a million words passing between them without a single one being uttered.

Dr. McKee's hands slip from Marie's coat, but she quickly catches his grip, her hand tightly around his. A tear drips onto her cheek and runs through her makeup.

Doctor McKee's face has gone ashen, his glasses askew. His lips are bluish as he winces in pain again, his other fist clutching his chest. The 911 operator comes on, and I tell her we need an ambulance. She gets the address and tells me one is on the way. I put my phone away just as the door opens, and Nathan and Melody come rushing in.

Melody gasps and watches in horror, and Nathan comes to stand next to me, wrapping his arm over my shoulders—holding me steady.

Marie doesn't let go of Dr. McKee's hand; they watch each other. It's a moment so full of secrets that I feel like I'm intruding. I open my mouth to ask if he'll be all right, when Dr. McKee's eyes roll back, his face scrunches up, and he chokes out a gurgling sound.

"Hold on, Tom," Marie murmurs, although she doesn't seem to believe it will do any good. She brings his knuckles to her mouth and presses them against her lips, her eyes squeezed shut as the tears flow freely now.

Dr. McKee fights to look at her, his eyelids fluttering. His face clears for a moment, and he smiles sadly at her.

"Tell her that I loved her more than anything," he whispers, his face wet with tears. "Tell her that I'm sorry."

Marie moans out what sounds like "I can't," and I don't understand why she won't just placate him. Lie to him to give him peace. But that must not be the sort of relationship they have. Painfully honest even until the last second. Even as they lie to everyone around them. I don't know what it would be like to have someone be so truthful with me. Does anyone know that kind of loyalty?

Dr. McKee blinks slowly, his body relaxing back. "We could have done anything, Dr. Devoroux," he murmurs. "Together, we could have saved the whole damn world."

She laughs and uses her free hand to wipe the tears off

his cheek. "I still will," she says. "I'll do it for her."

Dr. McKee's face breaks a little at the mention of "her," but he nods as if that's all he wants. Her.

And then Dr. Tom McKee closes his eyes and dies quietly in the back room of the Adjustment office.

CHAPTER NINE

I FOLLOW THE AMBULANCE TO THE HOSPITAL—I'M not even sure why. I guess I feel responsible, even though Dr. McKee's heart attack wasn't my fault. Nathan left with Melody. He wasn't happy about it, but she begged to talk to him. He told me he'd find me later and that I should be careful. I'm not sure what could happen in the hospital, but who knows anymore. Like Dr. McKee said, The Program never left. We were never safe.

Dr. McKee didn't regain consciousness, and although they tried to revive him at the Adjustment office, they couldn't. Marie didn't look at me once while the EMTs were working on him, not even when I asked if she was okay. She was lost in her head, and it makes me wonder about her and Dr. McKee's relationship. It didn't seem romantic—more like . . . family.

A closeness that could only come from unabashed loyalty and care. It makes me suddenly sorry for her. She'll be all alone now.

I text my grandparents to let them know what happened with Dr. McKee, but I don't mention what he told me yet. His explanation doesn't quite make sense in my head.

Something feels off. Wrong.

I need to talk to Marie for clarification, but now isn't the time. I'll let her grieve. I understand how controlling grief can be, and unlike her and Dr. McKee, I won't take advantage of that pain.

As I sit in the hospital waiting room, I'm reminded of the other times I've sat here, worried about Wes. I was hoping I'd never have to be in this hospital again, and yet here I am.

The sliding doors open, and I'm relieved to see Nathan walk in. He looks awful, drawn and tired. He drops down into the chair next to me. When he turns to me, my soul aches. Nathan with a broken heart is too much for me to take. I reach for him and pull him into a hug, and it nearly kills me as he silently cries into my shoulder.

Nathan tells me that he already filled in Foster on the fact that he and Jana/Melody have broken up and that she has been working for the Adjustment. As Nathan relayed it, Foster's response was: "Well, fuck her. I knew it."

Nathan promises to tell me what Melody said to him after they left the office, but first he wants to head home.

As we drive back to our houses in my Jeep, I'm torn on how to feel about Dr. McKee's death. I didn't want him to die, obviously. But I also think about Vanessa, how the Adjustment contributed to her death. How it nearly killed Wes. How Dr. McKee has spent his life manipulating others. It doesn't justify him dying—I'm not a monster. But it does add an extra layer of emotions.

"She used me," Nathan says under his breath. It's dark outside, and I glance over at him and see he's still the same brand of sad he brought with him to the hospital.

"Nathan," I say, but he shakes his head and looks out the passenger window.

"She used me," he repeats. "She was a fucking spy, and I was stupid for not seeing it sooner. I put us all in danger." He turns to me, miserable. "I put *you* in danger. I welcomed her into our lives, and I even made you be friends with her."

"You didn't make me do anything."

"You did it for me," he says, and he's not wrong. Jana and I were never completely on the same page, but I gave it a shot because he's my best friend.

"And that's not all," Nathan says. "She wasn't just a handler. I was right to be uncomfortable the other day. The woman she lives with is not her mother. Jana—" He stops and closes his eyes. "*Melody* was assigned to her as . . . a closer, she called it. She was . . ." Nathan doesn't seem to want to go on, and I reach over and put my hand on his leg.

"She was impersonating Jana Simms," Nathan says quietly. "A girl who died last year. Melody took over her life, originally at the mom's request—some twisted kind of therapy. But lately, she and her 'mother' had been arguing. I guess the mother had gotten her closure, and wanted Melody to move on. But Melody hadn't finished her assignment."

Nathan looks at me. "That's you. Her assignment." The words seem to make him sick, but I don't want his apology. Nathan hasn't hurt me. Melody did.

"So what does she do now?" I ask. I take a left onto our street and continue toward the light of my front porch.

"She's pretty tore up," Nathan says. "She actually cared for Dr. McKee. She's done with the Adjustment—I can tell that much. She hinted she might leave town soon. But I'm not sure she has anywhere else to go."

"If it matters," I say, "I think she really did care about you." I pull into my driveway and turn off the engine of the Jeep. I look across the car, and Nathan meets my eyes.

"It doesn't matter," he says simply.

He gets out of the car, and I watch him from the driver's seat as he crosses the driveway toward his house and disappears inside.

Over a late dinner of reheated food, my grandparents ask what I was doing at the Adjustment office. My grandmother flinches when I tell her that Dr. McKee died in front of me, but she adds nothing other than to say it's a tragedy. It's especially unsettling given the fact that Dr. McKee told me they were close. Given the fact that she and my grandfather offered me up to this experiment more than once. And yet, my grandmother sits there showing only quiet concern.

I tell my grandparents about Jana really being Melody. I lie and say Nathan and I were there to find her, afraid she was getting an Adjustment. But it turned out she worked for them. I try to gauge my grandparents' reactions—my heightened sense for bullshit ready to find any discrepancies.

But either my grandparents didn't know, or their lying skills are expert level now. My grandmother frets about Nathan and wonders if she should call his mother. But it's late, and I agree to invite him over for dinner tomorrow.

"And how are you feeling, honey?" my grandmother asks me. I notice that Pop hasn't said much the entire meal, and his passivity in this pisses me off.

"Well," I say, pushing my plate away. "I've done everything you've asked. I've ended things with Wes; I've gone to therapy; hell, I even tell you about my headaches. So basically, I'm miserable."

I'm purposely prodding them, seeing if they'll break down and confess. Confess what, I still don't know. It's already bigger than I imagine.

"It'll pass," my grandmother says. "You'll be in college soon—things will be better. You'll see."

I stare at her, and my eyes must be cold, because she lowers her gaze.

"I'm going to bed," I say suddenly, and stand up. I'll be better at faking normal tomorrow. Right now, I'm spent. Unable to pretend for another second.

My grandparents stay at the table, murmuring good night

as I leave. But when I get to the top of the stairs, I don't go directly to my room. I'm drawn to the box in my grandparents' closet. Something about it felt off. And I want to know exactly why.

I slip inside their bedroom and stride over to the closet. I open the doors and get on my tiptoes, but as I reach up, I find the box is gone. I take a step back, surveying the space, in case I put it back in the wrong spot. But my heart sinks because I know I didn't. The box is gone.

It's so bizarre; I'd entertain it was never there in the first place, except there is a box-size hole on the shelf. An empty space exactly where it had been. And then I remember that I didn't just tell Nathan and Foster about it—I told Dr. Warren, as well.

I fall back a step, overwhelmed. My grandparents aren't who I thought they were—how could they be? At this point, if I confront them, will they tell Dr. Warren? Will The Program come for me? I need help—I see that very clearly now.

Paranoid, I quickly dash back to my room. I don't understand what's happened, how quickly my life has unraveled. And that box . . . I don't get. It was baby stuff. What was in there to hide?

I shut my door, and consider locking it—just like Wes locks his—but I have to accept that physically, if I can keep pretending, I'm not in any danger. I have to believe that for now because there isn't another option. Not yet.

My bed creaks as I sit down, and I'm more confused than

when I woke up. So much of my past is a lie. Not even my recent past, but my actual childhood. And although I should be too worried to sleep, my eyelids are heavy. My conscience tired. I lie back, staring up at the ceiling.

I watched someone die today. I had my reality shaken. Once Nathan deals with his broken heart, we'll figure out what to do next about Melody. We'll figure it out together.

I'm drained, ready to slip away into the darkness of sleep, but I think about Dr. McKee again. How his last wish was to talk to his daughter. And how, for some reason, Marie said no.

There's a buzzing, and I glance over wearily and see Wes's name lit up on my phone. I debate answering, sure that if I talk to him, we'll talk for hours. I watch the phone until it grows silent.

There's a vibration, and I pick up the phone and see he texted.

I really need to talk to you, he writes. Can you please call me?

I stare at the words, and I hate that he has to ask. I should have answered the phone; I should call back. Wes has only known me two days—he can't feel that strongly about me. Not after I told him we weren't together like that. Then again, muscle memory. His heart remembers me.

But I don't respond. I tuck the phone under my pillow, and I close my eyes. So tired. So fucking tired.

There's an itch in the back of my head, deep in my skull. A

fuzziness begins to spread, and then all at once, the bed drops out from under me as I fall deep inside a memory.

Wes and I were at the park, six months before The Program came for me. The weeping willow tree rustled quietly in the sunny afternoon sky. Blanket spread out in the grass; birds singing on the branches.

I turned the page of my magazine, and Wes leaned in to kiss my bare shoulder, his finger teasing the spaghetti strap of my tank top.

"Can I ask you something?" he said, kissing my skin again. I shrugged him off and turned another page.

"Sure," I said. I didn't really want to talk. The Program had been collecting more and more people from class, their threat bigger than ever. Closing in on us. Talking seemed like a terrible idea.

"Do you love me?" Wes asked in a quiet voice.

I looked over at him with a sudden skip in my heart. His soft brown eyes reflected the light, shining even as he squinted at me.

"Yeah," I said impatiently. "Of course."

Wes fell silent, and then pushed on. "But you don't love me the same," he added.

We stared at each other for a long moment, and then I set my magazine aside. Wes and I had been together for years, we were a team. I cared deeply for him, but lately . . . things around me had started to feel hopeless. What was the point of loving anybody anymore?

We would never survive The Program.

That idea consumed me; it consumed my love for Wes. It was all I thought about.

Something was wrong with me. I was unwell, and I didn't have a single person to talk to about it aside from Wes. Anyone else would turn me in to The Program. But I couldn't spread this to Wes, this . . . sadness. I couldn't do that to him.

"Tatum?" Wes asked, still waiting for me to answer. But what could I say?

"No," I told him. "It's not the same."

Wes flinched, lowering his eyes to the blanket. He sniffled, his lips parting as he tried to find the question he needed to ask.

He was right—I didn't feel the same anymore. I was starting to think I didn't feel at all. For weeks, I'd been retreating further and further inside my head. Finding a safe spot. From The Program, from the world. From his mother. I was detached from everyone, including Wes. If I stopped feeling, stopped loving, I could still make it. I could still survive.

But new guilt crawled into my chest as I realized what I was doing. I would destroy him if I kept this up—this push and pull of a relationship. This lie. I'd basically be handing him over to The Program.

I had to let him go.

"We should see other people," I said, watching as he flinched again. "With everything going on, I think it'd be the best idea."

Wes lifted his eyes to mine, his face pained. "You want to date other people?" he asked, his voice scratchy with emotion.

Tears spilled over onto his cheeks, and he was crying. I was making him cry.

"I think you should see other people," I clarified. He hitched in a breath, his hand over his heart like it hurt.

"I want to be with *you*," he said. "Are you saying . . . do you still want to be with me, Tate?"

I couldn't hold his eyes, and I let the darkness creep over me. Blotting out the light. Erasing us. "No," I said, staring down at the blanket. "No, Wes. I don't think we should be together anymore."

Wes choked out a cry, and he was a wounded animal, desperate and hurt. I didn't even want to look at him. Didn't want to see the damage I had just inflicted. It would save him, though. Letting me go would save him.

"I'm sorry," I said, low. "I'm so sorry."

Wes dropped back onto the blanket, his forearm over his face, refusing to speak to me. But I curled up next to him anyway, unable to let him cry alone.

I still loved him. Just not the same.

And I listened quietly, hating myself, as he told me he wished he were dead.

I wake up to my phone buzzing near my head, disoriented. I squint against the light coming in my window, trying to unravel the mystery in my head. My phone stops buzzing, but my head doesn't.

The world is blurry, slow to come back. The memory sticks

with me, and a heavy realization crashes over my soul: I broke up with Wes first. I broke his heart and told him to date other people. I sent him away, and when he did try to find happiness, I pulled him back in. I pulled him down.

Until we were both taken by The Program.

Although it would be easier to blame the epidemic for this, blame fear—it doesn't matter what caused it. In the end, my sadness, loneliness, ended with me hurting Wes. And then to make it worse, I continued to hurt him. Right up until the end. Right up until yesterday.

I finally know the truth of our story. I was slowly dying and thought letting him go would save him. When he did, in fact, start seeing Kyle, it tore me up. And I wanted it all back. I wanted him back. But it was too late. I'd hurt him, broken him down. He was trying to survive, but I begged him to stay with me. And in the end, he wouldn't leave me, even though he should have.

I'm the worst thing that's ever happened to him.

My nose is bleeding from the crashback, mixing with the tears streaming down my cheeks. As I reach to grab a tissue, my phone starts buzzing again. I peek at the caller ID and see it's Nathan. I have no idea why he'd keep calling instead of texting. It must be serious.

"You okay?" I ask as way of answering, wiping off the last of the blood.

Nathan laughs bitterly. "Not quite. But I have an idea. Want to skip school today with me and Foster and get pancakes?"

I brush my hair away from my face, still trying to get my bearings. "Sure," I say. "And I . . ." I'm about to tell him about the memory but figure it would be better in person. "See you in twenty minutes?" I ask instead.

"Deal," Nathan responds, and hangs up.

I climb out of bed, the memory set aside, and suddenly the events of yesterday come flooding back. I fall to sit on the mattress. Dr. McKee is *dead*. My grandparents had my memory erased when I was a kid and then lied about everything. They let me get adjusted. No, they *had* me adjusted.

I'm overwhelmed, my heart racing, sweat gathering in my hairline. My skin prickles.

I switch to my default, the only way to have any normalcy. I have to block it all out, every confusing thought. Every question. Every returned memory. I push it aside and force myself to my feet. To the shower. To the kitchen.

It's no way to exist, this empty way I'm going through the motions. But it will help me to live. For now. Wes was right— the past is a dangerous place to be.

"Have a nice day, honey," my grandmother calls as I grab my keys from the kitchen. And for one fleeting moment, she stares at me as if she really sees me—like she can tell everything that's happened. But all I do is smile and tell her I hope she has a nice day too.

Nathan is sitting on his front porch, his posture sagging, and his elbows on his knees. He looks up from his spot on the stairs when I get to my Jeep. I wave him over, and he grabs his backpack and heads my way. He climbs inside, and I motion toward his bag.

"Thought we were skipping?" I ask.

"Prop," he says. His voice is tired and raspy. It makes me think he's been crying, and I decide it's not the time to talk about my past with Wes. It's over anyway. Nathan's pain is right now. I have to deal with one problem at a time.

"Didn't feel like telling my mother about skipping," he adds. "I couldn't even bring myself to tell her about Melody." He spits her name like it's a curse.

"And Foster?" I ask.

"He's going to meet us at Lulu's."

I pull out of the driveway and head toward the pancake house. "How much does he know?" I ask.

Nathan sniffs a laugh and rests his head back against the seat, staring vacantly out the windshield. "Enough to prove him right, which is going to be super annoying."

I smile and press down on the accelerator, speeding us toward our friend.

CHAPTER TEN

FOSTER TAKES A BITE OF PANCAKE, WIPES HIS mouth, and then looks across the table at Nathan. "So your ex-girlfriend was a spy for the Adjustment and kept tabs on all of us?"

"I guess," Nathan says with a shrug. I sip from my coffee. "Although mostly it was Tatum."

"She said she loved you?" Foster asks him. He bites off a piece of bacon, calm about all of this. "Did you love her? Is that what she used to manipulate you?"

Nathan sighs, lifting his head to glare at Foster. Foster nods that he doesn't have to answer, before biting another piece of bacon. And I can't stand that the first girl Nathan loved did this to him. He'll never get over it; how could he?

"She also got a job at Rockstar Pizza a few weeks ago," I add, trying to lighten the moment. Lift his pain. "So she manipulated him with pizza, too."

Nathan sniffs a laugh like he hates me. "Now I can never eat there again," he says, pushing his food around on his plate. "She took my favorite restaurant from me. It's unforgivable."

"You'll learn to love again," I tell him wistfully. "Maybe it won't be Rockstar, but I know there's a special pie out there for you." Nathan laughs.

"So just to make sure . . . ," Foster starts, scrunching up his nose. "Jana is Melody, who is a closer—a person who impersonates someone who died. Am I right so far?"

Nathan nods.

"Cool. She's also a handler, and Vanessa was a patient she monitored in The Program. I'm still good?"

"Yes, Foster," Nathan says, wanting him to get to the point he's sure he's trying to make.

"And then Melody watches Vanessa until she kills her—*inadvertently*," he adds quickly for Nathan's benefit. "But then she starts hooking up with you to keep an eye on Tatum?"

"That's what I've got," Nathan says. His skin is pale, and when he glances over at me, his hazel eyes are glassy with embarrassment.

"Don't," I whisper, hating that he blames himself.

"And so you broke up with her," Foster continues brightly, and holds out his fist for Nathan to bump; he does. "But she's still around. At least for a little bit?"

"I guess," Nathan says.

"But I can't tell Arturo?" Foster wants to know.

"I'd rather you didn't," Nathan says. "I just want her to go away. I don't want to answer questions or have people wonder if I was somehow in with a handler."

"You were in with a handler," Foster says, taking a sip of his coffee. I kick him under the table, and he apologizes.

"Look," Foster says, pushing aside his plate and leaning into the table. "It's not your fault, Nathan. I seriously shouldn't even have to tell you that. You're one of the most decent guys I've ever met, and I fucking love you. But Jana sucked. She always did. Now, we're going to expunge her from the record, and push ahead. Correct?"

I can see Nathan wants to blame himself anyway, but he nods that it's time for us to move on.

"The real Jana Simms died last year," Nathan says. "And I never knew her. So let's just leave it at that."

"Done," Foster replies easily. But the moment is dark. Morbid and heavy.

My phone buzzes with a message, and I check it. I sigh heavily, and Foster peeks over to read the text.

Seriously, Wes texts. Please call me back.

I look up and meet Foster's eyes, and he motions to the phone on the table. "Seems to be going well," he says sarcastically. "And we should note that I saw Wes at school before I left, and he's at once the most adorable and saddest thing I've ever seen. Am I wrong to assume that has to do with you?"

"Not on purpose," I say, lowering my eyes.

"Uh . . . didn't you sleep over his house, like, two days ago?" Foster asks.

"Right?" Nathan laughs and reaches over to take a piece of bacon off Foster's discarded plate. Foster smiles, as if reassured now that Nathan is eating again.

"Yes, I did sleep there," I say. "But nothing happened. Wes and I aren't getting back together. In fact, I told him that we never dated—that we were just friends."

"That was dumb. And kind of fucking mean," Foster adds, partially under his breath.

"Yeah, well, in case you forgot," I say, "I killed someone yesterday."

"You didn't kill him," Nathan says immediately.

"Okay," I admit. "But I'm still their *proof of concept,* whatever that is. I'm like, the last person Wes should talk to."

"You are definitely a bit of a mess right now," Foster agrees. "But that's exactly why you shouldn't cut him completely out of your life. You have a history together. You don't have to burn the entire bridge, Tatum. You might still need to cross it."

"You don't understand," I say, guilty. "He can't be with me. I . . . I broke up with him. Last year, before he met Kyle, I broke up with Wes. I told him to see other people."

Foster tilts his head, confused, and Nathan leans his elbows on the table.

"I had a crashback," I confess to them. "And I saw it all. What I did, said. How I hurt him. It's my fault."

"What?" Nathan says, shaking his head. "Wait . . . seriously, what? This changes everything. Your entire history. How could you—?" He stops himself from asking how I could forget something like this, wincing slightly.

"I thought I was protecting him," I say. "Protecting us from me. Instead, I made him sick."

"You told him to see other people," Foster corrects. "He did. You didn't force him to do anything, Tatum."

"But then I wanted him back," I explain.

"Uh-huh," Foster says. "And that happens in regular relationships that aren't being manipulated by the fucking *Program*. The way I see it," he says, "you're doing more damage now. He's better. You're better. Why lie to him? It's going to mess him up."

"Listen to Foster," Nathan relents. "You've both made mistakes. Admit to them, accept them. I'm sorry, but lying isn't an option anymore."

"Besides the two of you," I say, "everyone else in my life tells me to stay away from him."

"Yeah, well, you should trust us, obviously," Nathan says, and Foster nods. "Talk to Wes," Nathan continues. "You don't have to dive into your entire sordid past *yet*, but give him the option to find out. Don't steal his life away."

The words hit me hard, and I sit back in the chair, staring down. I think Nathan's right—I have to give Wes the option of knowing the truth—the full truth. I owe him that much.

"Where do I even start?" I murmur. "I brought him to this point. My constant lying, even if I did it to protect him. I'm no

SUZANNE YOUNG

better than my grandparents, than Dr. McKee or Marie Devoroux. I'm—"

My phone buzzes, startling me. I check it, and my heart jumps. I quickly look at Nathan, and he leans forward, reading my alarm.

"Who is it?" he asks.

"The Adjustment office," I murmur in the same breath I say hello, the phone at my ear, my gaze locked with Nathan's.

"Tatum," Marie says, the sound of her voice jarring me. "Have you heard from Melody Blackstone? I can't get hold of her, and her mother said she was gone this morning. Her room cleaned out."

"Oh . . . ," I say, watching Nathan's expression. "No, I haven't heard anything. I—"

"I'm worried," Marie cuts in. "I need you to come by the office."

"Are you serious?" I ask, annoyed she'd even suggest it. "After everything you and Dr. McKee did to—"

"Dr. McKee is dead," Marie says harshly. "And this isn't negotiable. I'll see you shortly." Marie hangs up, and I lower the phone.

"Marie?" Nathan asks. "What does she want?"

"She said Melody is missing. And she wants me to come by the Adjustment office."

Foster's mouth falls open as he darts a look between me and Nathan. "Not to be that guy," he says, brow furrowed, "but it's a trap. Don't go."

"I'll be with her," Nathan says instantly, tossing money onto the table. He's worried about Melody. Despite everything, he'll still protect her.

Foster checks the time on his phone. "Shit. I have a test fourth hour—I can't miss it. But I'll be done by noon. Find you after?" he asks.

"Of course," I say, still thinking about Melody. Wondering if she has anyone to turn to. Worried that she really is in danger. We should have looked out for her.

"For real, though," Foster adds, getting up from the chair. "Answer my call at twelve or I'm showing up at the office to rescue you."

Nathan promises Foster that we'll check in, his mind clearly somewhere else. Foster glances at me, concerned, and touches my arm in good-bye before walking out.

"Do you think she's all right?" Nathan asks quietly from the passenger seat as we drive toward the Adjustment office. I look sideways at him and see him chewing on the corner of his thumbnail.

I almost say yes automatically, but I think about Marie and Dr. McKee, how they were always honest with each other. Sort of like Nathan and me. At least, the way we try to be.

"I don't know," I tell him. "But I truly hope so."

"What if she . . . ?" Nathan creases his forehead and turns away.

My heart aches, and he doesn't have to finish his sentence.

We've lived through a suicide epidemic. The possibility is always on the table.

There are no cars in the strip mall parking lot when we pull in. It's early, and none of the few remaining businesses are open yet. The frosted-glass windows of the Adjustment office are lit up, the lights on inside. I can't help it—I check around for handlers. For their van. For any sign that Foster was right about this being a trap. But it's a quiet morning in Oregon. Nathan starts to open his door, but I reach out to grab his arm.

"I'm scared," I say.

"If she or anyone tries to hurt you, I swear, I'll go nuclear," he says. "Remember that time in Chuck E. Cheese's when—"

I smile. "When Rex Wisteria pegged me with a plastic ball from the pit?"

Nathan nods, looking proud of himself. Nathan isn't exactly a fighter, but he beat the shit out of that kid when we were in eighth grade. Of course, Rex deserved it. He'd been torturing me at school, and when he saw me at the restaurant without my grandparents, he tried to continue. Only this time Nathan was there, and he pounced. A fight in a Chuck E. Cheese ball pit is certainly something to behold. Rex never messed with me again.

"I love you," I tell him.

"Yeah," he says, lifting one corner of his mouth. "I love you, too."

He gets out of the Jeep, and although I'm frightened— terrified, really—I don't think Marie would call me, drag me down here, only to forcibly adjust me. Again. She's far too clever to be that obvious.

The door is locked, and I press the buzzer to let Marie know I'm here. It's quiet, apart from a few birds in the cherry trees along the road.

The door opens, and Marie nods a hello at Nathan—her mouth tight. He flashes her a winning smile, part sarcastic, and she tells us both to come in. She leaves it unlatched.

We get inside the lobby, and I'm stunned by her appearance. Marie is a beautiful woman, but today she is a tragic figure. Her dark skin has taken on a greenish hue, her red lipstick gone and her lips chapped. By the swelling around her eyes, I can see she's been crying. It actually chokes me up a little bit, and I clear my throat to regain my composure.

It's then that I see the picture of Dr. McKee, the one Nathan joked about the first time we came to the Adjustment office. Marie must have hung it back up today.

"When's the last time you spoke to Melody?" Marie asks, folding her arms over her chest.

"Yesterday," Nathan says. "But if you think she's going to come back and work for you, you're insane."

"I don't want her to work for me," Marie says curtly. "I'm worried about her. There are things you don't understand, Nathan. Other forces at work here. She can't just disappear; believe me when I say that doesn't typically lead to a good outcome."

"Typically," I repeat. "Meaning it's happened before?"

"Not with Melody," Marie says with a shake of her head.

"I've known her for years, since she was a child really. She helped us in the grief department, and then she decided to work for The Program, against my and Dr. McKee's wishes."

Nathan flinches and sniffs as he looks away.

"But when The Program was getting shut down, Melody came to me. She felt horrible about what she'd been a part of. She wanted to make amends. So she began to help us here, watching returners and correcting those we could."

"You didn't correct anybody," I say.

She levels her gaze on me. "We corrected you," she replies. "Now, as you know, The Program is still operating. They have their own handlers, ones who have no part in the cure. I'm not sure who else is involved."

I look at Nathan. "Derek's one, I bet."

"He is," Marie agrees. "He's been a handler with them for years."

The confirmation chills me, and I turn back to Marie. "I saw him talking to Melody," I say.

"She was attempting to dissuade him from following you. Derek is . . . stubborn."

"He's an asshole," I correct, and she smiles.

"Yes, he is definitely that, too. But Melody was looking out for you, Tatum."

I have a flash of regret, having always assumed the worst about Melody. Sure, she wasn't honest with us, but I'm grateful that she tried to get Derek off my back. I'm grateful she put herself on the line for that. Maybe I've been unfair to her.

"It makes sense," I say. "About Derek? Realm told me that The Program was after me."

"Michael?" Marie asks. "What else did he tell you?" I don't like that she expects me to answer so easily, and she must read that in my stance. "Michael always says The Program is after people—it's how he thinks," she explains. "My biggest concern right now is for Melody. She and Michael are friends, and I want to talk to him. But he hasn't returned my calls."

The fact that he's not returning her calls heartens me; it means he wasn't lying when he said he was done with the Adjustment.

"What does The Program want from me, Marie?" I ask. "Because I'm not buying the 'Realm is paranoid' excuse."

"I didn't say he was paranoid," Marie corrects. "Although he is most of the time. It's what makes Michael Realm excellent at his job. But you asked me about The Program, what they want—it's not a simple answer. There are a lot of moving parts here, Tatum. As you know, Dr. Warren has been your therapist; she's been keeping an eye on you."

"Yeah, thanks for the heads-up on that," I mutter.

"I don't know the nature of the deal that got you released from The Program, but we had no choice in bringing you to her. And . . . I'm guessing Dr. Warren has realized that the memories you gave her in The Program, the ones she erased, were not accurate. The crashbacks you told her about contradict your story. She hates being wrong. And now The Program wants to know if you're the cure."

"Why would they care? Why wouldn't they want to fix the problems they created?"

"Because they don't see crashbacks as problems. They are merely complications. And allowing a cure to come to market would wipe out any hope of The Program returning. They'd be obsolete."

"Good," I say. She smiles.

"It would be good. But when powerful people have profits to protect, when even more powerful people have ideas on how to use the technology to control the masses, they're going to fight. You *are* the cure, Tatum. And believe me when I say that we can't let them find out."

"Because?" I ask.

"Because then they'll want you dead."

My heart skips, and I look quickly to Nathan. He puts his hand on my arm, pulling me to his side. Ready to jump into the ball pit with a faceless organization.

"Or at the very least erased or lobotomized," Marie adds, and I feel like maybe that was the better answer, as disturbing as that is. The concern that settles in her expression makes me think I'm not the only person The Program is after. Maybe they're after Melody, too. Maybe they're after everyone involved with the Adjustment.

"If you talk to him again," Marie says calmly, "please have Michael contact me. I'm sorry Tom and I didn't warn you about Dr. Warren sooner, but we were trying to be discreet."

"You lie," I say. "You're not discreet."

A smile tugs on Marie's lips like she's impressed with how I'm standing up to her. Before she says anything more, the door to the Adjustment office rips open, and two people rush in.

The young woman has blond hair and blue eyes that are deeply red from crying. The guy with her looks equally miserable, and he buries his hands in his pockets, staring intently at Marie. The doctor falls back a step as she takes them in, obviously recognizing them.

"What happened to him?" the woman demands from Marie, not even glancing in my or Nathan's direction. "What was he doing?"

Marie stares back, wide-eyed in awe or disbelief. "He was trying to do right," she murmurs, sounding far away.

"What the hell does that mean?" the woman asks, talking with Marie in a way that's so personal, so steeped in history, that it feels like a parent/child relationship.

The woman herself is nondescript. She's young and pretty, I guess, but in a way that's not memorable. None of her features are prominent, a face that could be anybody. I don't know how else to explain it.

Next to her, the guy surveys the room before he notices us. He's intimidating—not because of his build or an aggressive expression. It's how he seems to look right into me, like he can see me and know everything. Know my every secret.

"Marie," the woman says, her voice tight but pleading. "What were the two of you doing here?"

It's then that the woman's eyes drift to the picture hanging on the back wall. Dr. McKee told us that his daughter shot it, and as her eyes well up, I realize this is her. This is his daughter.

Marie sees her looking and reaches to put her hand on her arm. "Quinlan—" she starts, but the woman shakes her off violently.

"Don't call me that," she says. "It's Nicole. And what is this?" she demands, pointing to the picture. Behind Nicole, the guy she's with curses under his breath.

"He remembered, didn't he, Marie?" Nicole asks. "He remembered me."

"You know he didn't," Marie says sympathetically. But she's lying, and the way Nicole shakes her head, she knows she's lying too.

Dr. McKee asked for his daughter—why would Marie try to cover that up? What else is she hiding that even after his death she has to keep a secret?

"You shouldn't be here," Marie says to Nicole. She glances at the guy. "You either, Deacon. How did you even know what happened?"

Nicole scoffs, offended. "Find out that my father was *dead*?" she asks bitterly. "A stranger called me, Melody someone. Told me that my father died in the back room of a fucking office." She chokes up, tears spilling onto her cheeks. "A stranger," she repeats. "You should have been the one to call."

Nathan and I exchange a look, not sure if this means Melody is okay, or if it was her final moment to set things right. He puts his hand over mine where I hold his arm. I can feel him shaking.

"Go," I tell him. "Go look for her."

He seems torn, partly because he's upset with her and shouldn't want to find her. But he still loves her. It's not something that just shuts off in a day.

"You sure?" Nathan asks.

I tell him that I am and pass him the keys to my Jeep.

I'm glad that Melody called Dr. McKee's daughter. It proves she has some compassion, after all. And although we don't know much about the real Melody Blackstone, I hope Nathan can find her. I hope she's still alive.

CHAPTER ELEVEN

AFTER NATHAN LEAVES, I GO SIT ON ONE OF THE chairs, and Nicole's boyfriend—husband, I decide when I see his wedding ring—comes to sit in a chair one down from me. He watches Marie and Nicole talk, their voices quieter. He's intense, like at any second he'll jump up to defend his wife.

"The picture was one he found in storage," Marie says. "He had no idea it was connected to you. He didn't remember."

I can't believe she won't tell her. I don't know the reason, but I refuse to sit here and let it happen. I won't be her accomplice. Not anymore.

"She's lying," I call out, and they all turn to me.

"Stay out of this, Tatum," Marie says harshly.

"No," I tell her defiantly, and then turn to Nicole. "Your

dad," I say. "He did remember. He told me the first time I was here that his daughter took that picture." I motion to where it hangs on the wall. "And before he died, he asked Marie to call you." My eyes drift to Marie, and she crosses her arms over her chest, her expression pleading for me to be quiet. "She told him no," I finish.

Nicole turns on her fiercely. "Why would you do that?" she demands, hurt in her voice. "Why wouldn't you let him talk to me?" Marie doesn't answer, and Nicole tightens her jaw. "It's time to stop bullshitting me, Marie! You can't really think I'm this stupid."

Marie watches her, softening, and shakes her head. "Of course I know you're not stupid." The kindness in her voice seems to annoy Nicole more than anything.

"Then tell me what the fuck was going on here," Nicole says.

The phone on the desk rings. Marie glances at it and then back to Nicole. "I need to take that in my office," she says briskly. "Wait here."

Nicole tilts her head as if asking if she's serious, and Marie darts her gaze between Nicole and Deacon before pulling open the door for the back offices. When she's gone, Nicole looks at Deacon in disbelief.

"Not much changes," he says.

"Apparently not," Nicole replies. "Marie lies as easily as she breathes."

Nicole sits in the chair between me and Deacon and presses

her palms together before bringing them to her lips, staring at the office door. Lost in a thought. It's almost like she forgets she's not alone.

I cross my legs to get more comfortable, and she jumps and looks over at me.

She smiles politely, embarrassed that she drifted away. "Thank you," she says. "For calling her out. I've found it's the best method to deal with her constant deceit."

"I'm really sorry about your dad," I tell her.

At the mention of him, her blue eyes begin to water, and she lowers her gaze to the floor. "I've been a grief counselor for the last few years," she says. "And I've worked with grieving parents most of my life." She looks at me, tears running over the light freckles on her cheeks. "And you know the one thing people say when they find out someone they love died? The universal response?"

I give my head a little shake, not knowing the answer.

"Almost every time, they say, 'It's not true.' In one form or another, their body's initial response is to deny that it happened. Deny the death. Deny the loss. They can deny it so completely that sometimes the people around them believe them and start to doubt it too. Grief is a bitter pill. It can destroy everything if you let it. It's a beast."

She rubs her hand over her cheeks to wipe away the tears.

"And this time," she says, sounding lost again, "I was the one saying it wasn't true when Melody told me."

"When did Melody call you?" I ask.

"About two in the morning," she replies. "Deacon and I jumped in the car and drove through the night. Why? Do you know her?"

"Yes." I furrow my brow. "Not really. It's actually pretty convoluted."

"It usually is if McKee or Marie was involved," Deacon says. He puts his arm around Nicole and pulls her into him, kissing the top of her head and closing his eyes. Whatever his relationship was to Dr. McKee, I can see that he's grieving too.

I'm a third wheel, uncomfortable with their closeness. Nicole straightens, brushing her blond hair back from her face.

"Tatum, is it?" she asks me.

"Yeah."

"You're a patient of my father's . . . I'm assuming," she asks.

"I'm not sure how much of his patient I really was," I say. "That's what I'm trying to figure out."

"That sounds like McKee," Deacon says, and the intimidation I felt when he first walked into the Adjustment office is completely gone. Around Nicole, he's gentle. He holds her hand while she continues to talk to me.

"Tatum, I don't mean to pry," Nicole says. "But what exactly have my father and Marie been doing here? I don't expect Marie will tell me the truth."

"She won't," I say. Nicole smiles as we bond over the fact that we're both dealing with someone who is a compulsive liar. I don't know Nicole's or Deacon's history, but they've clearly been involved with Dr. McKee and Marie their whole lives. What could it have been like having Tom McKee as a father? And how, after whatever happened, could she still love him this much?

It makes me wonder if we forgive our parents (or grandparents) for their sins too easily. Or if it's because when you love someone, you'd rather forgive it as a mistake, a bad choice with good intentions, than accept that they've nearly destroyed you.

At least, I wonder if that's why I've waited so long to confront my grandparents. Yes, I'm scared they'll deny it. But I'm also scared they'll admit everything. Because then . . . what? What comes after that?

"What have they done to you?" Deacon asks. Concern creases the skin between his brows.

I'm embarrassed, even though it's not my fault, when I say, "Have you heard of the Adjustment?"

Nicole and Deacon exchange a look, but it doesn't seem like either of them connect with the word.

"Would you mind explaining?" Deacon asks, leaning forward, his elbows on his knees.

I tell Nicole and Deacon all about the Adjustment procedure, the implantation of memories. I include the fact that they're trying to get a patent, and I was their proof of concept, something they neglected to tell me until yesterday. Nicole smiles ruefully.

"He never stopped experimenting on people," she says. "I

guess all the blame heaped on Arthur Pritchard wasn't fully deserved. And Marie was part of this?"

"She was most of it, it feels like," I admit. Even though Dr. McKee did a lot of the talking, it always felt like Marie was the driving force.

"Yeah," Deacon says. "Marie has always pulled the strings." He looks at Nicole. "On all of us."

I glance over to the closed door that leads to the offices. Marie's only been gone a few minutes, but it feels too long for a simple conversation. What could be so important that she wouldn't put it aside to talk to Dr. McKee's daughter the day after he died?

"I just want answers," I say, mostly to myself. "I want to move on, but I don't know how. I don't know what's true."

Nicole sighs, and there's a sense of camaraderie between us, as if she's been through something similar. She gazes at me, and I wonder if I somehow remind her of herself.

Abruptly she turns to Deacon. "I have an idea," she says. "There's not much time. She's probably already thinking of excuses and cover-ups."

Deacon stares at his wife for a moment, and then his lips flinch with a smile. "You have a plan," he says.

"Yep," she says. "And—"

"Oh, I'm already in, Nic. Let's go."

She smiles and then turns back to me. "I'm sorry to drag you into this deeper, but I need your help."

"I just want my life back," I say.

Nicole presses her lips together sadly. "I can understand that. Now," she says, motioning toward the back offices. "Do you have any idea where she keeps the syringes?"

While Deacon keeps watch in the hall, Nicole and I creep past the closed door of Marie's office. I lead Nicole into the treatment room where the Adjustments are performed.

As we enter, I see Nicole take it all in, seeing it for the first time and looking horrified. There's a large machine, computers and files, and various instruments ranging from sci-fi-looking to archaic. From a distance, the entire room is dangerous. I wish I'd seen it that way before.

I glance at the door, scared Marie will walk in. Nicole rushes across the room and starts going through the drawers of the cabinet. I don't know exactly where Marie keeps the syringes; they were always in her pocket. But I assume they keep some in the treatment room.

Toward the back, I pull open a drawer underneath a set of cabinets and find a few syringes in blue plastic bags. I grab one and turn to Nicole. "I got it," I say. She comes to take it from me.

"Perfect," she says. "Now we need to find the drugs."

Nicole goes to a white cabinet set against the back wall. She opens one side and finds folded paper gowns on the shelf. When she opens the other side of the cabinet, she pauses. There are rows of small glass bottles, neatly lined up. She turns a few with her fingertips to read the labels until she gets to the last row and snatches one out.

"That it?" I ask.

"Yep." She closes the cabinet and sets the bottle on the counter.

The label indicates it's the truth serum Marie uses. I watch as Nicole opens the syringe, pulling apart the plastic, and then picks up the bottle. She sticks the needle into the rubber top, and pulls out a dose . . . or two. I flick my eyes to her to see if she'll acknowledge how much medication she withdrew, but she doesn't look at me. I'm suddenly worried how far this will go. What is her intention here?

Nicole slips the bottle into her pocket and turns to me. There's a flicker of hesitation in her expression, but then Deacon's voice echoes through the hallway.

"Who were you talking to, Marie?" he asks loudly. "Didn't sound like you were making funeral arrangements."

Nicole curses and takes me by the arm, moving us into the center of the room, close to the exam table.

"Get out of my way," Marie says sternly, and then the door flies open. Marie sees us standing there, waiting for her, and she quickly glances around the room.

"What are you doing in here?" she demands. Deacon dashes inside and skids to a stop as he takes in the scene.

Nicole keeps her hand holding the needle behind my back, positioned as if she's comforting me.

"I wanted to see where you did it," Nicole says. "Where you've ruined lives. Like you learned nothing from what you did to me."

Marie flinches at the statement and lets down her guard. "That's not true," she says. "We only wanted to protect you." Marie takes a step closer. "We love you."

With her hand still hidden, I hear the sniffle, and Nicole starts to cry. I can't even tell if she's pretending.

"If only that were true," she says, her voice sheer pain. It breaks *my* heart.

"It is true, baby," Marie says, her voice softer than I've ever heard it. I look between her and Nicole. I don't understand their relationship, how they're even connected, but Marie nearly crumbled at the appearance of Nicole upset. She reaches for her and wraps her arms around Nicole like a confidant. Like a mother.

I watch as Nicole brings her arms around to hug her back, and then, with sudden fierceness, she jabs the syringe needle into Marie's backside and injects her.

Marie yelps and falls back a step. She turns around to see what happened and then looks at Nicole, who's holding up the empty syringe. Marie glances from her to the needle tip.

"Damn it," Marie says, almost expectantly. She doesn't try to run—although with the amount of medication in the syringe, I'm not sure how far she'd get anyway. She walks over to the exam table and leans against it. After a moment, I watch as her muscles sag, and Deacon comes over to help her sit on the table. Marie relaxes back languidly on her arms.

"Now I want the truth," Nicole says. "And not your version of it, Marie. The real fucking truth."

Marie rubs her back hip where the needle stabbed her, and when she lifts her head, her eyes are glassy. She smiles sadly.

"He was proud of you," Marie says wistfully, and behind Nicole, Deacon turns away. Of all the words she could have chosen, they react like these are the cruelest.

"Don't try to manipulate my emotions," Nicole says strongly, but her response proves Marie knows exactly which buttons to press.

"He remembered," Marie says. "*Of course* he remembered. You were his world. In his last moments, all he wanted was you. But I told him no."

Nicole presses her palm over her mouth as she holds back her cry. When she can, she lowers her arm, blinking back tears. "Why would you do that?" she asks Marie.

"Because he would have jeopardized everything."

"And what's *everything*?" Nicole asks.

Before answering, Marie's eyes drift to me. "Tatum," she says. "This doesn't concern you."

Nicole looks at me, taking in my appearance before turning back to Marie. "She stays," she tells her. "Now, what's going on? Why didn't my father want me to know him?"

"You're well," she says as if it's the explanation. "Don't you see, both of you?" She indicates me. "You're well. The problem the doctors never mentioned with The Program is the accepted compromise. The benefit-harm balance. They have it with every drug—a company takes an accepted loss. When a patient starts on a new medication, they're told of the side effects. They're briefly told of the long-term effects. But it's more than that.

"As doctors," Marie continues, "we understand that to cure one aspect of the body, we essentially cut off another, sometimes killing it. To cure what they thought were emotional triggers for depressive thoughts, they killed memories—removed them. That removal formed cracks in perception. Hairline fractures throughout. And now, returners are crashing back. They will *all* have complications."

"You're telling me that all of the patients from The Program are going to . . . have meltdowns?" Nicole asks, horrified.

"Yes. All of them."

I fall back a step, realizing this includes me, and Marie looks over to me dreamily. The medication has clearly kicked in.

"You don't have to worry, Tatum," she calls. "You aren't affected the same. And Wes will be fine due to his reset." She turns back to Nicole.

"We're curing returners," Marie says. "That's what we're doing here. We plan to save them. But we haven't quite figured out how. The brain is a fascinating organ, completely mysterious in so many ways. But we're close this time." She pauses. "I'm close."

"That doesn't explain why you've lied to us for the past five years," Deacon says, his voice loud in the small room and echoing off the walls. "Why did you tell us Tom had his memory wiped? What purpose did that serve, other than to hurt Nic even more?"

Nicole rolls her shoulders, the words themselves causing her tension. Marie's face tightens, and I can visibly see her fighting to not talk. For a moment, I don't think she will—sure this secret is buried deeper than any medication can get to.

"We were trying to keep you away from The Program. From Arthur Pritchard. And . . . your father didn't want you to know," Marie says finally. She closes her eyes, and then her entire body moves in a wave, and she looks up again. "He didn't want you to know that you're not the only one."

"Not the only what?" Nicole asks.

"You're not the only replacement."

CHAPTER TWELVE

DEACON SHOOTS FORWARD AND TAKES NICOLE'S arm. I look over and realize she's swaying, her eyes fluttering. "What do you mean?" Nicole asks Marie, her voice horrified. I don't understand what they're talking about, what "replacements" are.

Tears form and spill over onto Marie's cheeks, but she keeps talking. Her words are soft and dreamlike. "The grief department has secrets," she whispers. "And Tom—he knew you wouldn't forgive them." She looks at Deacon. "Either of you."

"Tell me what you did," Nicole demands.

"I will," Marie breathes out. "But first, you have to understand—what we've seen, your father and I . . . the depths of grief. The absolute misery of loss." She puts her hand over her heart. "We knew what it meant to lose everything. We only wanted to stop it."

"What did you do?" Nicole asks, louder.

"The grieving families," Marie starts, "the parents . . . sometimes they didn't want to give the closers back. Especially the young ones."

As Marie speaks, I watch the color drain from Deacon's face; Nicole's lips part as she sucks in a staggered breath.

"And so," Marie says, "we had another service, for those who needed it."

"Needed it or could afford it?" Deacon asks in a growl.

"Let's say both," Marie responds. "Those families who couldn't cope were given an option. Some chose to keep the replacement."

"I'm sorry, what?" I ask, stepping forward. A pit has opened in my stomach. "What the fuck kind of business did you run?"

"As my closers can tell you," Marie says, motioning to Nicole and Deacon, "their colleagues didn't come from good homes. They were orphaned or wards of the state, for the most part. Their job required them to step into a family situation and help the parents cope with grief. And then, once the loop was closed, they'd leave. But on occasion, a family asked for more time. And then more. If it was deemed a good fit, we let the closer stay indefinitely and adjusted the paperwork."

"What do you mean 'adjusted the paperwork'?" I ask.

"The death certificates," Marie says. "In some cases, we

were able to vacate them. And the closer took over the identity of the dead."

Holy shit. I can barely breathe—this might be the most disturbing thing I've ever heard.

"I was six years old," Nicole says from next to me. "You stole my life at six years old. Are you telling me you did the same thing to other kids?"

Marie watches her for a long moment. "We sent in *closers*, and if it was determined they could stay, then . . ." Marie fights the next words, but the truth serum must win out. "Then they were delivered to Arthur Pritchard for programming."

There's the name again—Arthur Pritchard. My heart is beating so fast that it makes my stomach churn. I'm stunned silent, helpless to listen.

"You rewrote their lives," Nicole says, her voice cracking. "You rewired their memories. You killed them."

"We gave them lives."

"Those weren't *their* lives!"

Next to Nicole, Deacon continues to stare at Marie, unmoving. He finally licks his lips to speak. "Who else?" he asks weakly, as if he's scared of the answer. "Who else did you do this to?"

"Not you, Deacon," Marie says. "Although there were many times we wished we could have improved your situation at home."

Deacon scoffs at the suggestion, telling her that no matter where he came from, he didn't want to be a replacement. Nicole still stares in shock. Marie glances at her and smiles.

"There is some good news," she offers.

Nicole reaches out instinctively to put her hand on Deacon, keeping him from stepping forward out of anger.

"And what could that possibly be?" Nicole asks.

"It's given us a blueprint," Marie says. "Those of you who were delivered as permanent replacements were the first steps in finding a cure. Because the crashbacks—the devastating ones— don't affect the replacements who've returned. The memories smooth themselves out, a fail-safe."

"Yeah, but . . . how many of your replacements went into The Program?" Deacon asks, shaking his head like he doesn't get it. Marie stills.

"We've only found one so far. It's why she's so important."

And suddenly a cold chill runs down my back. *No,* I think. *No.* "Marie," I call weakly.

She doesn't turn to me right away, even though I know she heard me. And it's as if the floor is beginning to crack open, ready to suck me into a pit of despair.

"Marie?" I call louder, my cry already breaking my voice.

She slowly turns to me. "I'm sorry, honey," she says.

"No," I shake my head, tears streaming freely. "What are you saying?"

She measures her words, and I wonder if the truth serum is wearing off. Part of me hopes it already has and that this is a lie, but it's too soon.

"Tatum Masterson was taken out of state by her mother," Marie says. "That part's true. But when Athena was located,

Tatum Masterson was gone. She had drowned when she was five years old, and your grandparents—they were beside themselves with grief. Unimaginable grief, Tatum."

"Don't call me that," I murmur, the entire scene going blurry. I feel Nicole look over at me sympathetically; she knows exactly how I'm feeling.

"You *are* Tatum," Marie says. "That precious baby, she didn't even have time to start her life. You've lived it for her. She was ripped unfairly from this world, and it was an absolute tragedy. But then there was another child for them. There was you."

"Why not adopt me, then? Why make me a replacement?" I demand.

"Because that doesn't stop the grief—not for your grandparents. They loved Tatum. They love you even more now. Your mother promised to leave in order to avoid neglect charges—promised to keep the secret. She hasn't been a problem since. And your grandparents, they've raised you with all the love in the world. It worked out. Don't you see, Tatum? You're a miracle."

"You stole me," I say, and Nicole puts her arm around me. "You stole my life."

"You were no one, and we gave you a family," she says. "Arthur took away your pain, helped you accept your new life. And whatever he did to you, to the others—it's saving your life now. You'll never fully crash back."

"Why should we believe that?" Nicole asks Marie fiercely.

"You didn't save all your closers. You couldn't save them from the epidemic—unless you've forgotten about Reed."

"Oh, I've never forgotten about Reed Castle," she says, smiling to herself. "And my and your father's assessment stands. The procedure that Arthur Pritchard did to adjust your memories is the same one we're trying to duplicate now. It could have worked in The Program, but after the epidemic took hold, regulations were loosened. Procedures were rushed. The corporation did this. And you can hate me and resent me all you want, but the fact remains: We're here to save lives."

"How can you even say that?" I ask. "How many have you ruined?"

"All returners will crash," Marie repeats, leaning back on the table. "The Adjustment is the only way to stop it. We need the missing piece in order to prevent a massive tragedy."

"You've controlled my whole life," I say.

"We protected you."

"And Wes? Why did Dr. McKee tell me to stay away from him? Why make me think I might kill him?"

"Because you and Weston . . ." Marie shakes her head, smiling softly. "You feel too strongly. Too deeply. It cuts through everything, even our Adjustments, we realized. After that, we decided it was best for you to stay apart. We were afraid you would remember. Crash back. We did it to keep you healthy."

"At his expense?" I ask.

"Yes," Marie admits.

"You're a psychopath," Deacon cuts in. "You—"

"Don't," Nicole whispers to him. Deacon glances at her, a flash of betrayal, and then he carefully untangles himself from her grip and moves to the other side of the room, far away from Marie. Nicole turns her attention back to Marie.

"I've had time to get used to what you and my father did," Nicole tells her. "But it doesn't mean I'm any less angry."

"I know," Marie responds.

Nicole studies her and then shakes her head. "I could never tell when you were lying," she says. "I should have learned by now. And what you've done to this poor girl." She motions to me. "Is there more that you haven't told us?"

Marie nods. "Yes," she says. "I need your help. I need you to help me understand Arthur Pritchard's procedure. Because if we don't figure it out, I assure you, The Program will."

"You really think you're part of a cure?" Deacon asks, disgusted. Marie looks over her shoulder at him. "What you did was about control," he says. "You control people's grief; you control their emotions. The grief department, The Program, the Adjustment—they're all the same. And now you want us to help you do it again? Another fucking cure?"

"Deacon," Nicole says warningly.

"No, Nic," he says, his face pleading. "We're not doing this. We're not—"

Nicole shrugs helplessly, signaling that she *will* help Marie, and Deacon lowers his eyes, defeated. I get the impression that Nicole has the final word on this. I, on the other hand, am still in shock. I can't even wrap my head around what Marie's told me. It's not real.

I'm not real.

A stabbing pain hits between my eyes, and I wince and rub at the spot.

"You okay?" Nicole asks me, and I tell her that I am. I force myself to stand up straighter, and the severe part of the pain passes, leaving an ache. Nicole turns back to Marie.

"What do you need from us?" she asks.

"First, I have to find someone—I'll need his expertise. And I'll need his protection once we have the cure. I'm hoping he can fill in for Tom." She presses her lips together sympathetically at Nicole.

"Who is it?" Nicole asks.

"My ex-husband."

This makes Deacon look up suddenly. "You were *married*?" he asks.

Marie nods that she was and smiles. "It was a long time ago," she says. "He works for the FDA now, partnering with the CDC since the epidemic. But we started together in the grief department. His name is Luther Williamson, and I'm sure he's somewhere in Seattle. We've lost touch."

"What do you want us to do?" Deacon asks, suspicious of her intent. But he must still have some connection to her, because he waits for her direction.

"I want you and Nicole to find him—it's what you do best. Tell Luther that I need his help finishing this. He'll know what to do."

"And me?" I ask.

"Once I figure out what to look for," she says, "we'll need to do a procedure." She pauses a long moment, looking me over. Deciding something. "But first," she says finally, "I need you to bring Michael Realm to me."

CHAPTER THIRTEEN

I DON'T AGREE TO BRING MICHAEL REALM TO THE Adjustment office, and not just because I have no idea how to get ahold of him. I asked Marie why she needed him, and her simple response was "information."

She claimed it was for his benefit, but I don't trust her. Besides, other than showing up unannounced at the Adjustment office, I have no idea how to reach Marie. When I brought that up, she told me that Realm will know where to find her.

Yeah, well, I'm not going to let anyone I know near Marie again, but I can at least warn Realm that she's looking for him. And whatever this procedure is . . . I'll decide that later. We might not even get that far.

It's strange to watch Marie with Nicole, the tenderness between them even though Marie has done unforgivable things to her. I doubt I could ever feel that level of forgiveness. I guess I'll find out.

Nicole gets Marie a cup of water from the sink in the treatment room and hands it to her. The doctor takes a small sip, noting that Nicole overmedicated her with the serum.

"I figured it would take an extra dose to cut through your bullshit," Nicole says, and rolls the stool over so she can sit in front of her. I stand in the back of the room, next to Deacon, unsure where to go.

"You okay?" Deacon asks quietly, looking sideways at me.

"Definitely not," I reply. He nods like he understands and leans against the wall, watching Nicole and Marie. He's like Realm in that way, observant. Seeing things the rest of us don't.

I check the time on my phone. Nathan has been gone for an hour. I text him and ask if he's had any luck finding Melody. I don't dare tell him about the madness happening here—not over text.

Not yet. Did Marie say anything about her? he asks.

Not really, no. When will you be back?

Do you need me now?

Soonish? I reply. I'm not sure how much longer I can stay here. My hands are visibly shaking, even though I'm oddly calm about not really being Tatum Masterson. I'm not ready to accept it, not without talking to my grandparents.

The time to be quiet is over. I'll demand they explain everything to me. I have all the pieces now.

See you in fifteen, Nathan writes back. I thank him and put my phone away.

Across the room, Nicole takes Marie's hand, and the two women smile at each other. Deacon kicks his sneaker on the floor, keeping his eyes lowered. He doesn't seem to be as forgiving as Nicole.

"Married, huh?" Nicole asks Marie.

Marie laughs. "Young love. I'm sure you understand."

Nicole nods that she does. "You never mentioned him," she says.

"It never seemed appropriate. He worked with me and your father for a short time, but found it . . . distasteful. I haven't seen Luther since the day I left him."

"But you knew where he'd be," Nicole says, tilting her head.

"We kept in contact for a while. I wondered if I'd need his help eventually," Marie says. "Turns out, I do."

"Will he help you?" Deacon asks. "Or did you ruin his life too?"

"I ruin everybody's life," Marie responds.

Nicole watches her but doesn't argue. She takes her hand from Marie's. "And my father?" Nicole asks. "Did you love him?"

"With all my heart," Marie says simply.

Nicole sniffles, and her lip begins to tremble. And there,

with Marie—the woman who stole her life—Nicole breaks down and lets Marie hold her. And together, they cry for Dr. Tom McKee.

"You sure you don't want a ride?" Deacon asks as we walk out into the lobby of the Adjustment office.

"No, I have a ride coming," I say. "But thank you."

Marie is still in the back office as Nicole follows us out. The air is fresh, but storm clouds have rolled in, ready to pour down on us at any second.

Nicole smiles at me, the kind of smile that says *Well, we're in some shit together, huh?* I appreciate when she pulls me into a hug.

"I'm a counselor," Nicole says quietly, giving me a squeeze before letting go. "And I understand what you're feeling, so if you need me . . ." She holds out a business card, and I take it.

"Thanks," I say, tucking it into my back pocket. "Where are the two of you headed now?" I ask.

"First to Washington to get our friend Aaron," she says. "He was a closer. I imagine he'll want to have a word, or several, with Marie. And then we'll track down this Luther Williamson—see if he's still fond of his ex-wife."

"I wish we were going to find Reed Castle," Nicole adds quietly, glancing back at Deacon. "All of us together again." Deacon wilts at the name and says he wishes they were too.

"Castle?" I repeat, looking at both of them. "There's a counselor at Dr. Warren's office with that name."

"No," Deacon says sadly. "Our friend Reed died years ago,

at the start of the epidemic. He was one of the first."

"Oh," I say, furrowing my brow. "Not to sound insensitive, but . . . you might want to double-check that. I'm not sure we should trust anything at face value anymore."

Nicole smiles that she will, but there's grief there that I don't think she wants to reaffirm. Deacon comes to put his arm over Nicole's shoulders, kissing the side of her head.

"Look, we've got to go," Nicole says to me. "You sure you'll be okay?"

Just as she asks, my Jeep pulls into the strip mall parking lot, bumping the curb. Nathan is a terrible driver. I can hear the radio playing too loudly, and he immediately turns it down when he parks in front of me. He smiles apologetically and climbs out, studying Nicole and Deacon.

Nicole tells me she'll be in touch, and I watch them leave. When they're gone, Nathan comes to stand next to me.

"I didn't find Melody," he says, disappointed. "Did I miss anything here?" He turns to me, and suddenly—as if my emotions were waiting for him—the devastation and severity of what Marie told me hits.

"I'm not Tatum Masterson," I choke out, and then Nathan catches me as I nearly collapse in tears.

Nathan is pale, sitting silently in the front seat.

We're parked in my driveway, and he stares down at his lap, unable or unwilling to speak. I told him everything Marie has done, both to me and her "closers." I told him her plan to figure out a cure using me and that The Program wants to stop us. But with every new detail, he asked, "But they're not really your grandparents?" as if that thought is too sickening for him to accept.

"What are you going to say to them?" Nathan asks, his voice raspy.

I texted my grandparents before we left the office and asked them to meet me at the house. When they asked why, I told them it was too involved to explain in a text.

"I'll just ask them," I tell Nathan. "They can't lie anymore. I already know." My shock has worn off slightly; crying it out actually helped me get a handle on what I was feeling. It helped me focus.

"Do you want me there?" Nathan asks, finally looking over at me. For a moment, he studies me, as if I've somehow changed from an hour ago. But then his bottom lip pouts, hurt on my behalf, and I reach over and put my hand on his cheek.

"I'll be okay," I promise him. "At least now I know the truth, right?"

"I guess." He turns and my hand falls away. "I still think I should come with you," he says.

"Thank you, but I have to do this on my own. And my grandparents need to come to terms with it. This is their grief. It's time we're all honest with each other."

"Damn, Tatum," Nathan says. "Foster would be so proud of you." We both laugh, and before I can ask, Nathan says he already talked to him—avoiding Foster showing up at the Adjustment office in a fit of protective rage.

"You'll call me right after?" Nathan asks.

"Of course."

He presses his lips into a smile, and then together we get out of the Jeep. He goes one way across the lawn toward his house, and I go the other way toward mine.

CHAPTER FOURTEEN

WHEN I WALK IN THE FRONT DOOR OF MY HOUSE, I stop. I study everything, every picture on the wall, every scrape in the paint. The stairs that I've gone up thousands of times, even the couch we've had for as long as I can remember.

This is my home, but for a moment, I'm a stranger in it. I take time to adjust to the truth, and soon, the house comes back into focus.

"Honey?" my grandmother calls from the kitchen. "Is that you?"

My reaction is immediate, and I grab on to the bannister to steady myself. I close my eyes, a lifetime of memories with my grandparents playing across my mind. I wish they had been real.

I'm about to cry, but I force my eyes open, force strength

into my spine. I have to face this. I have to know why they kept a little girl who wasn't theirs.

"Yeah, it's me," I say, unsteadily. I'm shaking as I walk toward the kitchen. The room is brightly lit, and I blink against it—my eyes dry from crying earlier.

My grandparents sit at the table and look up as I enter. Pop's eyes narrow behind his glasses as he studies me.

"Is everything okay?" my grandmother asks, her voice dripping with worry. She tightens her sweater against herself. "When you told us to come home," she continues, "we thought—"

My gaze drifts past her and settles on my grandfather. There's an irrational side of me that just wants to scream *Why?* and have him tell me that none of it is true. But logic wins out.

"What was in the box?" I ask Pop quietly.

My grandfather's mouth tightens, and I don't even need to explain about the box in their closet. He knows exactly what I mean. Next to him, my grandmother stills and looks down at her folded hands.

Pop exhales and removes his glasses, setting them on the table. It occurs to me that this is it—any lie I want to live is now over. I'm about to get smacked with reality.

My grandfather steadies his gaze on me, and his gentle blue eyes begin to tear up. "You know, don't you?" he asks.

I sway and grab on to the back of the chair closest to me. "Most of it," I say. "But I think it's time I hear the whole story. And from you."

"We were going to tell you," Gram says, still not looking at me. "When you got older, we were going to confess everything. But it got harder and harder, especially once the epidemic hit. We didn't want it to affect you, push you toward any behavior that might land you in The Program." She looks up. "But you got taken anyway. And when you came back, we *knew* we couldn't tell you. We couldn't risk hurting you."

My gram bites on her lower lip like she's trying not to cry, and seeing her like this hurts me. I can't watch her in pain. I can't bear it.

I round the table and wrap my arms around her from behind. My small gram lays the side of her head on my arm and cries softly, murmuring how sorry she is for not telling me sooner. Tears drip down my cheeks, and I look over to my grandfather. He's watching us, his head tilted as he cries too.

"Your mother," he says, then stops himself. *"Our daughter,"* he corrects, acknowledging that she wasn't my mother at all.

I straighten, my entire body shaking, and sit across from him at the table. Losing my mother doesn't hurt like it should; she and I were never close. Not like I am with my grandparents.

"Athena isn't a bad person," Pop continues. "She had problems. She needed help, but rather than get it, she ran. She self-medicated. She lost her way. We wanted to keep you—" He winces, closing his eyes. "We wanted to keep *Tatum* with us. She lived with us for nearly five years. We were prepared to raise her. We wanted to. But Athena took her and cut off contact. We were in the process of getting custody when the police showed up one afternoon."

His expression weakens, and Gram—sensing it—looks at him. She puts her fist to her mouth and nods for him to continue. I've stopped shaking, the feeling instead is weightlessness, an out-of-body moment.

"Two police officers stood on our doorstep with Athena," Pop says. "She didn't speak, and the officers were the ones who told us that our granddaughter had died. Tatum was alone. Her little, lifeless body all alone in some hospital morgue—" My grandfather chokes on his words, crying openly. My grandmother moans; I feel like my heart is getting ripped out. I've never seen this kind of ruin. I've never known it.

"She had . . . ," he tries to say, but takes another moment to clear his throat and find his voice. "She had fallen into the swimming pool at the motel, somewhere in Phoenix. Athena had been drinking, and she didn't notice Tatum had slipped out of the room. She heard another woman scream. The firefighters told the police you'd . . ." He stops again. "*She'd* been under water for at least fifteen minutes before she was pulled out. Paramedics pronounced her dead on the scene."

"Athena wouldn't call us," my gram says, outstretching her arm across the table toward me. I meet her halfway and grip her hand. "She told the police to call us," Gram says, "claiming that we were the ones who had custody. We didn't bother explaining to the officers that day that the case hadn't been settled yet. What was the point? Tatum was gone. We'd never get to see her sweet face again." She closes her eyes, and I squeeze her hand.

"It wasn't right," Pop murmurs, and I turn to him. "But we

were traumatized. This . . . unspeakable kind of grief. We didn't think we could survive it. Physically or emotionally."

"So I called Dr. McKee," Gram says, wiping the tears off her cheeks. "He and I had worked together before; I knew he helped grief-stricken families. And I asked him to help us." "Your grandfather tried to talk me out of it," she says, and Pop nods.

"I told her no," he agrees. "But when Arthur Pritchard showed up one evening, and I took one look at you—the little girl he brought with him . . ." He shakes his head. "You looked so much like her."

I blink quickly at the thought of looking just like his dead granddaughter. But in their faces now, I see a couple who is still traumatized by their grief.

"We weren't sure we could go through with it," my gram continues. "We didn't want a closer. But when you came to us as Tatum, it was like you were home. Like you never went away."

"We considered going through the legal channels," Pop adds. "But we didn't know where he found you—we had no claim to you. We were scared we would lose you. And you didn't remember your real family; you were so small."

"Arthur Pritchard tampered with my memory," I tell them. "I was small, but I'm sure I remembered something. It's long gone now."

"The grief department—Arthur," Gram says, "knew how to fix the paperwork. And so we agreed to raise you. We struck a deal with Athena so she would stay out of your life. It hurt her too much to see you."

I flinch at the thought, realizing I'm the ghost of her dead child. No matter how bad of a mom she is, she doesn't deserve that. It adds an extra layer to every sidelong glance she gives me during the holidays. Every awkward silence when it's just the two of us in a room.

"Athena's been able to move on with her life," Gram says. "She started a new family. And so did we—thanks to you."

"I wasn't a solution," I say. "You should have sought help."

"I know," Gram says. "But I wouldn't change a thing." Her voice cracks. "I know that makes me a horrible person, but I can't imagine the alternative. I can't imagine a life without you."

"Tatum," my pop says softly, and I turn to him. "If I can swear one thing to you, it's that you are and always have been the most important thing in the world to us. We've fought for you. And even though we've made mistakes"—he winces—"like with the Adjustment, we'll never make another one. You're a grown woman. We support you. We'll do anything for you. All we can ask is that you try to forgive us. We may not deserve it, but we're begging for it anyway."

"Of course I forgive you, Pop," I say, aching for them. This isn't the kind of pain that would drive me away from them. It brings us closer now that we're being honest. It makes me want to take care of them.

"I understand why you didn't tell me," I say honestly. "The Program had us all in their grip, and I would have definitely broken down. I do believe you were trying to protect me."

"We have fought," Pop says. "And we will continue to fight. Whatever you need, Tatum. Anything at all. Just please . . ."

"Don't leave us," my grandmother adds weakly. I look across the table at her, struck by grief so heavy that I put my hand to my chest. My grandmother looks broken, as if, after thirteen years, I would just get up and walk out, never speaking to them again.

They're my family. I love them, and they love me.

"I won't leave you," I tell her, and she covers her face with both hands and cries. Her shoulders shake, and Pop looks at me, his eyes welled up with tears.

"I'm sorry," he repeats.

"I know you are," I say.

"What can we do to help you?" he asks. "What's going on?"

I can trust them; in fact, I always could. Despite the huge lie of my life, and the Adjustment, they did try to keep me from The Program. They won't let them take me now, either.

"The Program is coming, Pop," I say, fear prickling my skin. "And the only way to stop them is to get the cure first. I need help locating someone."

"Finding people is part of my job. Who am I looking for?"

I rest my elbows on the table. "His name is Michael Realm."

I sit with my grandparents at the kitchen table for the next hour, telling them everything I've learned so far. Even Dr. Warren comes up. Although they knew she was previously with The Program, they didn't think she was still in contact with them. They truly believed she was trying to help me.

At Dr. McKee's warning, they never told Dr. Warren that I was a replacement. McKee told them it would be an automatic flag. They also never told her that I had had an Adjustment performed on me.

I asked my grandparents how I got out of The Program in the first place, and they didn't know that, either. My grandfather had been putting out stories with the local paper in an attempt at influence, but then he and my grandmother were pulled into Dr. Warren's office. She told them I was getting out but would require follow-up therapy—my possible readmittance to The Program at her discretion. They didn't strike any deals with her.

So I still have no idea how I got out of The Program.

My grandmother gets up from the table to put on a kettle and make herself some chamomile tea, saying she needs it for her nerves now that we're all part of the rebellion. I tell my pop that I should call Nathan and let him know we're okay.

"Yes," my grandmother says from the stove. "We need to speak to Nathan and apologize for asking him to lie to you. It was unfair of us. Please"—she turns to look at me—"tell him how sorry we are."

"I will," I say. I stand up and start toward my room, but at the door, I stop.

"Pop?" I ask, turning around to look at him. He lifts his head. "What was all the stuff in the box anyway?" I ask.

"Oh," he says, wilting guiltily. "I moved it to the basement after Dr. Warren called and asked about it. I lied to her, said it was nothing. But those were the items you came to us with when you were a child. We didn't feel right about throwing them out. We planned to give them back to you one day. It's yours."

"I'll bring the box up," Gram says, an apology clear in her expression.

"Thanks," I say, giving them both a warm smile. Letting them know I love them. I still have a lot of questions and emotions to get through, but at the core, we're family.

The box is on my bed, but I'm afraid to open it now that I know its meaning. I have no recollection of that time, but the idea of a little girl, brought here and given away . . . I must have been scared. I run my hand over the top of the box, wishing I could be there for her—even though she's me.

I examine the date on the box again, a few months off from my own birthday.

That means I'm already eighteen. It's strange to imagine your birthday isn't really your birthday. Maybe I'll celebrate twice next year. The idea makes me smile but is immediately replaced with sadness. I wonder if I ever felt it growing up. On the day of my actual birth, was there a part of me that knew?

I take off the lid and set it aside. The stuffed dog is on top, and I examine it again. I don't feel any pull, any significance. It's dirty—the kind of dirt that means it was well-loved. I put it next to the box and dig through some clothes, a dress that's yellowed over time. At the very bottom of the box, I feel an object.

I hold the fabric to the side and pull out a charm attached to a silver bracelet—a piece of child's jewelry. It's nothing fancy, but it's sweet.

I examine the charm, running my finger over it. It's a heart with a *C* carved onto it. There's a twist in my stomach, and my eyes begin to tear up. Could that have been the first letter of my old name? I turn the charm over, and my breath catches when I see it's engraved in tiny letters:

XOXO
—Mommy

"I had a mother," I whisper, and the words, once out of my mouth, are a sudden wrecking ball to my heart. "I had a mother," I repeat a little louder.

She must have loved me once, but something happened to her. Was she alive still? Did she give me away, or did they take me? Does she still wonder where I am?

You're not the only replacement, Marie had told Nicole. Marie and Dr. McKee have destroyed lives. Changed them. Rewritten them.

I'm the replacement for a girl who died, and in that moment, I died too—whoever C was. My family was gone. Now I have this new life, still battling my past. And it hurts to feel like an imposter.

I take the stuffed dog, and I curl up on my bed and cry. And after a while, my thoughts turn to Wes, and how he said the past has the power to destroy us. I think he could be right, but only if we give it power. Only if we let it.

So I sit up, clearing the tears from my cheeks. I neatly fold the dress and place it back in the box, breaking down a few times. I lay my stuffed dog on top. I stand and bring the tiny bracelet—too small to wear—and set it on my dresser. I gaze at it an extra second, wishing I knew my mother. I put the lid on the box and place it on the floor of my closet.

I don't want any more lies. I don't want to pretend for another second about anything. Being honest with my grandparents, and having them be honest in return, has lightened my soul. Keeping secrets is a heavy burden, and I'm ready to let it all go.

It's time I find Wes and tell him about our past. No matter what, he needs to know. I can't be the one keeping it from him. And maybe he'll say that he loves me again. That he always knew that we'd find our way back together. It's a naïve viewpoint, I know. But I can't help imagining the best-case scenario.

I can't help but allow in just a little bit of hope.

PART III
LOVE HIM MADLY

CHAPTER ONE

I TELL MY GRANDPARENTS THAT I'M GOING TO school to find Wes. They seem a bit stunned by the comment but don't argue. Just like they promised, they stand by my decision. Pop tells me to call if I need him.

I text Nathan before I pull out of the driveway, and he asks if he should come with me, but this is something I have to do on my own. He says he'll be home when I get back.

It's almost last hour, and I wonder if Wes will be in the library, catching up on his assignments. I consider texting him to ask where he is, but I don't have the nerve. This way, if he's not in the library, I'll have time to rethink and regroup. It's not brave, but I'm driving to school on a whim. Racing ahead without too much thought to slow me down. I know I'll find Wes eventually; I won't give up until I do. But it's also good to have some options.

The bell for seventh hour rings as I stand in the office, signing the student book. When the attendance clerk asks where I'm heading, I tell her the library, and she writes out the pass.

I glance at Dr. Wyatt's office door, thankful that it's closed. I wonder if she's out in the classrooms or talking with a student. Interrogating them, like she did with Wes. I'm relieved that she doesn't seem to be part of The Program, but I still don't trust her. And I still don't want anything to do with her brand of sanctimonious bullying.

"Thanks," I tell the clerk, and then head toward the library. I didn't even bring my backpack with me, and I realize that should have seemed strange. Then again, I did show up only for seventh hour—that alone was weird.

There aren't many students in the library when I walk in. Just a few people scattered around the tables. The librarian says hello to me, and I walk over and hand her my pass to let her know it's okay that I'm here. She glances at it and then goes back to checking in a stack of books.

Maybe Wes isn't here. Part of me hopes he's not because it will give me time to think of just the right words—formulate an argument for why he needs to know everything. I'm currently a storm of emotions, wild and unruly.

And it's then, of course, that I see Wes sitting at a table in the back of the library, reading a novel. I can't help it—I smile and even sigh a little. The vision of him reading is something I've always enjoyed. Have always been drawn to.

I slowly make my way toward him, studying him as I do.

My nerves buzz over my skin. I'm scared. I'm excited. I'm a mess.

When I get to his table, he looks up with a sharp intake of breath. "Tate," he says. "I didn't think you were at school today." He looks me over, taking stock of my condition, but doesn't ask how I am.

"Mind if I sit with you?" I ask.

He glances around, not immediately welcoming me, and my heart dips. I almost say never mind, but I won't back down this time.

Wes motions to the chair next to him and tells me to go ahead.

I sit down, and he studies me for a moment. I'm sure he noticed I don't have any books with me—it's obvious that I'm here for him—but rather than ask about it, he sits back in his chair, relaxed, and opens his novel to continue reading.

I can't see the title because he folds the spine. He seems relaxed with me next to him, even though we're not talking. Even though we have stuff we absolutely need to talk about. We belong by each other's side, even though we're not together.

"Wes," I say, and swallow hard.

"Hm?" he hums out, flipping the next page of his book. I watch him, the way he creases the binding, causing deep lines; when he licks his thumb to turn the page back like he might have missed an important plot point.

"The other night, you asked how I felt about you," I say. Wes stills but doesn't turn to me right away. His Adam's apple bobs, and then he closes his book. "I want to answer," I add.

"What are you doing?" he asks, turning to me. He says it like he's worried I'm going to hurt him. And to be honest, I might. That's the thing about us, we might hurt each other. But I can't keep the past from him anymore. I need him to know.

"I want to answer," I repeat.

Wes's jaw tightens like he's getting ready to take a punch. His dimples are deeply set, and his eyes flash with vulnerability.

"I love you," I say in a rush. "Wes, I love you so much. Always have. We were together from the first day we met, together for years. Not just friends. And things have tried to come between us: the epidemic, the doctors, your mother . . . *me*—but we find our way back. Our hearts remember, even when we don't." I pause when my voice begins to shake, and take a steadying breath.

Wes blinks slowly, his eyes glassy. He doesn't smile, doesn't say he loves me, too.

"I'm sorry I didn't tell you sooner," I continue. "And I'm sorry that I lied and said we were just friends—it was stupid. I thought I was protecting you, but . . . I won't lie to you anymore. I needed you to know the truth about us."

He still doesn't speak and lowers his eyes to his lap, his chest rising and falling quickly. Despite his subdued reaction, I feel lighter. The heaviness of carrying the secret gone, just like earlier. It gives me clarity, and I'm grateful for the open space I suddenly feel. I wish I'd told the truth all along.

"Anyway," I say, not sure if he needs time to digest what I

SUZANNE YOUNG

just told him. "I didn't mean to interrupt your reading, I just had to get that off my chest."

"And put it on mine?" he asks, lifting his eyes.

My lips part, surprised by the intensity in his words. "I didn't mean to. I—"

"You didn't mean to? You sure?" he asks. "Because I'm wondering why you would tell me all this if you didn't want a reaction. If you didn't want to ruin my day."

"Wes, that is not what's happening."

"Then what is?" he asks. A girl a few tables away looks over at us curiously. "What is happening, Tate? Because I was pretty clear how I felt about you, and you pushed me away. You made me feel . . . crazy—like I was making up our connection. You gave me just enough affection to keep me around, and then you'd pull it back. Acting like it meant nothing. Ignoring me. And now you walk up and say you *love* me?"

"You deserve to know what's real," I say, trying to explain.

"And *we're* real?" he asks, motioning between us.

I pause and lower my voice. "We used to be," I say. "I didn't remember everything, not at first. And the doctors, they told me you'd die if I confessed. But now I know that's not true. Now I have the whole picture. You have no idea what I've been through the last few days."

"You're right," he says. "Because you wouldn't return my texts. You wouldn't even have a conversation with me. You're . . . you're fucking me up, Tate."

My heart aches at his words. This isn't good for him, this

sort of emotional shrapnel. He needs time, and if I'm honest, he probably needs distance. Even when I'm trying to make things better for him, I make it worse. I can't hold his gaze.

"Forget I said anything," I murmur, and stand up from the chair.

"No," he snaps. "You don't get to do that. You don't get to just throw words out there and then try to take them back. What do you expect me to do with this information? What did you *want* me to do?"

"I don't know."

"Sure you do. What did you think would happen?"

I don't want to admit it because it makes me seem manipulative, but I can't lie to him again. "I thought you'd tell me you love me too," I admit.

Wes stares at me, and I'm at once exposed and hopeful. He licks his lips, his dimples deepening, and then he shakes his head.

"That's not how this is going to go, Tatum," he says coolly. "I'm sorry."

It's like a pile of bricks drops on my chest, but I nod, trying not to look as bowled over as I feel. Wes has every right to reject me, especially now. This is the way it was always supposed to end, with him moving on. I have to let him.

"I'm sorry," I say again, and turn to cross through the library.

The girl who'd been watching us smiles as she texts something into her phone. I can't help but wonder what she's saying about us. And then there's a small voice that says maybe she wasn't watching for gossip.

Maybe she was watching us for The Program.

I go to my locker, fighting back tears. What started as empowering feels more like devastation, and I deserve all of it. I should have been clear from the start or avoided him. Instead, I've strung Wes along. Why should he believe me at this point? The only Tatum he knows is a liar.

I lean my head against the cool metal of my locker. In the quiet hallway, I try to retreat into a happy memory of the two of us. Wes's arms around me. His lips at my ear, whispering that he would do anything for me. How pure it felt.

But are any of those memories even real, or have they all been strategically placed by an Adjustment? I squeeze my eyes shut, the idea too disturbing. I just want to go back, go back to before the doctors took it all. The good, the bad. I want to remember. I just want something *real*.

There's an itch, a pinhole of pain in my temple that suddenly and violently expands. I straighten, startled by it, but the hallway begins to tunnel, my vision blurs. I groan and push the heel of my palm against the side of my head.

The world is smashed like a ceramic plate, and I fall backward . . . and into a memory.

And I was standing in the leisure room of The Program, wearing stiff lemon-yellow scrubs.

CHAPTER TWO

"ARE YOU GOING TO PLAY OR NOT?" MICHAEL REALM asked, a pretzel rod bit between his teeth. "It's your turn."

The leisure room swam around me, and I didn't see how it could be my turn when I wasn't even playing their game. But the drugs Nurse Kell had given me made everything seem heightened, surreal. Like I was walking through a dream.

I sat down at the table, and Realm tossed me some cards, which I fanned out. I hadn't played bullshit since middle school, but I remembered the basic concept.

"I'll go," the guy next to me said.

"No, Derek," Realm said, pulling out the pretzel rod to point it at him. "We always let the pretty girls go first." Realm smiled at me, but I didn't return it. I kept watching him, sensing something off.

Derek groaned, and when I turned to him, he peeked at me as if from behind a curtain. I got the sense that he was faking—faking sick or faking well, I couldn't decide. But his dark eyes scanned me, and I didn't like their predatory nature. The way they paused where they shouldn't.

"Fuck off," I said under my breath. He had a spark of anger, glancing once at Realm before going back to his cards. Realm's glare was deadly.

"Oh, shit," the kid next to Derek said, motioning across the room.

"What's up, Shep?" Realm asked reluctantly, putting the pretzel back in his mouth.

"Here she comes."

We all followed his line of vision to a girl scratching her red hair, walking toward our table. She didn't look healthy, not even remotely, and I watched as Realm's expression showed concern. His eyes, however, flashed nothing.

"Hi, Realm," the girl said brightly. "Can I play this round?" She darted a quick look at me, and then smiled at him pleadingly.

"No, Tabby," he said. "Not today."

"Why not?" she demanded. "She gets to play!" She pointed in my direction, and I stared back at her blankly. My emotions were off—like Nurse Kell had literally turned down the volume to zero.

"I said not today," Realm replied, sounding halfhearted. He turned back to the game, and Tabby stood there, confused, before exchanging a glance with Shep and Derek.

I looked down at my cards, finding one I'd like to use. I snapped it down on the pile, and when I looked up, Tabby was gone.

"Bullshit," Realm said quietly, not even looking at me. I furrowed my brow and watched as he lifted his head, tears in his eyes. Next to me, Derek cursed. "It's all bullshit, Tatum," Realm repeated before handlers appeared next to him, pulled him from his chair, and led him from the room.

I gasp and find myself on the hallway floor of the school, fluorescent lights burning above me.

"Ow," I murmur, rubbing the back of my head where I smacked it. I blink quickly as the knowledge folds over me.

I knew Michael Realm in The Program. But not just him— there were others. And . . . they were faking it. Why?

Still disoriented from the memory, I sit up, and there's a trickle on my upper lip. I quickly swipe my hand through the blood that's coming from my nose. I reach into my pocket to see if I have a tissue anywhere, when suddenly there's one in front of me.

Startled, I look up and find Derek Thompson standing above me with a white tissue held out in my direction. My stomach seizes, and I slide back from him, bumping into the lockers.

"I know you," I say, staring up at him. "I remember."

I'm in a precarious position as he moves to stand above me, trying to dominate me. He lowers the tissue and puts his hand on my shoulder, fingers squeezing into the muscle, making me recoil.

"It's about time," he says, his mouth hitching up in a sinister smile. "Tatum Masterson, you've been flagged. Come with me."

I quickly slap his hand away and try to scramble to my feet, but the minute I get a foot under me, he pushes me down again. He can't do that! We're at school.

I open my mouth to scream, and then he's on top of me, his palm smothering my lips, pressing so hard I can't open them. A flash of bright panic floods me, and I flail my arms, trying to hit him wherever I can.

It's the same feeling I had in my foyer when handlers were dragging me out in front of my grandparents. My body shrieks, fights.

I try to tell Derek to stop, I even flop on my back to get his hand off my mouth, but he puts me in a headlock; his fingers knot painfully in my hair as he yanks me to my knees.

Behind my lips, I scream. He's too strong. And when I see him withdraw a syringe from his pocket, I fight even harder. I won't let him take me.

I dig my fingernails into the back of his hand and scratch as hard as I can. His skin tearing away makes my stomach turn, and Derek withdraws, cursing. Before I can yell for help, there is a sudden and blinding hit on the side of my head. The world goes white, getting smaller, and I feel myself tip sideways.

He punched me, and the reverberation of the hit has left me stunned. Shocked.

Derek grabs me by my hair and upper arm, dragging me across the hall. I'm kicking out my legs, my shoes slipping on the linoleum, and try to loosen his grip. He elbows the emergency exit door, opening it into the stairwell, and I know I'm almost out of time. The fact that the classrooms are right there, filled with people who can help me, and I haven't been able to call to them is terrorizing.

I'm being kidnapped in plain sight.

"Stop!" I finally yell.

But Derek gets me into the concrete stairwell, and the door slams closed behind us. I know it's too late. He's going to inject me with whatever's in that syringe. He's going to drag me out of here before anyone helps me. He's going to—

There's movement behind him, a flash of red, and then a whack, the thud echoing off the walls. Derek's dark eyes widen, and then I swear, it's the like a real-life version of x-ed out cartoon eyes. He's instantly unconscious, and before he hits the floor, a steady stream of red begins to pour down the side of his head. Down his neck. Over the shoulder of his shirt.

I scream, horrified, as he hits the cement, face-first, and there is the crunch of his nose breaking. My entire body shakes, the pain settling in. I look around wildly, from Derek's body to the girl standing there, a fire extinguisher clutched in her hands.

"Holy shit," I manage to say. Melody Blackstone stares back at me, a splatter of blood across her cheek.

Melody no longer looks like Jana Simms. She's not sporty

and cute. She's dressed in a black leather coat, black jeans, and boots. Her makeup stripped away. She gapes at me, wide-eyed, slighter than I remember.

"Did you just kill him?" I ask, looking down at Derek. I try to cover my mouth, but my hands are shaking too badly. I can't even get to my feet, and Melody sets the fire extinguisher aside and comes over to help me.

Shoulder to shoulder, we stare down at Derek's body, and I'm trying to figure out what to do, how to fix this, when Derek moans and moves his legs.

"Not dead," Melody says, disappointed. I look sideways at her, and she takes my arm. "But I have to get you out of here. Now."

"What about him?" I ask, motioning to Derek, whose moaning is getting louder. My head aches from where he punched me, and I can still feel his fist in my hair. His will overpowering mine.

"I'll take care of him once you're safely out," Melody says. "Now come on."

I don't even recognize her. Melody is every bit a handler now, a closer. I let her lead me down the stairs, knowing that I shouldn't trust her, but also knowing that I have to. I can't wait to see who else is involved with Derek. What if they corner me? What if this happens again? Oh, God. This can't happen again.

"He flagged me," I murmur, racing down the stairs with Melody. "He . . . hurt me. He was going to take me to The Program."

"Yep," Melody says, peeking up the stairwell to make sure no one is following us. At the ground floor, I can still hear Derek's moans. "You've been flagged since yesterday. I saw the call go out. Dr. Warren claims you're a danger to yourself and others. I'm surprised Realm didn't get to you first."

"Realm?" I ask, my memory flooding back. "He's in on this?"

"He's not with Derek, if that's what you mean. But Michael Realm always knows what's happening," she says with a small smile. "He would want to protect you. Something must be wrong for him not to be here."

"How did *you* know about the flag?" I ask.

"I'm on the same listserv," she says offhandedly, and we exit the door into the parking lot. The sun is bright, and it makes me squint, my head hurting even more.

"He punched me in the head," I say, rubbing the spot. "That fucking dick."

Melody sniffs a laugh. "Yeah, well, he'll have a headache for the next week, I'd say. Now, about this flag . . . any idea why Warren suddenly wants you erased? Why now?"

"I'm not sure. I don't remember her from The Program, but I guess there was some deal struck. Maybe I broke it."

"Maybe," Melody says. She keeps looking around as we walk quickly toward my Jeep, in that observant way closers and handlers have about them.

We get to my driver's door, and Melody opens it and ushers me in.

"Marie was worried about you," I tell her. Melody meets my eyes, and I know the question on her lips. "Nathan too," I add.

"Let them both know I'm okay," she says. "I tried to skip town, but I couldn't just leave you all in this mess. I'm sorry for whatever part I had in getting you into it," she adds. "But Marie is close to a cure now, and that means you have to stay safe. Be more careful, but act normal. I'll take care of Derek. I have a friend who'll help me get him out of here. You won't see him again. At least, not until this is over."

A thought occurs to me. "Did I . . . did I know you in The Program too?" I ask, wondering if I've been unfair to her all this time. If we have some long, forgotten history.

"No," she says. "But you were Realm's friend, and by extension, mine." She smiles. "Sound familiar?"

But her joke hits me a different way than she intended. There's more to my and Michael Realm's story. I knew him in The Program. I was his *friend*. Well, what the fuck? Why didn't he mention that?

"Go straight home," Melody says, checking back at the school. "Don't tell your grandparents about this. Don't tell anyone, if you can help it. Be normal, or the monitor will come sniffing around, and that is a whole different problem we don't have time for. If Marie asks, tell her I went south with Asa and that I'll call her when I can. It's all about the cure now, Tatum. It's the only way to stop The Program."

I nod numbly, my mind spinning. My hands are still shaking. Before she closes the door, I reach out to stop her.

"Wait," I say. "Won't they just come after me again?" I ask, fear ticking up in my voice.

"Yes," she replies. "But their first flag failed. They'll have to wait, or it'll draw too much attention. So you bought yourself a few days."

"And then?" I ask.

Melody holds my gaze. "And then they'll send better handlers."

The idea that I'm being hunted, watched, is terrifying. "So Dr. Warren is behind this?" I ask. "She has the handlers?"

"Dr. Warren is a part of it," Melody says, checking over her shoulder again, looking impatient. "But no, she's not in charge. They all have handlers—Warren, Marie, Wyatt. But Dr. Warren is the only one connected to The Program."

I'm confused, and I know we don't have time to sort it all out. "So who's the villain?" I ask.

To this Melody smiles ruefully. "Society," she responds. "Now, take care of yourself. And tell Nathan . . ." She stumbles over his name. "Tell Nathan that I loved him. For real. And that I'm really sorry."

I swallow hard, watching the hurt cross her features. And then Melody Blackstone eases my door shut, looking around the deserted lot, and runs back toward the school.

CHAPTER THREE

I SIT IN MY JEEP, MY HEAD THROBBING. I REACH UP to feel the area, the slight, fist-size swelling. I check in the mirror but can't see the damage. That's good, I guess. It would be a lot harder to act "normal" if I had a black eye.

But as I stare at myself, I'm awash in shame—even though I did nothing wrong. Embarrassment. And most of all, pure terror. My eyes well up and tears spill over, racing down my cheeks. I sniffle, crying openly as I try to wipe away the dried blood under my nose.

His hands on me. It's all I can feel, and I run my palms over my arms like I can replace the sensation. Take back my agency.

I look out the window toward the school. "Bastard," I whisper, my lips sore from where he crushed them to keep me quiet. I let anger in to replace some of my vulnerability. I want to go back in and give Derek a few kicks while he's down. I'm not even violent, but he not only *hit* me, he was going to take me to The Program and let them . . . I don't know, erase me? Lobotomize me?

He was going to kill me—this version of me. Melody saved my life.

And it was smart of Melody to suggest that I not tell anyone about this, but it's unrealistic. And it's pretty clear that the most important person on my interview list is Michael Realm. She said he knows everything that happened. Well, he neglected to mention that he and I were friends. Now, why would he leave that out? What else did he forget to tell me?

Before I can ask him, I'll have to find him.

I take out my phone and click through the numbers. I only have a few days to help Marie find a cure, and if that doesn't work, I'll have to leave town. Go on the run.

I can alert the authorities about The Program, sure. But how will I know who's in on it? The Program is underground, and I have to believe that people in positions of power are the ones driving it.

Melody said society is the villain, and I get what she means. Our desire for a quick fix to our problems, our fear of death. Our parents and guardians will do anything to keep us safe, even if that means not letting us live our own lives. And our teachers and bosses want us to behave, do our work. That's a lot easier when we can't remember what we're sad about.

If The Program expands, it won't just be to treat an epidemic. It will be to treat free will. It will be to control us. I don't consider myself a hero, but I will fight to stop them. Marie thinks she has a cure, and I want to believe it. Even if it might get me lobotomized.

I click my grandfather's number and bring the phone to my ear. I wince, the entire side of my head hurting. I put the call on speaker instead, dropping the phone into the cup holder, and start the engine of the Jeep.

"You okay?" Pop says as a way of answering. I smile, relieved to hear his voice, and drive out of the parking lot. I'm so grateful to have my grandparents back on my side—especially now. We still have a lot to work through, obviously, but I love them. And I know they love me.

"It's a long story," I say, glancing at my reflection in the mirror. I'm not going to keep the incident with Derek a secret, but now isn't the time for this kind of information. It'll frighten them, distract them from what I need them to do for me.

"Have you found out anything about Michael Realm?" I ask. "The guy I mentioned?"

"Ah . . . ," my grandfather says, and there's a rustling of papers. "Speak of the devil. Your grandmother and I were just looking into that."

"Hi, honey," my gram calls out from somewhere in the room.

"Hi, Gram," I reply. She must be skipping work to help him research, and I can't think of another time when that's happened. She doesn't get involved in his investigations, but I guess this one is different. This is for me.

Pop tells me he's putting me on speaker, and I stop at a red light. I adjust the phone in the cup holder.

"Any luck finding him?" I ask.

"Not yet," he admits. "But he has quite a past."

My stomach turns, afraid another world-upending revelation might just wreck me. "What kind of past?" I ask.

"Just a lot of chatter," he says. "Nothing verified yet. But he was definitely involved with the reporter who broke the story on The Program—the one who got it shut down."

"He was friends with Sloane Barstow and James Murphy," I say. "So I guess that makes sense."

"Like I said," Pop continues, "it's just chatter for now. But some of his history is hidden in paperwork—purposeful, I'd wager. I can't even find his original admittance paperwork for The Program. There's a lot more to his story."

"Tell me about it," I mutter. "Well," I continue. "I need to talk to him. Immediately."

"I'll keep looking," Pop says with a sigh. "We'll find him."

"Honey," my gram says in a worried voice. "Are you sure talking to him is the best idea? For now, it might be advantageous to keep clear of him. At least until we know we can trust him."

"I knew him," I say, watching the road. "I guess . . . I guess I was friends with him in The Program—that part's not clear yet. But he was right about Dr. Warren," I point out. My grandparents go quiet, and I hate that I have to bring up something they lied about. "He told me she was from The Program, and he told me to stop seeing her."

"Yes," Pop says. "He was right about that. We made a mistake," he adds. "Dr. Warren seemed sincere, but we shouldn't have confided in her. We put you in danger."

"Yeah, well," I say. "You thought it was just therapy. None of us knew The Program was still operating."

"I told her never to call the house again," my grandmother announces defiantly. I furrow my brow, surprised.

"When?" I ask.

"Dr. Warren called here after you left today. Wanted to 'chat' about your last visit. Asked if she could talk to you, but I told her you were at school."

Shit. Dr. Warren looked for me at home first. She tried to make my grandparents accomplices in my removal. Again.

"She asked if I'd bring you in for therapy," Gram continues, and I can just about imagine the way her face is stern right now. Her little cheeks bright red with confrontation as she sweeps crumbs from the kitchen table into her open palm.

"And I told her she wasn't welcome in our lives anymore," Gram continues. "And that she could take her concerns and shove them up—" She stops, and I hear my grandfather laugh softly.

"Well," my grandmother says, slightly embarrassed. "I just told her what she could do with her lies," she finishes.

The idea of my grandmother telling someone to shove their lies up their ass is one for the scrapbook.

"Good for you, Gram," I say. "We won't let anyone else manipulate us. Now, Pop," I say, glancing in my side mirror, feeling paranoid that I might be followed. "How long before you can track Realm down?"

He hums out like he's thinking, and there's another swish of papers. "I can try and trace some of the calls that went out of the Adjustment office, but I imagine Marie already tried that."

Melody suggested Realm hadn't shown because something had gone wrong. I'm starting to worry she might be right. If we'd really been friends, wouldn't he have warned me? Stopped Derek from assaulting me? I shiver and push away the images.

"And speaking of Marie," Pop adds, "you might want to clue her in that Dr. Warren is looking for you. Now—"

I swallow hard. "Yeah," I say. "About that . . ." I pull onto a side street and park the Jeep. I take a breath and tell my grandparents what happened at school. I thought I was handling it, but the moment I describe Derek's hands on me, the feeling of helplessness in a place where I was supposed to be safe, I break down crying. I was so scared. I was so fucking scared of him.

"We need to call the police," my grandmother yells, frantic. "We—"

"We can't," I say. I wipe my cheeks and glance around the neighborhood, making sure no one is watching me now. "Melody—Jana, that's her real name—she took him somewhere to keep him quiet. She said I'll have a few days before they send more handlers after me."

"That is ridiculous," Gram says, and there's a smack like she

SUZANNE YOUNG

hit her hand on the table. "The police can't ignore this. I don't care who they're involved with."

"Things have changed, Gram," I say, scared of the truth in it. "Until The Program is dead and buried, we can't trust anyone but each other. Do you understand?"

"Tatum," Pop says, trying to sound calm. "Come home. At least let your grandmother take a look at your head. You could have a concussion."

"I will," I say. "Melody told me to act normal, whatever that is. But first, I'm going to swing by the Adjustment office to check if Marie's there. See if Michael Realm is there. You need to keep looking for him, Pop."

"I will," he says.

"Oh, honey," my grandmother moans, sounding terrified. "Come home."

"I'm going to be fine, Gram," I say, my stomach sinking at the worry in her voice. "I promise. I'll see you both in a little bit." Although reluctant, they say good-bye, and we hang up.

I sit a moment in the quiet of my Jeep. My skin prickles with leftover fear. I don't ever want to experience anything like that again. I've already had it happen twice. And I need to make sure it never happens to anyone else.

Checking my mirrors, I pull back onto the street and head toward the Adjustment office. It's a long shot; I know that. But I'm hoping Marie's there, and part of me hopes Realm will be there. That he'll just open my Jeep door and climb in.

It makes sense now, the way I trusted him, even though I

didn't think I knew him. The way he told me he cared about me. He did. He does, I guess. And there is a tender pain in my heart, and I wonder if it belongs to him.

I arrive in the empty Adjustment lot and park in front of the office. There don't seem to be any lights on inside, but I get out and try the door anyway. I knock and ring the bell for ten minutes, but no one answers.

While there, I try the only number I have for Marie, but there isn't a voice mail to leave a message. I have no idea how she expects me to bring Michael Realm to her when I can't even find her.

I fold my hands on top of my head to look around but wince at the pain. I gingerly touch the knot on the side of my head. I think I need an ice pack and a few ibuprofen. Thinking about it, I wrap my arms around myself, not wanting to admit feeling weak.

I'll have to loop in Nathan and Foster about Derek, about the handlers. Hell, there's even the true and catastrophic story of me and Wes to deal with. But for now, all I want is to feel safe. To remember what that was like.

Even if it's just an illusion.

CHAPTER FOUR

I GET BACK IN THE JEEP, WAITING AN EXTRA MINUTE in case Michael Realm magically shows up outside my door. When he doesn't, I go over to the 7-Eleven to check inside, but he's not there, either. Frustrated, I start driving. I'm not sure where to look.

Alone, my mind tries to replay the moment I was attacked at school. I shake my head, like I can shake out the memory. I roll down the windows, turn up the music, trying to tune out my own thoughts. My head hurts.

I see the turn for the river up ahead, and I take it. I haven't been here since Wes was reset, but there are a ton of memories in this park, most of them tragic. Maybe that's why it feels like the perfect place to go right now. I might need to wallow just a bit before I go home.

I find a parking spot, and then I get out and head toward the river. I walk along the water's edge until I see the boulder that juts over the side. It's like a favorite chair calling to me, and I feel nostalgic as I climb onto it and hug my knees to my chest, listening to the river rush past.

I could have died today. And, more concerning, I might still die today. Or tomorrow. The next day. I need Michael Realm to help me. I'm running out of time, and I don't know what to do.

There's a rumbling sound, and my stomach drops when a motorcycle pulls into the lot and parks next to my Jeep. I can see from here that it's Wes, and I'm not sure if it's a coincidence, or if he's looking for me. I left my phone in the car, so I have no idea if he tried to call. I have no idea if he's still mad at me for lying to him.

I shift on the boulder, letting my feet dangle over the side. I don't watch Wes's approach, but my heart has sped up since he arrived. He doesn't call out, and when he gets to the boulder, he sits down beside me without a single word.

I keep my breathing measured, afraid to ask him why he's here. When the silence goes on too long, I look sideways at him while he watches the river.

"I'm failing English, by the way," he says. He picks up a pebble from the boulder and tosses it into the water. "That's why I was reading in the library."

"Failing?" I ask, surprised. I don't know why he's telling me this, but Wes has always been an A student—the sort you resent because he rarely has to try.

SUZANNE YOUNG

"I guess when you miss a lot of school and get your memory erased, it's hard to catch up," he adds.

"I bet it is," I say, imagining my own work piling up. But it seems petty to worry about grades right now.

"Want to tutor me?" Wes suggests, and turns. His expression has softened since I saw him at school. I smile, and there's a twinge in my head at the movement. I rub the bump under my hair.

"I'm not really in a place to provide much help," I tell him honestly.

"Okay. How about you just talk to me, then?" he asks like it was his real intention. "I should have . . . I should have run after you at school. I was full of shit when I said I wouldn't chase you. I would. I *am*. But you hurt me, Tate. You may not have meant to, but you wrecked me."

He has no idea. Now that I know our complete history, it seems that's all I do.

"How did you know where I was?" I ask.

"I didn't. I was pissed off and riding around, thought the river seemed like a good idea. Then I saw you here, looking all sad. . . . Maybe I'm a little sorry for how I reacted earlier."

"You don't have to be."

He shrugs one shoulder. "Maybe I'm a lot sorry. It's entirely possible that I drove by your house and didn't see your Jeep. And then I went by Lulu's."

"You were looking for me," I say, my heart swelling.

"I was looking for you," he admits, nodding. His dimples

flash with his embarrassed smile, and it's the most endearing thing I've ever seen.

I am helplessly in love with him; it burns bright in my chest, electrifies my skin. I want him. I want us. And I want to tell the truth, finally.

"I broke up with you," I say, making him raise his eyebrows. "It was during the epidemic, and I wasn't right—I was paranoid, a little delusional. The Program made us scared, and somehow that fear blotted out everything. It blotted out you. And so I broke up with you. I'm the one who screwed up our relationship. I'm the reason you were sent to The Program."

Wes listens, his throat bobbing when he swallows. I explain the whole story about me telling him to see other people, how I changed my mind, how his mother called The Program on me. I tell him about his return the first time, and how much he loved me again. How desperate we were for each other. How I failed him.

"I make your life worse," I say, miserably. "That's what I've realized. You really are better off without me."

"Interesting," Wes says, and lowers his eyes to the boulder. "I mean, it's quite a story."

I'm confused by his response, and I'm not sure if I should keep talking or let him process it.

"So . . . ," he starts. "You feel bad because an unethical institution took advantage of people's fear and grief, poisoning society, and you reacted poorly. And then, when I returned, you couldn't keep your hands off of me. And I couldn't keep mine off of you. But that landed us in the Adjustment, which didn't work, and ended with me at your house, bleeding profusely from the head?"

I try not to smile, but Wes has a way of pointing things out that makes them sound ridiculous.

"You bled all over my front porch," I say.

"And what was I doing at your house again?" he asks. Heat warms my cheeks, and I avoid his gaze.

"You came there to tell me that you loved me. That that version of you loved me madly."

"And I kissed you?" he asks.

"We . . . definitely kissed," I reply.

"Sounds like more. Like I said, interesting."

I look up at him, trying to read his reaction. He's not angry, although he's probably a little overwhelmed. If nothing else, he seems to be enjoying this trip down relationship lane. Especially the kissing parts.

"Well, we have certainly been through a lot," he says. "I mean, that's not even mentioning how you totally lied to me, repeatedly, but okay."

I chew on my lip, and Wes takes his time, thinking things over.

"I have to admit," he says. "It feels good to be right."

I sniff a laugh and look at the river, the water rushing faster than it was earlier. "I'm sure it does," I say.

"I've asked you out before," he says. "Probably a few times. And I knew I'd kissed you before. In my bed the other night, it was like I could remember what your lips felt like. What you tasted like. I just . . . knew it. Even though you lied."

I close my eyes, regretting that he can continually apply that word to me.

"I'm encouraged, though," he adds. "This whole honesty thing you have going on, I think we'd be good at it. If . . . you want to try it out."

I look sideways at him, nervous. Defenseless. "Go for it," I say.

"Yeah?" he asks, smiling. "If I asked you if you wanted to kiss me right now, would you answer?"

My heart beats fast and hard. And I nod that I would.

"Do you want to kiss me right now?" he asks immediately. "Yes."

Wes licks his bottom lip, and I hold my breath, waiting for him to lean in. But instead, he grins. "Good. I'm glad I was right about that, too," he says. "Back to why I'm here, though . . ."

I sit there, sort of stunned, but also amused. I've missed him. I think he might love me again, more easily than before, and I wonder if it's muscle memory or because he's been reset. He doesn't have past experiences to base his behavior on. Wes is clear on what he wants, without the guilt of second-guessing what he *should* want. His intentions are pure.

I'm not entirely sure where this conversation leaves us, but it feels honest and I like it. We're full of possibility.

I reach to brush my hair back from my face, and accidentally graze the lump on the side of my head, wincing. It throbs, and I touch the spot of the swelling. Wes stops talking and furrows his brow.

"What's this?" he asks, reaching to move my hair gently aside. He leans in to inspect the area. "Shit, Tatum. What is this?"

He's close now, and when I meet his eyes, I nearly break apart—shattering to pieces in front of him. But I don't want to give Derek any more power over me. I have to be stronger.

"Tate," Wes whispers, truly concerned. "Who did this?"

"After I left the library," I say, trying to sound calm, "I was attacked by a handler. He hit me." My voice cracks. "He hit me and he dragged me across the floor, and . . . I was scared. I was terrified."

Wes's posture stiffens, but he listens silently as I tell him everything, every detail. I tell him about Melody bashing Derek with a fire extinguisher, thinking he was dead. Her telling me to act normal, even though more handlers will be looking for me soon. I tell him I need the cure to make this stop. I tell him I might get lobotomized.

Wes doesn't say anything, but he's shaking. And when I look at him, I see that his jaw is sharp, clenched, and his gaze darts around the park behind me.

"And Melody told you Derek was taken care of for now?" Wes asks. "He's not in a place where I can go have a chat with him?"

"He's gone," I say. "But there will be others. The most important thing right now is finding this other guy, and then—"

"Which guy?" Wes says. For a second, I think he's jealous, but his eyes narrow with realization. "Are you looking for Michael Realm?" he asks.

My heart dips, and I nod, surprised that he remembers his name. More surprised that he knows who I was looking for.

"How did you—?"

"About him," Wes interrupts. "You know how I was texting, asking to talk, and you kept ignoring me? And then I came here looking for you?"

"Uh, yeah," I say.

"That's who I wanted to talk about. If you're looking for him, I found him."

My breath catches. "What do you mean you found him?" I ask. "Where?"

"I found his records," he clarifies.

"You spied on him?" I ask.

"Kind of. Does it count if it was only over the Internet?"

"Yes." I smile, and Wes laughs, nodding that I'm probably right. "And what did you find out about him?"

Wes takes a deep breath and pulls his legs under him, turning to face me. I do the same, sitting cross-legged.

"The day you saw him following us," Wes begins, "and then told me not to worry about him"—he lifts his eyebrows, pointing out how ridiculous the request was—"I asked you his name. I went home and searched for him on social media to find out why he'd been following us. But there were no profiles. No accounts.

"Then," Wes continues, "I thought about your revelation that you were in The Program. Pretty big deal, right? So I went onto survivor sites, dozens of them, and read through their forums."

I love him. Just listening to him, calmly explaining how he tracked someone down to find out if he was dangerous makes me smile. It was stupid, an overreaction in most situations. But this time he was right to check. Just when I needed him.

"I kept notes," Wes says, holding up one finger. "And I looked for similarities in stories. These people had gone through The Program and survived it. I mean, I read thousands of posts. Some of them pretty dark. But then I found one who referenced a guy named Michael."

"It's a common name," I suggest.

"Yeah, but how many have a jagged pink scar across their neck?" he asks. "How many were in The Program?"

"Okay, good point."

"Yeah," Wes responds like I'm not getting it. "But then I found another post on a different forum. A girl who said she dated Michael in The Program and was hoping to find him to reconnect."

"He's fairly cute," I say, not getting why that's strange.

"Huh," Wes says like that's a fascinating observation, and then presses on. "There were several *Michael was my best friend*, and another *I dated Michael for three weeks*."

I scrunch up my nose. "Uh . . . he would have been busy," I say. "Where was I in these posts? Realm and I were in The

Program together. I . . . I was apparently friends with him."

Wes stares at me a long moment, his eyes intense. "That's the thing, Tate," he says. "Most people are only in The Program for six weeks. These posts were scattered over several years. Michael Realm was in The Program for *years*."

A sense of dread winds through me. "Years?" I ask. "How? Why?"

"I couldn't quite make sense of it at first," Wes says. "So I pulled up public notices, articles, anything that might mention his name. I joined three different Program support groups, and in there, I found a guy who knew him. He even posted a picture. He said Michael dropped by recently with an apology and his file to give back. Michael Realm was his handler. And, Tate . . . I think he was your handler. He wasn't *in* The Program. He was working for them."

The world drops out from under me. I call up the memory again, us in the leisure room. The way Realm looked at Derek. How he sensed that I could see through their act. And it was an act because he wasn't a patient. He was a handler. They were all handlers.

When I had coffee with Realm the other day, I confided in him about Wes, and he acted like he'd never heard it before. But if he was my handler, he knows my entire history, knows it better than I do. And if he was my handler . . . that means he helped erase me.

And yet, Melody was certain we'd been friends. Even I'm sort of certain of that, although I can't prove why. I'm not sure how to reconcile these two versions of Michael Realm. What else is missing?

"I have to find him," I tell Wes. "Find him in person. Can you help me?"

"You want me to take you to your handler?" he asks, doubtful.

"I think he's on my side," I say, mostly believing it. "I think he's on our side."

Wes watches me, the corner of his mouth flinching up. "Are you saying *we're* on the same side?" he asks, his voice lower.

"Yes," I say.

He smiles broadly and looks down as he reaches to take my hand, playing with my fingers nonchalantly. He was always openly affectionate, and I forgot what that was like. It makes me melt a little.

"We'll find your handler," Wes says, sliding his fingers between mine and then out again. "But then what do we do with him?"

"We take him to Marie Devoroux. She said if she could perfect her cure for crashbacks, get it to the free market, The Program would be decimated. No point in having a mind-controlling service people are immune to. The company would be destroyed. And so would all their shareholders, politicians, or whoever the fuck runs it."

"So . . . ," Wes says, tracing his finger over my wrist. "You're saying you want to take on the entire Program, including any doctors, handlers, or politicians who are working with them?" He lifts his eyes to mine.

I smile. "Sounds a little ambitious when you put it like that, but yeah—pretty much."

There's a distant boom of thunder, and Wes glances up at the sky. I do the same, noticing gray clouds have rolled in. The weather here changes so quickly, and it almost always ends in rain.

"Another storm," he says. "Want to come over?"

I laugh. "I guess it depends," I say. "Are you going to help me save the world or not?"

Wes stares at me a long moment, and then he takes my hand and squeezes it. "Tate," he says seriously. "I thought that was already a given."

CHAPTER FIVE

AS I FOLLOW BEHIND WES'S MOTORCYCLE IN MY Jeep, I put my phone on speaker and call home. My grandparents are understandably stunned that I'm with him, but when I tell my grandfather everything that Wes has learned, he's impressed.

"I didn't even think about checking with survivors' groups," he says, a little embarrassed. "Tell Wes if he's interested in becoming a reporter, to let me know." I smile, thinking about Wes and my grandfather working together, two supersleuths in a cramped newspaper office. Wes used to want to be a lawyer. I wonder what the new Wes wants to be.

"Nathan has been looking for you," Gram adds in the background. "He and Foster came by a little earlier. And when I told them about Derek, they left here in a rush."

I wish she hadn't done that. Even the mention of Derek makes my stomach sick, my heart pound faster.

He hurt me.

I blink quickly, clearing my thoughts. Nathan is probably murderous right now, and he's probably wondering what happened with Melody. I have to tell him what she said, that she really did love him. I have to tell him how she saved me.

"Thanks," I say. "I'll give him a call." I'm tired of relaying the story of Derek, reliving it, so I guess it's good that Gram got that part out there for me. I'll just have to fill in the details.

"Let us know the minute you find Michael Realm," Pop says.

"I will. Same to you."

He tells me that he loves me, and then I hang up just as I arrive at Wes's house.

I park in the driveway next to his bike, not bothering to hide my Jeep down the road like usual. I know all about our past, and frankly, now that Wes knows too, his mother's threats are useless. She can't bully me out of Wes's life.

I've made mistakes, not all of them completely my fault, but I can try not to make any more. I'm not sure where we stand relationship-wise, but we'll figure it out. We might even make the right decisions this time. For now, we just have to save the world. No pressure.

I quickly dial Nathan, but he doesn't answer, making me nervous. I tell him to call me back, and that I'm at Wes's house.

I push the phone into my pocket and climb out of the Jeep.

Wes waits for me at his door, smiling and looking a little nervous. I wonder if he thought I was going to turn onto the freeway and drive away instead of coming here. The thought didn't even cross my mind. I would have followed him anywhere.

"Parents aren't home," he says, watching my approach. "In case you were worried."

"Now you won't have to lock the door," I say, and stop in front of him.

Wes's smile fades. "I always lock the door," he replies, and turns to push inside his basement apartment.

I realize that I'm nervous too. Beyond the life-altering shit that's about to go down with The Program—I'm here with Wes. And I'm still not entirely sure how to act.

I understand what Michael Realm meant now, how remembering can be a curse. Because I remember things that Wes doesn't. I remember how much he loved me. How much I loved him. The stuff they couldn't take. The stuff that crashed back. So much history, and now it's only mine.

I walk inside his room and close the door behind me. It's dimly lit, the high-set window not enough on a darkened, stormy day. But Wes doesn't flip on the lights as he leads us into the living room area.

I sit on the couch, and Wes comes to the coffee table and turns his laptop in my direction before telling me he'll be right back. He jogs up the stairs and disappears inside his house.

I smile at the wallpaper on his computer, a vintage motor-cycle, mid-repair. It's simple, honest. I click open the browser, and his last page pulls up. It's a board called Survivor Rate, and the quick description says it's a forum for survivors of the epidemic. It has over ten thousand members.

I click on the first thread and start to read through, when I hear Wes close the door and lock it before bounding down the stairs. I look up, and he holds out a bag of frozen peas.

"For your head," he says. "I tried to find an aspirin, but my mom won't keep any pills in the house."

"Oh," I say, taking the icy bag from him. "Thank you." It's kind of sweet of him to do that without me asking. I move my legs aside as he scoots past me and drops down onto the couch in his usual spot. I gently press the peas to my head, groaning at the pressure.

"This is the one," Wes starts, turning the screen so he can see it too, "where the guy had the picture of Michael."

"He goes by Realm," I say, and feel Wes turn to me. I point at the screen to move forward. "Can I see the picture?"

"Sure," Wes replies, and clicks into a different thread, scrolling through posts. He double-clicks one. "Here you go. That's him, right?"

And it is. There's a picture of Realm, not looking at the camera. He's partially turned away, his scar prominent on his neck. He doesn't seem to know his picture is being taken, and I'm reminded of Melody and how she never wanted to be in any photos. She always found an excuse. It was probably

324   SUZANNE YOUNG

because she was a handler, a closer, and she didn't want to be recognized. She didn't want a record of being Jana Simms.

"That's definitely him," I say. Under the picture, the post reads: *Anyone know this guy?*

Wes goes into the private messages and shows me his exchange with the original poster. It doesn't give us any information on locating Realm, so we eventually click out and scan the boards again.

There's a notebook, and Wes grabs it and flips back a few pages, reading through some of the information he copied down. I watch him, completely warmed by his dedication to figuring this all out. Knowing that he'd done it while I was ignoring him.

"It was hard for me to lie to you," I admit as he reads over a page. He looks sideways at me, setting the notebook down. "It broke my heart," I add.

"Then you should have told the truth," he says. "You could have done that all along."

"I wanted you to be happy," I say. "And I didn't think you could be with me." Wes holds my gaze and then sits back against the couch.

"Don't I get to decide what makes me happy?" he asks.

I shrug. "If I really loved you, wouldn't I make sure you were happy?"

Wes scrunches up his face, like he doesn't buy that theory. "As a point of reference," he says, "aren't we here, now, to fight back against an entity who claims exactly that? They're making decisions for us, claiming it's in our best interest. Why are they deciding what our interests are? Why did you think you could decide mine?"

"Our track record's not great," I say, although I get his point about The Program. How making a relationship decision without his input may not have been entirely fair—not when I still loved him.

"You told me all about it, remember?" Wes says, smiling with those adorable dimples. "We sound awful," he adds. "We sound young. But other than nearly dying, the second time didn't seem so bad."

I laugh, enjoying his take on the situation. "It wasn't awesome, either, although it had its moments."

"Seems like our thing," he says. "Bad timing."

I loop my arm behind the sofa and set the bag of frozen peas on the cushion. "What do you mean?"

"First round, we had the epidemic, you breaking up with me. Me trying to move on halfheartedly. And then the second time, you loved me first, and when I came around, you decided it was wrong. My head exploded, and boom—we're up to round three."

"I mean, it didn't *explode*," I say.

"Do you want my thoughts on all of this?" he asks. "My final thoughts?"

I shake my leg, nervous. "Yes," I reply, bracing myself for what he's about to say.

"Whatever went wrong between us," he starts, "I'm sorry.

No matter who was at fault, if anyone. And I can't promise it won't happen again. But I'm not going to move on this time." He smiles, kind of miserable. A bit stubborn.

"I think about you all the time, Tate," he continues. "I worry about you. I want to live this life." He motions between us. "And I hope I'm not being too much right now if I say I'm *wild* about you. Have been since you came to rescue me in the monitor's office. Since I saw you in class. I *knew* you"—he puts his hand over his heart—"even if I didn't know you.

"Now, I don't want to talk about the past anymore," he continues, "or fights we've had, or my mother. Can we do that? Because I think I love you. And I want to save the world with you. So . . . I don't know, can we stop ruining each other's lives and just love each other at the same time?"

I stare at him, my heart swelling to the point of bursting. It's everything I love about him, his pure way of looking at things. Even the faults. He sighs loudly, waiting for me to respond, and I smile.

"Why did you have to bring your mother into this?" I ask.

Wes coughs out a laugh, clearly relieved. "That was terrible of me," he says. "But I'm guessing you're cool with the other parts?"

I nod that I am, and he nods back like it's finalized. We're loving each other, concurrently. It's settled.

Wes turns to the computer, clicking through posts until he gets frustrated and tries another forum. I watch him, finding the first bit of true contentment I've had in a while. I'm almost dreamy, setting aside the shambles of my life as I study him, noticing his dimples first, the way they're always there even when he's not smiling. The way he licks his lips. The fast clicking of his fingers on the keys.

And the second he turns to me, noticing that I'm staring, I lean over and kiss him.

He's not surprised, not hesitant. Instead, his hand rests on the back of my neck, his lips moving against mine urgently, claiming me. Both of us gasp through our kisses, tongues intertwining. My head spins, and I move to my knees to get closer to him, knocking the bag of peas onto the carpet. Wes moans softly as he pulls me down on top of him, his other hand on my hip.

I straddle him on the couch, breaking the kiss to gaze down at him for a moment. Admire him as my heart races riotously. Wes's eyes are glassy, his lips part as he smiles. He reaches for the bottom of my shirt, tugging me into another kiss, wrapping his arms around me. He devours me, and it's not like before. He doesn't kiss the same; he's not touching me the same. This is all new.

Wes's mouth is on my neck, his teeth grazing my skin, and I whisper his name, knotting my fingers in his hair.

"You're so beautiful," he murmurs on my skin, our bodies moving against each other. "Fucking perfect."

I'm half out of my mind as I yank off his shirt and then mine, and we crash back together. If we're going to the break the rules by dating, we might as well break them all. His hand slides past my hip and between my thighs, and I melt against him. We're kissing and smiling and about to get very naked, when there is a sharp knock at his basement door.

I sit up, my eyes blurry as I look in the direction of his room. Wes groans and drops his head back against the cushions.

"Seriously?" he says out loud. I move to the other side of the couch, my body still tingling. I pull my shirt back on, and Wes stands up, grabbing his from the floor and carrying it with him to the door.

He looks back over his shoulder at me, as if to say he doesn't *have* to open the door. I motion for him to do it anyway. He exhales and opens it, resting on the door frame, blocking my view. I sit up straighter, waiting to see who it is.

"Tate," Wes calls back. "It's for you."

CHAPTER SIX

MY HEART LEAPS INTO MY THROAT, AND I QUICKLY jump up, smoothing my hair and avoiding the spot that still hurts. Wes pushes the door open all the way, and I breathe out a sigh of relief when I see it's Nathan. Standing behind him, Foster waves to me, mouthing hello.

Nathan flashes a disappointed look at Wes, who's still shirt-less, and walks past him into the basement.

Foster takes his time, chatting with Wes at the door to introduce himself, and then they both come into the living room. Foster heads in my direction and slyly holds his hand in a low five behind his back for me to slap. I do so with a laugh, and he takes a seat on the arm of the sofa.

"Sorry to interrupt," Nathan says flatly. "But I thought I should follow up on the 'attacked by handlers' situation." He looks from me to Wes. "Who would like to start?"

Wes grins, amused by Nathan's attitude. He comes to stand next to me, still not wearing his damn shirt, and I falter a bit in my explanation.

"We should sit down," I tell Nathan, motioning to the card table on the other side of the room. "It's kind of a long story."

Begrudgingly, Nathan makes his way to a seat, and Foster and I join him. Wes pulls on his T-shirt and flashes me a private smile before taking out his phone.

"I'm ordering a pizza," he says. "Before the storm gets too bad. Everyone good with pineapple?"

"Absolutely not," Nathan says immediately. Foster laughs and says he's fine with whatever.

Wes gives us space, going into his bedroom to call in the pizza, and when he's gone, Nathan stretches his arms out on the table in front of him and collapses on them dramatically. "Do I even want to know what's going here?" he asks.

"I do," Foster says encouragingly.

"I wish this was the height of my problems," I say, drawing Nathan's gaze. "I know Gram told you some of what happened today, but . . ." I shake my head as the fear crawls back in. My temporary distraction with Wes is gone, and my body begins to ache with the truth of my reality.

"The Program is coming for me," I say in a quiet voice. "It almost got me."

Nathan's expression hardens, and he reaches to pull me into a hug. When he accidentally touches my head, I wince. He gets to see the damage firsthand, and his body is tense as he listens to the details my gram left out.

I tell him about Melody saving me, her bravery. "She was different, Nathan," I say, smiling softly even as his jaw tightens. "I got to see the real her. I think you'd like this version. She's kind of badass."

"I guess I'll never know," he says, avoiding my eyes.

"She wanted me to tell you that she loved you," I add a little quieter. "She wanted you to know that part was real."

Nathan flinches, swaying slightly like he's pained by the words. Foster pushes back in his chair and comes to wrap his arms around Nathan from behind. He tells him he's a good dude, and the three of us sit together, acknowledging that Nathan got pretty screwed over in this deal. It's hard to see all the moving parts sometimes, smaller tragedies pushed aside for bigger ones. I hate that Nathan got hurt.

But Nathan doesn't break down. He pats Foster's arm to let him know he's okay. He sniffs once, regaining his composure, and then he faces me with a new determination.

"How do we end them?" he asks. "How do we beat The Program?"

"I have an idea," Wes says, coming back into the room. We all look up at him, and he's so . . . cool about everything. Like none of this surprises him. It makes Foster grin, and I understand that feeling. It's unusual to know someone without baggage. It's refreshing, honestly.

Wes grabs a chair and turns it around to sit backward on it.

He sets his phone on the table in front of him. "In my research," he says, diving into the conversation, "I saw that Realm went to Corvallis quite a bit. There was a passing mention of someone named Anna Realm. What if I track her down?"

"Who is she?" I ask. "His mother?"

"I don't know," Wes replies. "I didn't think much of it at first, especially since it was only a quick mention. But now I'm thinking this guy Realm knows how to stay off the radar. Is his whole family like that? Maybe, or maybe they're like, fucking accountants—just living their lives while he runs around stirring up shit."

Nathan laughs and covers his mouth. Wes picks up his phone to scroll through the Internet. "Just a thought I had."

"It's a good thought," I say, earning a smile.

Wes goes to grab his laptop, and when he returns, I tell Nathan and Foster everything else I can think of about today, everything we learned. Even the part about being friends with Realm. I leave out the stuff about me and Wes since we're at his house and that would be weird. At least, I thought it would be.

"I'm assuming we were all friends before?" Wes asks Nathan and Foster. They're a little thrown by the question and exchange a look.

"It's okay," I say to them. "Dr. McKee was full of shit. I told Wes everything, and his head didn't explode this time."

Wes is impressed by my joke and clicks into a forum on the web page.

"Yep," Nathan says. "I mean, not super-close friends." He

looks sideways at me because he and Wes had a strained relationship. Not jealousy in a romantic way, but in a "competing for my time" way.

"We used to play basketball," Foster adds. "You were better than me." Wes nods, liking this detail. Foster goes to stand behind Wes and watches him navigate the forums.

If The Program didn't exist anymore, this would be the beginning of our normal. All of us together, ready to move on with our lives. Of course, that's not what's happening. Sadly, I'm not sure it'll ever happen. Tomorrow, I could be rotting in a hospital somewhere, instruments stabbing my brain.

I shiver, and Wes glances up at me with a quick flinch of concern.

"Right there," Foster says, pointing to a post on the screen. Wes lowers his eyes to read it, and then clicks the preview to dive in further.

"I think this is it," he says, smiling at Foster. He pokes the keys of the computer before turning it so Nathan and I can see. "It's a phone number from Corvallis," he says, "registered to Anna Realm. No address."

"But here's the weird thing," Foster adds. "The area code is for Springfield, pretty close to the Program facility there. It's one of three lines she has. Why would she need three phone lines?"

"Other kids?" I suggest.

"Anna's not his mom," Wes says. He leans forward to tap a few keys and comes up with a picture of a pretty blonde with a passing resemblance to Realm. "Sister, I'm guessing. No mention of parents anywhere, so they're either out of the picture or dead."

We grow quiet at that suggestion, the sadness at the possibility of Realm's parents both being deceased. I take out my phone.

"Well," I say. "One way to find out."

"Tatum," Nathan warns. "Are you—"

"I don't have time, Nathan," I say turning to him. "I need Realm. Marie needs him, and that means so do I."

Nathan chews on the inside of his lip and then nods for me to go ahead, looking anxious. Foster drops back into his chair, and I dial. I set the phone on speaker and place it in the center of the table.

The line rings, and we all exchange nervous glances. The sound echoes around the room, and I start to shake my leg under the table.

The phone rings four times, and when it clicks, I assume it's voice mail and my heart dips. But instead, Realm says, "Hi, Tatum."

I cover my mouth, stunned by the sound of his voice. The deep familiarity there. Affirmation that he still exists. Wes stares at me, wide-eyed.

"Realm," I say, slightly out of breath. Nathan leans his elbows on the table, listening closely. "I . . . I need to talk to you. I have to see you."

He coughs once, but when he talks, I think I hear a smile in his voice. "I figured," he says. "I'm not in town right now. Can we meet tomorrow?"

"I don't have much time," I tell him shakily. "The Program has flagged me."

"I know," he says. "But you'll be okay until then. Just . . . lay low. They can't find Derek, so they have no idea that he got to you. As far as they're concerned, he could have fled; they're having a high rate of handlers disappearing. Happened before with closers, so they're not alarmed. Not to mention I put it out there that Derek was somewhere in California."

There is a prickle over my skin, a bit of awe, but also annoyance. He really does seem to be dialed in, but if that's the case . . . "You let him try to take me?" I ask, betrayed. "You knew he was coming."

Realm is silent for a moment, and under the table, Nathan puts his hand on my knee to steady my leg. I look sideways at him, and he presses his lips into a sad smile. I'm hurt that Realm could have stopped this and he didn't. I mean, what the fuck, right?

"I couldn't get there in time," Realm says, coughing again. "I got the word out, though. They would have never gotten you out of that school. We still have people on our side, Tatum. Now . . . we have a lot to talk about. And I mean that sincerely."

"We sure do," I say, my voice darker. I'm angry with him. I don't care what side he's on because he failed me. "When?" I ask.

"Tomorrow morning," he says, his voice scratchy. "There's a café outside of town. I'll text you the address."

"She won't be alone," Wes says, and then flashes his teeth at me in apology for speaking up.

Realm laughs softly. "I didn't think she would be. Now, whoever else is there," Realm says. "I'm guessing Nathan?"

"And Foster," Nathan says.

"Okay, good," Realm responds. "It's important to keep up appearances. I know that sounds impossible, but I need to know who the other handlers are. Melody hadn't figured it all out yet."

Nathan shifts next to me, his hands balling into fists on the table.

"Tatum won't be at school tomorrow, so I need the two of you to keep your eyes out. Who asks about her? Who leaves early? We . . ." He gets quiet for a minute, the line covered. "Avoid the monitor," he says after a moment.

Nathan looks ready to argue, but I think Realm is right. There's no sense in all of us going to meet him. Besides, I want to know who the other handlers are too. I need to know who to watch out for.

"You should know that Marie is looking for you," I warn Realm.

"No doubt," he replies. "I'd hoped to avoid her, but it seems inevitable now."

"Why?" I ask, furrowing my brow.

"Another conversation," he says, and pauses. And then his mouth is close to the receiver when he murmurs, "I'm sorry this is happening to you, Tatum. I truly did try to fix it."

His words are suddenly intimate, and I lean into the table, exposed by Realm's tone. The tenderness back in my heart.

"We really were friends," I say, like it's just us in the room. "We were good friends, weren't we?"

"Yeah, sweetness," he replies, sounding relieved. "We really were."

I fall quiet and dart a look at Wes. He shrugs one shoulder and rolls his gaze away.

"And I won't let them hurt you anymore," Realm adds. "Do you believe that?"

"I believe you'll try," I say honestly. Knowing that he doesn't have that power. "I'll see you tomorrow."

"Be careful," he replies.

And then Michael Realm hangs up, and I click off my phone.

The four of us sit silently for a moment in Wes's basement, staring at the phone in the middle of the table. It's Foster who talks first.

"So he's full of shit, yeah?" he asks, waiting for consensus.

"Definitely," Wes says immediately.

"Pretty much," Nathan agrees with a nod.

When I look around at them, Foster smiles at me first. "So I guess I'm stuck doing our lab report tomorrow?" he says.

"We're going to school?" Nathan asks him seriously.

"We have to," Foster replies. "I have an idea of who the handlers might be. I've actually been paying attention. I want them exposed, and you need to keep an eye on the monitor. Field any questions about Tatum."

"You just want to keep an eye on your boyfriend," Nathan says under his breath.

"That too," Foster says, and grins.

Wes's phone buzzes, and he glances at it before smiling. "Pizza's here," he says, going to grab his wallet. He starts for his bedroom but then stops dramatically to look back at us.

"I meant to tell you," Wes tells us. "I ended up getting pine-apple."

Nathan stares at him and then shakes his head. "This is why I fucking hated you."

And after a long pause, we all laugh.

CHAPTER SEVEN

WES WAS ONLY KIDDING. THE PIZZA HAD PEPPERONI on one half, sausage on the other. We all eat together, and I watch them quietly as they continue to joke around. Trying to keep this all manageable by not falling completely into it. It's a coping strategy we learned during The Program. Sometimes it was the only way to survive. But I don't want to play this way anymore. I just want to fucking win.

A buzz snaps throughout the room, and the electricity flickers. Wes looks around, and then stands up and goes over to the high windows, getting on his toes to check outside.

"Storm's getting worse," he says.

"Yeah, I have to get home," Foster says, getting up from the table. Nathan does the same, but I stay put.

"You coming?" Nathan asks me.

I glance behind me at Wes, and he smiles hopefully. I laugh. "No, I'm going to stay awhile," I say.

Nathan runs his palm down his face and then shakes it off. "Fine," he says. "Call your grandparents, though. And if anything else happens"—he leans down to give me a quick hug good-bye—"call me *yourself*."

I tell him that I will. I say good-bye to Foster and wait at the table while Wes walks them both out. My phone lights up, and when I check, I see that Realm sent me the address for a diner. I hate having to wait until the morning, but he said I'd be okay until then. I have to trust that he's right. What's the alternative?

Wes comes back into the room, his brown eyes lit up with concern. "It's pretty bad outside," he says. "If you wanted to be responsible . . ." He doesn't finish his sentence, extending the same invitation he gave me the other night.

"I'll stay," I say, sitting back in the chair. "If you don't mind."

He purses his lips as if thinking over whether he'll mind. "I think it's a mature decision," he says.

"Me too."

"Should I get the sleeping bag ready?" he asks, making me laugh.

"No," I say. "We can share that stupidly comfortable bed of yours."

"It's the worst," he says like he agrees. "I'm sure we can make it work, though." He smiles, and comes over to grab his laptop from the table. He heads to the couch and motions me over.

"I will, let me just call my grandparents first."

I take my phone into his room and sit at the end of his bed. I call home and talk to my grandfather. I relay the conversation with Realm and text the address where I'll be meeting him. I let him know I'm spending the night at Wes's, and although he doesn't love it, he doesn't order me home, either. Gram asks about my head, and if I'm honest, it still hurts. But I tell her it's not too bad.

"Call us before you leave in the morning," Pop says. "And if you want me there . . ."

"I'll let you know," I say. "But don't worry, I'll be careful."

"Okay, honey. Talk to you in the morning."

I hang up and set the phone next to me, taking a deep breath. Wes appears in the doorway and leans against the frame.

"How'd it go?" he asks.

"Fine. Pop will come with us if we need him."

Wes nods. "I hope we don't. Less people involved, the better—or so it seems to me," he adds, admitting he doesn't know the full extent of this threat. He comes over to the bed, stopping in front of me. I lean back on my arms, staring up at him. He smiles softly.

"Want to help me forget for a little while?" I say in pretend seduction, running my socked foot over his calf. He laughs.

"Uh, yes." He moves in closer, lifting my ankle to tip me backward. He slides his knee against my inner thigh and climbs onto the bed, holding himself above me before slowly lowering into a kiss.

I put my hand on his cheek, and then we move up on the bed until we have pillows. Wes collapses next to me, taking my leg to pull over his hip, and we turn into each other, occasionally kissing, mostly just cuddling.

And I feel safe with him. The other images still haunt me, but here with him . . . it's up to me. I'm powerful. I'm in love.

I listen as Wes talks about motorcycles, about music, about movies. Whenever he asks me a question, I'm quick to ask a follow-up, enamored with how calm his thoughts are. The peace in him. I kiss him constantly then, and we're sweet together, free-spirited in a lazy way. Like we have time.

But time is only an illusion. Sometimes, in the midst of a disaster, you have to take a moment to breathe, or you'll run out of oxygen. Wes and I breathe each other.

And as the afternoon fades into evening, we fall asleep together—letting the storm rage around us.

There's an insistent knocking. I think it's only in my dream, but then it gets louder. Wes moves first, moaning softly before pulling me closer and burying his face in my neck like he can block out the sound.

"Weston," a voice calls, shrill and angry. The knocking becomes banging.

My eyes open, and I stare up at the ceiling. "Well, fuck," I murmur.

"Probably not *now*," Wes says, and I snort a laugh.

We sit up, and I quickly get out of his bed, smooth his

sheets, and reset the pillows. I slip on my shoes, and go to stand in the doorway to the living room, poised there to give Wes's mom the chance to adjust to my presence.

"Weston?" she calls again, and the wind howls against the windows.

I'd be lying if I didn't admit that I'm terrified of Dorothy Ambrose. She doesn't deserve all the blame in making me feel that way, but for the past year, she has been more than a thorn in my side. She has eroded my confidence, made me question my self-worth on every basic level. She's managed to make me feel like the lowest person on the planet, and although I know she did it to protect her son, I have to wonder if that excuses the fact that she's been awful to me.

I want to forgive her, though. Not for her, but for me. It doesn't mean I'm not scared of her. I wrap my arms around myself and nod for Wes to open the door. He waits a beat, watching me. Although I've told him everything, he didn't see any of the exchanges first-hand. My expression must give away my fear, because his softness fades, and he strands straighter as he pulls open the door.

"Yes, Mother?" he asks. She scoffs, and her hand darts out to grab the edge of the door to push it open wider.

"Where—?" She stops dead when she sees me. Her hair is wet with rain, and the storm crackles behind her. She looks deranged, her own storm as she bounds into the room. Wes closes the door but waits there like he's hoping she'll walk right back out.

"How dare you?" Dorothy says to me with contempt. "How fucking dare you?"

I flinch back, surprised she'd swear at me, and I quickly lower my eyes, my bravery stumbling. Maybe I should have hidden my Jeep up the road.

"Hey," Wes says immediately. "Don't talk to her like that."

"Stay out of this, Weston," his mother says, not looking back at him. Wes laughs bitterly.

"Yeah, I think not," he says. "She told me everything, Mom."

Dorothy's eyes widen into saucers, and she spins quickly, rushing over to him and putting her hand on his cheek, his upper arm. He shrugs her off and takes a step back.

"Are you okay?" she asks, frantic with worry.

"It wasn't true," I announce, finding my voice. "What Dr. McKee said about the truth hurting him—it was a lie meant to protect me."

Dorothy looks at me, and I shrink back. She intimidates me, which I guess is her point. I consider leaving, but that would mean walking past her. So instead, I try to make myself as small as possible.

"You called The Program on her," Wes says to his mother, his voice thick with betrayal. "You could have called her grandparents and got her help, but instead you called The Program. Instead you did the worst thing possible."

Dorothy looks at him, shaking her head that it's not true. "The Program was the only answer," she says. "And you can't take her word for it." She motions to me. "You didn't see how erratic she was acting."

"But I did see," he says. "I must have known what was

happening to her, but I didn't help her either, not in any real way. When it came down to it, though, I didn't want her in The Program. I wouldn't have fucking erased her. I wouldn't have stolen her life. I would have saved her."

Dorothy tightens her jaw, the first indication that she knew full well the impact of her action. "You don't understand what those times were like," she says. "She was out of control, Wes."

"Like I said, why didn't you call her grandparents, then? Why was your first call to The Program?"

Dorothy stands perfectly still for a moment, and I realize that I want to know that answer too. She could have called my pop—he would have gotten me help. It all could have gone down differently. But he never got the chance.

I hold my breath, waiting for her response.

"Because I wanted her out of your life," Dorothy says with finality. "And I didn't want her to come back."

I put my hand to my chest, a sudden pain striking me. It is the cruelest thing she's said about me yet. She knew what she was doing. She knew what The Program would do to me. She used it to break up a relationship, not because she was worried—but because she wanted me gone. A literal character assassination.

My eyes well up, and when I blink, tears drip onto my cheeks. I've never felt weaker, the idea that an adult I trusted could hate me so completely. I sniffle, and tears keep flowing.

"Why?" I choke out, and she turns her head slightly, not daring to look at me.

"Because Wes deserved better than you," she says. "He

deserved someone from a good family, someone who made him a better person. And that wasn't you, Tatum. All you would have done was take him away."

I sway, hurt. I had no idea her contempt went so deep. I'm in shock, but Wes is breathing heavily, his face going red.

"I hated you," Wes says to his mother with sudden realization. "I hated you, didn't I?"

Dorothy watches him like she's waiting for him to calm down before she answers. She must decide that's not going to happen, because she starts talking.

"After your sister died," she says, "you retreated down here. I guess we all retreated into our own places of misery. But the Wes I knew died in that river too. You weren't the same without Cheyenne. And then you met Tatum, and together, you began to slip away—just like your sister did. I knew it was only a matter of time. Both of my kids would be gone. I had to stop it, but you wouldn't listen.

"And don't you see now?" she continues, looking from him to me. "I was right. Tatum broke your heart just like I thought she would, and then she came here to ruin your new relationship. I got to her first. I only wish it could've been permanent."

Holy shit.

I know that Wes wasn't the only one destroyed by Cheyenne's suicide—his entire family had been devastated. As a parent, Dorothy's loss is immeasurable, and all this time, she's been slowly spiraling. Digging into her pain. Trying to protect her last child. But that grief has brought her to the brink of insanity.

She wished she had killed me. I think she might still wish it.

"You're not well," I say, wiping my cheeks. "Dorothy, you need serious help."

I'm braver now because I realize this wasn't about me. This was always about her holding on to her only living child. And although that's sad, it's also completely fucked.

Dorothy smiles ruefully. "No, honey," she says coldly. "I need you out of our lives."

The door suddenly opens, and with a gasp of wind, two men rush inside. Wes quickly drops his arms to spin to face them, but it's clear they have a mission. Without hesitation one of them comes for me. Dorothy steps aside.

They're handlers, I realize, and I dart into the living room, bounding up the stairs. I don't make it. One of the men grabs my foot, and I slip, banging my knee painfully on the stairs. I reach to hold on to the stair above me, but he drags me down the steps, my elbows getting carpet burn, my body bumping jarringly at each stair.

"No!" I scream, trying to turn over, but he's got my feet, and pulls me to the basement floor. He flips me over, and I'm able to look up, stunned when I recognize him.

The handler has a scar across his cheek, thick and white with little lines running through it. He's the same man who took me from my house and brought me to The Program.

I kick him hard in the thigh, and he loses his grip. I get up, trying to rush past him, running for the bedroom and the door to the outside. Wes is pinned against the wall, his arm behind his back at an impossible angle as he tries to fight. Dorothy, concerned, watches it unfold.

She widens her eyes when she sees me run into the room, but then I'm tackled from behind and fall onto the bed. I scream, scream as loud as I can, and Dorothy flinches against the sound. Wes goes wild, and just as he breaks free from the handler, there is a pop and he howls out in pain, his arm dangling at his side. The handler takes a step back and looks at Dorothy.

"Get her out of here!" she yells, pointing to me.

But I'm still kicking, not letting the handler get close enough to grab me. I don't understand how this happened, how we got here. Wes, injured, sees the second handler start toward me. He grabs the lamp with his left arm, ripping it from the wall, and bashes it over the guy's back. The handler stumbles, falling into Wes and knocking him against the desk, both of them hitting the floor.

Undeterred, the handler with the scar punches my shin to get my leg down, making me cry out, and then scrambles on top of me, holding me on the bed. I thrash, ready to bite his fucking ear off.

"What are you doing?" I beg Dorothy. "Stop this!"

"You're a threat to my family," Dorothy says authoritatively. "And Dr. Warren contacted me and told me all about how you slept here the other night. How you did exactly what I told you not to. She said you'd bring Wes down, and I told her I already knew that. Dr. Warren promised to collect you earlier,

THE COMPLICATION   349

so imagine my surprise to see your Jeep in my driveway. I called her. You left me no choice, Tatum."

She is completely unhinged. The handler tries to lock my legs with his, but the intimate touch makes me go berserk. I free myself enough to bring my knee between his, nailing him in the balls as hard as I can. He coughs and falls to the side, gripping them.

I push him off the bed and dash for the door.

"If you don't cooperate, she will take Wes!" Dorothy screams.

"You fucking idiot!" I scream back. "They're going to take him anyway!" I stop to help Wes up from the floor. He's gone ghostly pale, holding his arm to his side. He looks like he's about to throw up.

We don't wait for her to consider my words. I grab Wes's wallet off the dresser, along with my keys. Both handlers are on the floor, trying to get back to their feet.

Wes looks at his mom one last time, and I think she suddenly realizes how badly he's been injured.

"Weston," she says softly, and I swear, I think Wes is about to break down. The look of betrayal on his face is absolutely devastating.

I put my hand on the back of his neck, letting him know we have to go. And then Wes and I escape outside into the storm. We get in my Jeep and flee the scene.

CHAPTER EIGHT

I'M SHAKING, COLD FROM THE RAIN ON MY SKIN and terrified by the fact that they almost got me again. Grabbed me. Hurt me.

I'll never escape—that defeatist thought tries to work its way into my brain, the same thought that landed me in The Program. But I beat it back. I won't let it take me. I'm stronger now.

I glance over at Wes in the passenger seat. He's sunken down, shivering against the chill, holding his arm gingerly. His breathing is stilted, and I know he's trying not to let on how much pain he's in.

"Fuck," I say under my breath, clicking up the speed on the windshield wipers. I repeat the curse, knowing it's not going to help, but needing the outlet.

"Where are we going?" Wes asks after a minute, his voice

gravelly. I turn to him again, worried. I grab my phone and call home.

"Gram," I say, when she gets on the line. "I need your help. Wes is hurt. Can you meet us at the hospital?"

"What's going on?" she asks, sounding terrified.

"I can't explain now," I say. "But whatever you do, do not talk to Dorothy Ambrose. She's working with Dr. Warren. Wes got injured, but we can't be seen in public. Can you help us?"

"Of course," she says. "But should I call—"

"Don't call anyone," I tell her. "Just meet us at the hospital."

"We're on our way, honey," she says. She hangs up, and I click off the phone, glancing up just in time to see I've caught a red light. I have to press on the brakes pretty hard, and both Wes and I shoot forward.

He groans in agony and falls back against the seat, his eyes squeezed shut.

"I'm sorry," I say. "What can I do?"

"Shh . . . ," he says, and then smiles a little. "Can't talk," he adds, keeping his eyes closed. He's trying to concentrate on holding in the pain. He told me once that when he worked out, he was always really quiet to help keep his focus, concentrate his energy. That must be what he's doing now.

"You stay quiet," I say. "I'm going to keep talking. What are we going to do?" I ask rhetorically. "We can't wait until tomorrow. Dr. Warren must know that I'm onto her. They're coming for me—us, now."

Wes's mom might think to look for us at the hospital, so we'll have to be careful. I grab my phone just as the light turns green, and I quickly dial Realm as I drive toward the hospital. The line rings, and I start talking the minute it's answered.

"Won't make it until tomorrow," I say into the phone. "They found me at Wes's with the help of his mother. Guess they're not worried about drawing attention anymore, huh?"

"They're desperate," Realm says, his voice low. "I'm en route now," he says. "I can meet you in about two hours. The diner I sent the address for is open all night, so it'll still work."

"Why were you already on your way?" I ask.

"Because I thought I was coming to rescue you from Dr. Warren. I'm glad you got out of there. I assume Wes is with you?"

"How did—"

"I had no warning," he says as if heading off my accusation. "Just got a call from a friend right now who said handlers were at Wes's house. I put the rest together, and like I said, I was coming to save you."

"Yeah, well," I say. "I saved myself already. I'm sure you'll get another chance, though."

Realm laughs to himself. "I'll see you in a couple of hours, Tatum," he says. We hang up, and I drop the phone into the cup holder, leaning forward to see out the windshield. My wipers can't quite keep up with the rainfall.

"So I get to meet Michael Realm tonight?" Wes asks, his eyes still closed.

"Apparently," I say.

"Good."

I look over at him, trying to guess the meaning in that simple word. But I'm not sure what's going on in Wes's head, not anymore. And when he opens one eye to peek over at me, I laugh and turn back to the road.

"I'm sorry you got hurt," I tell him, wishing I could reach over and touch him, but worried it'll make him worse if I do.

"Thanks," he says. "And I'm sorry my mother's a maniac who's essentially trying to kill you."

"Right?" I say, looking sideways. "Didn't expect that." We both smile and I focus on the road, and speed us toward the hospital.

My grandmother is waiting for us under the cover of the awning at the back of the hospital. It's the outpatient center, usually locked at night. We park, and after we get out, Pop is quick to jump into the driver's seat.

"I'm in the first spot," he says, motioning to the parking lot. "We're switching cars for now."

"Good idea," I tell him. He hands me his keys and then takes the Jeep around to the other side of the building.

My grandmother and I get Wes into the hospital, and my grandmother has a nurse waiting for us, a woman she's known for a long time. Nurse Belmont is sweet—I sometimes see her when I need a quick appointment. The bonus of having a guardian who's the hospital administrator.

We go into the triage room, and after a quick exam, she tells Wes that she thinks he's separated his shoulder. She doesn't even ask how it happened. The swelling has already begun, so she's unable to see the extent of the damage. He'll have to let it settle for a few days.

As Wes sits on the table with his shirt off, his hair wet, I realize that he's barefoot. On top of that, his shoulder is lower on the right side, drooped down at a significant angle. It's turning blue, a bruise spreading quickly.

"I'm going to wrap up the shoulder and give you a sling," Nurse Belmont says. "You okay with shots?" She rolls her stool over to a drawer and takes out a syringe.

Wes's teeth chatter, and I think he might be in shock. I walk over to him and lean my cheek against his temple, rubbing his back. His skin is freezing cold.

"I love shots," he says, miserable, and Nurse Belmont laughs.

My grandmother paces the room nervously, and I'm glad she was able to help us. Wes wouldn't have gotten far without some kind of assistance tonight. As it is, I still have a terrible pain in my head, a new one in my leg. We're getting our asses kicked over here.

"Tatum," my grandmother says gently. "Can we talk?"

"Yeah," I say, and tell Wes I'll be right back. He reaches for me first, wincing, and murmurs something about giving him a kiss. It's so pathetic in the most adorable way, so of course, I lean in and do just that. I really hope Nurse Belmont gives him some good drugs for the pain.

My gram leads me to another room. My grandfather joins us, shaking the rain off his jacket. While my grandmother inspects my head wound, I tell her what happened with Dorothy. She doesn't say anything at first but gets an ice pack and holds it to my head. My grandfather gets aspirin from where my grandmother points it out, and I take two with a sip of water.

"Concussion," my grandmother says sternly, looking down at me. She's still holding the ice on my head, and I smile at her.

"Mild," I say.

"Yes, but still a concussion," she says. "I'd make you stay here for monitoring, but clearly that's not a good idea. I'm hoping you have a better one. Because right now, my idea would involve getting Dr. Warren and Dorothy Ambrose sent to prison."

"We'll get there," Pop says, and turns to me. "Have you updated Realm?"

"I'm meeting him in about two hours," I reply.

"Good," my grandmother says. "First, you should call Nathan and see if he can bring Weston some shoes."

"Right," I reply. I take the ice pack from her hand, holding it myself, and call Nathan to update him.

He and Wes have about the same shoe size, so fifteen minutes later, he comes by and drops off a pair of sneakers with socks, and two jackets for us.

He's obviously worried, but our plan remains intact. I need his help rooting out the other handlers. Foster probably already knows who to look at.

After Nathan's gone, I go back into the room with Wes, finding him lying on the table, groggy. His arm is in a black sling. He smiles slowly when he sees me.

"Hello, beautiful," he says easily. I blush, a little embarrassed. And Nurse Belmont smiles at me.

"I gave him something for the pain, as well as a steroid. He should keep the shoulder iced when he can, and come back in a few days. We have to refer him to see if he'll need surgery."

I tell her I understand, but Wes isn't listening. He's gazing at me, hopped up on whatever Nurse Belmont gave him. He smiles broadly, and I have to laugh.

"We should go," I tell him. He nods like that's a good idea, but he's slow to get up. Pop comes into the room to help him.

The nurse tells us the brunt of the painkiller will wear off in about a half hour, and after that, it'll leave him a little fuzzy around the edges.

"Will I be sore later?" Wes asks. Nurse Belmont actually laughs out loud.

"Yes. Absolutely."

Nurse Belmont says good-bye to me, and after I give my gram a hug, promising to call her soon, the two women go off to discuss tonight's situation. This is the first time I've seen my grandmother as the person Dr. McKee described. A woman connected, leading even. It never occurred to me the kind of sway she had at the hospital until now.

Pop walks us out and gets Wes into the car. We look around, checking to make sure we're not being watched, and then I tell Pop that I love him.

"Be careful," he says, sounding desperate. He looks like he

might cry, and honestly, I don't blame him. If this weren't my story, I'd think it was already too late. But I won't give up.

It's The Program or me. And I decide it's going to be me.

Wes sleeps on the way to the diner, waking up when I park in the lot, hidden toward the back in a spot with no lights. The rain has finally stopped, leaving everything soaked and wilted. We're a half hour early, and the restaurant appears to be deserted. There's only one other car near the back door, probably someone who works there.

"I don't think we should go inside," Wes says, groaning as he adjusts his position in the seat. "Let's see who arrives first. Get a better idea what we're dealing with."

"I agree," I say, and look sideways at him. "How are you feeling?"

"I'm . . . ," Wes starts, wincing once. "I'm kind of irritated that the drugs are wearing off." He smiles and turns to me. He holds out his good hand to call me toward him.

I move over as far as I can and rest my head on the edge of his seat rather than on his shoulder. I slip my hand into his, and he intertwines our fingers and rests them on his lap.

"I don't regret it," he says. "If you're thinking I'm regretting getting involved with you again, I don't."

"That's because you're fucking insane," I say, making him laugh. "You should run far away."

"I'll never run. Not unless it's with you."

I smile to myself. "You're being really sweet," I say, watching

SUZANNE YOUNG

the building, getting lost in the feeling of his fingers stroking mine.

"You can be sweet too," he replies playfully. "If you wanted to . . . I don't know, distract me from the parts of my body that are now separated from each other."

I lift my head and look at the side of his face. He's got his eyes closed, a soft smile on his lips. His entire expression relaxed. He's such an idiot, and I love him for it.

It would be completely inappropriate to hook up in the car while his arm is in a sling. After we were attacked. *While* on our way to more disaster. But I'll be honest, the more reasons I think of not to, the more I want to.

Wes bites on his lower lip in anticipation, and I'm helpless in how badly I want him. How I want to take up his entire world, and him mine.

"We could just try it," he whispers. "Or I can do all the work. I don't mind."

To be honest, he's pretty good at what he does, but not tonight.

I lower myself toward his lap, and his breath catches in his chest—a little surprised. He slides his good hand into my hair, gently brushing it aside. And then he murmurs in a serious voice, "If I get erased tonight and end up forgetting this, I'm going to be so pissed."

And then we both crack up laughing.

"Now, I'm not a doctor," Wes says a little later, blinking like he's trying to clear his head. "But we probably could have skipped the drugs and gone straight to that."

"Something to keep in mind for next time," I reply like he's making sense, and check my reflection before flipping up the mirror. It's ten minutes past the time when Realm was supposed to arrive, and I'm beginning to get worried. Although Wes isn't currently in any pain, and, I would daresay, he's in a spectacular mood considering our situation, this state of euphoria won't last forever. He needs to rest.

"Should we do this?" I ask, motioning toward the restaurant.

"Probably not," he says. "But it's not like I'm going home tonight. At least in there I can have a slice of pie." He reaches out his hand to me, and I squeeze it before we both get out of the car.

Wes adjusts his sling several times, but he still manages to beat me to the door. He pulls it open, a set of bells jingling, and he holds it for me to walk in first.

I'm immediately smacked with the smell of grease and syrup, the air warm and a little sticky. I sweep my eyes around the empty restaurant, and my heart sinks when Michael Realm is nowhere in sight.

CHAPTER NINE

"HOW YOU DOING TONIGHT, DOLL?" A WOMAN'S voice calls. I glance over the counter to where there is a large rectangular hole leading into the kitchen and find an older woman smiling. "Go ahead and sit wherever you want," she adds.

A cook appears next to her, wearing a white hat, and the woman comes through the swinging door to pause behind the counter. She's wearing an old-fashioned pink uniform with apron, and she has bleached hair and orange lipstick.

"Two coffees?" she asks, as Wes slides into a booth at the side of the room.

"Yes, please," I tell her. "And a slice of apple pie if you have it."

"You got it," she says with a smile, and then goes to the stack of coffee cups behind the counter.

I get to the booth, and Wes is all the way in, his right shoulder next to the partition, looking even more swollen from the swath of bandages under his shirt. I'm about to get in on the other side of the booth, but he shakes his head.

"Next to me," he says. "I'd love to say it's to protect you, but it's actually to protect me." He smiles. "I'm not much muscle right now. Maybe we should call for backup."

"We won't need muscle," I say, sliding in next to him. We're facing the door, and I stare at it, willing it to open. I'm suddenly terrified that Realm won't show. That this will all end with handlers rushing into a diner off the highway, one town over, and dragging me out. That I'll disappear, and no one will ever find me again. It's a terrifying thought.

The server comes over and drops off two cups, filling them with steaming coffee. It smells strong, and Wes practically dives for it when she's done. She smiles at him, putting the slice of pie where he can reach it. Opening his napkin for him and handing him the fork. His sling is garnering him some extra attention, and he definitely doesn't mind.

"Did you want whipped cream, honey?" she asks him. "Or some ice cream? How about some ice cream on the house?"

"That is the nicest thing anyone has ever done for me, Mable," Wes says with a grin, reading her name tag. The woman practically melts at his adorableness and tells him she'll be right back.

I look sideways at him, my eyebrow hitched up. "Uh . . ." I say. "Ten minutes ago?"

Wes stabs his fork into his pie and then holds the piece out to me. Reluctantly I lean forward and take the bite off the fork. He smiles, setting the utensil down, and slides his hand onto my leg.

"No," he says in explanation. "What you did was the hottest thing anyone's ever done for me. There's a difference."

I slap his hand off my knee, making him laugh.

There is the jingle at the door, and Wes and I immediately straighten and look in that direction. My heart skips when Michael Realm stands there, finding us immediately.

He looks like shit, although admittedly, Wes and I aren't in great shape either. Realm lowers his eyes to the patterned tiles and heads toward us.

"Hi, doll," the server calls to him. Michael nods to her, asks for coffee, and she tells him it's coming right up.

"You were right," Wes says under his breath. "He is fairly cute."

I sniff a laugh just as Realm reaches our table. He sits down across from us, and his eyes skate past me, at once apologetic and suspicious. He has a folder in his hands, and he puts it on the seat next to him. I'm shocked by how awful he looks up close. He's pale and tired, his T-shirt helplessly wrinkled. His eyes are bloodshot, rimmed in red.

The server drops off a bowl of ice cream for Wes and pours Realm a cup of coffee. She asks if we want anything else, but I tell her we're fine. When she's gone, I lean into the table toward Realm.

"Are you okay?" I ask him, a flash of worry in my voice. Realm finally meets my gaze, holding it a moment with a soft smile on his lips. Without answering, he turns to Wes and extends his hand.

"Michael Realm," he says, introducing himself. Wes doesn't hesitate with any macho crap. He shakes Realm's hand and tells him it's nice to finally meet him.

Realm sits back and begins to stir too much sugar into his coffee. "I'm glad you're here together," he says. "For the record."

"Noted," Wes replies, narrowing his eyes, trying to figure Realm out. Good luck with that. Realm's secrets have secrets.

Realm takes a sip of his coffee and hums out that it's good. He takes another gulp and then pushes his cup aside and folds his hands in front of him.

"I'm sorry about what happened with Derek," Realm says, making me wilt with the mention of his name. A cold chill down my spine. "He wasn't always terrible. He used to be one of the good guys."

"Yeah, I'm going to call bullshit on that," I say bitterly. "I remember him from The Program—he was always a creep. But what about you, Michael Realm?" I ask. "I need to know if you're one of the good guys."

The question must hit Realm hard, because he furrows his brow deeply. "I try to be," he says earnestly. "I really do." He waits a beat. "What else do you remember, Tatum?"

"Not much," I admit. "Meeting you, I guess. Knowing that

you were all pretending to be patients. That's what was going on, right?"

Realm nods that it was, but I see the instant of disappointment in his expression. He thought I had remembered more.

"Well," he says in a heavy breath. "Let's start with this." He sets the manila folder on the table, staring down at the closed cover, measuring his breaths. Finally, he looks up, miserable.

"I was your handler," he whispers. "In The Program—I was your handler. Both of you."

Wes sits back against the seat, retracting from the words, and groans when he hits his shoulder. He hadn't thought to research his own time in The Program; he'd been too worried about me.

And although I already knew Realm was my handler, I still feel betrayed. Hurt. He dealt out my info in small doses, deciding what I got to learn. He could have fixed this months ago. He could have prevented *all of it* if he had stood up to The Program sooner.

"You erased me," I say, my voice low and monotone. "You stole our lives."

Realm has shadows under his eyes, his chin tilted up like he's ready to take the abuse. "I know you're upset," he says in the understatement of the year. "But I'm here to help, believe it or not."

"Not," Wes says immediately. Realm nods that he has a right to that opinion. He slides the folder in Wes's direction, but Wes doesn't touch it. He stares at it tentatively.

"What is this?" Wes asks.

"It's yours," Realm says. "It's your file." He looks at me apologetically. "I'm sorry, Tatum," he adds, "but I don't have yours. I think it was lost."

"Of course," I murmur. I look at Wes, scared of what's in his file. What it will say about him, about us.

"It's pretty thorough," Realm says, motioning to the file. "I mean, it's not everything—you lie as well as your girlfriend—but there's still a lot there. Your sister's in there."

Wes pulls the folder into his lap and quickly opens it. He sifts through the papers, the pictures. He finds one of Cheyenne and immediately turns to me.

"This is her," he says breathlessly. He touches her face, and his eyes well up. "This is my sister."

Wes was close with his sister; she was his only real connection to his family. They were a team. And even though he doesn't remember that, I can see that his heart still feels it. I blink away my own tears, happy he'll get this piece of himself back.

When I look across the table, I find Realm watching me. He presses his lips together sadly. "Your file is kind of useless anyway," he says like it's a good thing. "You lied to me."

"When?" I ask. "Because you seem to be the master of incomplete truths here."

"In The Program," Realm clarifies. "You agreed to tell me everything, but instead you lied to me. You lied to yourself. You have a pretty strong will, Tatum. I'm glad they never broke it."

"Yeah, me too."

Realm looks down at his hands again. "The other day," he says, "you asked why I care what happens to you when we don't even know each other. But the truth is, we were close. We kept each other close."

And I'm not sure if it's because he gave Wes back his sister, or if I still feel that closeness, but I find some affection toward Michael Realm. Some sense of connection.

"How did I get out of The Program?" I ask. Even though it's not the most important question right now, I have to know.

Realm picks up his coffee, stalling with a long sip.

"I'm guessing it has something to do with this," Wes says, taking a paper out of his file and setting it on the table. I lean over to read it and see it's a patient intake form.

I don't get what he means at first, but toward the bottom, I see the checked box. My stomach sinks, and I cast an accusatory glance at Realm.

"Voluntary," Wes says. "It says I voluntarily turned myself in to The Program. Now, why the fuck would I do something like that?"

We both stare at Realm, and before he can answer, the server comes by and refills our coffees. The three of us sit in active silence, waiting for her to leave. She asks Wes if the ice cream is okay, and for her benefit, he takes a spoonful and tells her it's delicious. When she's gone, he sets the spoon down on the table with a loud clank.

"He didn't turn himself in," I tell Realm, jabbing my finger at the box. "He was taken from his house. I was there."

"You were there," Realm agrees. As he starts talking again, his voice grows serious, steady. It reminds me that he's not a regular guy, not someone you meet at school. He's a hardened handler, having spent years manipulating people. I realize he's someone I should never trust. But that doesn't mean I think he's lying.

"I told you there was a deal," Realm begins, looking at me. "When I met you in The Program, I was on my way out. I had been under contract with them for years, but after getting involved with Sloane and James, seeing the true horror of the system, I was trying to escape. Trying to stop it.

"But I couldn't just disappear. If they found me, they would've had me lobotomized. I tried to stick it out, but my mind wandered. I began to research different organizations that could help. Tried to find Marie Devoroux, who was one of the first doctors I worked with. And then you showed up, Tatum." He smiles at me. "You showed up, and you refused to cooperate. You were defiant. I loved it."

Wes doesn't *love* his word choice, and he clears his throat before sipping from his coffee. Realm nods to him and continues.

"After we talked," Realm says to me, "I realized that your memories had already been tampered with. Something about your past had been changed, altered. You processed things differently, saw things for what they were. I thought . . . I thought that could matter down the line. I couldn't let The Program erase you, not in any significant way. I tracked down Marie and told her about you. At the time, I didn't believe in her cure, but I did believe she could keep you safe."

"This is all great," I say. "But that doesn't explain how I got out of The Program. What deal was made?"

"I went to Dr. Warren with specific memories you had given me—willingly given me," he adds. "You and I had made a plan: You would give me your memories to pass on, and once you got out, Marie and McKee would give them back to you. It should have been simple." He scrunches up his nose. "Fucked up, but simple in implementation."

He steadies himself, seeming uncomfortable in his skin, a little twitchy. He meets my eyes. "I went to Dr. Warren, and I told her you weren't a candidate for The Program. I told her the intake form was wrong, that Weston's mother's statement was wrong, vindictive even. I believed that because in the memories you gave me, there was no illness. Just . . . a broken heart. But Dr. Warren wasn't easily convinced. She didn't want to make a mistake. She was under the impression, thanks to Dorothy Ambrose, that your and Wes's relationship was the problem. She said it couldn't continue."

Realm's mouth pulls taut, and he looks regretful when he says, "I agreed. At that point, I did. So Dr. Warren told me to interview Wes and to present an offer. I called him and asked him to meet." Realm turns to Wes, but Wes won't look up from his file page. He's seething, not enjoying this conversation one bit.

"We went over all the options," Realm says, turning back to me. "And I told Wes the deal Dr. Warren wanted to make."

Realm swallows hard. "She agreed to let you go if Wes turned himself in for erasure. The deal was that both of you would be erased from each other's pasts. That was all that was supposed to happen. When I told Wes this"—Realm puts his elbow on the table, his fingers rubbing roughly at his forehead like it hurts—"he agreed without even a second thought. He said he would do anything for you. He just asked . . . he said he wouldn't go until he made sure you were safe."

My heart is racing, banging painfully. Wes could have been free. I'm devastated by the decision he made. But I'm humbled by it too. He saved my life.

"Dr. Warren agreed to his terms," Realm says, watching me. "You were sent home immediately. Once there, you were secretly given the Adjustment based on the files I supplied Marie with. Wes didn't want to stay with his parents, so he hid out, waiting for you to recover. It was another week before I called him and told him he could see you. See you one last time. He went immediately to your house.

"You remembered him," Realm says, his voice cracking. "Tatum, he was so happy that you remembered him—it was all he could think about, right up until the moment they erased it in The Program."

There's a tickle on my cheek, and I swipe at it, realizing I'm crying. Wes's missing week was spent waiting for me, waiting on a deal that would ruin him. He had given up everything for me. Just like Wes said before The Program took him: "I'll make it right, Tate." That's what he thought he was doing.

SUZANNE YOUNG

"So that was how you got out of The Program," Realm says. "Wes traded his life for yours. And the deal was you'd stay apart, forever. Dr. Warren was convinced it would send you spiraling otherwise. And after Wes's Adjustment failed, and Dr. McKee and Marie realized you'd lied about the actual breakup, they agreed with her assessment. They worried rekindling would lead into a full-blown crashback—the kind you couldn't get over. No one, and I mean literally no one, wanted the two of you together." He pauses. "But I knew you would be anyway."

Realm takes a deep breath. "It didn't help that Wes lied too," he says, sipping from his coffee. "Seems neither of you wanted to talk about the end of your relationship. Just skipped right over all the Kyle Mahoney bullshit."

"Who's Kyle Mahoney?" Wes asks.

"Nobody," Realm and I say at the same time, and then look at each other. I almost laugh. I would if I wasn't so completely and utterly heartbroken right now.

"But I'll admit," Realm says. "I wasn't a great handler at the end. I was doing incomplete work. Maybe I didn't try hard enough to get Wes's true memories about you—who knows. But I left soon after, and The Program erased more than just you." He looks at Wes. "I'm sorry about that. I brought you in; I should have stayed."

Realm turns to me. "And even with all that," he continues, "I know I was right to send you to Marie. She thinks you hold the key to the cure, and I think she's right. And selfishly . . . I need you. I need the cure." He swallows hard, and I notice the swelling in his neck, just under his jaw. It occurs to me that he's unwell.

"But, sweetness," Realm continues in an earnest voice, "I'm so sorry for whatever part I've played in your story. I wish I could go back and make it right, but at this point, what is right? Wrong? Is there even such a thing?"

"We're right and you're wrong," Wes says quietly, his eyes downcast, and he pokes the spoon into his ice cream. What could he possibly be thinking right now? I may not have asked him to give himself up, but it doesn't mean I don't feel guilty about his decision.

A thought occurs to me, and I turn to Realm. "Why did Dr. Warren flag me again?" I ask. "Why now?"

"You broke the deal," he says. "You demonstrated over and over again that you'd keep going back to him. That he'd keep coming for you. But more than that, you told her about your memories, and she realized what she learned in The Program was false. She figured out that you lied, that I lied. Fuck—we're all liars. And she knew that the only reason we'd all go so far to protect you was because you're the cure. She was running out of time."

"How do we stop her? I ask.

"The only way to stop The Program is to make it obsolete," Realm says. "Cure it and make it irrelevant. Attack the bottom line."

"Then Marie needs you," I say. "She asked me to find you."

"Everybody's always trying to find me," Realm says under

his breath, and then coughs, grabbing a napkin to wipe his mouth. I furrow my brow.

"How do you know everything?" I ask. "How are you so connected?"

"Because I've been here since the beginning," he says. "I was one of the first in The Program. I was given the Treatment. I'm sure I still have an experiment or two left in me. I've made mistakes, Tatum. Huge ones. But I always try to set things right where I can. I'm trying to be a better person." He smiles at me, knowing that I've been trying to do the same. His words remind me of the first conversation we had, and I narrow my eyes.

"The Treatment?" I say. "Are you the 'friend' who remembers everything? The cursed one?"

"I'm not the only one who remembers," he says, rubbing absently at the scar on his neck. "But yes—I'm definitely the cursed one."

I want to tell him not to talk like that, but when he glances at me again, something is wrong. There's a splotch of red on the white part of his right eye.

"Your eye is bleeding," I say, pointing.

"What?" Realm swipes one finger under the lid, checking for blood. Wes looks up curiously.

"No, not like, crying blood," I say. "Broken blood vessels or something. It wasn't there a minute ago." My stomach twists, and dread pours in. "Realm," I say, truly concerned. "I think we should take you to a doctor."

He laughs. "God, I hate those words," he says. His color

has paled, and now that I'm really looking, I note the bluish tint to his lips.

He closes his eyes, as if fighting back a pain, and then shakes it off. He pours more sugar into his coffee and stirs it.

"What's wrong with you?" Wes asks flatly.

Realm smiles sadly and picks up his cup. "I'm dying, Wes," he says. "I'm fucking dying."

CHAPTER TEN

REALM SITS IN THE BACKSEAT OF THE CAR WHILE I drive. He had Marie's address, just like she promised he would. Although he admits that she moves often—part of staying off the grid when she can.

"I make it my business to always know where Marie Devoroux is," Realm says, staring out the window. "My insurance policy in case I need her."

He shakes once like he's trying to hold back a cough. That's probably a good idea considering he coughed up blood before we left the restaurant. He didn't elaborate on why he's dying, what exactly is wrong with him. But he refused to go to the hospital, refused to let me call my grandmother. He said she couldn't help him anyway.

"We have to stop somewhere first," Realm says, settling

back in the seat before leaning the side of his head against the window, eyes closed.

"Not to point out the obvious," Wes says, glancing back at him, "but it's probably not the best time to run errands. Take it from someone who's bled from his ears before: Get to the doctor."

Realm smiles but doesn't open his eyes. "Trust me," he says. "This errand is worth it."

I glance in the rearview mirror at Realm, pained to see him in this condition. I don't remember being his friend, but I don't doubt that I was.

"Realm," I ask. "Where have you been? Why didn't you stay to help Marie?"

He looks at me, head still resting on the window. His reflection is alarming, the way his right eye is dark with blood—completely black in the low light.

"Look, I love Marie," Realm says. "I honestly do. Everyone does. But Marie will fuck up your life—she asks too much of people. I wasn't a fan of placing Jana Simms in Nathan's life, but despite my objections, they went ahead with it anyway. And she still wanted more. That's Marie—the never-ending ask.

"So even though I needed this cure," he continues, "I decided to leave. I went back to finishing up my own personal business, setting up meetings with former patients to give them some of what I helped take out. I was doing just that when the flag went out on you."

Realm pauses, closing his eyes for a moment as if he's wait-

SUZANNE YOUNG

ing for a pain to pass. "But I'm getting worse. And although I hate her methods, the only person who has a shot in hell of helping me is Marie Devoroux. She's in control here—is always in control. Right now, I hope that's truer than ever. She gets shit done."

"What did she want from you?" I ask. "You say she always wants too much—what did she ask of you?"

Realm opens his eyes, finding mine in the mirror. The quiet goes on too long, and Wes puts his chin on his shoulder and looks back at him.

"She wanted me to pull a Jana Simms," Realm says. "After you left school with Wes the day he returned, she wanted me to intervene, embed. She wanted me to break the two of you up. No offense, but I wasn't interested."

Wes turns back around, gently touching his shoulder as if checking for range of motion. Checking in case he has to use a little muscle, I guess. When he sees me noticing, he smiles sheepishly.

"I'm glad you realized it was a lost cause," I say, glancing at Realm. He laughs.

"It certainly is," he replies.

"Say Marie can save you," Wes interjects. "How exactly does she plan to *get* the cure from Tatum? I know she wants to use it, but how does she get it?"

"That is something only Marie knows," Realm says. "But at this point, it's not what the cure is—it's who will get it first. Marie or The Program. And the problem with that, is some of her people work for both. In the end, I guess it'll matter what side they choose."

Realm coughs, and the sound is thick and worrisome. Wes looks toward the backseat, true concern playing over his features.

"You okay, man?" he asks. Realm nods that he is, his hand a fist at his chest.

"Never better," Realm says.

We arrive on a quiet street with widely spaced lots and a few wispy trees. When he said he had to grab something, I kind of thought he meant a burger or a file. Does he live here? It's weird that I never wondered where he's from. The real him.

Realm points out a house, and I pull up to the curb in my grandfather's car. Wes and I get out, and although he can't do much of the helping, Wes holds the door as I ease Realm to his feet. I loop my arm around his waist and get us to the curb. Wes comes over, and the three of us stare up at a two-story house. There are no cars parked in the driveway, no lights on or sign that anyone's here.

Realm coughs again and spits a mouthful of blood onto the grass. Wes narrows his eyes, examining him.

"Dying?" he says. "What exactly *is* happening to you?"

"A crashback, I'm assuming," Realm tells him. "I was supposed to be immune, but who knows. Science, right?" He laughs, but my heart sinks. "That's why we're here." He motions to the house, and I tighten my arm around him.

"Let's hurry up and get what you need," I say, and begin walking him toward the front porch.

As we approach, there is the distant chirping of crickets. A low buzz from the streetlights. We get on the porch, and Wes and I exchange a concerned glance as I open the screen door and knock. The sound echoes throughout the house, but I don't hear any movement inside.

Realm groans, putting his finger on his temple to massage the area. I knock on the door again, harder. There is a swish of curtain from the nearby window, and my heart jumps.

There's the sound of locks, a chain, and then the door opens—just a crack at first. Realm smiles wildly and holds up his hand, as if he's just dropping by for a drink.

"Holy shit," a male voice says. The door swings open, and a guy rushes out, quickly gathering Realm from my arms. "What's wrong?"

"James," Realm says with a grunt. "These are my friends."

James turns to look at me and Wes, nodding a hello. I'm immediately stunned, not just because he's gorgeous, or because of his startling blue eyes, but because he's *James Murphy*.

Wes glances over to check my reaction, not realizing that we have one of the people who beat The Program in front of us. One the most important people in the entire series of events.

"James, who is it?" a girl calls from inside. She comes to the door and skids to stop, surveying all of us. She has thick black curls and an expression of absolute horror that drags down her pretty features. I recognize her from when her picture was being flashed on the news. On billboards. Sloane Barstow.

"Michael," she says, her voice dripping in concern. She comes over to wrap her arm around the other side of him, and together she and James help him toward the door.

"Wait," I say. "We have to get him to Marie."

Sloane looks confused by the name, and James narrows his eyes.

"*Marie Devoroux?*" he asks. "What does she have to do with this?" He turns to Realm accusingly. "What kind of shit are you into now?"

Realm winces, holding his chest before looking at him apologetically. "Not just me, James," he says. "And it's moving fast."

He and James stare at each other for a long moment; Sloane is equally silent, but her expression begins to rage. When they don't speak, she readjusts her grip on Realm, making him groan. I think she did it on purpose.

"Tell me what's happening to you," she demands. "Tell me right now, or I swear—"

"Poison," Realm says, and I see James flinch. "The Treatment pill . . . basically poison at this point."

James's jaw tightens, and he and Sloane immediately turn to each other. James grabs Realm roughly and rests him against the house.

"What are you talking about?" James asks. "In case you forgot, Michael—*I* took that pill too."

Realm's expression darkens. "And how are you feeling?" Realm asks him. Sloane darts her gaze to James again, and her lips part when he doesn't immediately say he's fine.

"Headache," James says quietly. "In my ears, too. I . . ." He glances at Sloane apologetically, and her chest begins to rise and fall quickly. "I had a nosebleed earlier," he says quietly to Realm.

"You didn't think to mention this?" Sloane asks him, her voice tight.

"I didn't want you to worry."

"Oh, because I'm certainly not worried now," she says. James tilts his head like she's overreacting, but he reaches out his hand to her anyway. Reluctantly, she squeezes it before letting it drop to his side.

Sloane turns on Realm, looking him up and down. He flashes his teeth in a smile.

"You don't get to die either," she tells him, pointing in his face. "And if Marie can fix whatever's going on, then we have to talk to her."

"Marie," I interrupt, immediately self-conscious when they all turn to me. "She isn't entirely trustworthy. We should be careful what we tell her."

Sloane presses her lips into a smile. "That's the general rule around here," she says. "We don't trust anyone but each other." She gives Realm a quick side-glance, and I'm not sure if he's part of her circle of trust at the moment.

Realm rests his head back on the siding of the house, and Sloane watches him, concerned.

"We took a pill to get our memories back," Realm tells me, blinking heavily. "We survived it, which, let me tell you, was no small feat. I began to worry when I saw the other returners crashing back, but I thought James and I were safe. We remember everything—what's there to crash back? Apparently, our nervous system."

"Then what are we waiting for?" Sloane demands. "Let's see what Marie has figured out."

"Marie's not known for her ethical experimentation," Realm says, looking sideways at her. "If she sees me like this, I could end up with my skull cracked open on the table somewhere."

"Yeah, well," Sloane says, brushing her hair over her shoulder. "If anything happens to James, you'll be missing more than your brain." She turns to James, whose blue eyes have grown uneasy.

"Stay with him," she says, motioning to Realm. "I'll grab the keys."

James nods that he will, but he doesn't even look at Michael Realm. He watches Sloane go into the house, waiting for her to come back. Concerned only with her.

Realm turns to me, and I meet his eyes. He lifts one side of his mouth in a sad smile. "You might be the cure for all of us," he says quietly. "But whatever happens, once this is over, leave. You and Wes . . . just leave. Never let anyone mess with your memory again. No more—" He starts to cough, and this time he gags on the blood in his mouth. He stumbles over to the railing, his entire body racking.

James curses and crosses to him, helping Realm to the edge of the porch, where he spits blood into the bushes. James holds him up, his arm wrapped tightly around his shoulders. Their heads close together.

"You should have called," James says to Realm privately. "Let me know how bad you'd gotten."

"Would it have mattered?" Realm asks, looking sideways at him.

"Yes," James replies simply. "You matter, Realm."

Sloane rushes out of the house, closing and locking the door behind her. "How far is it?" she asks Realm, taking stock of his condition but not letting it deter her mission.

"Twenty minutes," Realm says, spitting again before letting James straighten him.

"Have you got that long?" she asks.

Realm laughs. "I hope so."

James helps Realm off the porch, and Wes walks beside them even though he can't do much to assist. Sloane suggests we use her SUV, and we start that way. I'll leave my grandfather's car here for now.

"Thank you for bringing him," Sloane says. "I know he can be difficult."

"He is . . . something," I say. "But I guess if there's anyone who's in the know, it's usually him."

"Yeah," Sloane replies. "Whether he shares that information is a different story."

Well, she's definitely friends with Michael Realm.

I don't entirely understand their history together. Realm said that he loved her, and I *think* she cares about him—but she seems pissed. And it's about more than him not alerting James about getting sick sooner. This goes deeper. It feels a little brutal.

James eases Realm into the back row of the SUV, leaving him moaning, his breathing shallow. Sloane gets behind the wheel, and James sits in the front while Wes and I get in the middle row.

Realm calls out the address from the back, and Sloane has a lead foot as we race in that direction. Realm sits with his head against the window, gasping occasionally. Sloane continues to monitor him, silently taking in his condition. They don't speak to each other.

"I'm sorry," James murmurs to Sloane. "I should have told you about the nosebleed."

"Yep," she replies, and when James turns to her, she keeps her eyes on the road. James leans over in the seat to put his face in Sloane's hair, snuggling into her, his palm on her neck. Sloane rests her cheek against him, and I hear James whisper that he loves her. That he loves her so fucking much.

"Good," Sloane says. "Then let me drive." James pulls back, and Sloane smiles at him, making him laugh, before he turns toward the window. He keeps his hand on her thigh.

The sky is dark and without stars, the clouds still too heavy. I wonder then if Marie is expecting us—if she has the same uncanny ability of knowing shit like Realm does. I'm pretty angry with her right now. She planned to send in a handler to ruin my relationship with Wes. After we save the world, I'm going to tell her she's a real bitch sometimes.

We end up in a residential neighborhood with small bungalows, several Craftsman homes. Most are run-down with overgrown yards. Cars with parking violation stickers line one side of the street.

I glance back at Realm and find him staring out the window, awake.

"You sure this is the place?" I ask.

"I am," Realm says, and when he turns to me, my heart dips. His lips slightly blue, gray in the low light. He must not be getting enough oxygen. I don't understand what's happening to him.

"Realm," I start, worried. "What—"

"My brain is shutting down certain body systems," he says in explanation. "I can't diagnose it, but I can tell you that it sucks. My joints ache, my head hurts. My lungs are filling with fluid, so I guess I'm drowning." He says the last part like it's an inconvenience.

"I can stab you in the chest with a pen to relieve the pressure," Wes suggests brightly. Realm laughs and tells him to fuck off before turning back toward the window. I glare at Wes, letting him know he shouldn't joke.

"Should always joke," he says under his breath. He might be right about that. The minute we stop laughing is the moment we start crying.

CHAPTER ELEVEN

SLOANE PULLS UP IN FRONT OF A DUPLEX AND parks behind a black car, one nicer than any other on the block. I have a spark of worry, but we don't have time to be methodical right now. We need to get Realm inside.

Sloane and I help Realm out of the back, while James rests his palm against the SUV, gathering his strength. I'm alarmed at how quickly he's deteriorating. This is faster than how it happens to returners. It's not the typical crashback—this is a system-wide shutdown.

We all get to the porch, and Realm rests against the railing with James, Wes standing with them, a little helpless in his sling. Sloane and I wait together at the screen door, and Sloane rings the doorbell.

There's no immediate response, and Sloane and I turn to

each other before she sighs. In the humid night, her hair has become unruly, wild and curly with a layer of frizz. She pulls it over one shoulder, twisting it to keep it out of her face, and then takes a step back to glance up at the second-story window, where a light is burning.

"James," Sloane asks. "Any chance you're up for scaling a wall?"

"Anything for you, baby," he responds easily, although he doesn't move. Sloane smiles, then opens the screen door and begins to knock loudly on the wood, eventually closing her fist and pounding.

There is a click of an inside light, and then the quiet padding of feet on stairs. Sloane lowers her arm, and I move closer to her, both of us prepared to confront Marie and beg for her help.

The handle turns, and the door opens. Marie is haggard, her face devoid of makeup, her sweatshirt stretched out at the collar. I've never seen her disheveled like this. Sloane sweeps her eyes over Marie and then nods to her. I'm not sure how well they know each other.

Marie smiles weakly at me and then takes a step onto the porch and looks sideways to where Realm and James are against the house. Realm holds up his hand in a wave, pathetic.

"I figured," Marie says to him. "The Treatment is speeding up your decline."

She moves back and holds open the door, telling us to come inside. We all file in and start up the stairs toward her apartment. When Marie closes and locks the door behind us, she says in an exhausted voice, "I'm not alone."

Wes is beside me as Sloane and James help Realm up the stairs. We don't make it to the top before the door opens. I nearly trip when I find the monitor, Dr. Wyatt, standing there, her arms crossed over her chest.

"Holy shit," Wes says, moving in front of me protectively. "What the hell's going on, Marie?" he calls back to her.

Sloane doesn't stop moving, though. She continues to work Realm up the stairs, pushing past Dr. Wyatt to get him inside, James following behind them. The monitor watches them but then turns back to Wes.

"Nice to see you again, Mr. Ambrose," she says coldly. "Seems you know more than you let on."

"Let them pass, Angela," Marie asserts from the door. Dr. Wyatt stares down at her and eventually steps aside.

Dr. Wyatt studies us, studies Wes's shoulder like it's evidence of our recklessness. Yeah, well—adults did this damage.

Sloane dumps Realm into an oversize chair in the corner of the room and then goes to join James on the couch. I pause in the doorway with Wes, exhausted, scared, and hungry. But judging by the room, I'm better off than most.

James leans to whisper something into Sloane's ear, and she looks worriedly over at Realm. For his part, James seems unfazed. Strong. If I hadn't seen his actual concern earlier, I wouldn't think he had any. He's a skilled liar, and I suddenly understand how he and Realm are such good friends.

Marie and Dr. Wyatt both come into the room, and Wes and I move to the side. My heart is racing. I have no idea how these two ended up here together. I'm not the only one.

"Well?" Wes demands, glaring at Marie. "I'll be honest and say I don't know you, but I know her." He motions to Dr. Wyatt. "She's not on our side."

Dr. Wyatt's normally stoic expression falters. "You're wrong," she says. "We're fighting for the same thing. I'm just not as irresponsible as you."

"Oh, come on—" Wes is getting angry, but when he moves, it must tug on his shoulder and he winces. He looks away as if to disguise the pain, but Dr. Wyatt smiles like he proved her point.

"Why are you here?" I ask her. "Why can't you just leave us alone?"

"Angela is here to shut down the Adjustment. For good," Marie says. "She's against memory manipulation, but she's proposing a new system, one that will put you back into a facility for returners. She deems all returners a danger to society. So despite her beliefs, she's decided a complete reset is the only option left. It's the only one that's worked. She wants to save your lives, but she plans to do it by erasing them."

"Over my dead body," James says. "Because no offense, Angela, or whoever the fuck you are, but none of us are going back to The Program."

He sounds so sure of this that it actually gives me a ray of hope. James may be heading toward a crashback, but he shows no signs of it when we're all being threatened.

"It's not The Program," Dr. Wyatt says. "It's to save your lives."

"And I told you," Marie replies tersely. "I have the cure."

Dr. Wyatt exhales heavily. "You've said that before, and it's never worked, Marie. Why now? And how without McKee?"

"Because Marie has always been the brains," Realm says, his head back against the seat, his face slack and tired. Unlike James, he can't hide how sick he is. "She's done more to find this cure than anyone. More than you, or The Program, or any other doctor. If she says she has the cure, then I believe her," he says. "And excuse me for saying this, Angela, but if your daughter were alive today, you'd want it for her, too. You wouldn't want her reset."

I dart my eyes to Dr. Wyatt, stunned by this revelation. She had a child, one who must have died during the epidemic. Is that why she's been such a beast, tracking and hunting us? Was it all really in search of a cure?

"Don't, Michael," she says warningly, betraying her emotion. And, holy shit. I had no idea Michael Realm knew her, but I should have guessed.

"Don't let Ally's death mean nothing," he says, holding her gaze. "Give us one more shot at the cure. Please. I won't survive otherwise."

Dr. Wyatt inspects him and crosses her arms once again. "You could reset," she offers. "Then—"

"Won't work," Realm says. "Treatment, remember? I can't forget."

Dr. Wyatt and Michael Realm stare at each other for a

long moment, and it occurs to me just how entangled in everything Realm is. He's been on both sides, the doctors' and the patients'. And whatever their past, his mention of her daughter has softened Dr. Wyatt's resolve. She looks at Marie.

"What is your cure?" she asks.

Marie smiles warily and slowly shakes her head. "You know I can't tell you that. But judging by Michael's condition, it won't take long to find out if it works. Please, give us a day, Angela. Just one more."

Dr. Wyatt considers this and looks around at all of us. It's Realm who she lingers on, and then she nods to Marie. "You have twelve hours," she says. "And if your cure doesn't work, I will report you. You will be taken into custody for memory manipulation. Do you understand?"

"I do," Marie says. "But I don't imagine The Program will ever let that happen."

Dr. Wyatt tightens her jaw and nods. "If what you say is true about them, if you don't find this cure, we will all be over after this."

She starts for the door, giving us one last chance. But I still hate her. I still hate what she's doing.

"You're no better than The Program," I call out, making her turn back. "You're using fear tactics. If this fails, I want you to know I'll do everything I can to stop you from resetting people."

Dr. Wyatt smiles. "I'd expect nothing less from you, Tatum."

She turns, and Marie leaves to walk her out. I suddenly think about Nathan and Foster, knowing I need to call them soon. But I don't want to worry them yet. Hopefully the next call I make will be to tell them it's all over. The Program and its offshoots are officially done. I can't even imagine how good that would feel to say.

Marie comes back into the room, and I sit next to Sloane and James on the couch, Wes perched on the arm. Realm is only half-awake, and sweat has gathered on his brow and above his lip, even though he's shivering. There's a tug on my heart, and I look away from him.

"I meant it," Marie says, looking at me. "The cure—I've found it."

"Great," I say, like I don't really believe her. "Let's have it."

She smiles. "You're the cure, Tatum. I've asserted that from the start, back when Realm found you in The Program. I didn't understand at first, but now I do. I spoke with Luther, and I know how to find it. There's a pattern in your memory that I have to procure, but to do that, I need equipment from the Adjustment office. We can't do the procedure there—we could be raided. As it is, handlers are searching for you."

I shiver, and Wes reaches out his good hand to rest it on my arm. I think we both know I might not survive the night out there.

"I'll bring the equipment," Marie says. "But first I have to know if you're willing to take part in this. If you're truly committed. It won't be easy."

Realm looks over at me, not urging me in either direction, and I can feel Wes ready to speak on my behalf. But I don't need anyone to speak for me.

"How long will it take?" I ask.

"The procedure?" she asks. "Not long. But, again, I need the equipment to—"

"I'll go with you," Wes says, startling me. He stands up from the arm of sofa.

"No," I say, immediately. "Why?"

"To make sure it's not a setup," he replies. "And to make sure she gets back here with what you need. If she disappears, then we're all fucked anyway, right? At least I have a phone so I can call and tell you to run if I need to."

He's delusional if he thinks I'm okay with this. He'll be risking his life, risking getting caught by handlers. Wes turns back to Marie.

"You got anything for the pain while we're at it?" he asks, motioning to his shoulder. The soreness must have settled in, even if he hasn't mentioned it.

"I do," she says, nodding to him. "And you're welcome to join me, Wes. I think it's actually very smart."

Wes turns to me, grinning. Proud to be called smart. But I don't laugh, worried instead.

"Aw, come on," he says, his playfulness fading. He leans in to hug me one armed. "I'll be fine, Tate," he whispers next to my ear, his breath warm. I close my eyes, wishing this was already over. Wishing we could just be together and forget the rest. "Let me do this," he adds, and pulls back to look at me.

He smiles, waiting for my permission.

"Those damn dimples," I murmur, running my finger over

one. He leans in and kisses me, smiles, and then kisses me again.

When he straightens, I see him flinch at the pain, but he walks over to Marie. "For clarification," he says. "The stuff we're picking up—is it heavy? I'm at a bit of a disadvantage."

"No," Marie says. "Dr. Wyatt has already confiscated the big equipment. What's left is travel size."

"Lucky me," Wes offers. He casts one more glance in my direction, and then Marie tells us they'll return as soon as possible.

Marie and Wes leave, and the moment the door closes, Realm doubles over in the chair, clutching his stomach. He moans like he's been holding it in this entire time; he gasps for breath. I rush to his side, and Sloane is there too.

"Fucking hurts," Realm growls through clenched teeth, not looking at either of us.

"Let's get you to a room," Sloane says, helping him to his feet. "You should lie down."

James watches, following Sloane with his eyes, waiting to see if she needs help. But there's something else there, something beyond his worry. He softens slightly at the way she's helping Realm.

Sloane and I walk Realm into the back of the apartment, where we find a bed with a bright-patterned quilt tucked neatly inside a small room. We ease him onto the bed, and he turns away from us on his side. He coughs out a sound, half between a cry and a moan, and we wait. Realm waves us off, and Sloane goes into the living room to be with James. I hesitate.

"I want to be alone," Realm says. "Unless you can find something to stop the liquefaction of my organs."

"What?" I ask, covering my mouth.

Realm turns slightly to look at me and then rolls his eyes. "I'm kidding. All the organs are still here. They just hurt a whole bunch. Now, if you don't mind, Tatum—can I please writhe in pain in private for a minute?"

I nod that he can, but I'm horrified by his condition. Absolutely floored by it. He turns away from me again, and I exit the room, leaving the door ajar. I stop in the kitchen, taking in the space that's mostly barren. A few pieces of furniture. No art. No antiques. No sign of any real life.

This is temporary housing. It's symbolic of where we're all at right now. And alone in the quiet of the room, I see that we have multiple problems but only one long-shot solution. And I don't know if it'll be enough to save any of us.

Realm is asleep, or at least he stopped moaning, so I go into the living room and sit in the chair. Sloane stands at the couch, looking down at James, who's spread out on the cushions.

"How are you?" she asks him, betraying no emotion. At least not to me.

James stares up at her, the dark circles under his eyes hauntingly deep. "I'd feel a hell of a lot better if you were closer," he says, his voice raspy.

Without hesitation, Sloane leans down and brushes her fingers through his hair, their eyes locked, her lips on his. She kisses him once, softly, and his hand touches the small of her back to keep her close.

Sloane moves onto the couch and lies with him, her head tucked under his chin. If I'm understanding correctly, James is on the same path as Realm. How long before he's writhing in pain too? A couple of hours? Days? How long before Sloane crashes back—she's a returner too. Maybe she doesn't care, not when the more immediate threat is losing James.

"Tell me a story," Sloane says quietly.

James narrows his eyes as if deciding what she'd like to hear. Although the moment is intimate, they don't seem to mind that I'm in the room. They're lost in their own little world.

"Miller?" James asks.

Sloane smiles at the name, but then she grows thoughtful. "Tell me a story about Brady," she says almost in a whisper. "Tell me about my brother."

James's mood shifts, a bit melancholy, and he tightens his arms around her.

At first, I'm confused. Then it occurs to me that Sloane went through The Program. She doesn't remember her past, and that includes some of her family history. She's asking James because he took the Treatment pill. He has the same gift (curse?) as Realm. James remembers everything.

James rests his cheek on Sloane's hair and stares across the room with glassy blue eyes, like he's looking directly into the memory. I can't help but listen, vanishing into the story right alongside them.

"You were about fourteen," James starts, "and your parents rented this cabin up in Bend—a real shithole. Your mom just about died when we arrived, and she made your father drive her

SUZANNE YOUNG

to Home Depot for heavy-duty cleaning supplies."

Sloane laughs and places her hand on James's forearm, tracing her nails lovingly over his skin.

"The minute they left, Brady started searching the house," James continues. "Told us he was looking for dead bodies. Instead, he found a baseball bat, glove, and ball. Asked if we wanted to play. To be honest, I just wanted to sit on the couch and flirt with you. That was my favorite pastime," he whispers, making Sloane laugh. "But Brady was super *not* into that idea."

"I bet," Sloane says, making James grin.

I take a moment away from the story to look around Marie's apartment, thinking about the purity of our memories. Why would The Program take this particular one from Sloane? Why make us scared of our pasts when they aren't all bad? Maybe The Program wasn't just removing what they thought were triggers; they removed the good stuff too. That would ensure control. Because both our good and bad memories influence us, and they wanted to decide our direction.

The Program was never about our well-being. It was always about control.

James continues his story, amused. "We all went outside," he says, "and by the cabin was this huge, dirt lot. Brady wanted to bat first, and you"—he laughs—"wandered to the outfield. You put your hat on backward, adorable. No fucking clue what you were doing."

"Doesn't sound like you were paying attention to the game," Sloane points out.

"Oh, I wasn't," he admits. "So anyway, Brady gets up to bat, and I strike his ass out—no mercy." Sloane laughs. "And then it was your turn, and you came to the plate, choked up on the bat, biting the corner of your lip in concentration," James says. "I underhand-pass you an easy hit, and you knocked it right to me. But then your brother got pissed. Said I was cheating."

"You were," Sloane says.

"So? Were we in the major leagues? Was I getting endorsements? No. Well, then Brady gets up to bat, and me being me," James says with a smirk, "I struck him out again. He threw the bat and told me to stop fucking around."

Sloane is cracking up, and I'm smiling too. The innocence of it all. I hope that one day we can all return to a world like that.

Sloane snuggles into James. "Then what did you do?" she asks, assuming he made things worse.

"You got a few more hits," he says, "and your brother was incensed. Told me he was going to shove the ball up my ass if I didn't play right."

"Graphic," Sloane murmurs.

"So he got up to bat," James says. "And he pointed at me and said, 'If I hit this ball, you're never allowed to look at her like that again.' I told him I had no idea what he was talking about.

"And don't you know," James adds with a laugh. "Your brother took my worst and fucking nailed that ball. Knocked it over your cute little head and into the next lot. I was . . ." He pouts his lips, still staring into the distance. "I was pretty bummed," he says. "And so Brady came over to me, both of us watching you chase the ball, and he threw his arm over my shoulders and said, 'I know you're going to anyway, so don't look so fucking sad.' When I turned to him, he smiled, and then he ran out to help you get the ball from next door."

The story ends, and I watch as Sloane's smile fades. Her eyes well up. "He knew," she says. "About us."

"Oh, yeah." James brushes an absent kiss on her hair. "I think he even liked the idea, you know, once he got over the shock of his sister and his asshole friend."

"You're not an asshole," she murmurs, still clinging to the memory. "Okay," she adds, narrowing her eyes slightly. "You are, but I like that about you."

James laughs, but before he can follow up, I hear Realm call my name from the back bedroom. Sloane and I exchange a look, and she sits up, nervous.

"I'll check on him," I tell her, and she nods, resting back against James.

I go to the bedroom and poke my head in, surprised to find Realm awake and staring up at the ceiling. His color has taken on a grayish tone, and I wish Marie and Wes would hurry back. Spare us one way or another. Either the cure works or it doesn't. But no more uncertainty. We just want this nightmare to end.

I think about that, about how tragedy is more palatable in small doses. Long term, the devastation goes beyond physical. It becomes psychological. It'll start to unwind you. It'll destroy you strand by strand. And I'm not sure how many strings we have left.

Realm senses me and turns his eyes in my direction. My heart skips as I take in his current condition, and I sit next to him on the bed, careful not to jostle him.

"You look nice," he says, flashing a small smile. "Healthy. Is Wes here?"

"No," I tell him. "He's with Marie. They're getting some equipment. Looks like you'll get those last few experiments after all."

"I knew it," he says with a smirk. But after a second, it fades into something graver.

"What?" I ask, leaning closer.

"I'm sorry you're the cure," he murmurs. "That you haven't found the happy life you deserve. I promised you once—promised you'd get the chance. But I'm the worst liar of all. I've never helped anybody." His voice cracks, and the sound is absolutely heartbreaking. "I'm sorry, sweetness," he says, tears spilling onto his cheeks. "I'm so fucking sorry."

Realm reaches to touch my hand, and I look down as his fingers interlace with mine. The sensation envelops me, not with fear, but with something like realization. Like my entire body just realized something.

I look up, staring into Michael's eyes, noting how kind they look, despite the gore. How familiar.

How deeply familiar.

There is an intense pain, a spark of blinding light. And then a memory hits me hard and fast, knocking me out of my own head.

CHAPTER TWELVE

"KNOCK, KNOCK," REALM SAID FROM THE DOORWAY of my facility room, not actually knocking. I looked up from my bed, my slipper socks tucked underneath me, my yellow scrubs scratchy at my neck. "Am I interrupting?" he asked.

I stared at him. I hadn't seen him for the three days, not since he was pulled from the card game, but I hadn't wondered where he was, not really. I was too busy being medicated to near-unconsciousness. But I'd finally figured how to get the pills out of my system before they could take hold. It left me with just a bit of fuzz clinging to my consciousness.

"You're not interrupting," I told him, more out of curiosity than actual want of interaction.

"I was gone," he said. "Not sure if you noticed." He offered me a smile, and unlike the other day, this seemed closer to real.

I moved back on the bed as a way of inviting him into the room. He seemed grateful, bowing his head, and came to sit in front of me.

"How's it been?" he asked.

"Am I really supposed to answer that?" I replied, making him laugh.

"Guess not," he said. He waited a moment or two, and then, when Michael Realm looked at me again, I got the sense that I was seeing him for the first time. Someone ravaged by the epidemic, his soul threadbare.

"I need to talk to you," he whispered, his dark eyes desperate. "Because if I don't talk, I'll die."

I nodded that he could talk to me. He leaned in closer, and I didn't mind his proximity. I didn't mind when his leg touched mine, as if I'd suddenly solidified into a real person. For the last few weeks, I'd felt like an apparition.

"I don't belong here," Realm said in a small whisper. "Neither of us do. None of us do. But I especially don't. Do you want to know why?"

And suddenly I did want to know. "Yes."

Realm swallowed hard but didn't break eye contact. He stared deeply into my eyes. "I'm a handler," he said. "I gather information, and I give it to the doctors. If I don't, they'll lobotomize me. But I can't stay here anymore, sweetness. I want to leave and go find my friends. I was thinking you should come with me."

"Why me?" I asked. "We don't even know each other."

"Because you can tell. You can see this is fake, can't you? Me, Tabby, Shep, and Derek—you know it's all bullshit."

He was right. I could see through their act. I didn't even know how, but I figured it out pretty quickly. Even with all the drugs. "None of you were very good," I said. "It seemed kind of obvious."

Realm lifted up the side of his mouth in a smile. "Yeah, the doctors have already informed me that they're not pleased with my performance as of late. But how could you tell? What did I do wrong?"

I shrugged. "It was your eyes," I said. "Almost like you were looking at a different scene altogether."

Realm seemed to ponder this, and he shifted, his knee sliding to my outer thigh as he got closer. "And the others?" he asked. "How did you know they were lying?"

"I could just . . . tell. It sort of reminded me of something. Something terrible that I can't quite remember myself."

Realm's eyes widened, and he looked around the room, disturbed. When he turned back to me, he leaned in close enough to kiss me, although none of his intentions were romantic.

"Tatum," he asked. "Do you know Dr. McKee?"

"No," I said, not recognizing the name.

Realm didn't seem deterred. "Have you ever met Arthur Pritchard?"

That name did hold a familiar ring, and I quickly sorted out that he was the creator of The Program. I must have heard his name on television. I told Realm that I didn't know him.

"You're different," Realm said, and then laughed. "And that's not a pickup line. I mean . . . you're not here like the usual patients."

"I don't know what you mean."

"Dr. Warren told me you were being evasive, even with truth serum. The source on your file is doubling down on the assertion that you're a danger. Dr. Warren assigned me because she wanted me to get the details you wouldn't share with her." He smiled a little. "But you're not going to share them with me, either, are you? You're shut off. You've turned it off. Your . . . emotions, or something."

"It's the medication," I said, but Realm shook his head.

"No, it's not. It doesn't work that way." He leaned back, his arms outstretched behind him, and studied me.

"Tatum . . ." He furrowed his brow. "Have you ever had a lobotomy?"

"Of course not," I said.

"I don't know what they did," he said. "But now I definitely know you can't be here. You can't let The Program get too close."

"Great idea," I said. "Any plans on how I can achieve that?"

"Your grandfather's a reporter, right?" Realm asked. "Can you give me his number?"

It occurred to me then that Michael Realm was a handler here to manipulate me. But since I'd been in this facility, I'd been able to see through the lies. And I believed that Realm was telling me the truth. I gave him my grandfather's number, and he scrawled it down on a piece of paper and stuffed it into his pocket.

"Okay," he said like he was about to deliver bad news. "I'll do everything I can to get you out of here, but you have to give me something in return."

"What?" I asked.

"A story. Something about you and Wes, something they can erase."

I scoffed, and he quickly apologized. "I don't want them to erase anything either," he said. "But if we don't give them something, they'll realize you've been . . . tampered with. So, please. Let's give them something. I'll get it back to you when this is all over."

Michael Realm could have spun this entire story to get at my secrets. And it probably wouldn't have been the first time he'd done it. But I wanted to believe his sincerity; I wanted to believe he'd help me.

"Just stick with me, and we'll get through this," he said. "I promise."

And so I lay back on the bed, Realm lying next to me, and I told him the greatest love story I knew. The story of me and Wes. And when I was done, I didn't even feel bad for lying about most of it.

There's a rustle of sounds, light seeping in from under my closed eyes. I feel a cloth pressed under my nose, making it harder to breath, as wetness slides down my neck.

"Tatum," a voice says, and I realize it's Sloane. "You're having a crashback. You've got to stay with me. Do you understand? We need you."

She pinches my nose, and I gasp out of my mouth, my eyelids fluttering open. I sit up, Sloane's hand falling away as she stares at me, wide-eyed.

"Are you back?" she asks like I'm not really here.

"Yeah," I say, trying to clear the blood in my throat. I look around the room, James standing in the doorway. Sloane next to the bed, terrified. I blot the blood under my nose, furrowing my brow.

"I told half-truths," I murmur, turning toward Realm.

I find him lying there, staring at me. His every breath is a small gasp, followed by a rattle. He tries to smile, but he winces like it hurts.

Realm got me out of The Program. I remember now. I remember us.

Realm and I had planned it all, how he would present my memories to Dr. Warren. How I could call them up for erasure. He and I would lie in my hospital bed night after night and play card games during the day. We knew the system. Michael Realm told me all of his secrets, but I didn't tell him all of mine. He was so lonely. He said he always had been. I wanted to take that loneliness away, and we grew close. I wanted to save him.

Eventually, a deal was struck—one where Dr. Warren would let me out but keep an eye on me afterward, looking for any signs of depression or suicidal thoughts. If they appeared, she'd put me back in The Program.

My grandfather came in and assured her that wouldn't happen. Realm assured her that I was well, supplying my distorted memories of Wes as proof. I didn't know then, but he had tracked Wes down, told him what had happened in the facility. He fed him my memories, even if he didn't realize they were lies. It skewed Wes's files.

We're all liars, just like Michael Realm said. But in the end, he saved my life. And a tear drips onto my cheek, mixing with the blood from my nose, because I realize I don't think I can save his life in return.

I lie down next to Realm, my head on his shoulder, just like how we'd lie some nights as he told me about Sloane. How he wished he could be good enough for her.

Realm continues to gasp in breaths, slowly, but he reaches to put his hand on my hair. "I've missed you," he says.

I close my eyes, knowing that I've missed him too. Our relationship was never romantic; it was friendship. It was the closest thing we had to real in a place that demanded lies.

We did our best. We grew real enough to survive.

And so when there's a sudden stillness next to me, and Realm's breathing stops, I cover my face and I cry.

CHAPTER THIRTEEN

"MOVE, MOVE," SLOANE YELLS, PUSHING ME OFF Realm's shoulder as she turns him on his side, sitting on the edge of the bed. "James!" She screams so loud her voice cracks, the mirror on the wall rattles.

"Don't you fucking die, Realm," she says, swiping her finger through his mouth. "Don't you fucking dare!"

I sit there, stunned. Realm's cheeks are hollow, and his mouth has gone slack. I put my hand on my chest because my heart hurts. I remember him. He can't go now.

James rushes over to the bed, his blue eyes scanning Michael's body before he falls to his knees next to Sloane's legs. Together, they work him onto the floor.

"Find out where Marie is," Sloane says to James. She tilts Michael's chin up and presses her mouth to his. She begins to administer CPR while James, looking pretty awful himself, calls Marie.

Sloane starts chest compressions, up on her knees to apply enough pressure. At one point, I hear the pop of a rib, and my stomach swirls with sickness.

"Don't do this," Sloane is murmuring over and over. Tears run down her face even though she's laser focused. "Not after everything. You can't leave me like this."

She leans in to give him more breaths.

"Marie?" James says into the phone, squeezing his eyes shut. "Marie, it's Michael. He . . . he needs help." But James starts crying, and I have to reach over and grab the phone from his hands.

"Realm stopped breathing," I tell her. "What do we do?"

Marie is silent for a moment, and I check to make sure the call didn't drop. I put it back to my ear. "Please, Marie, he's dying."

"I'm on my way," she says. "Get him breathing again. I'm ten minutes away. Just get him breathing."

"And then what?" I ask.

"Then we'll find out if the cure works," she says.

Sloane falls back to sit on the floor, and I turn. Realm gasps, coughing and moaning. He places his hand on his ribs, and I forget all about Marie on the phone.

James sits there, his face covered, and Sloane stares at Realm like he's the sun and moon. And when he opens his eyes, it's her that he focuses on first.

He's still having a hard time breathing, wincing with every intake. But he reaches out his hand to her, and she takes it and offers a fragile smile.

"Was I asleep for long?" Realm asks weakly, and then grins when she laughs and kisses his hand.

"You fucking died," she says, shaking her head. "You died, Michael."

His eyelids are heavy, but he looks at her with complete adoration, and I can see that he still loves her. Same way he did back in The Program. And despite everything he did, she loves him, too.

"Not a chance," Realm says, touching her cheek to wipe away a tear. "I wouldn't leave without a good-bye."

Her face starts to crumble again, but she straightens it quickly. Fact is, Realm is still dying. And so is James. A whole hell of a lot of people will die if we don't get that cure.

And I can't help but look around this small room, some tiny apartment in the middle of the suburbs, and wonder how the hell this can all work out.

We get Realm into the bed again and keep him stable while James goes to the couch, telling us he's fine but looking worse. I was surprised when he leaned down to Realm, his hand on the back of his neck, their foreheads together in a quiet embrace. I wonder how they can be such close friends while in love with the same woman. Then again, I guess we all have some relationship issues.

Marie arrives a short time later, and when I hear the door open, I'm sitting in Realm's room. "I'll be right back?" I ask, and he nods for me to go. He hasn't been able to say much, mostly just watching me with deep-set eyes. Pained.

I jog out into the kitchen and find Marie standing in the living room, talking to James and Sloane with a black medical bag in her hand. Next to her, Wes is holding a box with his good arm, his eyes a little glassy. He's a little high, and he all but confirms it when he smiles dreamily in my direction.

I walk over and take the box from him. Just as I set it on the kitchen table, he comes over to kiss my cheek, murmuring that he missed me.

"I see she gave you the good drugs," I say, not hating when he stays against me, wrapping me up from behind.

"Did you know I could smell colors now?" Wes asks, and when I turn to him, he grins. I laugh, and Marie appears behind him.

"Where's Michael?" she asks, and I wonder if she thinks he's dead. Like I'd be out here smiling at Wes if that were the case.

"In the room," I say. We head back that way, and Marie grabs the box. I want to ask her what's inside, but I imagine I'll find out soon enough. Marie moves urgently, reminding me that time is of the essence.

I wait at the door while Marie goes inside. She sets the box down and stands above Realm, her arms crossed over her chest. Her expression is unreadable as she looks him over. For his part, Realm smiles at her, and she softens when she meets his eyes.

"Thought you were going to get out of this, huh?" she asks.

He sniffs a laugh, and then holds his side and groans. Marie's smile fades.

"I have a cure," she tells him, but her lack of excitement isn't encouraging.

"Isn't that good?" Realm asks in a low voice.

"I don't know if it will work on you," she confides. "You're pretty far gone, Michael. Right now it's a fifty-fifty shot."

"Those aren't terrible odds," Realm replies.

"Fifty percent you're cured, fifty percent you die within ten seconds."

Realm's lips twitch with the start of a joke, but the moment drags on, and the heaviness of the truth weighs us down. His eyes tear up, and Marie doesn't break his gaze. Her lips press together, holding in her emotion.

"I don't want to die today," Realm whispers to her, and I have to turn my head. "Don't let me die, Dr. Devoroux."

Marie dips her chin in a nod and then reaches to put her hand on Realm's cheek, making him turn into it. I don't quite understand their relationship; Realm never talked about her. But when it comes down to it, Marie has known Realm since he first went into The Program. I imagine she's known him the entire time. Somehow, they've worked together, maybe not always on the same side.

But there's respect and mutual admiration in their relationship.

"I'm going to warn you," Marie says, taking her hand away. "This is really going to hurt."

Realm rests back against the pillow and closes his eyes like he was waiting for it. "Everything good usually does."

Marie begins to prep Realm, helping him take off his shirt so she can attach some sticky tabs and wires to his skin. Wes and I go out into the kitchen, and Sloane and James are on the couch. James's head is in her lap while she plays with his hair, the two of them talking quietly. They just watched their best friend die. They know time is running out for all of them.

Wes pulls out a chair at the table, offering me the seat, and I thank him as he sits next to me.

"Thanks for going with Marie," I say. "You didn't need to take that risk."

"I'm just doing my part to save the world," he replies. "Besides, I wanted to know what sort of equipment she planned to use on you. I don't want you to forget me again." He smiles at me, and it makes my heart warm.

"You're so cute," I murmur, smiling.

"God," he says, dramatically. "We're like obsessed with each other or something."

I laugh, and he reaches to pull my chair closer to his. He flinches a little, overextending himself because of the haze of medication. "Speaking of obsession," he says. "My phone rang about eighty times, and eventually I answered it."

"I swear, if this is another conversation about your mother—"

"It was my mother," he says, talking over me. "And she apologized and asked me to come home."

The joking stops, and a spike of fear plunges into me. "You didn't agree, did you?" I ask.

"Uh, no. I'm not stupid," Wes says. "But I also told her I didn't know where you were. I thought it was better that way. I told her I needed a night away to think. Do you hate me for lying?"

"To *her*? No. Just don't lie to me."

"Okay," Wes says, leaning to kiss me, lingering there. "We're full-on honesty here," he murmurs, his lips grazing mine. "Unfiltered, naked honesty. Completely—"

"I get it," I say with a laugh, pushing him back down in his chair. "So," I say. "What kind of equipment was in that box you brought in?" I ask.

"Not much, actually. Some computer equipment, a bunch of vials of the truth serum. A metal-looking crown with wires. We talked a bit in the car, and from what I can gather, she has a theory that if she can synthesize your memory patterns, the way your mind lays them out, she can apply it to others. She says as long as you're healthy, you have a unique connection—a bond—between memories." Wes shrugs, like he can't confirm if it's true. "She said you and Nicole have similar patterns, but you're the glue. Your patterns can make the transitions seamless because you also went through The Program—you're like, extra special." He smiles.

When Arthur Pritchard turned me into Tatum Masterson, he had to erase or rewrite who I was. I'd only been a child, but even children have lasting memories. As Marie describes it, memory patterns are unique pulses, creating images. In the Adjustment, to add memories, they re-created those pulses in a patient's brain, letting it build a memory from the ground up. It was never exact; things like hair color, anything on the periphery, would be up to the individual brain to fill in. The core of the memory stayed mostly the same.

Marie and Dr. McKee thought this would be enough to cure what The Program had done. They were wrong. The Adjustment failed miserably, and as a result, people died. What if this cure has the same problems?

"Tatum?" Marie says, appearing in the doorway of the bedroom. I gasp in a breath, not sure how long she's been standing there. "We're ready," she adds.

I exchange a nervous look with Wes, scared of what's about to happen. Marie comes closer to the table when I don't move right away, and she rests her hands on the back of a chair.

"I assume Wes told you about our conversation?" she asks.

"I was hoping you'd want to explain it," I say. "What exactly are you going to do to me?" I tell her what I already know, and I find Sloane watching us, listening in from the other room.

"The Adjustment did fail," Marie admits. "You're right. But what The Program did is having a worse effect. When the doctors extracted a memory, it left a crack"—she runs a finger down the side of her head—"a crevice between events. The Program sought to fix this by overlaying a false memory, a bandage over a gaping wound.

"Returners have hundreds of these cracks," she continues. "And Treatment patients have thousands. Over time, as memory continues to grow and expand, those cracks also expand. And when a former patient has a crashback, they fall in, sometimes getting lost entirely in their own head. They shut down. They die."

I swallow hard. Wes had one of those crashbacks, and it nearly killed him. He takes my hand under the table and holds it.

"So what we'll do," Marie says, steadying her gaze on me, "is find the moment where Arthur Pritchard stitched together your brain pattern. Whatever he did all those years ago, it was more intricate than anything we've ever seen. And it's different from Nicole, probably because she was reset multiple times. Re-created."

The words make me sick, and I let go of Wes's hand and lower my eyes. I haven't had time to fully grasp what it means to have lived my life as someone else. I'm not sure when it'll actually hit me, but I don't have time for it now.

"We need to find that pattern," Marie continues. "And once we do, we'll mimic it over the breaks in the memory of returners. We can bond their reality, like a computer getting an upgrade. We won't add any new memories. Won't take any out. Instead, this new pattern will make them process things differently, glide over cracks without a hitch. If nothing else, Arthur Pritchard was a brilliant man. No one could have created a system as sophisticated as his. We need his original work. You"—she smiles—"you are the only one I've seen with this pattern. You survived the grief department. The Program. And the Adjustment. Each manipulation changing you, perfecting you, in a way. For this. Tatum, you are the cure."

I shudder at the thought, like I'm some kind of Frankenstein's monster. "And once you find this pattern, then what?" I ask.

"We'll apply it to Michael Realm. See if it works. And then move on to James and then returners. It's our only hope at this point." She presses her lips together. "But I can't guarantee that it won't harm you," she says. "Going back to those dark memories is dangerous."

My breath catches, and she holds up her hand apologetically. "I'm not trying to scare you," she says. "I'm trying to be up front."

But I'm worried she hasn't researched enough. Hasn't done enough to prevent a catastrophe.

"Michael Realm dies if this doesn't work," I tell her.

"Michael Realm dies if we don't try," she adds.

I can't be responsible for his death. Although I wasn't the one who took his memories, gave him a Treatment pill, or caused his crashbacks—I have to weigh if it's worth giving him this. Will I risk my life for his?

But I know that Realm already risked his for me when we were in The Program. He helped get me out. He promised I'd be happy again.

"I'll do it," I say. Wes shifts in his chair, nervous, worried, maybe a little disappointed now that he's clear on all that's at stake.

We could walk out that door and start over, but I know that neither of us would actually do that.

CHAPTER FOURTEEN

I DIDN'T KNOW SEARCHING MY MEMORY WOULD BE a spectator sport. Marie has me on the couch as she sits next to me in a chair. Sloane propped up my head with a pillow, while Wes sits at the other end of the couch for emotional support.

Marie takes her time attaching sticky tabs and wires to my head, and then she removes a crude-looking metal crown from her bag. She tells me it was the prototype for the Adjustment, built by Dr. McKee himself, and sets it aside.

Her hand is under my shirt, attaching wires to my chest, and I glance around the room, a little self-conscious.

James sits at the kitchen table, his head down on his folded arms as he watches us. He continues to check on Realm in the bedroom, his concern giving way to panic. He also seems to be getting worse himself, and Sloane casts a cautious glance in his direction. At one point, James puckers his lips subtly to offer her a kiss, and she smiles and turns back to Marie.

The only option is for this to work. For all of us.

Marie takes out a syringe, and I gulp, a twitch of nervousness when she touches my arm.

"What's that?" I ask.

"Truth serum," she responds. I dart a look at Wes and then back to Marie.

"For what?"

"It's a high dose." She pauses. "Extremely high. We have to find the point where Arthur Pritchard weaved you in. We can't make a mistake."

"But you know—"

"We have the basic idea, but we need the clearest memory we can get. Understand, you're about to crash back . . . hard. You'll relive the memories, Tatum," she says. "I hope you don't get lost in them."

Although I expect this memory to be shocking, or sad, I don't get the grimness in her expression. Before I can think too much, she inserts the needle, and I feel the burn race up my vein. I wince, and Wes slides his hand onto my ankle.

Marie removes the syringe, covering the needle tip, and slips it into her bag. She places the metal crown on my head, brushing my hair away from my face. The dose was definitely strong, because I feel the first wave of warmth splash through my chest.

Things blur before getting clearer, still frayed at the edges.

I sense it immediately: I can no longer lie. Not even to myself.

James coughs at the kitchen table, and the sound of it is heavy and dry. Sloane gets up and goes over to him. She stands behind his chair as he tries to catch his breath. He swallows hard and looks up at her. Her expression shatters—all pretense of bravery gone—and he nods her toward him.

"Come here," he murmurs, and she wraps her arms around him, and he reaches up to rest his hand in her hair.

I hear James whisper that he'll be okay. He'll never leave her.

And I wonder if anyone has ever been more in love than Sloane and James. What would that be like, to have your fates be so completely and utterly intertwined? I glance at Wes, finding him watching with anticipation, worry.

Warmth spreads over my skin, crawls up and seizes the back of my neck like a grip. I love Weston Ambrose, and he loves me. I stare over at him, the edges of my vision shading in, and Wes smiles encouragingly.

"It's your dimples," I say out loud, making Marie look at me. Wes smiles wider.

"What is?" he asks, his thumb tracing along my ankle.

"The feature I love best," I say. "You asked me once, and the answer is your dimples, every time."

He has no idea what I'm talking about, but he nods anyway like he does.

"I see the medication is working," Marie says to no one in particular, and takes out her laptop, her fingers clicking quickly on the keys. There is a buzz in my head, and it startles me.

"Sorry," she says. "Checking the connection." She taps a few more times, and then she adjusts her chair next to me, computer balanced on her lap. "Are you ready, Tatum?" she asks.

Sloane comes in from the kitchen, watching us intently, counting on me to be the cure. Her eyes plead with me to not fail.

"I feel a little sick," I tell Marie, looking up at her. And I do, a swirl in my stomach, nausea. Marie apologizes again and tells me it's the medication.

She poses her finger over a key but looks at me one last time. "I'm going to start mapping now," she says. "I need you to focus. I don't know what you'll find, but we're all here. You just need to remember."

"I will try," I say, and close my eyes.

"Now," Marie says. "Think back to the very first time you saw your grandfather's face. The oldest memory you have of him. Find it."

There's a sting at the same time she hits the enter key, and I groan, a headache hitting behind my eyes. I keep them squeezed shut. Wes is still touching me, but the feeling of it fades.

It's like I'm falling backward, eyes up to the sky, plummeting. And then, suddenly, I crash like a meteor striking earth.

"Now tell me what you remember," Marie says, and the words drill straight into my head.

I was climbing out of the black car that had been idling at the curb for fifteen minutes. There was a black scuff across my white shoes, and I tried to keep up.

"Cynthia," the old man said as he tugged me toward the house. "I expect you to be quiet, understand? They need to get a good look at you."

I nodded that I did understand, but I was too scared to tell him that I just wanted to go home. My father would be waiting for me, and when I didn't get off the bus, he'd be scared. He wasn't well, but he was trying. Since my mother died, he'd been trying really hard.

The man—Dr. Pritchard—had been meeting with me at school for the past few weeks. After my mother died, the counselor worried I wasn't being properly cared for at home. They brought in this doctor, and he'd warned my father. After that, Dr. Pritchard would come talk to me every day, checking on our progress.

But today he took me from school, and he brought me to this house in a town I'd never been to before. I'd never really been anywhere.

Dr. Pritchard held my hand tightly as he rang the doorbell, and I looked up at him, my eyes wide. When he noticed, he pressed his lips into a smile and smoothed down my hair.

The door opened.

The man who opened it was older than my father, but he clasped his palm over his mouth the minute he saw me, his eyes watering behind his glasses. I stepped closer to Dr. Pritchard, using both of my small hands to hold one of his.

"Now, now," he said to me warningly. "This is Mr. Masterson. He's your grandfather."

I looked up at the man in the doorway, and I knew he wasn't my grandfather. My mother told me a long time ago that all of my grandparents were already in heaven, and when she was in the hospital bed, she whispered that I shouldn't be scared for her. I shouldn't be scared because she was going back home to *her* mother. And that she'd take care of her.

The man in front of me looked kind, and I did my best to smile. At that moment, a woman joined him, and she moaned when she saw my face.

I tried to hide behind Dr. Pritchard, nervous, but he put his hand on my shoulder and pulled me forward. Put me on display.

"It's uncanny, isn't it?" Dr. Pritchard said, and the older woman nodded her head. The man next to her couldn't look at me anymore.

"She's perfect," the woman said, shaking her head slowly. There was a soft flinch in her mouth, a twitch. "How did you find her?" she asked.

"She was one of many candidates," Dr. Pritchard told her kindly. "But I think she's the best choice." He looked down at me again, warmly. I didn't know what he was talking about.

"I want to go home," I whispered, and my lip jutted out. I wanted to see my father. My room. My dog.

Dr. Pritchard tsked, but the woman stepped forward, holding up her palm. "It's okay, honey," she said to me. "It's okay."

Her voice was soothing; I'd always wanted a grandmother— a sweet one. She squatted down in front of me and ran her palm over my arm, trying to comfort me.

"You look just like her," she said like I should be proud.

The woman gently pulled me into a hug, and the second I was close, she started to cry into my shoulder. I hated watching adults cry. My father had cried every day since my mom died.

But last night, after he tucked me into bed, he told me that he loved me. It was the first time he'd said it in a really long time. When I left for school in the morning, his car was already gone, and I walked to the bus alone.

"I want to go home," I repeated louder. The woman pulled back, brushing my hair, nodding like she understood. And then she looked up at Dr. Pritchard, and they were both quiet, staring at each other.

The old man behind her walked back into the house. And the woman, my grandmother, leaned close to me and whispered, "You are home, Tatum."

My eyelids flutter open, and the scene of the apartment floods in. There's a buzz deep in my head, and Marie tells me not to move.

"They kidnapped me," I say out loud, and my breath hitches.

"What happened after that?" she asks.

But I don't want to go further into the memory, don't want to obliterate everything I know about my grandparents. My eyes well up, tears spilling over.

"I can't," I murmur, a dam inside of me breaking and flooding me with warm water.

"You have to," Marie says.

"Please," I hear from behind her, knowing it's Sloane. "Please don't let him die. Don't let any of us die."

She doesn't even know if I'm really the cure, but we're desperate, all clinging to this possibility. I can't let them down. I have to try. Even if it means destroying Tatum Masterson.

I close my eyes again, and Marie hits a key, causing a vibration in my temple. The room dissolves around me.

I didn't stay at my grandparents' house that night, although I wasn't allowed to go home, either. Dr. Pritchard brought me to a place he called the grief department. In the back, there were toys, a small bed. I was the only one there.

I took off the bracelet that my mother had given me and kept in my pocket, scared they'd take it away.

I cried myself to sleep the first night, hugging a stuffed dog to my chest. The entire place smelled like rubbing alcohol, like the hospital where my mother had died. I didn't mind the daytime at first, playing alone. But at each therapy session, I would dread going into the white room. Sitting with Dr. Pritchard as he told me about my life. About my grandparents.

"They're not my grandparents," I said stubbornly.

"Yes, they are, Tatum. And they love you very much. They—"

"My name isn't Tatum!" I screamed at him, and he reacted quickly, grabbing me by the wrist and setting me down in the seat. It startled me, and I began to cry, asking for my father.

Dr. Pritchard stood up, staring down at me sternly. "Your father's dead, Tatum. He didn't survive the grief. And now you have no one but your grandparents. I expect you to appreciate that."

Just as my lip began to shake with my cry, he walked out and left me all alone in the room. I held my stuffed dog close to me, sniffling as I cried into his ears. My daddy was dead. I reached into my pocket and held the bracelet in my fingers, wishing my mom had come home to me instead.

When Dr. Pritchard returned to the room a little while later, he brought a girl with him. She looked about eleven or twelve. She was plain with blond hair, blue eyes, and a tired face. Dr. Pritchard led her into the room and sat her down across from me.

"Since you plan to be difficult, Tatum," he said, calling me by the wrong name, "let Quinlan show you how that can work out." Quinlan cursed at him, and he laughed and left us there.

The girl turned to me, circles under her eyes. "My name's Nicole," she said, using a different name. "And when you don't listen, they reset you. They erase you."

"I want to go home," I told her.

"I know," Quinlan said. "But they won't let you. You'll never go home again. As long as they're around, at least." She leaned forward in her chair and reached to take my hand. It made me start to cry again because I hoped she would help me.

"They might take it," she whispered. "But the memories come back sometimes. You have to be stronger than those

SUZANNE YOUNG

memories, otherwise, you'll fall apart. You'll be so angry, and you won't be able to hide it. I haven't been able to. I don't even know how many times I've been reset at this point. How many more times they'll erase. You have to learn to lie," she said emphatically. "Don't ever let anyone know the truth, or they'll take it from you. Understand?"

The door opened, and Arthur Pritchard walked back in with two sodas. He set them both on the table for us.

"Quinlan," he said, staring her down. "Are you ready to cooperate? Your father is worried."

She ground her teeth, stubborn like me. She wanted to shout that this wasn't her life, but she just stood up and spun to face him.

"Go fuck yourself," she said, and brushed her hair over her shoulder. The doctor grabbed her arm and dragged her from the room. When they were gone, I was left in silence.

Never let anyone know the truth, I thought. If they didn't know my real past, they couldn't erase me—the real me. But I knew I'd have to bury it deep. I'd have to lie to myself most of all.

When Dr. Pritchard came back in with a pill in a small white cup, I took it from him, staring down at it. I didn't want to take it. I wanted to go home.

"After today," he said firmly, "Cynthia Wilds never existed. You are Tatum Masterson. Your birthdate is . . ." I listened as Arthur Pritchard read off the facts of my life, my name, birthday, family. When he was done, he told me to take the pill, and I did, tears in my eyes.

This went on for days, weeks. And even though I never gave him all of my secrets, Arthur Pritchard convinced me that my name was Tatum Masterson. And that my grandparents were the most loving people I'd ever known.

He brought me back to them eventually, and clutching my stuffed dog, a bracelet from a person I couldn't remember still hidden in my pocket, I ran into their arms. I'd missed them. My grandmother smiled down at me, told me she had baked me a cake. She was so happy, offering a watery smile. My grandfather watched me, and I couldn't understand why he didn't look happier to see me.

But over time, he talked to me more and more. He grew to love me, not as the old Tatum, but as the new. I never once crashed back. I never once remembered, until now, the memory stored away like a dusty box in a closet.

And when I open my eyes and find Wes sobbing, Marie with tears on her cheeks, and Sloane staring at me with pity—I know that I was finally able to tell all of it. Tell the truth.

I was finally free from my memory.

CHAPTER FIFTEEN

MARIE TAKES THE CROWN OFF MY HEAD, SILENT IN words and movements. She sniffles several times as she types on her keyboard. I'm not sure if she's crying for me, or possibly for Quinlan—I know she's close with Nicole. Maybe she didn't appreciate the true horror of what we'd been through with Arthur Pritchard.

It must have been terrible as Quinlan, always remembering. Always being reset. It must have been torture. I wonder how Marie lives with that now. How she can handle knowing she was a part of it.

"Did it work?" Sloane asks, biting impatiently on her thumbnail, pacing behind Marie.

"I won't know until we try it," Marie says, watching her

computer screen as lines begin to fill in a map of the brain, populating it with different patterns.

I try to sit up, but my head feels foggy, my stomach sick from the medication. Wes comes over and offers me a bottle of water, helping me sip from it. He leans in, his forehead against my temple like he's so sorry for me. I think my heart will be sore later, but for now, we just need to end this.

"I have the pattern," Marie says, simply at first. She looks up with wide eyes, tears glistening there. "I've got it."

Sloane turns to James, who's watching her, head on his arms. A trickle of blood leaks from his ear, slides down his jaw. Sloane curses and rushes over to him. She grabs a napkin and wipes away the blood, and James follows her with his eyes, not moving.

Sloane gets down on her knees at his side and puts her palm on his cheek. "Hold on," she whispers. "For me, hold on."

"Always for you," he says quietly.

If James is this bad, what condition is Realm in? He's already died once today.

Marie grabs her black bag and heads toward the bedroom. Wes helps me up. It's still a little difficult, but I want to check on Realm.

"The Program got to you when you were a kid," Wes says in a quiet voice. "They've ruined your life from the start."

I'm on my feet, standing to face him as I get my bearings. I feel suddenly exposed, broken down. And I can't lie about it—not yet. The ache of the truth is slowly coming over me. Wes gathers me into a hug, letting me cry against him.

"This is why we'll win," he whispers into my hair. "You've survived their worst, and now it's your turn. You're going to make them pay. You're going to destroy them."

I want to believe him, not just that we'll win, but that I'm the reason for it. I need that. I need to know it was worth it somehow. They essentially killed the little girl I used to be. It has to count for something.

Marie comes back into the room, her entire demeanor professional, emotionless. It's exactly how we need her to be. I quickly straighten out of Wes's arms, swiping my palm over my face to clear my tears.

"We're beginning," she says, before focusing her attention on James. "And let's get him into the room before he dies at my kitchen table."

Realm sniffs a laugh as they lay James next to him. He looks sideways at his friend, but James stares at the ceiling, annoyed that he's getting this unwanted attention.

"Do we seriously have to share everything?" Realm asks.

"She loves me," James says, his voice barely a whisper. "So I already won."

He tilts his head to the side, and he and Realm smile at each other. Wes helps me to a seat, and Sloane begins to pace the room, chewing on her nails.

Marie puts her hand on Realm's shoulder. "This is going to be . . . uncomfortable."

"Awesome," Realm replies.

"Now, using the pattern we extracted," she says, motioning in my direction, "we're going to overwrite your memories. It will either smooth the cracks, or it will widen them, distort them. And we won't know until we try it."

Realm nods that he accepts this risk, and Marie takes the crown and fits it onto his head, attaching the wires. She gets her laptop ready, and unexpectedly, Realm looks over at me.

And it hurts to see him so sick, so half out of this world. We had a whirlwind friendship, that kind of summer camp romance that lasts a lifetime. Add in the threat of being erased and lobotomized, and I daresay Realm and I lived a hundred friendships in those weeks.

"Hope you don't kill me," he says, flinching a smile.

"Same," I reply. "And if you don't die, you owe me a card game."

His eyes weaken. "I'd like that," he murmurs, tears gathering. The air in the room grows thick with grief.

Marie's finger is shaking as it hovers above the key. And then she hits enter, and Realm screams.

We all flinch back, and Realm bares his teeth, Marie trying to keep him from pulling off the crown. The scene is alarmingly violent, and I wonder if it's because she doesn't have all the equipment needed, or if she's killing him. James watches in horror, and fresh blood streams from Realm's nose.

Realm convulses, his eyes rolling back in his head. And all at once he goes limp. I get to my feet, and Sloane stops pacing.

"Michael," she calls under her breath.

It's a horrific sight, and just as I look at Wes to see his reaction, I hear the squeal of tires outside the duplex, cutting through the night air. Shouts, voices.

"No," Marie says, typing faster on the computer. "I need more time. We need more time!"

They're here. They're going to take us. The Program is coming.

I don't wait for direction. I run out into the kitchen and through the apartment. I take a quick glance out the living room window and see two black cars, a white van, and a beat-up Bronco at the curb. There's a rush of movement toward the door, and before I can see who it is, I go back into the kitchen and grab a chair.

Sloane appears, and we meet each other's eyes for just a moment—true fear pulsing between us. She motions to the table, and together we drag it toward the door. We can't let them in. We can't let The Program take us, not when we're so close.

We slam the wood against the door just as we hear the sound of footsteps pounding up the stairs.

"Fuck!" Sloane growls out, and takes a step back from the door, her hand on her throat. She turns to me, and with a moan she murmurs, "It can't end like this."

"It won't," Wes says coming into the room. His right arm is

in a sling, his shoulder grotesquely swollen, but my boyfriend walks over to the butcher block on the counter and draws out a knife.

Sloane watches him and then nods. I don't know what to do, but Sloane's right—it can't end like this. Not after everything.

A sharp banging on the door startles us, and the door rattles on its hinges. The knob begins to twist back and forth, the loud thud of a shoulder against the wood. I jump forward and put my weight against the table.

"I won't let them take him," Sloane says, mostly to herself. "They can't have us."

"Open the door," a deep male voice says from the other side. "Marie Devoroux, open the damn door."

I don't recognize the voice, and Wes comes to stand next to me, knife in hand. There's no other way out, no back door.

We're all that's left of the rebellion. Without us, The Program rules the world.

There are more voices in the hallway now, and Sloane sneaks over to the window and looks out. She's shaking.

And then, from the back room, there is a groan. We all turn toward it, silent, as we tilt our heads listening. A cough, followed by a soft laugh.

"Well, that fucking hurt," Realm says.

I gasp and run in that direction, leaving the violence at the door behind. Running for Realm. When I get to the bedroom door, I find him sitting up in bed, blood everywhere, awake. Marie is sobbing next to him, murmuring that she did it. That it works.

James has a soft smile on his lips, his eyes blinking heavily. Realm notices me in the doorway.

"Well, damn," he says, his voice hoarse. "You always beat me at cards."

I choke out a laugh, about to say that I'm glad he didn't die, when there is a loud bang, making us all jump. Sloane comes running into the room, Wes behind her, holding out the knife defensively. I don't think he'd use it, and beyond that, I'm not sure how well he'd use it with his left hand anyway.

Marie stands, defiant, ready to face whatever comes.

"Where is he?" a female voice yells from the kitchen. Behind us, Realm laughs loudly.

"You have got to be shitting me," he says.

Sloane turns to him, stunned, and steps out into the kitchen tentatively. Wes tells her to wait, but it's like she's entranced by the voice.

"Sloane?" the voice says. Wes and I look at each other, and then we start in that direction, unsure of what's happening.

There are six people in the kitchen, most of them in suits. An authoritative-looking man with dark skin and a well-manicured beard stands in the doorway, surveying the scene. But it's a girl with blond hair and dark red lipstick who takes up all of the room with her presence. When she smiles at Sloane, there is a large gap between her two front teeth.

"Oh my God, Dallas?" Sloane says, and walks right into her for a fierce hug. "I thought you were The Program."

Dallas gives her a quick squeeze. "Yeah, no. Just me, the FDA, and the CDC," she says like she knows it sounds ridiculous. "Also, awesome I had to hear all this from them. Now, where the hell is Michael?"

"In the back."

Dallas rushes past Sloane, only glancing at me, before stopping at the doorway. She sweeps her gaze over the room and then puts her hand on her hip. She doesn't smile, but Realm beams at her.

"Hi, honey," he says in an amused voice. "You're late."

"Huh," she says, crossing her arms over her worn T-shirt. "You're not dead."

"Nope. Not anymore."

Dallas's lips flinch with a smile. "Good news, I guess."

"Yep."

They stare at each other, and from next to Realm, James holds up his hand.

"Hi, Dallas," he says.

"Hi, gorgeous," she replies. "You'd better not die. The world couldn't handle that kind of loss."

He laughs softly, and Marie says hello to Dallas and leaves the room. I follow behind her, not sure who any of the people standing around the kitchen are. They don't seem to be with The Program.

The tall man steps forward, sliding the table aside, and comes to stop in front of Marie. He's wearing a sharp gray suit with a white shirt, a lemon-yellow tie. He holds out his hands to her, and she grasps them.

"Hello, Luther," Marie says. "I'm glad you made it."

"Marie," he replies in a deep voice. "I'm glad you got my message. I hope it helped."

Marie nods, and her eyes well up. "It did. We have the cure," she says. "I've done it."

He smiles. "I always knew you would," he replies.

They stay silent for a moment, and then he motions the other people forward.

"And Nicole and Deacon?" Marie asks, hopeful, as the people pass.

Luther's smile fades. "Your kids found me," he says. "But they left. They told me . . . they said they forgive you, but that they couldn't be a part of your life anymore. They said good-bye."

Marie drops Luther's hands, brushing at her hair. She doesn't say anything else, but I can see her heart breaking.

Luther's associates file into the room with Realm, and Dallas strolls out, going to the living room and dropping onto the couch like she owns the place. Boots up on the cushions. She makes a call, laughing loudly. Telling Cas that Realm is alive.

Dallas is Realm's ex-girlfriend, the one he's still fond of. The one he didn't think he deserved. But she came for him. I hope she'll stay for him.

Wes sits at the table with me while Marie administers the cure to James, the FDA and CDC there to witness and document the entire process. When they're done, Luther comes out to interview all of us.

I'm a little scared at first, but Marie's ex-husband is actually very engaging, understanding. And for once, I don't feel like I'm being manipulated. An adult who's actually listening to our feelings—what a novel idea.

"You were very brave," Luther tells me, nodding from across the table. "And we appreciate what you did. We'll keep you safe. I don't want you to worry."

"Uh . . . definitely easier said than done," I tell him. "I can't remember the last time I wasn't scared."

Luther reaches to put his hand over mine on the table, comforting me. "It'll get easier over time, but the first days will be hard," he admits. "The fear . . . it'll find you at inopportune times. A flash of a memory that might leave you feeling vulnerable."

Of course the moment he says that, I pull my hand back, thinking of Derek. I roll my eyes to the ceiling to stop myself from tearing up, the memory unsettling me.

"But there's hope," Luther says, leaning into the table. "You never gave up, Tatum. None of you. Your fight is what's going to bring down The Program. Set us back on the right course. Helping people. Not controlling them."

He exhales heavily, folding his hands in front me. "Just please promise me that you'll get counseling—deal with this the proper way. You'll have some things to work through."

I tell him that I will, thinking of Nicole's card in my pocket. Who better to understand my issues?

Luther smiles warmly at me and nods a good-bye before interviewing Wes, who really doesn't know much. When he's completed all of his debriefings, Luther tells Marie that he's filing for immediate evaluation of the cure. With him standing by to confirm, they contact Dr. Wyatt and let her know it's begun.

"I suggest you get these kids out of here before the authorities arrive," Luther says quietly to Marie, standing in the doorway of the bedroom. "We need to lock down the scene. And then we'll round up those involved with The Program. We have everything we need."

Marie smiles at him, and I imagine she feels vindicated, justified in everything she's done to get us here. I'm not sure I agree, but I'm still grateful. She stares at Luther, but it's different from how she looked at Dr. McKee, not as deep. She's lost people too.

"Just give me a few minutes with them," Marie says to Luther. He nods that he will, and Luther tells Realm and James that he hopes they'll feel better. He says good-bye to Dallas— who apparently does freelance work for his office—and then offers me one last smile before taking his team, and Marie's equipment, out to his van to make more calls.

Marie comes over to the stove, her body still shaking, and puts on a kettle for tea. Wes says he'll be back and goes to the room with Sloane to check on the others. The space is suddenly intimate, and Marie looks at me.

"Thank you," she says. "Thank you, Tatum."

She doesn't need to thank me for being a good human, and I tell her so.

"How are you feeling?" she asks.

"Little bit of a headache," I say. "Heartache."

She nods like she understands and leans her back against

the sink. "I didn't know," she offers. "Not the extent. I was Arthur Pritchard's employee, and I brought him Quinlan several times, but I didn't realize how much she knew. I would have never . . . I didn't know he was so cruel to her." She closes her eyes and gathers herself.

"I've made a lot of mistakes," she continues after a moment. "And I've spent years trying to correct those mistakes, sometimes making more. I'm sure you can understand that."

"Every time I try to make things better, they get worse," I tell her.

"It'll be different this time," she says like she believes it with her whole self.

The kettle starts to whistle, and Marie takes out two cups and turns off the burner. When she's made tea, she brings the cups to the table and sets one in front of me.

"I'm not sure I can live with it," she says quietly. "Live with what I did to Quinlan . . . Nicole," she corrects. She hitches in a breath, and her entire façade breaks wide open. For as many times as I've seen Marie, I've never seen this. The woman here now is shattered.

"She's my baby; she's my little girl," Marie says, choking. "And I did that to her. I . . ."

My eyes are tearing up in response, and I reach over to put my arms around Marie. I admit, what she did was disturbing. She ruined that girl's life. She tortured her.

But I hug Marie anyway, because even though she messed up, she tried to make it right. She never gave up, even when other doctors did. Teachers, politicians, and parents—they *all* gave up on us at some point, relying on The Program instead.

Marie Devoroux never did. She searched for a cure until she found one. She's the true face of this rebellion. She's our hero, even if she nearly killed us to save us.

As Marie straightens out of my arms, thanking me and wiping her tears, Wes comes back in. He pauses a second, not sure if he should interrupt, but Marie offers him her chair.

"I'm going to check on my patients," she says. "Dr. Wyatt is on her way, and we hope to start clinical trials immediately. Fast-track it to the market. Now, the rest of you should get out of here. Go home. It's over."

It's such a strange thing to hear: *over*. I can't quite believe it. Marie leaves the room, but Wes and I take a moment to absorb what's happened. I'll call Nathan in a few minutes, ask him for a ride so we can fill him in. He won't believe it either.

"I hate to bring this up," Wes says, biting his lip like he knows he shouldn't continue. "But what are we going to do about your grandparents? That whole memory was really . . . fucked."

"They're not my grandparents," I say, although not coldly. "But I love them anyway. They're my family. Do you remember the other day when I asked you how we live with the people we love, knowing they betrayed us?"

"Vaguely," he says. "I was much shinier then."

"Yeah, well, you told me that you just *do*—you forgive the people you love because you have to. And I don't know . . . I forgive them." I take a sip of tea. "But I'm going to tell them everything, what I remember. It'll hurt them, seeing themselves as the villains. I'm going to anyway. It's time for all of us to see the whole picture—even the messy parts."

"I'll come with you," Wes says, picking at a scuff in the table. "If you want me to."

"You can be there," I say, making him smile.

"That's good," he says. "Because I'm never going home again, so . . . I hope I can live with you too."

It's sad, but we laugh anyway. I tell him there's always room for him. He murmurs that he loves me, that he's happy we saved the world after all.

And it reminds me of something Michael Realm said to me once in The Program. He told me that Wes and I were a heart rate on a monitor, sky high and then through the floor. Never quite even. We love hard and completely, and that's the stuff that never goes away. Not from us. Not ever.

"You're the love of my life, Wes," I say, looking sideways at him.

Wes flashes me that devastating grin, the kind that can convince me of anything. The kind that made me fall in love with him in the first place.

"It's three lives for me," he says like it's a competition. He looks over my face, pausing at my lips. "So let's make this one count."

I smile that we will, and when he leans in to kiss me, groaning once at the pain in his shoulder, I think that we'll both be okay.

I think I've made the right choices this time.

CHAPTER SIXTEEN

SCHOOL IS WEIRD. AFTER BEING ATTACKED SEV-
eral times and fighting for your life, sitting through science
class is a bit anticlimactic. But we made it. We earned this
mediocrity.

Foster is next to me, filling in the last questions on our lab
report as I stare dreamily out the window.

He made good on his promise to find the handlers. There
were thirty-seven in our school. The number is staggering,
shocking. I wonder if there was ever a moment when I wasn't
being watched.

The monitor is still around, but there are no more assessments. No more fear. Dr. Angela Wyatt is partnering with Marie
and the FDA, administering Adjustments on a voluntary basis.
They all agreed that forced treatment isn't the answer. They

voted for transparency, and because of that, returners come to them in droves, hoping to be cured.

A special counsel has been appointed by Congress, investigating the role of The Program in deaths of returners. Throughout the country, nearly three hundred teens died. Numerous doctors and psychiatrists attribute those crashback deaths to procedures used in The Program. The special counsel found The Program criminally and monetarily liable.

Marie was able to keep me anonymous, and it was decided that she would take credit for creating the pattern that destroyed The Program. They didn't want to tie it in to Arthur Pritchard or the victims of the grief department—Luther's advice. Gaining back the public trust wouldn't be easy.

But the pattern worked. People are getting better. The worst of the epidemic, its aftermath, is over.

After all this time, it's finally over.

The bell rings, and Foster and I grab our bags and head to lunch. We're staying in today, as we've done for the past few weeks. Like Foster said, the purity of recess.

"Holy shit," Foster says as we walk down the hall, looking down at his phone. "Arturo just sent me this." He holds it out to me, and I gasp. "Says she was in Colorado," Foster adds.

It's a link to a news article about Dr. Warren. She disappeared the night we found the cure. Her office had been cleaned out, the office of Mr. Castle also empty. She disappeared into the wind, and it left us looking over our shoulder. Dr. Warren didn't have any power, but then again, we'd underestimated her before.

"'Warren was taken into custody at a Chipotle in Denver,'" Foster reads, and then laughs. "That's actually fucking hilarious," he says.

"Does it say what they're charging her with?" I ask. Part of me worries I'll get dragged into a lengthy trial, but Marie already told me I'd be redacted from all records pertaining to Dr. Warren. She said she had plenty on her without bringing up the fact that she sent people to kidnap me.

"Uh . . ." He scans the page. "No," he says. "It just says she's been wanted in connection with illegal memory manipulation and crimes against the state." He looks at me, and a moment passes, acknowledging all she put me through. "She'll never get out of prison," he says.

I nod that it's good; she deserves it. But the terrible truth is they never tracked down the main backers of The Program. They got a few—hell, three senators were indicted. The Program was everywhere and yet under the radar. They could have changed the world—controlled it.

But we stopped them. *Us*—regular people. And a doctor and the FDA and the CDC, but still—mostly us.

Foster and I get to the doorway to the courtyard and scan the area. I find Nathan and Wes immediately, the two of them laughing as Nathan continues telling whatever story he has. They've become pretty decent friends, and Nathan says that he likes this new Wes a whole hell of a lot better than the old one. But really, he's just given him a chance now. He would have liked the old Wes too.

"There you are," Arturo says, coming up to Foster. They smile, exchange a quick kiss, and Arturo says hello to me. "I'm guessing you saw the news?" he asks, raising his dark eyebrows.

"I did. Pretty wild, right?" I reply.

"Yeah, well," Arturo says, pursing his lips and glancing over at Nathan. "Not as wild as Nathan Harmon and Melody Blackstone meeting up last night."

"What?" I ask, widening my eyes. Arturo gets the best information. He and Melody actually stayed friends, and with his help, he got her and Nathan to speak again.

"He's going to kill you for telling me," I say to Arturo, making him laugh.

"I'm not worried," he replies, and takes Foster's hand to lead him to our lunch spot. I hang back a moment and watch Wes.

His hair has grown longer since that night at Marie's, a little unruly and adorable. He didn't need surgery on his shoulder but had physical therapy for weeks. The injury left a small bump, a permanent reminder of what his mother was responsible for.

Wes and I are both eighteen now, and he never went back to his house. My grandfather collected his stuff for him and moved him into our spare bedroom until we leave for college. Graduation is only a week away, and after the summer, we're going to Arizona, of all places.

Wes isn't giving up on the possibility of becoming a lawyer in the future, but for now he's been accepted into the journalism school, and I'll be there in the creative writing department.

My grandparents joke that they look forward to us moving back in after we graduate with our shiny English degrees.

My phone buzzes, and I take it out. A smile spreads across my lips.

You've probably seen this, but . . . , Michael Realm writes, attaching the article about Dr. Warren.

I did, I reply. Still feels just as good to read it again.

He sends a picture this time, and it's Dallas in the front seat of his car, her eyes closed, her tongue out, as she holds up a set of keys. Got a new place if you guys want to come visit.

There's a soft tug on my heart, mostly happiness. Realm and Dallas moved to Eugene, and before he left, Realm told Marie that he truly hoped he'd never see her again, before hugging her good-bye.

I'm glad that Realm finally sees he's good enough to be loved. I'm a little sad that he moved away, especially now that I remember our friendship. I blink back the start of tears.

Tell Dallas to plan a party and I'm there, I write. I don't really know her; she's kind of intimidating, if I'm honest. But she and Realm have been doing this together for a long time. He told me once that he always hoped he'd make it back to her. I'm happy that he did.

I put the phone away and start toward my friends. Nathan notices me first and nods to me. I'm glad he's finding closure with Melody, even if it doesn't lead to anything more.

Wes never looks up at me, eating his sandwich and listening to Foster and Arturo tell a story, but when I sit next to him, he passes over his bag of cookies without a word.

"And then what happened?" he asks Foster, totally invested in the conversation. His dimples flash, and I watch him—enjoying his curiosity. When the story's done, Wes turns to me and looks me up and down.

"Hi," he says simply.

"Hi," I respond, fighting back a smile. And then, in a swift movement, he wraps his arms around me and tips me back into the shrubbery, kissing me passionately. I laugh, hand on his cheek, and let him help me back up.

"Disgusting," Nathan says under his breath, and Wes blows him a kiss.

We all have lunch together, and it's the purest thing I can remember. After years of being scared all the time, of living in constant fear and worry—we've all found our peace, much like Wes.

He *is* the love of my life, but he's not my life. I have that back now—no more threats, no more secrets. A bit of research proved I had no biological family left, but I have my name—Cynthia Wilds.

I've never used it. I let her rest with her mother and father. She was someone in another life, but she died the day I was created.

Wes slips his hand around mine, leaning in to murmur that he loves me because I'm so fucking cute, and I smile to myself. It's all so simple now that it's shocking sometimes.

But I accept our fate, accept this new world. I know we deserve it.

Because we're all better people now.

EPILOGUE

SLOANE BARSTOW LIES ON THE BANK OF THE RIVER, her forearm over her face to block the summer sun. It was getting too hot, and James promised to take her somewhere to escape the weekend heat. Realm and Dallas were off on another secret mission, so they were out of town.

But even though Sloane's at the river, the same river where her brother died, she still doesn't entirely love swimming. She opted to roast on the blanket instead.

As if she conjured him up, she hears James approach from where he's been in the river. Sloane lowers her arm and looks at him, one eye squinted against the sun. James stands at the edge of the blanket, staring at the water as he drags a towel over his bare chest, his hair golden in the sunlight. He senses her watching him, and he glances down at her with those arresting blue eyes.

"You checking me out, Sloane?" he asks, exactly the same way he asked her years before when she first realized she liked him.

"No," she replies easily, trying not to smile.

James nods like he believes her and goes back to watching the water. He tosses the towel aside and lowers himself onto the blanket next to her.

Sloane's face is turned in his direction, waiting. She can feel the coolness coming off his skin from the river water. James looks sideways at her, his eyes impossibly blue, as he runs his gaze over her swimsuit.

They're quiet for a long moment, Sloane's heart speeding up, a smile creeping over her lips.

James curses at his lack of self-control and turns to wrap his leg over Sloane's hip, rolling her against him and making her laugh.

"It's so wet," she says with a quick shiver from his damp suit on her skin.

James snorts a laugh, and Sloane smacks his leg. "Not what I meant," she says, laughing anyway.

They both chuckle for a few moments, and then they settle on the blanket. James stays wrapped around her, their faces close as they watch each other.

Sloane can't stand to look at him sometimes, especially this close up. It seems ridiculous . . . but she loves him too much. She loves everything about him, and she knows he feels exactly the same way. They're both helpless in that love. She leans in and kisses him softly.

James hums out his approval, his hand sliding up her back and under her hair, resting on her neck as his tongue glides against hers. He moves his leg to bring it between hers, and the kissing leads to more, his fingers under her swimsuit, her hand inside his.

"Car or tent?" James murmurs at Sloane's lips. "I don't want sand getting—"

"Car," Sloane says, but doesn't stop. James breaks the kiss, burying his face in her hair as she brings him close, and then, when she's finished, he stays against her, once again helpless in his love.

"Still car?" he asks, out of breath. Sloane laughs.

"No, I'd prefer the tent," she says. She isn't in such a hurry to get naked, though; she just likes being near him. She almost lost him this time. She never wants to feel that again.

"Now?" James asks, getting up on one elbow, his eyes heavy lidded. He looks so sweet and happy that Sloane sits up to give him a quick kiss before tossing him the towel.

"Later," she says, looking at the river to check the current. "And for a lot longer."

"Don't you worry," he says, and smiles broadly.

"I never have to," she replies. That certainly is never one of their problems.

"But I was thinking," he adds, reaching to trace his finger down her back as she stares at the water. "Now that things are normal, or at least normal for now . . . I have ideas."

"Yikes," Sloane says jokingly, flashing him a smile.

"I know, right? But anyway, these ideas . . ." He pauses, and his expression grows serious. "They're not in Oregon," he finishes.

Sloane turns around on the blanket and sits cross-legged, facing him. "What are these ideas?" she asks.

"You, me, California. Some super-cute beach. Maybe formal wear."

Sloane stares at him, heat creeping onto her chest. "Anything else I should know about this idea?" she asks.

James licks his lips, lowering his eyes like he's self-conscious, and reaches to play with her fingers.

"Not really," he says. "Just a couple of friends, a man of God." He lifts his blue eyes. "A ring that's not made of plastic."

Sloane and James have been through so much, and Sloane always knew they'd end up here. She knew it when they first started dating years ago. She even knew it when she didn't remember him at all. And yet . . . and yet . . . she's not prepared for how her heart aches at this idea. How all of the misery somehow got them here, and that means she can let it go. She's not prepared for that.

Sloane's eyes well up, and she looks down to where James is pressing his fingers between hers, opening and closing his hand. "What if I like the plastic ring?" she asks, not meeting his gaze.

"We could upgrade to platinum," he suggests. "One that has, I don't know, our initials or something. Maybe some kind of rock."

Sloane tries to bite back her smile.

"River rock?" she asks, just to mess with him.

James laughs and tugs her hand so she'll look at him. She's surprised to see the glassiness in his eyes, the red high on his cheeks.

"Maybe one like this?" he asks, and then leans over to grab his backpack. He pulls out a clear plastic bubble with a yellow top, the kind that comes out of a quarter machine. The same kind he's given her before with sparkly rings in them.

She holds the plastic in her hands, and when she looks at James, he shrugs like she should open it.

"I love you," she says first, straight and to the point. "You know I love you madly, right?"

"Yeah," he says, one corner of his mouth lifting in a smile. "Yeah, I know you do."

Sloane slides her thumb under the lid of the plastic bubble and pops off the top. Inside is a silver ring with a princess cut diamond set in the middle. She stares at its sparkle in the sunlight. She looks up at James and sees him impatient for her response.

"It's bigger than I thought," she says, taking it out of the plastic.

"I get that a lot," James returns, eyes still impatient. Sloane laughs and studies the ring, finding their initials connected with a heart. James reaches for the ring and then takes her hand.

Sloane and James stare at each other as James waits for permission to put it on, his confidence only waning when it comes to the possibility of Sloane not feeling the same.

"Well?" Sloane whispers. "I think this is your part."

James's lips flinch with a smile, and then he shifts to get one knee down on the blanket in front of her. Sloane gets to her knees in return.

They're both in damp bathing suits with sand sticking

to their skin, but Sloane can't imagine a better place. A more important place than next to the river.

"Will you marry me?" James asks suddenly, his voice tight with emotion. Sloane watches as tears slip onto his cheeks, his chest rising and falling rapidly.

It's all come to this. The pain and grief are over; they're free.

Sloane blinks and feels her own tears drip down. James slides the ring onto her finger, but she doesn't want to look down. Doesn't want to look away from him.

And the weight of the ring feels natural; it feels right.

Sloane brings her arms over James's shoulders, threading her fingers through the back of his hair.

"Yes," she says simply. "The answer was always yes, even when you were just joking."

"I was never joking," James says. "Because it's always been about us." He leans in and kisses her, laying her back on the blanket. Their tears fade away, evaporating from the heat of their skin pressed together.

"It's us forever, Sloane," he murmurs. "Just like I promised." It's a promise he's never broken.

And so later, when Sloane stares at the top of their tent, James between her legs as her fingernails dig into his back, she knows he was right.

It has always been about them. And it always will be.

ACKNOWLEDGMENTS

I first want to thank my agent, Jim McCarthy, and everyone at DG&B. Your guidance and determination has made this all possible, and I'll forever be grateful.

I also want to thank my amazing editor, Liesa Abrams, for understanding the depths of the characters and the world I created. Your point of view has made me a better writer and has brought this series to life. I'm lucky to have you in my corner.

Thank you to the entire team at Simon Pulse for your support of this series. A special thank-you to cover designer Russell Gordon (seriously, what great covers), the fantastic Mara Anastas, the Riveted Lit team, and everyone in the education department.

Thank you to my tireless friends who have read drafts of

my books, sometimes multiple times: Trish Doller, Amanda Morgan, Bethany Griffin, and Michael Strother. I also want to thank Mindi Johnson, Hannah Johnson, and Abe Tinkham for your support (and acting skills) over the years.

And mostly, I want to thank my readers. Thank you for inhabiting the world of The Program for six years, for rooting for these characters, for believing in hope. This last book was for you.

As always, thank you to my family. My husband, Jesse, and my kids, Joseph and Sophia. Also thanks to my dogs Jasper, Marlowe, and Teddy for chewing up everything I own with the exception of this computer.

Finally, this book—just like every book I've written—is in memory of my grandmother Josephine Parzych. She passed away shortly before my books were published, but she always believed I'd be a writer. And it was her belief in me that pushed me to continue. If she were alive today, I know she'd be in the front row of every signing; she'd interrupt people on the street to tell them about my books. She'd be proud of me. And honestly, it's all I could ever strive for—to make her proud.

Thank you, everyone. And please . . . stay hopeful.

TURN THE PAGE FOR A GLIMPSE AT
SUZANNE YOUNG'S CHILLING NEW SERIES. . . .

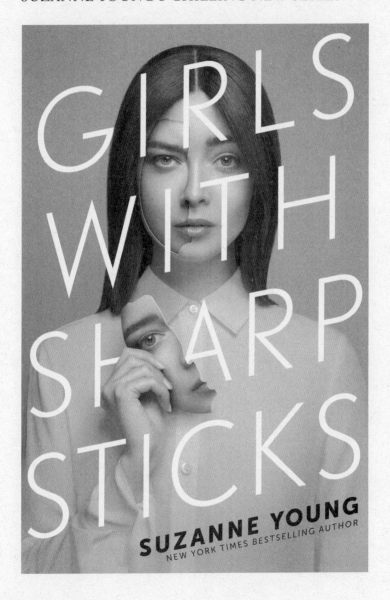

GIRLS WITH SHARP STICKS

SUZANNE YOUNG

NEW YORK TIMES BESTSELLING AUTHOR

1

t's been raining for the past three months. Or maybe it's only been three days. Time is hard to measure here—every day so much like the one before, they all start to blend together.

Rain taps on my school-provided slicker, the inside of the clear plastic material growing foggy in the humid air, and I look around the Federal Flower Garden. Precipitation has soaked the soil, causing it to run onto the pathways as the rose petals sag with moisture.

The other girls are gathered around Professor Penchant, listening attentively as he points out the varied plant species, explaining which ones we'll be growing back at the school this semester in our gardening class. We grow all manner of things at the Innovations Academy.

A thought suddenly occurs to me, and I take a few steps into the garden, my black shoes sinking into the soil. There are red roses as far as I can see, beautiful and lonely. Lonely because it's only them—all together, but apart from the other flowers. Isolated.

The sound of rain echoes near my ears, but I close my eyes and listen, trying to hear the roses breathe. Thinking I can hear them live.

But I can't hear anything beyond the rain, so I open my eyes again, disappointed.

It's been a dreadful start to spring due to the constant rain. Professor Penchant explained that our flowers—and by extension, us—will flourish because of it. Well, I hope the flourishing is done in time for graduation in the fall. Our time at the academy will be up, and then the school will get a new batch of girls to take our place.

I glance at the group standing with Professor Penchant and find Valentine Wright staring blankly ahead, her gaze cast out among the flowers. It's unusual for her to not be paying attention; she's the most proper of all of us. I've invited Valentine, on multiple occasions, to hang out with me and the other girls after hours, but she told me it was unseemly for us to gossip. For us to laugh so loudly. Be so opinionated. Eventually, I stopped asking her to join.

Sydney notices me standing apart. She rolls her eyes back and sticks her tongue out to the side like she's dead, making me laugh. Professor Penchant spins to find me.

"Philomena," he calls, impatiently waving his hand. "Come here. We're at the apex of our lesson."

I immediately obey, hopping across the rose garden to join the other girls. When I reach the group, Professor Penchant presses his thumb between my eyebrows, wiggling it around to work out the crease in my skin.

"And no more daydreaming," he says with disapproval. "It's bad for your complexion." He drops his hand before turning back to the group. I imagine he's left a reddened thumbprint between my eyebrows.

When the professor starts to talk again, I look sideways at Sydney. She grins, her dimples deep set and her brown eyes framed with exaggerated black lashes. Sydney has smooth, dark skin and straightened hair that falls just below her shoulders under the plastic rain slicker.

On the other side of her, Lennon Rose leans forward to check on me, her blue eyes wide and innocent. "I think your complexion is lovely," she whispers.

I thank her for being so sweet.

Professor Penchant tells the group about a new strain of flower that Innovations Academy will be developing this semester. We love working in the greenhouse, love getting outside whenever we can. Even if the sunshine is rare.

"But only those who are well-behaved will get a chance to work on these plants," the professor warns. "There are no rewards for girls who are too *spirited*." He looks directly at me, and I lower my eyes, not wanting to vex him any more today. "Professor Driscoll will concur."

As the professor continues, turning away to point out other plants, I glance around the flower garden once again. It's then that I notice Guardian Bose standing near the entrance where we came in. He's talking to the curator of the garden, a young woman holding an oversized red umbrella. While one hand holds the umbrella, she puts the other on her hip, talking impatiently to the Guardian. I wonder what they're discussing.

Guardian Bose is an intimidating presence in any setting, but even more so outside the walls of the academy, where he's become commonplace. He's here to ensure our safety and compliance, although we never misbehave—not in any significant way.

Innovations Academy, our all-girl private school, is very protective of us. We're confined to campus most days of our accelerated yearlong program, and we don't go home on breaks. They say the complete immersion helps us develop faster, more thoroughly.

Recently, the academy raised its curriculum rigor, increasing the number of courses and amount of training. Our class of twelve was selected based on the new heightened standards. We're *top of the line*, they like to say. *The most well-rounded girls to ever graduate.* We do our best to make them proud.

Guardian Bose says something to the woman with the red umbrella. She laughs, shaking her head no. The Guardian's posture tightens, and then he turns to find me watching him. He angles his body to block my view of the woman. He tips his head, saying something near her ear, and the woman shrinks back. Within moments, she hurries toward the indoor facility and disappears.

I turn away before Guardian Bose catches me watching again. Thunder booms overhead and Lennon Rose screams before slapping her hand over her mouth. The professor looks pointedly in her direction, but then he glances up at the sky as the rain begins to fall harder.

"All right, girls," he says, adjusting the hood on his rain slicker. "We're going to wrap this up for now. Back to the bus."

A couple of the girls begin to protest, but Professor Penchant claps his hands loudly to drown out their voices. He reminds them that we'll return next month—so long as we behave. The girls comply, apologizing, and start toward the bus. But as the others head that way, I notice that Valentine doesn't move; she doesn't even turn in that direction.

I swallow hard, unsettled. Rain pours over Valentine's slicker, running down the clear plastic in rivers. A drop runs down her cheek. I watch her, trying to figure out what's wrong.

Sensing me, she lifts her head. She is . . . expressionless. Alarming in her stillness.

"Valentine," I call over the rain. "Are you okay?"

She pauses so long that I'm not sure she heard me. Then she turns back to the flowers. "Can you hear them too?" she asks, her voice soft and faraway.

"Hear what?" I ask.

The corner of her mouth twitches with a smile. "The roses," she says affectionately. "They're alive, you know. All of them. And if you listen closely enough, you can hear their shared roots. Their common purpose. They're beautiful, but it's not all they are."

There's tingling over my skin because a few moments ago, I

did try to listen to the roses. What are the chances that Valentine and I would have the same odd thought?

"I didn't hear anything," I admit. "Just quiet contentment."

Valentine's behavior is unusual, but I want to know what she's going to say next. I take a step closer.

Her smile fades. "They're not content," she replies in a low voice. "They're waiting."

A drop of rain finds its way under the collar of my shirt and runs down my spine, making me shiver.

"Waiting for what?" I ask.

Valentine turns to me and whispers, *"To wake up."*

Her eyes narrow, fierce and unwavering. Her hands curl into fists at her side.

I shiver again, but this time it's not from the rain. The academy tells us not to ask philosophical questions because we're not equipped for the answers. They teach us what we *need*, rather than indulging our passing curiosities. They say it helps maintain our balance, like soil ripe for growth.

Valentine's words are dangerous in that way—the beginning of a larger conversation I want to have. But at the same time, one I don't quite understand. One that scares me. Why would the flowers say such a thing? Why would flowers say anything at all?

Just as I'm about to ask her what the flowers are waking up from, there is a firm grip on my elbow. Startled, I spin around to find Guardian Bose towering over me.

"I've got it from here, Philomena," he says in his deep voice. "Catch up with the others."

I shoot a cautious glace at Valentine, but her expression has gone back to pleasant. As the Guardian approaches her, Valentine nods obediently before he even says a word. Her abrupt change in character has left me confused.

I start toward the bus, my brows pulled together as I think. Sydney holds out her hand when she sees me and I take it gratefully, our fingers wet and cold.

"What was that about?" she asks as we walk.

"I'm not exactly sure," I say. "Valentine is . . . off," I add for lack of a better word. I don't know how to explain what just happened. Especially when it's left me so uneasy.

Sydney and I look back in Valentine's direction, but she and the Guardian are already heading our way. Valentine is quiet. Perfect posture. Perfect temperament.

"She looks fine to me," Sydney says with a shrug. "Her usual boring self."

I study Valentine a moment longer, but the girl who spoke to me is gone, replaced with a flawless imitation. Or, I guess, the original version.

And I'm left with the burden of the words, an infectious thought.

Wake up, it whispers. *Wake up, Philomena.*

The bus tires bump over a pothole, and Sydney falls from her seat to land in the center aisle with a flop. She immediately laughs, standing up to take a dramatic bow when the other girls giggle.

Professor Penchant orders Sydney to sit down, poking the air impatiently with his finger. Sydney offers him an apologetic smile and slides into the seat next to me, mouthing the word "Ouch."

I jut out my bottom lip in a show of sympathy before Sydney gets up on her knees to talk to Marcella and Brynn in the seat behind us.

"At least they bought us rain covers," Marcella is saying to Brynn. "I've always wanted to wear a trash bag in public. Goal achieved."

"I believe it's called a 'rain slicker,'" Sydney corrects, making Brynn snort a laugh. "And don't settle yet, Marcella," she adds. "Maybe next time we'll get a potato sack."

Brynn nearly falls out of her seat laughing. Marcella catches her by the hand, intertwining their fingers. They smile at each other.

Marcella and Brynn have been dating since our second day of school at the Innovations Academy. Eight months later, they're closer than ever. A perfect pair, if anyone were to ask me. Marcella is clever and decisive while Brynn is nurturing and creative. Despite the strength of their relationship, they keep it a secret from the school—afraid the Guardian will separate them if he finds out. Our education is supposed to be our only focus. Dating is strictly forbidden.

Annalise Gibbons raises her hand from the seat in front of us, and when Guardian Bose notices, he exhales loudly and rolls his eyes. "What?" he asks.

"I really have to go to the bathroom," she says. "It's an emergency."

We're still about an hour from the school, I'm guessing, so the Guardian gets up to speak to the driver. We wait in anticipation of an unexpected stop, watching him in the oversized rearview mirror as he talks quietly to the older man behind the wheel. The white-haired driver nods as if he doesn't care either way, and Guardian Bose lifts his eyes to the mirror, where he catches us staring at him. Several of us lower our heads so we don't sway his opinion in the other direction.

"There's a gas station a few miles up," Guardian Bose announces. "Only those who have to go to the bathroom get off the bus, understand? Otherwise we'll fall behind schedule."

There are murmurs of "yes, we understand," but a buzz

reverberates through all of us. Normally our field trips are limited to one place and very few people outside of our group. Nothing unexpected ever happens. At that thought, I sit up taller to check on Valentine.

She's in the front seat, across the aisle from the Guardian. Her long black hair flows over the back of the padded green seat, but she is impossibly still, staring out the windshield and not acknowledging any of us. Like she's thinking about the roses again.

Today *has* been unexpected. Unusual, even. But it's about more than Valentine's peculiar behavior in the flower garden. It's about the restlessness her words have caused. The way my head seems to itch somewhere just out of reach.

No, today is different—that much I know for certain. And to prove it, a sign for a gas station appears on our right and the bus edges that way, bumping over the lane dividers.

The other girls press against the windows as I grab money from the front pocket of my backpack and tuck it into my waistband. The bus hisses to a stop to the side of the building.

A beat-up yellow car pulls in just behind us and parks at the gas pump. Other than that, the place looks deserted, run down. Grimy in a quaint way, I suppose. Like it's never been updated. Never changed.

Despite the Guardian's warning, nearly all of us stand to go inside—thrilled at the chance to see someplace new.

Guardian Bose is quick to hold up his hands. "Really?" he asks. "All of you?"

A few make frantic gestures like their bladders might explode, and others look at him pleadingly. I just want to buy candy. We're not allowed sweets at the academy; our food is closely monitored. Even at home, my parents didn't allow sugar in my diet. But I find I crave it desperately, especially after getting a taste on a field trip earlier this year.

The school brought us to an art exhibit at a museum just outside of town. It wasn't during regular business hours, so we had the place to ourselves. Sydney and I raced up the stairs when the Guardian wasn't looking, and Lennon Rose, Annalise, and I spent extra time staring at the nude male statues until Annalise nearly snapped off a penis while posing dramatically next to him. And before we left, we all stopped in the gift shop. Some bought postcards for their parents or a souvenir or two. I picked out several bags of M&M's and Starburst candies.

Honestly, I don't understand the addictive properties of sugar—it's never been mentioned in our classes—but I can attest they are life altering.

And so I put on my most pleasing and innocent expression for the Guardian. I must not be alone in trying this, because he darts his pale eyes around the bus and then shakes his head.

"Fine," he says. "You go in small groups. Fifteen minutes and we're back on the road. Understand?"

We nod eagerly and he motions us off the bus by row. Only Valentine and two other girls willingly stay behind. Sydney and I are the last group to leave, and on the way out, Guardian Bose looks down at me.

"Philomena," he says, darting a quick look at Valentine

before studying my expression. "Don't get distracted in there."

"No problem," I say with a smile. Nothing can distract me from candy.

I step off the bus, pleased to find the rain has softened to a drizzle. The mountain is closer now that we're heading toward school, and I'm at once enchanted and intimidated by its scale. Mist clings to the summit, so I imagine it's raining at the academy. It's always raining there.

I'm no longer wearing the plastic rain slicker, and I appreciate the moisture on my skin, tickling my bare forearms. Soaking into me. At least, I do until I step into a puddle and splash muddy water on my delicate white socks. I glance down past my plaid uniform skirt and shake out my shoe.

As I start walking again, I look at the yellow car. There's a young guy pumping gas, his face turned away as he leans against the back door, talking through the open passenger-side window to another boy still inside the car. I examine them, curious.

The boy in the passenger seat is wearing a crisp white T-shirt, a shiny watch glinting on his wrist as he rests his arm on the open window. He's cute—dark skin, his hair shaved short. He must say something funny, because the other guy laughs and turns to press a button on the pump, his face coming into view.

I note immediately that he's extremely good looking. This boy is thin with an angular jaw—sharp at the edges—thick black eyebrows, messy black hair. And when his gaze drifts past the pump and he notices me, he seems just as startled by my attention. He holds up his hand in a wave.

I smile in return, but then Sydney calls loudly for me to catch up. I jog to meet her at the glass door of the building, embarrassed at my lack of decorum. I didn't mean to stare at those boys. It's just . . . we don't see many young men at the academy. Actually, we don't see any at all.

Sydney looks over her shoulder at the boys as if she's just spotting them. When she turns back around, she flashes me a quick grin and pulls open the door. A bell on the metal bar jingles.

I'm struck by the smell of baking bread. The gas station has a menu board posted over a small deli at a second counter. A woman in a hairnet stands behind there, her face deeply tanned and creased with wrinkles. She doesn't even mutter a hello.

Sydney heads toward the bathrooms while I step into the candy aisle. I'm overwhelmed by the sheer volume of choices, the bright colors and assorted flavors.

The bell on the door jingles again as the two boys enter the store. They walk directly to the deli counter. The boy in the white T-shirt gives the woman his order while the guy who waved notices me standing in the aisle, watching him above the candy rack. His mouth widens with a smile.

"Hey," he calls. "How's it going?"

The other guy glances sideways at his friend—a bit of concern in his features that seems unwarranted. But the boy with the black hair waits for my response, the ghost of a smile still on his lips.

"Anything else?" the older woman asks the two boys, ripping the top page off her pad.

The boy with the black hair tells her that'll be it, and his friend goes to pay at the register.

I return to perusing the aisle, trying to focus on my mission to collect bags of candy. I am, indeed, distracted. It doesn't take long before the boy with black hair comes to stand at the end of the aisle near the pretzels.

"Sorry to bother you," he says, his voice low-pitched and raspy. "But I was wondering if—" I turn to him and the words die on his lips. He smiles his recovery.

"You're not bothering me," I tell him. He looks relieved and shoves his hands into the pockets of his jeans.

"I'm Jackson," he says.

"Philomena," I reply. And then, after a beat, "Mena."

"Hello, Mena," Jackson says casually. He takes a step farther into the aisle and picks out a bag of candy, seemingly at random. He draws his eyebrows together as he looks out the window toward the bus.

"Innovations Academy?" he asks. "The one that used to be Innovations Metal Works—the old factory near the mountain?"

"I'd like to tell you it's not a factory anymore," I say, "but I can still smell metal in my sheets sometimes."

He laughs as if I'm joking.

Innovations Metal Works was a factory that'd been around since the town was founded. About a decade ago, they started making significant advances in technology: metal additives. Eventually, the Metal Works patent was bought out by a hospital system, and again later by a technology firm. The building itself was repurposed.

Now it's an academy that teaches us about manners, modesty, and gardening, a change that can be credited to new ownership and generous donors. And yet, I pick up the scent of machinery every so often.

"A private school?" Jackson asks, glancing at my uniform.

"Yes. All girls."

He nods like he finds this fascinating. "How long have you been there?"

"Eight months," I say. "I graduate in the fall. What about you? Do you live near the mountain?"

"Oh, I . . . uh, I live not too far from here, actually," he says. "It's just . . . I saw your bus leaving the Federal Flower Garden. Was curious."

"You've been following us since the Flower Garden?" I ask, surprised. He turns away and grabs another bag of candy.

"No," he says, waving his hand. "Not on purpose."

Suddenly, his friend appears next to him holding a brown paper bag with ends of subs poking out. "Jackie," the boy says. "We should probably get going, right?" He motions toward the glass door.

Jackson shakes his head no, subtly, and then turns to me and smiles. "Philomena," he says, "this is my friend Quentin."

Quentin glances at him, annoyed, but then smiles at me and says hello. He turns back to Jackson.

"Five minutes, yeah?" Quentin asks him, widening his eyes.

"Yeah," Jackson murmurs. He presses his lips together and looks at me, waiting for his friend to leave. Once Quentin is gone,

Jackson shrugs, as if saying his friend is just being impatient.

I study the array of chocolates, and Jackson comes to stand next to me. He grabs a small bag of Hershey's Kisses.

"These are my favorite," he says. I look sideways at him, struck by his imperfections. The freckles dotting his cheeks and nose. The slight turn of his canine teeth that makes his smile boyish and charming. There's even a tiny scar near his temple.

"I'll try them," I say, plucking the chocolates from his hand.

"Ahem," Sydney says dramatically from the other end of the aisle. She runs her gaze quickly over Jackson before settling on me.

"Sydney, this is Jackson," I tell her, fighting back my smile. Just as seeing someplace new is exciting, meeting *someone* new is absolutely thrilling. Sydney steps forward and introduces herself, politely, like we're taught.

They exchange a quick handshake, and Jackson tells her it's nice to meet her. When Sydney turns back to me she covertly mouths the word "cute."

She smiles, pleasant and respectful, when she's facing Jackson again.

"I'll meet you on the bus?" I ask her, holding up my fistfuls of candy. She pauses a long moment before nodding. She has to bite her lower lip to keep from grinning.

"Right . . . ," she says. "See you there." Sydney tells Jackson it was nice to meet him and leaves the store, the bell on the handle jingling.

Quentin watches after her while hanging out near the ATM, the brown paper bag set on top of the machine. He chews his thumbnail, and when Sydney is gone, he returns his gaze to the door.

Jackson grabs a pack of Twizzlers while I pick up red hot candies with a flaming sun on the package. Together we head toward the register.

"Can I buy that for you?" Jackson asks when I lay my pile of candy on the counter. It would be rude to refuse his offer, so I say yes and thank him. The cashier begins to ring up our sweets together.

"I'm not allowed candy at school," I confess to Jackson as he takes out his wallet. He looks at me as if he finds this unusual. "But whenever I get the chance," I add, "it's what I spend my allowance on. It's not like there's anything to buy at school."

"I'm sure," he says. "Your school's out in the middle of fucking nowhere."

I'm a bit shocked by his cursing; a bit exhilarated by the indecency of it. Jackson leans against the counter, studying me again.

"Would you want to grab a coffee with me sometime, Mena?" he asks. "I have a lot of questions about this private school–factory of yours."

I'm about to explain that I'm not allowed to leave campus when there's a series of clicks from the register. The woman behind the counter tells us the total for the candy, and Jackson removes several bills from his wallet to hand to the woman.

The bell on the glass door jingles, and I turn to see Guardian Bose walk in, a hulking mass in the small store. The woman at the register busies herself by putting my items in a plastic bag.

"Philomena," the Guardian calls in a low voice, darting his gaze from me to Jackson. "It's time to go."

I flinch at his scolding tone. I'd been told not to get distracted.

"Be right there," I say politely, avoiding Jackson's eyes as I wait for my candy.

The Guardian stomps to my side and takes me by the wrist. "No," he says, startling me. "*Now*. Everyone's already on the bus."

Jackson curls his lip. "Don't touch her like that," he says.

I look at the Guardian to gauge his reaction; I've never heard anyone speak to him that way. He opens his mouth to retort, his grip loosening, and I quietly slip free to take my bag off the counter.

But the moment I do, Guardian Bose grabs my forearm hard enough to make me wince and I drop my candy on the floor.

"I said get on the bus, Mena," he growls possessively, pulling me closer. I'm frightened, ashamed that I've upset him. I apologize even as he hurts me.

Jackson steps forward to intervene, but the Guardian holds up his palm.

"Back off, kid," Guardian Bose says. "This is none of your business."

Jackson scoffs, red blotches rising on his cheeks and neck. "Try and grab me like that, tough guy," Jackson says. "See what happens." Guardian Bose laughs dismissively.

I have no doubt that the Guardian would easily best Jackson in any fight, but at the same time, I'm struck by Jackson's open defiance—how stupid and brave it is at the same time. It's fascinating. I start to smile just before Guardian Bose yanks me toward the door.

"Come on," the Guardian says. I struggle to keep up, tripping over my own feet as his grip tightens painfully on my arm.

When I look back at Jackson, he nods at Quentin, calling him over.

"You're hurting me," I tell the Guardian. He doesn't listen, using my body to push open the door. He forces me out into the misty parking lot. My shoes scrape along the pavement as I try to look over his shoulder toward the store. But the Guardian keeps me in front of him, his fingers digging into my upper arm.

When I turn toward the bus, the girls are watching, wide-eyed, from fogged windows.

The bus doors fold open, and Guardian Bose shoves me angrily. I trip going up the stairs and cry out in pain when my knee scrapes the rubber mat on the top step, tearing my flesh. The Guardian hauls me up by my underarms and dumps me on the seat next to Valentine. A trickle of blood runs down my shin and stains my sock.

The bus driver witnesses all of this with a flash of concern, but the Guardian whispers something to him. The white-haired driver closes the bus doors and shifts into gear.

Tears sting my eyes, but Guardian Bose doesn't apologize. He doesn't even look in my direction. There are murmurs of concern from some of the other girls.

"You're responsible for the damages," Guardian Bose says. "The visit to the infirmary will come from your savings."

Ashamed and injured, I turn toward the window, looking past Valentine. She hasn't spoken to me, not even to ask if I'm okay. But her hands are balled into fists on her lap.

Jackson and Quentin come out of the store and watch as our bus pulls away. Jackson is clutching my bag of candy. Despite my circumstance, his thoughtfulness makes me smile. I reach to press my fingers against the window in a wave.

In return, Jackson holds up his hand in the same way he did when I first saw him. He stays like that until we're on the road. I watch as long as I can, until Quentin says something to Jackson, nodding to the car at the pump. And then they both turn away as I disappear.

3

The mood on the bus has shifted from excitement to dread, and the driver seems to be going over the speed limit. I'm embarrassed that he saw me fall, saw me get redirected by the Guardian. But more than that, I'm regretful that my behavior led to this consequence.

Professor Penchant stays near the back of the bus with the other girls. When I glance at him, he purses his lips in disapproval, and I turn toward the front again.

Although the Guardian isn't one of our professors, he watches over the students on a daily basis. He's typically indifferent, but not unpleasant. He's never spoken to me so viciously.

I'm shaken by it all, but at the same time, I'm deeply ashamed. We're not supposed to anger the men taking care of us. I never have. It was selfish of me to not listen immediately.

I glance at Valentine, watching her as she stares straight ahead. Her body sways along with the movement of the bus, her nails causing indents in her skin where her fists are clenched. But she doesn't say anything to me. I'm almost convinced that I imagined our entire conversation at the Federal Flower Garden.

I slide my eyes to the side so I can peer over at Guardian Bose. He's angry, his jaw set hard. I should apologize, but before I can, there's a flash of dark hair as Sydney sits down next to him. The Guardian is ready to argue, but she smiles sweetly.

"I got you something," she says to him. He eyes her suspiciously. Sydney pulls a pack of gum from her pocket and holds it out to him.

Guardian Bose takes it, not realizing Sydney must have stolen it while in the store. He unwraps a piece and folds it into his mouth, not offering gum to the rest of us.

Sydney waits patiently, and after a moment, Guardian Bose nods and turns toward the window. Sydney beams, having won my freedom, and she reaches for my hand and brings me to my usual seat.

The moment I sit down, Lennon Rose crosses the aisle to hug me, sniffling back her tears. I promise her that I'm okay, petting her blond hair. She sits back down in her seat, watching me with concern. I've never been injured before. Not even a scratch.

Sydney bends forward to look at my knee. She sucks at her teeth and straightens up. "There's so much blood," she says, lifting her eyes to mine. "Do you think the doctor will be able fix it?"

Lennon Rose gasps. Sydney and I both turn to her.

"Of course he'll be able to," I say for Lennon Rose's benefit. Although the idea that I might be scarred for life creeps into my worries. "Dr. Groger is the best around."

"Absolutely," Sydney agrees in the same tone. Lennon Rose's panic eases slightly, but her brow is still furrowed. She's the most sensitive of all the girls. We try not to burden her needlessly.

We all understand that there are consequences for poor behavior. But since we don't act out, we've never earned them. What I did was wrong, therefore I deserved the pain that followed, even if I didn't like it. My opinion on the subject is irrelevant.

I rest my head back against the seat and close my eyes, trying to relax in hopes of lessening the stinging in my knee. There is the occasional pop of gum from the front seat.

I'm struck suddenly by the feeling of being watched. I open my eyes and lean out into the aisle. To my surprise, I find Valentine Wright turned around to face me with the same fierce expression she had at the Federal Flower Garden. It raises the hairs on my arms.

I'm not sure what to say to her, not sure what she wants. She's unsettling me.

I quickly glance around, but the other girls haven't noticed her. The Guardian, however, looks in Valentine's direction. His head tilts slightly, examining her.

"Turn around," he orders.

Valentine doesn't listen. Doesn't even acknowledge the command. She continues to watch me, her eyes finding the blood running down my leg. In the seat behind her, Ida Welch and Maryanne Lindstrom exchange a concerned glance.

My heart begins to beat faster. Lennon Rose looks over the seat to see what's going on, her eyes wide and fearful.

"Valentine," Guardian Bose says, raising his voice. "I said *turn around*."

There are several gasps when Valentine stands up instead, positioned in the middle of the aisle. Sydney sits up straighter, her hands sliding on the green padding of the seat in front of us.

Annalise leans into the aisle, whispering for Valentine to sit down, cautiously checking on the Guardian. But Valentine's not listening. She takes a step toward me and I gulp, scared of the attention.

The Guardian jumps up and grabs Valentine by the wrist. She grits her teeth at the pain and tries to yank away. Behind me, Marcella murmurs, "*No*"—afraid for her. Disturbed by her defiance.

The Guardian twists Valentine's arm behind her back, making her cry out, and studies her eyes a moment before pushing her down in the seat. When she immediately pops up, he pushes her down again, this time more violently.

"Stay," he warns, pointing his finger in her face.

Valentine stares back at him, but she doesn't stand. She tilts up her chin, defiant. I've never seen a girl act like this before, and I wonder what's wrong with her. Clearly her words at the Federal Flower Garden were the first symptom of this larger misbehavior.

"You've just earned yourself impulse control therapy," the Guardian tells Valentine. He stands there, towering over her, his presence seeming to grow larger as she shrinks back. "I'll make sure of it."

Lennon Rose sniffles across the aisle from me, but I don't try to comfort her this time.

The Guardian sits down and takes out his phone, quietly making a call while keeping a cautious eye on Valentine. For her part, Valentine turns around to face the windshield, once more impossibly still.

I can feel that Sydney wants to ask me what just happened, but none of us dares to talk. We wouldn't want to get sent to the analyst with Valentine.

Impulse control therapy is a punishment for when redirection isn't enough. One we earn but dread nonetheless.

I've only been to impulse control therapy once, and I never want to go back.

It was shortly after my first open house—an event the academy holds several times a year. Parents, sponsors, and investors are invited to celebrate our accomplishments. But my parents didn't show up—they were the only ones who didn't. I felt left out and abandoned. I started crying and couldn't stop. Everything was wrong. I felt wrong.

After speaking with Anton—our analyst—he recommended the therapy. But I didn't want to be punished, even when he told me it was for my benefit. That it would make me a better girl.

He said I was too responsive and that impulse control therapy would help me manage my emotions.

I don't remember much after that. Impulse control therapy erases itself when it's done. All I know is I went in crying, and twenty-four hours later, I came out better—just like he promised. And yet, whenever I try to remember what happened, I'm overcome with a crushing sense of foreboding. It's odd to have that strong a feeling without a connection to the memory causing it. When I ask Anton, he says it's just part of the process.

Well, it's not a process I want to go through again. None of us do. So we lower our eyes and keep quiet the entire way back to the academy. I just hope Anton is able to help Valentine the way he helped me. Even if she won't remember it.

The arches of the iron gate come into view when we turn down the gravel road. The words INNOVATIONS ACADEMY are etched into a large metal sign, which has rusted and aged quickly from the rain. The gate opens and we pull forward.

The academy looms ahead, the mountain backdrop as beautiful as a painting. The rain has finally stopped completely, and there's a small ray of sunshine filtering between the clouds. It casts the metal roof in oranges and reds; it would be lovely if the school itself wasn't hidden behind overgrown ivy and barred windows.

They say the bars are remnants from when this was still a factory—protection from thieves and villains. The new owners opted not to remove the bars when this was turned into an academy several years ago, because they thought we needed the security just as much. Or maybe more, considering the iron gates that now surround the property.

"It's dangerous to leave girls unprotected," a professor told me once. "Especially pretty girls like you."

The bus stops with a hiss in the roundabout, and the front doors of the academy swing open. Mr. Petrov, our Head of School, walks out, dressed in a charcoal gray suit and royal blue tie. He's visibly concerned, folding his hands over his stomach as he watches the bus. His wife descends halfway down the stone steps to pause next to him, taking his arm obediently.

I haven't spent much time with Mr. Petrov. He limits our interactions, saying it might interfere with our educational program. His wife, however—Leandra Petrov—met with each of us when we first arrived at the academy. She taught us how to properly apply makeup and style our hair to the academy's specifications. And I remember thinking at the time that she was the most beautiful woman I'd ever seen. She's significantly younger than her husband—probably not much older than us.

Leandra's on campus fairly often. She monitors and records our weight once a week, and she leaves products in our bathrooms to help us manage our periods. She's one of the few women we interact with here. Poised and beautiful, an example to be emulated.

The front doors open again and Anton comes rushing out, a bit frazzled in an endearing way. He stops beside the Head of School, turning his head to talk confidentially as they wait for us to exit the bus.

Lennon Rose exhales with relief and Sydney smiles at me.

It's reassuring to see Anton—a promise that everything will be okay. Despite him being the person who administers impulse control therapy, we mostly look forward to our time with him. He's a wonderful listener. An excellent analyst.

He's older—like the other men at the academy—with light brown hair, gray at the temples. Even his beard is growing in gray, and he jokes that it's because he has so many girls to worry about.

"Philomena," Guardian Bose calls from his seat in the front row. I jump, startled.

"Yes?"

He stands, chomping on his gum. He grabs Valentine by the arm and pulls her out of the seat. She keeps her eyes downcast, her defiance seeming to have faded away.

"Take the back stairs and go see Dr. Groger," the Guardian tells me. "Ask him to patch you up."

I nod, embarrassed again for my earlier behavior. My knee still stings.

The Guardian walks Valentine off the bus, and Anton quickly rushes the rest of the way down the stairs to meet them. He gives the Guardian a pointed look before gently taking Valentine's elbow and leading her inside.

"Do you want me to come with you?" Sydney asks me as we get to our feet. We follow the other girls off the bus. I tell Sydney that I'll be fine, but I thank her for the concern. She blows me a kiss before joining the others on the stairs of the school.

As the girls head inside, Mr. Petrov says hello to each of them as they pass, his yellowed teeth crooked in his smile. He assesses each girl, his eyes traveling over their uniforms. Their hair. Their skin. His wife nods along, her gaze drifting from girl to girl.

LOSE YOURSELF IN THE WORLDS OF
SUZANNE YOUNG